BLOOD

and

MOONLIGHT

BLOOD

and

MOONLIGHT

ERIN BEATY

FARRAR STRAUS GIROUX
NEW YORK

Farrar Straus Giroux Books for Young Readers
An imprint of Macmillan Publishing Group, LLC
120 Broadway, New York, NY 10271

fiercereads.com

Our books may be purchased in bulk for promotional, educational, or business
use. Please contact your local bookseller or the Macmillan Corporate and
Premium Sales Department at (800) 221-7945, ext. 5442, or by email at
MacmillanSpecialMarkets@macmillan.com.

Library of Congress Cataloging-in-Publication Data is available.

First edition, 2022
Book design by Veronica Mang

Printed in the United States of America

ISBN: 978-1-250-75581-0 (hardcover)
1   3   5   7   9   10   8   6   4   2

This book I write day and night
For Dear Reader's thrill and fright.
If treated low, you must know,
Ill winds through your life will blow.

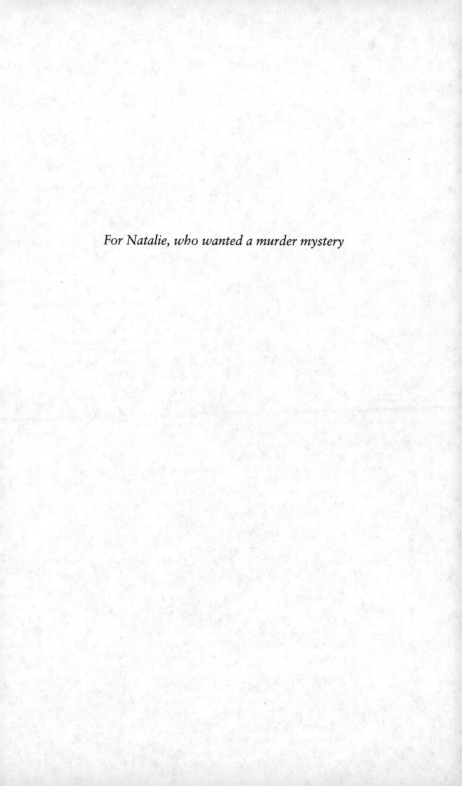

For Natalie, who wanted a murder mystery

BLOOD

and

MOONLIGHT

CHAPTER 1

I'm waiting for the moon.

All other ground-level windows in the neighborhood are shuttered for the night as I lean out of ours to look. A breeze whisks up the deserted street, carrying the scent of rain and the distant rumble of thunder from the west. The city of Collis covers a large hill rising from the flat plains, but my view of the approaching storm is blocked by angled roofs. If I balance on my hips and crane my neck as far as it will go, the rose window and towers of the Holy Sanctum to the east are just visible through a gap between houses. Even without moonlight, the white facade glows against the ebony blanket of sky, washing out all the stars.

Not high enough yet.

I sigh and lever myself back inside as Magister Thomas comes down the stairs into the workroom behind me. The architect pauses when he sees me, his eyebrows so high they disappear in the chestnut hair peeking out from under his cap. "Catrin?" he says. "I thought you went to bed hours ago."

"No, Magister." I remove the angled support and lower the shutter, sliding the bolts into the frame before turning to face my employer's frown.

"If I didn't know better," he observes, "I'd say you're dressed for climbing."

After dinner I'd traded my calf-length working skirt for a much shorter one over a man's breeches and bound and pinned my dark curls into submission. "I am," I admit. "I wanted to check on a bowed crossbeam I noticed this morning on the southern scaffolds."

The master architect's frown deepens, creasing his forehead. "Why didn't you do it earlier?"

"Well . . ." I count the reasons on my fingers. "Between showing the Comte de Montcuir around the work site all morning, verifying the alignment of the drainage system, writing up the stone orders for you to sign, and visiting the market in search of fresh rosemary for Mistress la Fontaine, I ran out of time." I drop my hands and shrug. "Besides, it's easier to inspect when the scaffolds aren't crawling with workers."

"Hmmph." The architect eyes my belt, which doesn't hold the small hammer I usually carry. "And no wandering hands to smash. How many this week?" he asks severely.

His ire isn't directed at me, so I smile. "Only three or four."

If the apprentices—and some of the older craftsmen—would just keep their hands to themselves, they wouldn't have to worry about their fingers. I don't hit hard enough to break bones the first time, and once is usually enough.

"Show me where your concern is, then." Magister Thomas nods to the scale replica of Collis's Sanctum which dominates the room. The model is as old as the Sanctum itself, started decades ago.

I walk around to the far end of the table, and the architect joins me from the opposite side. Really, to call this representation a "model" doesn't do it justice. Every stone, window, and shingle of the structure is perfectly and proportionally rendered, from the two square towers at the western entrance and down its long nave, to the arms extending north and south from the altar at the center—or rather, what will be the center once the holy building is finished. Our expansion project now underway will lengthen the building far beyond its current T shape. The transept wings mark the beginning of the work area, all of which is also portrayed and updated with our progress, including the scaffolding.

"Right here." I point to a scarlet thread I've tied as my own reminder of the location, then back away so he can see. It's in a support section as complicated as a spider's web, tucked within the shadow of the high tower at the end of the southern transept.

As Magister Thomas leans closer to look, the parchment nailed to the wall behind him flutters. The light is too dim for me to read the names written on it, but I know them all by heart: fourteen fathers, husbands, brothers, and sons lost in the collapse of scaffolding and wall five years ago. Above the list rests the gold-plated hammer used in setting the markers of the latest construction project as it was blessed by the high altum.

The placement of those two items is significant: The master architect will never look at the symbol of his greatest achievement without also seeing an account of his greatest failure.

To prevent such a thing from ever happening again, the scaffolds must be as safe and reliable as the limestone walls themselves, and the only way to ensure that is to have someone climbing around them regularly, checking for cracks and warps.

That someone is me. It's a job I take very seriously.

Magister Thomas is still studying the model, measuring distances with his fingers, when the gentle toll of the Sanctum's bells drifts through the cracks in the shutters. It's nearly midnight, which is when a full moon peaks, meaning its light will finally be where I need it to be to see by. While I wasn't trying to hide my plan to go out tonight, now I feel like I need to wait for permission, but with the storm coming I can't afford to waste time.

"Do you ever wonder why the brethren even bother going to bed before their last devotions?" I ask, mostly to call the magister's attention to the hour. The holy men who make up the religious order attached to the Sanctum have probably only slept two hours before being wakened for midnight liturgy.

"Seeing as they're up again at dawn for the next series of chants, I imagine they catch sleep whenever they can," is his absentminded reply. He tilts his head to look at the indicated beam from several angles. Though the architect is two years past forty—old enough to be my father—two white streaks running back from his temples are the only obvious signs of his age. The one on the left appeared after the accident five years ago, but the other is more than a decade old according to the housekeeper. Given the tragedy associated with the more recent one, I've never had the courage to ask what caused the first.

Magister Thomas shakes his head. "I can see how a problem there could have gone unnoticed, but it's going to be a difficult spot to reach, even for you."

The scaffold supports are set at unusual angles due to the carved statues that stick out from the walls. Gargoyles are part of the drainage system, which makes them necessary, but working around them is likely the reason a problem has developed. It *is* high, and I'm not quite sure how I'll reach it yet, but I've been climbing trees and scaling the sides of buildings for nearly all of my seventeen years.

"I'm not worried," I say.

"You never are." He stands straight to look at me again. "Maybe I should go along. I can hold the lantern."

I doubt I'll need his help—or the light—but a sharp pounding on the door in the kitchen interrupts us. That's odd. Who would call at this hour, and from the alley rather than the street?

Mistress la Fontaine shortly appears in the doorway to the kitchen. The housekeeper's gray-white hair is halfway escaped from the bun at the top of her neck after a full day of baking bread and chopping vegetables, and she wears a sour, disapproving expression as she wipes weathered hands on her apron. "There's someone here to see you, Magister."

The architect's jaw tightens as he narrows his gray eyes suspiciously. "Who is it?"

"Perrete Charpentier."

A daughter of one of the fourteen builders killed in the accident, about my age. Nothing good comes of her visits, but the architect feels responsible for her father's death, and so he's tried to make sure she had enough to live on. Lately, however, it's been obvious she earns plenty—doing exactly what Magister Thomas had wanted to prevent—and sees him only as a source of free money.

"Tell her to come back tomorrow," he says.

The housekeeper shakes her head. "She says if you don't talk to her now, she'll go straight to the high altum."

It's easy to picture the stance Perrete took as she made her threat, hand on a hip jutted out, scarlet lips pouting, her face rouged to play up the natural beauty mark on her cheek. No doubt she waited until the midnight bells so she could actually carry out that threat and approach Altum Gervese as he walks back to his palatial home from the Sanctum after prayers.

"I'll be fine without you, Magister," I tell him. "I'd already planned on going alone."

He shakes his head, though I can tell he's torn. "Maybe we

could block off the area first thing in the morning and inspect it then."

"You know it can't wait," I say. "The altum is already frustrated by our recent weather delays. He'll be angry if we halt work tomorrow."

Angry is an understatement. He's been out to replace Magister Thomas for over two years, and his incessant, underhanded campaign from the pulpit is finally turning some people against him. As a result, donations have decreased, slowing our progress and seeming to back up the altum's claim that it's time for a new master architect to take charge.

Which was why I spent the entire morning showing the city provost and his sons around the expansion site. Fortunately, the Comte de Montcuir was impressed and promised a hefty contribution. I took him straight to the window maker, who then sketched his face as an inspiration for one of the stained glass pictures he'll create. Nothing opens a man's purse wider than public evidence of his generosity.

The master architect considers my argument for several seconds. At last he sighs. "Very well. I'll speak with her, Mistress, in private. Let her in."

Relieved, I open the door to the street. "I'll be back before the rain starts."

"Catrin," calls the architect. "You're forgetting something."

I stifle a groan as I stop in the doorway. "Magister Thomas, I have never fallen."

"Until last summer, the bell tower had never been hit by lightning," he says sternly. The western facade tower, the shortest of the Sanctum's four by a few feet, had been damaged by the severe strike. "Never only means 'not yet.'"

With a heavy sigh, I take the coiled safety rope from its hook next to his cloak by the door. I'm about to walk out with it in my hand, but I catch the architect's glare and pause long enough to knot one end around my waist. "Better?"

His beard shifts with the skeptical tilt of his lips. "Will you use it?"

"Yes, Magister," I assure him, though it will probably be in the way more than anything.

"Be careful," he says, waving for me to go. "Mother Agnes would come at me with her bare hands if anything happened to you."

I grin as I sling the rope over my shoulder. Despite the fact that the prioress of Solis Abbey just celebrated her seventieth birthday, I'm not sure it's a fight she'd lose.

Perrete sweeps into the workroom then, wearing the simpering, one-sided smile that hides the rotten gap in her teeth. A wave of perfume from her dress wafts over me, and I grimace as I pull the door shut. Last time she was here, it took a whole day of airing to get that lingering scent out of the workroom.

From the street, I can see enough sky ahead of the approaching storm clouds to assure me I'll have time for my inspection, but I still have to hurry. I turn and trot uphill toward the Sanctum, the wind at my back.

CHAPTER 2

The problem is shockingly easy to see by moonlight. Something about the way the shadows play across the lines and angles of the supports nestled against the new stone structure. It's almost as if the darkness coaxed the flaw into revealing itself when it thought no one would be looking—which is nonsense.

Observing it from the ground isn't enough, though. I have to inspect it up close if I'm to justify stopping work tomorrow.

There's nothing nearby to support my weight other than a stone gargoyle extending three feet from the Sanctum wall. The doglike creature is designed to spew channeled rainwater from its mouth, away from the building. Like most sculptures, it's supposed to look fierce, but the circular opening between this one's teeth makes it appear comically surprised. Wind whistling across the mouth creates a shrieking sound, like a housewife who's spotted a mouse, adding to the effect. With the scaffolds built around it, I have to balance across the statue's back and stretch out to reach the warped pole. My fingers immediately find a split in the wood which is invisible from every vantage above and below.

Falling Skies, it's *huge*. It's a miracle it hasn't failed already. By day, the scaffolds above are crawling with dozens of workers. Had they collapsed, few would have survived the six-story fall onto the stones in various stages of cutting and shaping below.

I angle myself to feel along the length of the crack. The gap is almost as wide as my forearm—too large to simply reinforce with lashing—and the tiny, fresh splinters I encounter mean it's expanding rapidly. As much trouble as this will cause, I'm relieved to have such a clear answer: The entire scaffold here will have to come down and be reassembled.

Two days of construction, lost. One more reason for the high altum to complain.

A sharp sliver of wood jabs my middle finger, and I reflexively yank my hand back. Blood wells from under the nail as I bring it to my mouth. The coppery taste hits my tongue with startling intensity, but it's not bleeding that badly. After a few seconds, I raise the wound up to the moonlight to look for any remaining fragments of the splinter. Fortunately, there are none.

My arm, still extended to hold the beam, begins to tremble from bearing so much weight alone. Before I can reach back with the other, a strong gust of wind causes the gargoyle's whistling to pitch higher and louder, and the shrill screaming sound sends a jolt of lightning down my spine and out to my limbs. All the muscles in my body contract, and my already precarious grip on the pole slips.

Suddenly I'm plunging headfirst toward the stones below, tumbling and twisting as sky and scaffold and Sanctum and moon streak across my vision. An arc of blood splashes the wall in front of me, and in that instant, I think—*I know*—I'm going to die.

I never thought it would end like this.

My vision fades on the edges, and I arch my back and grab at my throat in a desperate attempt to stop the bleeding. The other hand claws at the wall with equal futility until an impact across my stomach rips me open.

Pain is the only thing left in my world. All I can do is wait for the last of my consciousness to drain away.

Until it doesn't.

My surroundings slowly come back into focus. It takes several seconds for me to understand I'm not lying dead on the ground but dangling about thirty feet above it, the safety line agonizingly tight around my waist. Dazed, I look up to the gargoyle where the rope angles back to the place I'd attached it to the scaffolding on the other side—rather reluctantly, I might add. The whistling sound continues as though it had never changed. Did that horrible shriek come from the statue's mouth? It had sounded . . . human. Like someone terrified or about to die, or both. If I wasn't absolutely positive the noise came *before* I fell, I would've thought it was me who screamed.

There's no blood on the wall next to me, either, and as I raise my shaking hands into the moonlight, they, too, are clean.

But I'd *seen* the blood. I'd *felt* it.

I was going to die. I'm not entirely sure I didn't.

Someone who was dead wouldn't hurt this much, however. Grunting, I wriggle into a position where I can brace my feet against the stone wall. My leather boots are specially made for climbing, and the ascent is fairly easy, even with trembling hands and bruises forming across my middle. The hardest part is heaving myself over the gargoyle so I can stand and jump back to the woven-reed platform.

I collapse against the smooth limestone of the Sanctum as soon as I'm safe, promising myself never to complain about using a safety line again. As I work the length into a loose coil, I notice my fingertips and nails aren't ravaged from clawing at the wall. Other than the clotted splinter wound, which has expanded into a perfectly round bruise, they're undamaged. Shaking my head, I untie the line from my sore waist and gaze out over the homes and shops which ring the paved area around the Sanctum. Most of my view is blocked by rooftops three and four stories tall. All is quiet but for the scream still echoing in my brain.

Did that sound come from out there?

Throwing the rope over my shoulder, I stand and begin climbing the scaffold to the top of the Sanctum, bothering with ladders only half the time. The uppermost level is even with the main gutter along the edge of the new section's roof, and the wind snaps and pushes me along the length of the expansion to the far east end, where the leonine form of a chimera watches over his domain.

"Good evening, Pierre," I say, dropping the coiled line behind the statue. Unlike gargoyles, these serve no purpose but decoration. I name each of them as I watch them take form over several weeks under the master carver, but this one is my favorite so far. Its face resembles that of a snub-nosed bat, with long fangs that curve all the way around its mouth, which is open wide in a snarl. I pat one of the wings stretching vertically from its muscled back and continue speaking, though I'm not silly enough to expect an answer. "Have you seen or heard anything strange tonight?"

From this vantage I can see the entire hill Collis is built on and miles of countryside beyond. My childhood home, Solis Abbey, nestles near the bottom of the southern slope. Beyond it lies the ivy-covered walls of the Selenae Quarter, home to the reclusive religious sect whose members keep the hours of the moon rather than those of the Blessed Sun. A glow too steady to be a bonfire comes from the open plaza in the center of that neighborhood. Even at this distance, the haunting melodies of their midnight hymns reach my ears.

Outside the Quarter, the city is devoid of nighttime revelers, probably in anticipation of the storm, quiet as the dead except for the rapid rhythm of footsteps ricocheting off walls and paving stones. I lean forward, unthinking, to look, and Pierre's outstretched arm almost seems to point at a lone figure below. A cloaked form—definitely a man—moves too quickly and purposefully to be a drunkard stumbling home from a tavern. The direction he's moving suggests he came from Madame Emeline's or another similar establishment, but he almost seems to be running *from* something.

As I watch, the shadowed figure darts into a side street, out of sight, and in the quiet that follows, a ghostly voice cries out.

Someone help me. Please.

The words flutter through my head, weightless as moonlight, yet carrying a despair so heavy I struggle to breathe in its wake. What Mother Agnes always called my wayward imagination connects the voice and its pain to the fleeing man. Perhaps he robbed someone, leaving them sobbing and injured in the street. Would the city's night watchmen find them before the storm, or am I the only one who can help this person? How would I even begin to search for them?

"Go home, little Cat."

I spin around, heart pounding, pressing my back to the statue. Those words I actually *heard*. Someone speaking that softly would have to be nearby, if not right behind me, but there is only empty air. I search the nearby portico, roof, and scaffolds with wide eyes, unable to find the source of the gravelly whisper even as it continues.

"This is not a night to be out."

It feels more like a warning than a threat, and between the weather and seeing a strange man running through the streets,

I'm inclined to agree with this phantom voice. Until the silent cry comes again.

Please. Anyone.

Suddenly, I'm hurrying back the way I came, climbing down poles and hopping across reed and wicker platforms, driven by a compulsion I cannot explain. Once on the ground, I jog in the direction the cloaked man came from. In the back of my mind, I know this is stupid to do alone. But while Perrete is surely gone by now, Magister Thomas would never agree to prowl the streets at this hour, especially with such flimsy reasoning.

I turn down the road connecting the Sanctum Square to the centuries-old Temple of the Sun, a relic of the Hadrian Empire which established our Faith. While the street's official name is the Pathway of Prayer, it's more commonly known as Pleasure Road due to the high number of brothels along the way. Many of Collis's orphaned or foundling girls are raised in convents, but those who decline to take vows as Sisters of Light unfortunately often have trouble finding reputable employment. Many end up here.

I'm panting as I pass the fourth block of row houses, and a sudden assault on my senses makes me stop to look around. The brightness of the moon creates harsh, angular shadows that cut the scene into jagged pieces, but it's the sweet metallic tang hanging in the air which makes me shudder. The last time I smelled it this strongly was when passing a butcher shop as a hog was being slaughtered on the front steps.

Blood. Lots of it.

But I don't see any.

A chilling gust blows dead leaves past my ankles, drawing my eyes down to a large, muddy footprint. Several more continue in the direction of the Sanctum, fading at some point not far away, but they came from the dark alley on my right. I slide under the awning of the building next to it and peer cautiously around the corner.

"Hello?" I call softly.

There is no answer. A slash of moonlight shines on the opposite wall, so bright I can see nothing outside it. I can't recall ever being here, but a strange familiarity draws me forward into the shadowed mouth of the alley.

Darkness closes around me like a curtain. The smell of blood is now overwhelming, and I cover my mouth and nose with one hand and stretch the other out in front of me into the pitch black. I take one hesitant step toward the light, then another, my toes pushing aside what I hope is rubbish. When I reach the illuminated wall, I find an arc of crimson spatter at eye level, eerily similar to what I saw as I fell from the gargoyle's back.

That's impossible. Yet now I also recall my vision then hadn't been of the immaculate limestone of the Sanctum—it was rough and grimy. Like the wattle and daub in front of me.

There is also one place where the pattern differs. It's smeared in the middle, like a grasping hand was dragged across the wet stain. The fingertips on my left hand ache as though they had done this, and I reach out, hypnotized, needing to know if the feel of the wall matches my memory.

When I'm only inches away, the alley suddenly bursts into light with the strength of a thousand candles. Everything around me becomes visible—walls, crates, barrels spilling over with refuse, scurrying rats . . . and the shape of a woman lying on the ground.

She's on her back with her feet toward me, with pale, white calves and worn, wooden heeled shoes exposed beneath a rumpled skirt. Blood pools like black ink around her head and shoulders, so much that the packed dirt can't absorb it all, leaving a flat liquid surface which reflects the stars and scudding clouds above. Her stomach is a mess of torn fabric and internal parts I've only seen in butchered animals.

All that is horrible, but it's not the worst.

The woman's jaw hangs open in a silent scream, half the teeth missing or broken. Her face has collapsed inward, crushed, and her eyes are a hollow mess of ravaged tissue. A stream of blood trails from the gory sockets, running like a tear past the beauty mark on her cheek.

I gasp, inhaling so deeply that the floral perfume layered under the thick scent of blood becomes recognizable, but I already know who this is.

Perrete.

CHAPTER 3

My arm is frozen in midair, reaching for the wall, and still the entire scene is bathed in light as bright as day—brighter, perhaps, for it is a place the sun rarely shines.

I've seen dead bodies before. I've seen death from sickness, from accidents, and even from violence.

I've never seen anything like this.

Please. Anyone. Help me.

A wetness seeps into the toes of one of my leather boots. When I realize my right foot is standing in a puddle of blood, I recoil, drawing my hand back just as the alley plunges into darkness once again. Unseeing and disoriented, I trip over my own feet and fall in my haste to get away.

Help me . . .

The jolt from hitting the ground jars my teeth and sends a painful shock around my already-bruised waist, but I don't care. I know what soaks the ground and into my clothes. Rolling over, I push to my hands and knees, scrambling for the entrance to the alley.

. . . someone . . .

Screams echo off the walls, and I only realize the shrieking is mine when I reemerge onto the street and the sound expands to fill the open space. I collapse to my knees and vomit on the cobblestone, heaving and sobbing until I'm empty of everything but the memory of what lies behind me.

As I sit back on my heels, a shutter on the second floor several buildings away crashes open, and a woman I can see with startling clarity peers out. Her eyes are ringed with dark circles and the top of her dress is loose. From behind her comes a soft wailing.

"Silence, you drunkard!" she shouts. "My babe was just asleep!"

Before I can react, she slams the window shut, and I'm alone again.

I look around. No one else appears disturbed by my noise, but I suppose if no one cared enough to investigate the screams of a woman being murdered, I shouldn't be surprised that no one is reacting to me now. The heavy taste of blood in my mouth tells me I bit my tongue when I fell, and I wipe my face with the back of my hand, leaving a trail of scarlet from my wrist to my knuckles.

What should I do? Perrete is dead. No one can help her now, yet leaving her feels wrong. Magister Thomas would know the right course of action.

Grace of Day! If anyone knows Perrete went to see the magister tonight, he'll fall under suspicion. His innocence won't matter. Just the taint of accusation and his association with her could cost him his position as master architect. I need to warn him.

The scattered clouds of the storm finally cross over the moon, briefly extinguishing its light. A cold wind sprinkles the ground in front of me with the first drops of rain. I put my hands down to push myself to a stand, and one brushes my blood-soaked boot.

Please. Anyone. Help me.

"All right!" I shout back at the sky.

My voice is lost in a roll of thunder. I wipe my fingers clean, leaving bloody streaks on my short overskirt. Madame Emeline's isn't far. She's likely one of the few who will even care what happened to Perrete.

I turn and run down the road as the moonlight vanishes again, making the world dark and muffled, this time for good. The downpour catches up to me just as I arrive on the madam's doorstep. Emeline herself answers, and I push my way inside, half soaked.

"Perrete," I gasp as she closes the door.

"Doesn't work here," Emeline finishes. Her hair, bleached to a shade of orange, is curled and mostly in place, and her face is fully painted. The makeup exaggerates the pinch of her thin lips as she raises a candle to peer at me. Concern quickly replaces irritation. "What about Perrete?"

"She's dead," I say. "I found her body."

Some of Emeline's alarm eases. "Are you sure she just wasn't passed out from *skonia*? It wouldn't be the first time."

The madam's own voice is husky from use of the euphoria-producing drug, which is burned and inhaled in its cheapest form.

"I'm sure. She was—" I choke, but manage to finish with, "It was horrible."

Emeline sighs. "You can tell the night watchmen. They'll inform the provost." She turns to the stairs in the back of the room.

"I, ah, couldn't manage to find any of them before the rain started," I say, though I hadn't searched for them at all. "That's why I came here."

The madam glances over her shoulder. "Then it's fortunate that two of them are upstairs now."

——— • ✳ • ———

Madame Emeline assures the city guards she won't disclose where they were as long as they sound the alarm to her satisfaction, which they do, rousing the whole neighborhood despite the storm.

While one watchman runs to the Palace of Justice, the other is unable to keep the first gawkers out of the alley until more guards arrive. Those lucky few tell everyone what they saw, and the story grows more gruesome with each telling. Most people huddle under the meager shelter offered by awnings and doorways, but I slink around the edges of the crowd, listening for anyone who knows where Perrete went tonight. So far I've heard nothing. Madame Emeline stands just outside the alley, arms crossed, her bloodshot eyes simmering with rage. The provost should've been here by now.

I'm worried the magister will come searching for me, but I don't dare leave yet. My toes are numb with cold, and liquid squelches from my boots as I shift my stance, sending faint tendrils of blood spiraling out into the puddle at my feet.

. . . help me . . .

My jaw clenches as the plea echoes through my mind. Perrete's ghostly voice has been as constant as the rain dripping down my face. I brought attention to what happened to her. Isn't that enough for her to leave me alone?

Within an hour the storm has passed, and the western half of the sky glows with the full moon behind thinning clouds. A number of people approach from up the street, and a tall, cloaked figure among them makes me freeze. Unlike the man

I saw from the scaffolding at the Sanctum, however, this one's cloak is a nondescript gray color, and the clothes beneath are a blue so dark as to be black. He glides between shadows like he's one of them until he catches sight of me and stops midstep.

"There you are."

He's too far away for his gruff whisper to reach me, yet it does. I know the voice, too. I heard it earlier, standing next to Pierre. "*Go home, little Cat.*"

My stomach plummets as I recognize the silver-ringed irises gleaming against the thick outline of black kohl from deep within the hood. He's Selenae.

I wouldn't call it fear, but I'm as wary of them as anyone in Collis. Selenae are among our most skillful physicians, so much so that many consider them magicians. Only the richest citizens can afford their services, but it's said they extract a price only worth paying if one is on the edge of death. And, if rumors are true, the People of the Night are also the source of *skonia*, the drug many use in an effort to bear their terrible lives. The reclusive sect rises and sleeps as the moon does, rather than the Sun, and they govern their own members—not outside of Gallian law, but not precisely within it, either. Above all, they have two unbreakable rules: Keep strictly to the Quarter at night and shun all non-Selenae matters. Something has made this man disregard both.

From his actions, that something could only be me.

I'm still as a Sanctum statue as his gaze sweeps down and up. When his eyes refocus on mine, he nods ever so slightly. His broad shoulders relax, causing a silver chain to shift and glitter against his neck. Despite the darkness, I can see the face within the hood is marred by a number of scars, and his nose sits decidedly off-center. If Selenae weren't such strict pacifists, I would presume him to be a former soldier, or at least a barroom brawler.

The Selenae man steps back, deeper into the shadows, never relinquishing my gaze. "Go home," he whispers.

As before, it feels more like a warning than a threat, and I'm tempted to obey, until I see the Comte de Montcuir coming.

By his appearance, it seems the provost did make some effort to hurry—his clothes are wrinkled and his russet beard and mustache aren't oiled into their usual shapely arrangement. Trailing behind him is a tall, unfamiliar young man in an even more disheveled state, though he's dressed in fabrics as fine as the nobleman's own, tailored to fit his lanky frame. He—like most people present—was obviously roused from bed. His dull, blond curls are flat on one side and flying wildly on the other, and his expression is trancelike.

The pair brush past the Selenae man like he's invisible. Perhaps he is, because he vanishes as soon as they cross between us. When I find him again, he's half a block away, leaving as silently as he came.

There's no chance I'm going home now. I join the crowd swelling in response to the Comte de Montcuir's arrival and the easing rain. Relief is plain on every face. The king's appointed executor of justice is here. Order will be restored.

"What goes on here?" Montcuir booms, throwing the weight of his authority into his voice. He and his companion step into the circle of torchlight, the latter slowly blinking pale blue eyes against the relative brightness. There's something odd about the left one, but I can't see what from this angle.

A watchman steps forward. "The body of a woman was found, your Grace, about one hour ago."

The provost grunts. "Any sign of the perpetrator?"

"No, your Grace." The guard shakes his head. "He was gone long before the alarm was raised."

Montcuir isn't impressed by the watch's failure. "Who was she?" he asks no one in particular. Then, spying Madame Emeline, the comte raises a rust-colored eyebrow. "One of your girls, madam?"

She bristles. "If you're asking if we share the same profession, the answer is yes." Her makeup runs in trails down her cheeks from standing in the rain and perhaps a few tears, but the madam's voice is clear and unapologetic. "That doesn't make her worth less than anyone else under law. And what was done to her will shock even you."

The provost holds her accusing stare for several seconds but doesn't address her subtle insolence. "Who discovered the body? You?"

Emeline's eyes find me, questioning whether I want to admit my part or not. She will allow me to escape involvement, should I wish. I rub my palms against my breeches in indecision.

. . . help . . . me . . .

"I did," I say, startling myself.

Montcuir and dozens of other faces swing around to stare at me, and I swallow to keep my voice steady.

"I heard her scream."

The comte recognizes me, of course. Only this morning I was showing him and his sons around the Sanctum. He curls a meaty finger at me in a command to come forward. "Bring a light and follow me."

I don't want to go back in there. My hands shake so badly I nearly drop the torch someone thrusts at me. Montcuir also gestures to the stranger. "Simon, you come, too."

The young man balks. "Why?"

"You know why."

I'm confused. The comte has been provost of Collis for over two decades, while this Simon doesn't even look to have twenty years in age. What does Montcuir think the young man can observe that he cannot?

Simon's pale eyes spark in anger, and his face twists in defiance before suddenly going blank again. Then he steps forward, his movements stiff and mechanical. I let him go ahead of me, wanting any excuse to keep my distance from the body. Madame Emeline also follows, and no one tries to prevent her. The alley feels darker than before, even with the light I carry.

Comte de Montcuir stops next to Perrete's still form, which lies under a dingy linen sheet soaked with rainwater and blood. Bright red spots spread out from her middle and face. "Who covered the body?" he asks.

"I did," says Emeline. "You'll shortly see why."

Montcuir leans down to fling the sheet aside. Though much of the blood has washed away, Perrete's ravaged features are just as horrible as before. I don't expect much of a reaction from a veteran of the Second War of the Eclipse, but the comte seems shocked.

Simon barely flinches.

No one moves for several seconds. "Well?" Montcuir finally says as he stands straight. "What do you think, Simon?"

"She's dead," he replies dully.

"And?" The comte crosses his arms. "Is this madness or something much simpler?"

There's a long pause, during which neither Madame Emeline nor I breathe. "Yes," answers Simon quietly. "This was done by a madman."

Emeline exhales in relief, but I don't see how the acknowledgment changes anything.

Without another word, Comte de Montcuir turns and stalks

back to the street. The madam is on his heels, and I rush to follow, immediately returning the torch to the man who gave it to me. Simon lags behind and stops at the entrance of the alley, as though to block the way.

Outside, the comte's adult sons are just arriving. The older, Lambert, is about Simon's height, and he propels the much stockier Oudin along with a firm grip on his arm. Once they're in the cleared area, Oudin jerks his elbow free from Lambert's hold and stumbles another step before catching his balance.

"I was coming," he growls. His clothes and breath reek of alcohol from several feet away. Oudin is nearly always drunk and almost as often belligerent.

"Not fast enough," says Lambert calmly. I've never heard him raise his voice before, and tonight is no exception. "Father said we were to hurry."

"Yes," says Montcuir sourly. "You weren't at home when I left; where were you?"

"Enjoying the pleasures of the night." Oudin has no shame. Half a decade separates him from his older brother, but in maturity they're a lifetime apart.

Simon sighs. "Why did you bring Juliane, Cousin?"

The comte's daughter stands behind her brothers with a brass lantern in her frail hands and a guilty countenance on her face. Lady Juliane's loose overdress was obviously thrown over her nightgown, making her barely presentable. Auburn hair hangs in damps strings over her shoulders, and purplish circles ring her brown eyes like deep bruises in her painfully thin face. I haven't seen her in months, but her appearance makes me think she's been ill. Eight years ago she was considered one of the greatest beauties in all of Gallia. Now, at twenty-four, spinsterhood would appear to be her fate.

Lambert frowns at Simon's question. "She was already awake. I didn't want to leave her alone."

"What's happened?" says Oudin. "I heard someone was dead."

"Perrete Charpentier has been slain," hisses Madame Emeline. "Murdered and left to rot in an alley."

Almost all color drains from Oudin's face, leaving two clownish splotches of crimson on his cheeks—evidence that he's not just been drinking, he's been using *skonia*. Not as a smoke, however. He can afford a concentrated powder either sniffed or placed under the tongue. "Perrete?" he whispers in a strangled voice. "That's not possible."

"How is that not possible?" demands the comte. "Were you with her tonight?"

Oudin closes his mouth and tries to swallow. After several seconds of struggle, he nods. "Yes," he admits. "But . . . not in that way. And she left me hours ago saying she'd meet me later, but she never came back."

An alarm louder than the Sanctum's largest bell rings in my head. It's obvious Perrete visited Magister Thomas in that time, but does Oudin know that?

Montcuir glances around, no doubt noting the suspicious looks being cast on his younger son. He sets his jaw. "A formal inquiry will be opened immediately."

The crowd shifts and murmurs. Murder of a prostitute isn't generally considered worthy of such attention, but the nature of this crime and the comte's son's possible involvement have apparently changed that.

"Simon of Mesanus." Montcuir pauses dramatically as he turns to face him, and the young man tenses like he wants to flee. "You will conduct this investigation."

"Why me?" he spits back. "I have no official position in Collis."

"No, but I'm the one who assigns such offices." The comte turns away, waving his hand dismissively as he steps off, clearly done with the situation. "Put your experience to use."

Madame Emeline frowns at Simon. "What reason could the comte have for giving you this task, sir?"

Simon's fists clench like he's gripping the rails of a ship in a storm as he glowers at the provost's back. "Because I'm the resident expert in madness," he whispers ruefully.

CHAPTER 4

City guards encourage the crowd to disperse. Most people obey, but the Montcuir siblings stay, and I'm not leaving if there's a chance of learning whether Oudin knows Perrete went to see the architect. A cluster of women also wait nearby, some holding hands. Their bare shoulders and painted faces make their reason for staying obvious—Perrete is one of their own.

The last watchman shifts his feet and eyes Simon, who hasn't moved a muscle in two minutes. Finally, the guard coughs for attention. "Venatre . . ."

Simon jumps. "What did you call me?"

"Venatre," the guard replies uneasily. I've never heard of Mesanus, but Simon must not be from Gallia if he doesn't know the word. "That is the title of one who investigates a crime."

Emeline nods as she pushes a soggy clump of flame-colored hair from her face. "As venatre, you have the authority of the provost himself."

"I see." Simon's mouth twists up on one side. "I don't suppose either of you knows what *venatorae* means in the tongue of the Old Empire?"

Personally, I'd be surprised if either Emeline or the watchman could read. And while the ancient language is still used in holy rituals, *venatorae* is not a word I recognize.

"It means 'hunter,'" says Juliane from behind her brothers. "Or, more precisely, 'one who tracks an animal to its lair.'"

Simon meets her glance and they share some secret communication. Whatever it is causes him to relax slightly.

Oudin rolls his eyes. "May I leave then, *Venatre*?" He coats the word with sarcasm. "I'd like to go home."

His callous attitude makes me ill. Even if he's truly unaware of what was done to Perrete, a woman he knew is dead.

Simon frowns. "We need to discuss your movements and actions tonight."

I hold my breath, hoping to witness the conversation. Next to Juliane, Lambert stares into the alley like most of the people who gathered earlier. I want to tell him he's better off not seeing what lies within.

"Cousin," Simon calls out to him, "would you please escort your brother home and keep him there until I can question him?"

My heart sinks, but of course I cannot voice my protest.

Lambert shakes himself out of his reverie and nods, reaching for Juliane's elbow rather than Oudin's. "Come along, Sister. Simon was right, I never should have brought you along."

Juliane sidesteps his grasp. "I would stay and assist," she says. "I can record Simon's observations." Her eyes meet Simon's again and silently beg for him to agree. *Please*, she mouths. *I'll be good.*

To my surprise, he sighs and nods, motioning her to join him.

Lambert scowls. "These are not things she should see, Cousin."

"It's not your decision," Juliane says, moving away from him.

Simon holds up a hand before Lambert can protest again. "She'll be safe, Lambert. And you're the only one I can trust with Oudin."

With obvious reluctance, Lambert grabs his brother's arm and urges him up the street. "I'll sober him up, too."

"Thank you. Hopefully this won't take long." Simon turns to address Madame Emeline. "After I'm finished here, will you take—" He stops, embarrassed.

"Perrete," Juliane supplies.

"Yes, Perrete." Simon nods his gratitude. "Will you carry her away?"

Emeline glances at the group of women off to the side. Most are weeping openly. "Yes, Venatre," the madam says. "We will tend to her."

They know no one else will care enough to bury Perrete properly.

Simon looks down on Emeline. "I'll need to examine her before she's redressed, in as much light as you can provide."

The idea of poking and prodding the body of a naked dead woman turns my stomach, but the madam nods eagerly. "If it will help."

Simon thanks her and steps away to instruct the guard in how he wants this area watched for anyone who lingers or passes by more often than seems reasonable. Apparently he believes the murderer may come back to look at the place. Though he acted earlier like he was the wrong person to lead the investigation, he clearly knows what to do.

My gut also says the man running across the Sanctum Square was important, but I'm not sure how to approach the venatre with my information. Maybe I should speak to Juliane. Though she was schooled at the abbey under Mother Agnes, I was too young to have had much contact with her, and I highly doubt she remembers me. Even so, I suspect she's my best chance of being listened to.

One doesn't simply grab the arm of a comte's daughter,

however. I settle for sidling up next to her and saying quietly, "My Lady, I may have seen the man who did this."

Instead of acknowledging me, Juliane snaps the fingers of her right hand twice, making Simon look around to her. His eyes—there's definitely something odd about the left one—shift to me, and he gives a tiny nod. Only then does she turn to face me, asking, "What did you see?"

Did he just give her permission to speak to me?

"I heard a scream, sometime after midnight," I answer, aware the venatre is watching us. "A bit later I saw a man running across the Sanctum Square."

Simon draws his brow low. "What did this man look like?"

"I don't know. It was dark, and when he turned down a side street, I lost sight of him."

"Why were you out at such a late hour?" The venatre steps closer, studying my unusual outfit.

"I was doing an inspection for the master architect."

Simon's gaze stops at my feet. "There's blood on your trousers and boots." His eyes snap back up to my face. "Oh yes, you're the one who found the body."

I nod, fascinated by what I can now see. Both of his irises are colored like the azure sky in the panes of the Sanctum's north window, but in the left, a wedge of brown mars the ring of blue, something I've never seen before and didn't know was possible.

"Who are you, then?" he asks. "The architect's daughter?"

Magister Thomas is the closest thing I have to a father, but I can't say that. Nor can I call myself his apprentice. "I work for him," I say simply.

Juliane lifts her lantern to peer at my face. "You used to live at the Abbey of the Sisters of Light."

If she indeed remembers me, it's probably from the afternoon I released a sack of brown toads in the prioress's sitting room, bringing an embroidery lesson to a shrieking halt. "Many years ago," I answer.

She brightens. "Ah yes. 'Caaaaaaah-TREEEEN!'" Juliane perfectly imitates the way Mother Agnes had screamed that afternoon.

I cringe. "Yes. That was me."

Simon raises his eyebrows but doesn't ask for more information. "I'll need to take your full account of tonight, Miss Catrin. Can you come to the provost's home this afternoon, or should I call on you?"

"I can come to you," I offer quickly. I don't want the venatre anywhere near Magister Thomas.

"Thank you. Until then." He turns his back on me, and I realize I've been dismissed. "Are you sure you want to assist?" he asks Juliane. "It won't be pleasant."

Juliane shrugs. "Killing people never is."

Her choice of words startles me. Simon winces, but rather than respond, he faces the alley and takes a long, deep breath. Then he straightens his shoulders and plunges into the darkness. Juliane follows, her brass lamp swinging.

I back away as Emeline's women crowd around the entrance. The guard, too, is very interested, allowing me to slide unnoticed into a gap between houses farther up the street. This one is narrow enough for me to climb with one foot on either side. The last time I did something like this was the day I met the architect, when he watched me escape a group of street thieves I'd just pick-pocketed. This time, rather than tuck myself into the dark eaves and hide, I swing up onto the roof on the left, smothering a grunt from the raw bruises under my shirt.

The rain-slick roof tiles and the need to be silent have me moving slower than I'd like back to Perrete's alley. Once I reach it, I lay flat on the side slanting away from the street and peer over the edge. The moon is visible again, low on the horizon and not much help, but I can see Simon crouching beside Perrete.

He raises one of her bloody hands and studies her stiff fingers. "I can't tell if she managed to scratch him." The walls reflect his voice up to me as clearly as if I were standing next to him. "Cuts on her fingers are probably from clutching her abdomen as he stabbed her." Simon sets Perrete's arm down. "The killer is likely to have similar incidental wounds on his hands from wielding the knife."

"Spell abdomen, please." Juliane's voice is grating and loud in contrast to Simon's. "I don't know this word."

"*A-B-D-O-M-E-N*," Simon replies, rising to his feet. "It's a word physicians use for the stomach area."

Simon is a physician?

"I can't tell how many times she was stabbed." Simon speaks absently as he motions for Juliane to raise the lantern higher, and he slowly rotates around, scanning the area. "I'll know when I look at the body later. Meanwhile . . . there."

He stops, focusing on the blood on the wall, then steps past Juliane to stand in front of it. "He must have cut her throat from behind right here." Simon gestures to the pattern so strangely familiar to me, then lower to more I hadn't noticed. "Then he started stabbing her, too. These vertical streaks of blood are from that."

I don't know whether it's more disturbing that he understands what he sees or that I know he's right.

Simon follows barely visible tracks in the mud back to the body. "He dragged her over here, but she didn't struggle, so she was unconscious if not dead by then."

"Small mercy," says Juliane.

"Agreed," he murmurs, pacing back to the area near Perrete's head. "He removed her eyes and crushed her face with something heavy, but I'm not sure which he did first."

Simon looks around again, this time taking almost a full minute, before shaking his head. "I don't see anything he could've used to do that, though." Then he sighs and rubs his temple. "Everything is disturbed. Footprints, heavy rain, the body covered and moved from how it originally lay . . ." I realize he's correct—Perrete's position is not quite as I found her. "I don't think there's much more I can learn right now," he says. "Best to let them take her away."

Juliane lowers her lantern. "Will we go with them?"

"*We* will not," Simon emphasizes. "We'll go home and speak with Oudin. When I come back, I might bring Lambert, but not you."

"But I can make sure nothing is for—"

"Juliane," Simon says firmly. "You know how tired you'll be by then."

She sighs. "Yes, you're right. More tired tonight."

Simon holds out his elbow like he's inviting his cousin for a stroll, and they exit the alley, arm-in-arm. I ease away from the edge and crawl back across the roof. As an extra precaution, I spring nimbly across the gap and creep across another block of houses to the next alley before climbing down.

I haven't learned whether Magister Thomas will fall under suspicion, but if I arrive at the Montcuir house while Juliane is alone, I might be able to find out from her what Oudin says.

In the meantime, I have to warn the architect.

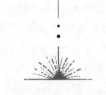

CHAPTER 5

I'm halfway home when I hear a shout.

"Catrin!"

Magister Thomas runs at me, cap askew and black cloak flying out behind him. "Thank the Light!" he gasps. "Where have you been? I heard there was a murder."

I don't realize how precarious a hold I have on my emotions until I'm in his arms, sobbing.

"Rising Sun," Magister Thomas whispers into my hair. "You're cold as ice." He strokes my back for several seconds, then pulls me back and holds my face inches from his. "*Why*, Catrin?" He keeps his voice low, but I've never heard him so angry. "Why were you here and not at the Sanctum?"

Tear flow down my cheeks and over his thumbs. "I'm sorry, I'm sorry," I babble. "I was there, but I saw—I saw . . ."

The architect's hands tighten. "*What* did you see?"

"A man. Near the Sanctum," I gasp. "And I heard—"

I break off. What *did* I hear?

"You heard the woman who was killed?" he whispers, horrified.

It's hard to nod with him holding me as he does, but his hands keep my teeth from chattering. I also remember why the architect can't be seen anywhere near here. "We n-need to go," I tell him.

"Yes, yes. I'm sorry for being so upset. I was just frightened." Magister Thomas pulls his cloak off and settles it around my shoulders. The warmth steadies me enough for him to guide me along minor streets to our back door, where the housekeeper waits for us, wringing her hands.

They seat me near the kitchen hearth fire, and Mistress la Fontaine starts pulling the pins from my wet hair. Magister Thomas kneels and takes my filthy hands in his, looking up into my eyes. "What happened, Catrin?"

Slowly, I tell him about the scream which startled me, though I don't mention my fall or seeing blood on the wall. Then I describe the man in the square and going to look for the source of the cry, also leaving out the whispers telling me to go home.

Magister Thomas sighs and shakes his head. "What possessed you to go into that part of the city, at that hour, alone?"

How can I explain? "I don't know. I just—I just knew someone needed help."

The architect exhales slowly and glances up at the housekeeper standing over my shoulder, clutching a handful of pins. "*How* did you know?" he asks. "Did you hear something? Something more than just a scream?"

"I don't know," I repeat, shaking my head and sniffling. "I just knew." A fresh sob breaks from my chest. "And I was too late!"

Magister Thomas rises higher on his knees and grabs my shoulders. "Praise the Light you were."

I lean away. "How can you say that?"

"Because you wouldn't have been able to stop him!" He shakes me with every word. "He would've had to kill you, too, to keep you silent!" The magister stops and reels himself in slowly, like a kite he's afraid will break free if he pulls too hard. "Cat, what happened to that woman was *not* your fault."

"It was Perrete," I whisper. "And the killer did . . . terrible things. Her eyes—" I squeeze my own tight in a vain attempt to shut out the vision.

Mistress la Fontaine crosses her arms. "I knew that girl was up to nothing good."

"Quiet," Magister Thomas snaps. "No one should speak ill of the dead. Especially one who died so horribly."

I've never heard him speak this sharply to the housekeeper, not even after a kitchen fire burned half the house and all his sketches. Nor has he ever been as cross with me as he has been tonight—twice.

"What if someone knows she was here?" I ask. "The venatre will want to question you."

Magister Thomas blinks. "A venatre has been assigned? For someone like Perrete?"

I nod. "His name is Simon. I've never seen him before, but he's a relative of the Montcuirs."

There's a long silence as the architect strokes his beard and stares into the hearth fire. Then he pulls his hand away and rubs his fingers with a frown. I suspect the coarse hairs have irritated what appear to be a number of fresh cuts on them.

"What will we tell him if he comes?" Mistress la Fontaine asks, her voice trembling.

"The truth," he answers, dropping his hand. "She came here, and I sent her away empty-handed."

The housekeeper presses her lips together. "What about the man—"

"He is nothing," interrupts Magister Thomas. "You will not mention him." The architect focuses back on me. "Does the venatre know what you heard and saw?"

"Yes. He wants me to answer questions this afternoon."

The magister doesn't look pleased. "Then you must do so, but you will only speak of things you know and in the plainest terms. Don't mention Perrete was here unless asked, and then say only you left as she arrived, so you know nothing. Make no speculations on what *may* have occurred." His gray eyes bore into my face. "Do you understand?"

"Yes, Magister," I whisper.

"Good." He sighs and sits back on his heels. "Now, tonight has been an ordeal, but did you find anything at the Sanctum while you were there?"

I nod eagerly. "There's a huge crack in that beam I was worried about. It could fail at any time." I start to rise. "Let me show you on the model."

He pushes me back down before I'm more than a few inches off the chair. "Don't bother. Do you think work should stop?"

The architect has always trusted me, but he's never made such a major decision without verifying it himself. I swallow. "I think the whole section should be taken down."

"That's good enough for me." He comes off his knees with a groan, and I realize he's wearing different clothes from earlier. "The first workers will be arriving within the hour. I'll get that started as soon as there's enough men on the site."

Mistress la Fontaine is already bustling around the kitchen, collecting cheese and meat and sawing on a loaf of bread with a long knife. Magister Thomas bends down to kiss my forehead. "Get cleaned up and get some rest. When you're recovered you can . . ." His voice trails off, and he chokes a little. "You'll see what needs to be done," he finishes.

The housekeeper shoves a hastily prepared breakfast into his hands before he can leave the kitchen. Once he's gone, she forces me to eat a slice of bread with butter and pulls out the wash-tub.

The rain barrels outside are overflowing, so every kettle and pot she can fit over the fire heats up while she fills the bath one bucket at a time. It takes an hour to get it warm enough for her satisfaction, during which I doze off in the chair at least twice.

Once I'm finally in the water, Mistress la Fontaine rinses my breeches and jacket in a smaller basin. Seeing all the blood on them has me scrubbing to get any trace of it off my skin. The housekeeper indulges me as she works to brush the mud from my boots, adding another kettle of hot water to the tub every time it's available. Then she insists on fully unbinding my hair and combing it out—a project that could last all day in lesser hands.

When my curls are tamed and rebraided, the housekeeper pulls a drying sheet down from a high shelf and wraps it around me twice. "You get to bed. Once you're rested you can meet with the venatre. Then we can put all of this behind us."

"He's from Mesanus," I say. "Do you know where that is?"

"Never heard of it." She leads the way to the front room like she intends to dress me and tuck me into bed. "Best grab your boots, you'll need them."

I'm confused, but I bring them as she says.

At the doorway to the architect's workroom, I halt in shock. The magnificent model of the Sanctum lies in pieces all over the floor. Some of the bigger walls are still partially intact, but tiny stone blocks and chunks of mortar are scattered everywhere. On the wide ledge under the closed shutters, tiny shards of colored glass from the miniature windows sit in piles. Several are arranged in patterns, like Magister Thomas had begun piecing them back together. "What happened?" I gasp.

"That girl happened, that's what." Mistress la Fontaine takes a broom and works to clear a path to the stairs. "The magister said not to speak ill of her, and I won't, but I won't speak well of her either."

Perrete did this? How?

Broken glass glitters on the floorboards even where it's been swept, so I slide my boots on. Before standing straight again, I pick up a wadded parchment near my feet. It's the one with the names of the dead, ripped from the wall and thrown across the room. I glance up. The golden hammer is gone from its mount.

That was what Perrete used to wreak such havoc. And in a grisly parallel to the scene in the alley, the scent of her perfume lingers in the air.

My stomach twists and mist fills my eyes as I look over the wreckage again. It will take months to repair and rebuild. This is what Magister Thomas meant when he said I would know what needed to be done.

"Come now," the housekeeper calls from the bottom of the stairs. She sets the broom aside. "You can worry about this after you've had a good sleep."

I walk numbly across the room and up the steps. My suspicion that Mistress la Fontaine would put me to bed like a child is correct, but I let her. I'm consumed with the worry that anyone who learns what happened will assume Magister Thomas would've been more than just upset with Perrete over it.

But angry enough to kill her? Angry enough to do such terrible things?

I can't believe that. I *won't* believe that. Ever.

But would the venatre?

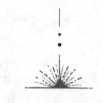

CHAPTER 6

It's almost noon when I wake. My eyes water from the pain of the deep bruises across my stomach as I dress in a clean working skirt. The skin, too, is raw and scraped, and protests every touch and movement. The injuries remind me how lucky I am to be alive, but I can't shake what I heard and saw in my head while falling. Part of me still believes *I* was the one who died last night.

Even with boots on, I tread carefully through the dim workroom. The front shutters are still down, but I'm glad for the darkness. It feels wrong that the Blessed Sun should shine so brightly when everything in our lives is turned inside out and hanging by a thread.

My mood changes a bit when I see the young man sitting at the kitchen table. He looks up and grins. In the last six months, his face finally seems to have grown enough to fit his giant nose, and his upper lip now has a substantial black mustache rather than just the beginnings of one. When he stands to greet me, I see he's also several inches taller.

"Light of Day, Remi!" I gasp, flinging myself into his arms. "It's good to see you."

The rumble of laughter in his chest resonates into mine as he hugs me back. Before I can sink too deeply into the embrace, I suddenly remember how we'd parted last fall. Does he?

I lean back, feeling awkward. Remi's rough hands come up to either side of my face and hold me there as deep green eyes study mine. I pull my lips between my teeth as he does the same. Oh yes, he remembers.

He wrinkles his brow. "Your eyes look different."

"Nonsense," says Mistress la Fontaine from the counter on the other side of the kitchen. Everything I see and smell tells me she's preparing all of her son's favorite dishes.

"No, truly." Remi cocks his head to the side. "They used to be darker, and now the outer edges are . . . more distinct."

My eyes are hazel, a mix of blue and brown. That he knows their color so well—or thought he did—says much.

"It's just the light." The housekeeper slams two cast-iron pots together loud enough to make us jump apart. She obviously doesn't like what she sees between us, which is . . . Well, I'm not sure what it is.

When he left for further study in Lutecia, Remi kissed my cheek like a brother bidding a sister goodbye, saying things would be different when he returned. I'd assumed he was referring to the fact that, Sun willing, he'd have tested out of his apprenticeship. Then he'd called me Catrin—which was unusual—and kissed me again. On the mouth. In a very *not* brother-like way.

It hadn't been unpleasant, but it didn't give me the thrill I'd expected from a first kiss, either. Maybe I was just surprised.

Remi sits back down and kicks a chair out for me like nothing strange had ever passed between us. I drop into the seat, asking, "When did you arrive?"

He glances at his mother. "Early this morning."

"You must have stopped just outside of town last night," I say. "Why not come all the way in?"

"And cause a fuss right before bed? Mum needs all the beauty sleep she can get." Mistress la Fontaine scowls at him over her shoulder, but Remi only smiles. "Though I heard she was up anyway with all the excitement last night."

My appetite immediately vanishes. "Excitement is not the word I'd choose."

"That reminds me," says the housekeeper. "The venatre was here earlier. He wanted to speak with you, but I told him you were asleep and intended to call on him as agreed."

Remi shakes his head in disbelief. "I still can't believe there's an official investigation for Perrete."

"Oudin Montcuir admitted to being with her last night," I say. "And dozens of people heard him say so."

Mistress la Fontaine's shoulders stiffen, but Remi leans forward, focused on me. "The comte's son is suspect?"

"I think the investigation is mostly to clear him," I answer. "It's also why the venatre isn't the comte or his other son."

"Who is he?"

"Someone called Simon of Mesanus. I think he's a relative of the Montcuirs."

Remi sits back again. "Keeping it in the family, then."

"Do you know where Mesanus is? I've never heard of it." I study the plate of muffins between us, not sure I can stomach one.

"Prezia, I think," Remi says. "Near the coast."

That's several days to the north, outside Gallia. They speak a different language, but Simon didn't have an accent like other Prezians I've met.

Remi plays with a fork on the table, spinning it with one finger. "What's he like?"

"The venatre?" I shrug. "He was reluctant at first, but I think he'll do a thorough job."

"How thorough?"

Again I shrug, this time to hide my unease. "I guess I'll find out when I answer his questions."

Or avoid answering them.

"You'd best let the magister know you're here, Remone," says Mistress la Fontaine abruptly. Her use of his full name leaves no room for argument.

I glance at the plate in front of him. Not a crumb is on it, so he must have licked it clean. No doubt he missed his mother's cooking.

Remi stands and stretches with a groan. "It's good to see you again, Kitten," he says. "We'll catch up later, eh?"

I hate when he calls me Kitten. "Goodbye, *Remone*," I retort, wishing I had a better name to torment him with.

After he vanishes out the door to the workroom, Mistress la Fontaine turns to me, chopping knife in hand. "You be careful what you tell the venatre today," she says. "I don't like the look or sound of him. Foreigners should have no business in our affairs."

Odd she would take such a stance when her late husband was from Tauria, which isn't even on this continent. No one who looks at Remi could doubt his foreign father's business in *her* affairs. "Prezia isn't exactly far," I say. "Less than a week's journey."

"I don't like his eyes," she insists. "They aren't natural."

I roll my own at her superstition. Then, remembering Remi's comment, I ask, "Have my eyes changed like Remi said?"

"No." The housekeeper turns back to her vegetables with a series of vicious *thwacks*. "It's just the light." *Thwack*. "Nothing more."

CHAPTER 7

The Montcuir family lives only a few blocks away, but after last night I have no desire to stray from the main roads even in broad daylight, so I take the longer route to their house via the Sanctum Square. While the section of scaffolding I inspected last night is a long way away and blocked from view by the transept arm and tower, I can hear it coming down. I'll have to swing by later and sketch what's been done so I can change it on the model.

Then I remember there's no model to update, and it's like a blow to my bruised stomach. Now that Remi has returned, however, I might actually have time to start piecing it back together.

A woman I recognize as Lady Juliane's former governess answers the door. From the cloth over her hair and the smudge of flour on one round cheek, it's a fair bet she stayed with the household, working in the kitchen, expecting someday to care for Juliane's children. If so, she's been waiting a long time. She barely speaks as she leads me to the third floor. In a room at the end of the passage, Juliane sits at a long table, writing. Behind her on the wall hangs a wooden carving of the sun, polished smooth and reflecting the light coming through the open window. The far corners of the room have a medium-size bed and an oak wardrobe, but otherwise it's so bare I assume it must be unoccupied.

"Miss Catrin"—the woman pauses in her announcement as though to emphasize that I don't have a surname—"says she's here at Master Simon's request."

Juliane sets down her quill and stands, smiling in a way that says she's glad I'm here, and not just because Simon asked me to come. "Thank you, Madame Denise," she tells the woman, who curtsies and departs without another word.

Once we're alone, Juliane gestures for me to come inside. "I hope being in Simon's room doesn't make you uncomfortable, but it guarantees some privacy."

"The venatre lives here?" I look around again for signs of life but find none other than a worn chest with a bronze candlestick on top of it. Given the house is at least four times larger than the architect's, it must have more than enough bedrooms on the second floor, and I wonder what that says about Simon's place in the family. "It's so . . . empty."

She shrugs. "I think he's used to a simpler life. Please, have a seat."

I nod politely and sit on the bench across from her, waiting until she lowers herself down again.

"Simon isn't here at the moment," Juliane continues. "But he should return soon." She pulls a clean piece of parchment—no *paper*—from the messy pile between us. Not even the architect uses paper. It's too expensive and can't be reused like parchment. There's more in front of me now than I've ever seen in my whole life. "If you like, I can begin recording your account now," she offers.

My mouth goes completely dry. I'd come early in hopes of learning what Simon knew so far and hadn't expected to answer questions from her. "All right."

"Excellent." She speaks like we'll be discussing something pleasant and benign, like the weather, rather than murder. "Let's begin with your employment. You said you work for the architect, yet you aren't an apprentice?"

"Um, no, not really." I twist my hands in my lap. At one time I'd thought to work alongside Remi in that position, but though I have a good eye for load-bearing structures, I could never master the mathematics required or produce designs with enough accuracy. That's why my specialty is the scaffolds; they don't require precise measurement like the Sanctum itself. "I'm his assistant," I explain. "Mostly I inspect the building site."

Dipping her quill, Juliane records my exact response in ink, including the *Um, no*, and also her own words before and after. "And that's what you were doing last night?"

I clear my throat to see if she'll write an approximation of the sound, which she does. "Yes, we were behind schedule so I went out once the moon was up." I omit my fall as I tell her about hearing the scream, and how I went to the top of the Sanctum to look out over the city.

The pen scratches across the paper for several seconds, then stops as Juliane looks up. Her eyes are dilated so widely the deep brown of her iris is barely visible. "Then what?"

"I saw a man, running." I describe him as much as I can and the directions he went.

"Was he Selenae?"

The question takes me by surprise. "Ah, not that I could tell."

Scritch scritch. Pause. "Did you hear anything else?"

Besides a disembodied voice telling me to go home? I shake my head. "No."

Juliane frowns in what might be disappointment. "Please continue."

From there I relate the search that led me to Perrete's body, running out of the alley screaming, the woman who yelled at me, and how I eventually raised the alarm. I include as many details as possible to make up for what I leave out, like the strange whispers and how the alley seemed alight with a thousand candles.

"Did you see a Selenae man in the crowd which gathered?" Juliane asks.

"Um, yes?" Though she'd asked about Selenae earlier, I'm so startled I answer without thinking. I'm not sure I want to get this man into trouble, though. "But he left right after I noticed him."

"Do you think he was following you?" says a male voice.

We turn to see Simon's lanky form leaning on the doorframe, arms crossed. Lambert stands behind him, flushed and sweating in contrast to the venatre's pale composure.

"How long have you been there?" Juliane asks, frowning.

"Just a minute or so. You were doing fine." Simon turns his gaze to me. "Do you think the Selenae man was following you?" he asks again.

"From where? The Sanctum?"

Simon nods, the tired shadows under his eyes briefly spilling over his sharp cheekbones.

"Why—why would you think so?"

The venatre purses his lips for a few seconds, his expression revealing nothing. Finally he nods at Juliane. "Show her Oudin's account."

Juliane drops the quill and begins sifting through the mess of papers as Simon and Lambert come into the room. She picks out three pages and puts them in order before handing them to me. I can't believe my luck—I'm going to see exactly what Oudin said.

Like what she's written for my questions, these pages appear

to be a word-for-word record. Even with the occasional abbre-
viations, I wonder how she was able to keep up. The sheet on
top isn't the first, however, so I'm missing the beginning of his
account.

S: *Then?*
O: *I went to find Perrete.*
S: *Did you go to her home?*
O: *Of course. I don't rut in an alley like an animal.*

I clench my teeth. What a horrible thing to say, especially
given where Perrete ended up.

S: *Did you find her?*
O: *Yes, but she said she had business to attend first.*
S: *Did she say where she was going?*
O: *No, but she was smiling like she had a secret. She was
always a tease.*

He didn't know she went to see Magister Thomas. I slowly
release the breath I was holding, aware Simon is watching me.
Lambert drops heavily into a chair on the far end of the table.

S: *What did you do after that?*
O: *Went back to the alehouse. She said she'd meet me there
if things went well.*
S: *Did you consume* skonia *while there?*
O: *Will you have me arrested for that?*
S: *No, that is none of my concern.*

I wonder if the venatre ignores it out of family loyalty or true
desire to solve Perrete's murder.

O: Then yes, I did. Had to do something to pass the time.
S: Was that your only dose of the night?
O: Yes. What–Ah! Get away!
S: Slightly delayed reaction.

My guess is Simon snapped his fingers or clapped his hands right in front of Oudin's nose. City guards do that to assess people they find wandering the streets in a drug-induced haze. Apparently Simon can judge exactly how long it's been based on Oudin's eyes, because he continues,

S: Moderate dilation. Time of consumption approximately five hours ago. If that was soon after seeing Perrete, that puts Oudin Montcuir in her company at—
J: One hour before midnight.

She doesn't leave a single word out, even her own. I've noticed something else about Simon. Even if he's not a physician, he knows quite a lot of methods and phrases they use. Perhaps he's a scholar of some sort, though the room bereft of books implies otherwise.

S: Thank you, Juliane. Then what?
O: She never came to the tavern, so I decided to go home.

Foreboding unwinds in my stomach like a spool of ribbon. The Sanctum Square would've been the most direct route.

S: Did you see or hear anyone else on your way?
O: It—it may have been the skonia.
S: I will judge that. What did you see?
O: A Selenae man. Standing in the shadows. Looking up at the Sanctum.

Juliane's writing conveys a choppiness to Oudin's speech, and perhaps fear. I'm feeling the same unease.

S: *What was he doing?*
O: *He was—He was communing with one of the demon statues high on the wall. He spoke to it, and it flew away.*

Skonia delusions often start with seeing or hearing something real but unexpected, then diverge from what's truly happening into a flat-out hallucination. If Oudin indeed saw a Selenae man, it means I was being watched—and followed—long before I left the Sanctum.

I'm also certain Oudin saw me standing by Pierre. When I moved away, his drugged mind interpreted it as the statue taking flight. The unspooled ribbon of anxiety in my belly feels like it's caught fire at one end, spreading rapidly through the twists and turns. Somehow, I know what's coming.

The next speaker is Lambert, someone I hadn't realized was present.

L: *Did the Selenae man say anything?*
O: *He said, "Go home, little cat. This is not a night to be out."*

CHAPTER 8

I drop the page and slap both hands over my mouth to hold back the scream that tries to burst from my lungs.

Impossible. There's no other way to describe what I've read.

Yet those were the exact words I heard while standing on the Sanctum wall. The Selenae man's voice reached me then just as it did later, and neither time should have happened.

Impossible.

Simon is at my side, one hand on my shoulder. The gesture is too familiar coming from a stranger, but I'm grateful for the steadiness it offers. "Juliane," he says, "can you get us some calming tea?"

"Right away." She leaves, but I hardly notice.

When I remain silent, Simon ventures to speak again. "I'm sorry, Miss Catrin. I didn't anticipate that would be so frightening."

He believes my horror is from realizing I was being watched. That's an assumption I won't challenge.

"Do you think you could describe the Selenae man you saw later, or recognize him?" Lambert asks, sitting forward, all concern.

Yes, I could. I don't imagine there are many as scarred as him. Yet I have no reason to believe he was malevolent. In fact, he was trying to protect me. Why else would he have urged me—twice—to go home?

This is not a night to be out.

"I—I don't know if I would recognize him," I stammer. "It was so dark. I was upset from finding . . . the body."

A cup of tea appears in front of me. The steam carries the pungent odor of valerian root and other herbs I don't recognize. "It tastes better than it smells," says Juliane kindly.

The liquid scalds my tongue, but what flavor I taste is positively floral. I take several slow sips, letting the warmth spread through me. With each inhalation, my body feels lighter, like I'm floating upward. I half expect my head to brush against the rafters.

"How are you feeling now, Miss Catrin?" Simon asks.

"Better." I smile and raise the cup to my lips again, but Simon grabs it with impossible speed, splashing hot tea on his fingers and my lap. He brings the drink to his nose and sniffs.

His eyes dart to Juliane. "Did this brew all night?"

Juliane wrings her hands, and I'm struck by how visible her knuckles are in her thin fingers. "I brought what was in the pot," she says. "Is it over-strong?"

Simon looks back at me. "Most definitely. I've never seen it affect someone this much so quickly."

"Will she be all right?" Lambert peers at my face. When he blinks, the short fringe of his eyelashes sweep the dust motes around him, making them dance in the sunlight streaming through the window.

"I'm fine," I tell him. I can't even recall why I was so anxious.

Simon frowns and sets the cup aside. "She only drank about a quarter of it, so I'm not too worried." He sits next to me, straddling the bench. "But I don't think she'll be able to answer questions for much longer."

I scowl, annoyance pushing through the fog of contentment. "Please stop talking like I can't understand you."

"Of course," says Simon. "My apologies, Miss Catrin."

"Cat," I say thickly. My tongue feels as heavy as a Sanctum stone.

His blond eyebrows come together. "What?"

"I'm just called Cat." Each word requires concentration. "'Miss Catrin' makes me think you're speaking to someone else."

The tiniest of smiles tugs the corner of Simon's mouth. "Very well, Cat. Was there anything else you heard or saw last night?"

I heard Perrete's despair and the Selenae man's words. I saw blood on the Sanctum wall just like in the alley. Or did I see the alley wall from the Sanctum? I shake my head to clear that thought. "I saw what was done to Perrete," I answer, conscious of the double meaning.

"Perrete." Simon leans back at my casual use of her name. "Did you know her before?"

My answer comes before I can stop it. "She visited Magister Thomas sometimes."

No, I mustn't say that.

"But not for what you think," I rush to add. What was in that tea? I put a hand over my eyes. *Concentrate.* I have to explain what I've admitted without revealing anything that would raise suspicion.

"Her father worked for the architect years ago, but he died." Truth is the easiest path, and I walk down it, picking my words as carefully as roses from thorny vines. "Magister Thomas tried to make sure she wasn't destitute, but . . . he hasn't given her money in a long time." The tears that rush to my eyes are real. "Her death was a shock to him."

Simon nods in understanding. "I can imagine." He sighs and looks to Lambert. "Cousin, I think Miss—Cat needs to go home. Would you mind escorting her there?"

"Certainly." I hear Lambert standing, though the noise sounds like it's coming from the bottom of a well. "I'll be back in a few minutes," he tells Simon as he helps me to my feet.

"Don't bother." Simon yawns. "I'm too tired to do anything more today. You probably are, too."

Lambert guides me out of the room, his gloved hand holding my arm as we navigate the hall and staircase. Somehow I make it down two flights and out the front door, though I'm not sure my feet ever touch the ground. Lambert anchors me with his steadiness, but I feel like I'm drifting above him as we walk up the street. The Sanctum looms ahead, bringing a smile to my face. "Beautiful, isn't it?" I ask.

"If you like that sort of thing," he replies.

"I do," I say. "Do you know there hasn't been an accident in five years? Do you know why?"

"Why?" His voice is laced with amusement.

"Because of me," I answer solemnly. "I climb all over the scaffolds, looking for problems. That's why I was hired."

"Where were you before that?"

"At Solis Abbey."

Lambert nods. "Ah, yes, Juliane said she recognized you from there." He directs our path the same way I came, probably because cutting through side streets with a young woman leaning heavily on one's arm isn't very proper.

My focus remains on the Sanctum despite the brilliant sunlight reflecting off it. It's magnificent. I never understood Mother Agnes's objection to my work, as it's for the glory of the Sun.

"The prioress was upset when I left," I say, filling the silence with my thought. "I used to have tea with her once a week, but

I haven't in a while. I miss her." The last admission is a surprise to me.

It's her fault, though.

"Someone is waving at us," Lambert says. We've reached the open plaza. Remi runs toward us, wearing a scowl.

"That's Magister Thomas's apprentice," I say brightly.

Remi's close enough to hear me. "Not anymore. I'm a journeyman now, remember?" Without waiting for an answer, he asks, "What's wrong, Cat?"

"Nothing. No thing. Not a thing." I burst into giggles, though I'm not sure why the words are so funny.

"Is she *drunk*?" Remi yanks me away from Lambert, and I stumble into his side.

"No, no." Lambert shakes his head. "She only had some tea. Some of the questions we asked about last night were distressing, and it was meant to help."

"What in Sun's Light was in that tea?" Remi nearly yells. "*Skonia*?"

"Don't be mad at him," I say, leaning into Remi's shoulder. He smells like stone dust and sweat. The scent of hard work. "The venatre gave it to me."

"Then he'll answer for that." Remi leads me away. "I'll take her home from here."

Lambert watches us go. Something deep inside me cringes in embarrassment as I blow him a kiss goodbye.

CHAPTER 9

I sleep straight through to the next morning, which allows Remi to give Magister Thomas his account of my return first.

"It wasn't meant to do that," I try to explain. For some reason I feel compelled to defend what happened, though if the architect knew I was being watched that night, he'd probably never let me out of doors alone again. "As soon as they realized how strong the tea was, they took it away. I only had a few sips."

Remi stabs his sausage with a knife. "I'd hate to see someone under the influence of a full cup," he mutters. "You could barely string two words together."

"That's because I was asleep," I snap. "I went straight to bed."

"I know, Kitten. I carried you there." Remi rolls his eyes, then glances at the architect. "I mean, I took you to your door." Not entering my room is the one rule he's never attempted to stretch.

In response to that hated nickname, I rake my fingers through the air like claws and hiss at him.

"Enough," Magister Thomas says. "What did you tell the venatre, Catrin?"

I straighten my face before answering. "I said I heard a scream, saw a man running, went looking, and found her body, Magister. Nothing else."

"Nothing about Perrete coming here?" the architect asks, and Remi's green eyes bulge.

Technically I didn't. "No. I said we knew her and that you sometimes gave her money," I admit. "But that you hadn't done so in a long time."

Magister Thomas's lips push out from his beard, a sign he's displeased.

Remi chokes down his mouthful and gasps, "She came *here*?"

"She came, she demanded money and I refused, she threw a tantrum, then she left," the architect says. "That's all."

"Threw a tantrum?" Remi points a thumb to the workroom door. "*She* did that?" The magister nods wearily. "Did she take the hammer, too?"

He sighs. "After she used it, yes."

My eyes widen. I hadn't realized the hammer was actually missing. If Perrete had it with her, robbery could've been the motive for her murder. The tool is engraved with the architect's name, though, so it would probably be melted down for the gold plating.

The magister focuses on me, a deep sadness in his gray eyes. "Does the venatre suspect anyone?"

I nod. "Oudin says there was a Selenae man in the Sanctum Square that night. I think the venatre will be looking for anyone else who saw him."

Magister Thomas throws his two-pronged fork down on his plate in disgust. "Curse that idiot! He's going to get someone killed."

Remi snorts. "Just a Selenae."

"The People of the Night are exactly that," says the architect sharply. "People."

"Moon worshippers," Remi mutters at his remaining sausage. "Magicians and heretics."

Magister Thomas sits forward. "Don't be ignorant, Remone. They no more worship the moon than we worship the Sun."

The theology is something few bother to understand, but Mother Agnes drilled into us how the Blessed Sun is a gift from a higher power. We honor and praise it with temples to capture its beauty and show our appreciation, but it is not a god. I have no idea how Selenae could feel the same way about the moon, however. Its light isn't strong or constant enough to support any kind of plant life on its own. Even the moonflowers which cover their walls need the sun. But that something greater lies Beyond the Skies is something we all agree on.

The architect continues, "If you don't understand our religion, you cannot expect to properly build a Sanctum like ours."

"I don't need your lectures!" Remi jumps to his feet. "I'm not a child!"

The magister only raises his eyebrows. "Then don't act like one."

Remi storms out without another word. A few seconds later, we hear him stomping up the stairs to his room on the third floor. I turn to the architect, astonished. "What was that about?"

Magister Thomas rubs his face tiredly, then pulls his hand back to grimace at the cuts on his fingers. "I wouldn't promise to put him in charge of the transept expansion in two years."

"Why not? He's passed his apprenticeship."

"Yes, but he still has a lot to learn. Even I wasn't a master until I was twenty-five."

After eight years of study and work, Remi was being told he had to wait another five at least. "How did you feel at his age?" I ask.

The architect smiles, though it's a bit strained. "Arrogant. Full of myself and grand plans. Unable to appreciate those around me."

"Well, then he's right on schedule."

That earns a chuckle. Magister Thomas stands and tugs a stray curl by my ear. "Do me a favor and make repairing the model your priority for the next few days."

"It'll take weeks." Starting with several days of just cleaning up the mess.

The architect bends lower to look me in the eyes. "And valerian tea aside, the more time you spend with the venatre, the more likely it is you will say something you don't want to. You've given him your account. That's all that's necessary."

I nod in agreement as much as in obedience, and the magister departs.

By the time Remi passes through the workroom for the Sanctum, I've swept nearly everything that can't be saved into a barrel. After that, I divide the remaining stone blocks into piles according to their size. The model's cornerstone is still intact. Everything can be rebuilt from that point, but first the table will need to be fixed.

The front window is propped open for light and air, and all morning, people pause and look inside. Around noon I'm sitting in the center of the room, scraping mortar off blocks when another shadow stops to stare. I've ignored everyone until now, but something makes me look up this time.

It's Simon of Mesanus.

"How are you feeling today, Miss Catrin?" he asks cautiously.

"Well enough, sir." His expression is so much like a child who expects to be scolded that I look back down to hide my smile. "I slept over twelve hours."

He clears his throat. "The tea wasn't meant to be that strong. I'm sorry."

"Apology accepted." I glance up. "But I remember telling you to call me Cat. Everyone else does." Except Mother Agnes. And Remi.

"That's actually why I'm here," Simon says. "May I come in?"

I nod and indicate the half door, unable to refuse a venatre's request, but also curious. "It's not latched."

Simon pushes it open and steps inside, his strange eyes sweeping over the ruins. "What happened in here?"

"It was a model of the Sanctum." I stand and brush dust from my hands. "One side of the table collapsed, and, well . . ."

I shrug. It's another half-truth. Perrete had kicked out one leg and smashed a second.

He studies the tiny shards of colored glass the architect had been arranging. "It must have been extraordinary."

I point to the year stamped on the cornerstone. "It was as old as the Sanctum itself. We updated it with every expansion."

Simon picks up a tangle of twigs and reeds from a pile. "Even the scaffolding?"

"Even that. It was useful for reference." I wait for him to set the splintered pieces back down. "What is it you wanted?"

He walks around the broken table, hands clasped behind his back. "Something was bothering me yesterday after you left, but I was so tired I gave up trying to figure it out. After a good night's sleep and sorting through all of Juliane's notes, I realized what it was." Simon reaches the far side of the room and turns to face me. "Your name is Cat."

"And?" I rub my sweaty palms on my work apron.

"'Go home, little Cat.'" Simon quotes. "That Selenae man was talking to *you*." When I don't say anything, he takes a few steps closer. "And you realized it. That's why you were so upset."

Simon's face is all planes and angles except for the end of

his nose, which is rounded and slightly turned up, giving him a boyish look despite his seriousness. "What difference does it make?" I ask, then lie for the first time. "I didn't hear him."

"But that means he was watching you, and likely followed you. That's very interesting."

Again I feel uneasy. The man did nothing wrong as far as I can tell, and Magister Thomas was worried about the venatre's interest in finding the man. "I'm sorry, but I couldn't see him that well."

Simon sighs like he knows I'm not being entirely truthful. "Will you keep watch for someone following you, though? And take steps to keep yourself safe?"

I nod before he can define how. "I will."

"All right then." Simon clears his throat. "Now I'd like to talk about the things you *did* see and hear."

My eyes drop to the pile of rubble by my left foot. "I already told Lady Juliane everything."

"I know," says Simon. "But there are a few inconsistencies." I look up in alarm, and he raises a hand to reassure me. "By that I mean there are things I don't quite understand, and I think you can clarify. That's all. You're not in any kind of trouble."

The more time you spend with the venatre, the more likely it is you will say something you don't want to.

I chew on my bottom lip. "What do you want me to do?"

Simon relaxes a little at my tentative offer. "I'd like you to question people in the neighborhood with me." He pauses. "You're not a stranger in Collis. People will be more willing to talk to you. Then I'd like you to help me better visualize what you saw that night."

In the corner of my vision, Mistress la Fontaine appears in the doorway to the kitchen. From the frown which creases her forehead, she's been listening to the whole conversation.

It's dangerous, but I *want* to help Simon. He genuinely seems to care, both about Perrete and finding the truth.

Magister Thomas is innocent; the truth cannot hurt him. And if I know what the venatre is thinking, I can lead him away from the architect if necessary.

"I'll go."

CHAPTER 10

"Where are Lambert and Lady Juliane today?" I ask Simon as we skirt around the edges of the Sanctum Square. "Aren't they assisting you?"

"They're elbows deep in wedding preparations. Lambert was recently engaged to Lady Genevieve d'Ecre." Simon runs a hand through his blond curls, then hooks one thumb in a pocket of his tunic. "It'll be quite an event."

That explains why the comte was so concerned during his tour about when the vaulted ceiling in the expansion would be finished. "What part do you get to play?"

"The easiest. I just have to dress up and stand where I'm told." Simon's grin is hesitant, like he hasn't smiled in a long time and isn't sure he's doing it correctly.

He's still the venatre, though, and it's safer to center the conversation on him. "How exactly are you related to the Montcuirs?" I ask.

"My mother's sister was married to the comte's younger brother." Simon hunches his shoulders and kicks a stone the size of a small plum, sending it skittering to rest against a cart selling sweetmeats. "It's a distant connection, but they're the only family

I have left." He smiles self-consciously, again like he's trying to remember how. "I came to Collis last winter hoping for help finding an apprenticeship or other work, but . . ." His mouth tightens. "They had other ideas."

Not a physician, then. I steal a glance at Simon's hands, searching for hints of what kind of work he's done in the past, but his palms are smooth and his fingers uncalloused. "What kind of apprenticeship did you want?"

He shrugs, this time with only one shoulder. "Whoever would take me. I have no experience or skill."

The statement shocks me into staring at him. "Aren't you a little old to be starting from nothing?"

"Old?" Simon raises an eyebrow. "I admit eighteen is later than most to begin an apprenticeship, but it's not *old*."

"Eighteen?" I face ahead to hide the color I feel spreading across my cheeks. "I thought you were at least Juliane's age."

"Nineteen now," he replies. "Though, given my task, I hope other people assume as you did."

The Pathway of Prayer is visible, but we're still only halfway across the square. Simon clears his throat. "May I ask about your family?"

A hollow forms in my chest. "The family that gave birth to me, the family that raised me, or the family I have now?"

Simon chuckles ironically. "I see we have similar problems, but whichever you would prefer to talk about."

His empathy unlocks something inside me. "I was left with the Sisters of Light when I was a few days old. The prioress makes it her mission to educate any girl she can get her hands on, so I was well schooled, but I left the abbey to work for the architect when I was twelve."

"To climb scaffolds." That's what I told Juliane and Lambert, so it's not a question.

I nod. "That was the initial reason, but now I assist him in other ways."

We pass the transept before Simon speaks, raising his voice to be heard over the noise of construction in this section. "And so he's your family now."

"Well, him and the housekeeper. And Remi."

"Who's Remi?"

"Magister Thomas's apprentice, but he just finished several weeks of examinations in Lutecia under another master, so he's a journeyman now," I explain. "He's also the housekeeper's son. Mistress la Fontaine needed a home after her husband died, so it was an arrangement that suited everyone."

"Ah," says Simon knowingly. "That must have been the woman who watched us leave. Does she mother you?"

I shrug. "We get along." Mistress la Fontaine has always been concerned with keeping me well-fed and presentable. Mother Agnes and I fought constantly, but in some ways her nettling showed she cared about me on a deeper level.

Which only makes her lies worse.

We reach the Pathway of Prayer and turn away from the Sanctum. The noise level drops quickly, but Simon doesn't continue our conversation, for which I'm glad, as I half expected him to ask about my parents. The prioress told me years ago that she had no idea who they were. That was her first lie.

After a minute of silence, I realize Simon hasn't said a word about his own mother or father, either.

A city watchman comes into view, sitting on a barrel outside the alley as he picks his fingernails with a small knife. When a passerby stops to peer into the alley, the man looks up and growls for him to keep moving. So much for observing anyone who lingers beyond reason. As we approach, his challenging expression turns to Simon.

"I don't think he realizes who you are," I murmur.

Straightening his back, Simon walks right up to the watchman. "I am the provost's appointed venatre." The title doesn't roll easily off his tongue, but he's apparently decided it has some uses. "Do you have anything notable to report?"

The man jumps to his feet, pulling his halberd to his side. "No, sir!" he answers respectfully. "No one has tried to get past me or the watch before."

His ready acceptance of Simon's authority is likely due to a passed-down description. That left eye of his is a pretty distinct way to identify him.

Simon sighs in exasperation. "No, I wouldn't think so. I have some inquiring to do, so consider yourself dismissed for the next hour."

"Thank you, sir." The guard hurries off, eager to make use of his sudden free time.

"Well, Venatre," I say. "Where do we start?"

Simon scowls. "We can start with you never calling me that again."

I knew the word made him uncomfortable, but it's obvious he actually hates it. "Sorry, Master Simon."

"*Simon*. Just Simon." He shakes his head. "Light of Day, we're the same age."

"You're two years older," I correct him.

He blinks. "Really?" Suddenly he flushes and looks away. "Close enough. I'll call you Cat if you call me Simon, agreed?"

"Agreed. So where do we start, Simon?"

He glances around. "Let's begin with the woman you saw after finding the body. Where were you exactly?"

I move to stand next to the barrel. "Here."

Simon steps up beside me and looks down the street. "And which window did she look out of?"

"That one." I point to the house six doors away. "The one with the repaired board that's not painted yet."

He frowns and squints where I indicate. "You saw that at night?"

My fingertips tingle with a sudden anxiety. "The moon was very bright."

"All right. We'll start there." Simon leads the way to the door below the window. The woman who answers his knock holds an infant to her shoulder and looks very much like the face I saw that night.

"Good day, madam," Simon begins, and she raises her eyebrows almost into the fringe of the sweat-stained cap on her head. "I'm investigating the murder two nights ago. I need to know if you saw or heard anything."

"I heard nothin' till everyone was on the streets." She steps back to close the door.

"Wait!" I say quickly. "What about the woman who was up with the baby?" Ignoring Simon's confused look, I push on. "One of your neighbors said she yelled at someone for waking the child."

The woman snorts. "Wait here." She closes the door.

Simon frowns. "She wasn't the mother you saw? She had a baby, so I just assumed."

I study the grain of wooden door to avoid looking at him. "That woman's eyes were blue."

"You saw that from this distance?" Simon glances back at the alley. "If the guard was over there, I'm pretty sure I wouldn't be able to distinguish his eye color, and it's broad daylight."

Fortunately the door reopens at that moment, and a woman close in looks and age to the first one peers out. They must be sisters. "What do you want?" she asks.

"Nothing difficult to answer," Simon says amiably. "Just that I was told you saw someone on the street the night of the—"

"Murder?" she finishes, and he nods. "Aye, I did. I leaned out of that window"—she points upward while tilting her head up the street—"and saw a fellow emptying his guts over there."

"So you were already awake?" he asks. "For how long?"

"Hadn't a wink of sleep thanks to the babe. I'd finally got his eyes t' close when tha' idiot's screaming woke him." She shrugs. "Later I figured mebbe he found tha' girl, but what does it matter? I dinna see more than that."

A queasiness twists my stomach as Simon tries again. "What about before? Did you hear anything?"

"No." She starts to shut the door.

"Wait!" I put out a hand to stop her. "You didn't hear the woman scream at all? Please, we're just trying to establish what time she died."

"No." She peers at me through narrowed eyes. "It was a quiet night. Quieter than most, even with the storm coming."

I couldn't have been the only one. "Do you think the baby's crying kept you from hearing her?"

The woman steps back, shaking her head. "No, I was nursing him. It's the only way to get him t' fall asleep, but he just wouldn't tha' night."

I lurch into the doorway. "Please—"

"Cat," says Simon gently. "She didn't hear anything."

The door slams shut in my face.

CHAPTER 11

"I don't understand," I whisper.

Simon regards me carefully. "Do you mean why you heard her but no one else did?"

Nodding numbly, I step away from the door.

"There are several possible explanations," he says. "First, that the woman could be lying."

I shake my head. "Why though? Shouldn't she want the crime solved?"

Simon gestures for me to follow him up the street. "She doubts it will be, and for good reason. The less she's involved, the better, especially if the provost's son is implicated."

I wonder if Simon considers the case equally hopeless. We continue knocking on doors, but no one admits hearing anything before I screamed and the woman yelled at me. Such disturbances are common in the area, and none bothered to investigate the commotion until the guard was called.

"Why else might no one have heard anything?" I ask Simon as we approach the last home within sight of the alley. "You said there were several possibilities."

"The acoustic nature of the walls may have kept the noise from traveling out to the street but not from going up." He pauses. "Do you know what that means?"

"Of course," I say, feeling patronized. "Acoustics are a major part of the Sanctum's design." Though I was never able to grasp the geometry required, I understand the concept. Angles and curves of walls are used to reflect and amplify voices from the altar to all corners of the building. I'd also noticed that very effect when listening to him and Juliane from the roof, but I refrain from mentioning that. If Simon understands acoustics and the language of physicians, however, his education was on the same level as Remi's—or better.

When no one answers the last door, we return to the alley. "Let's start at the beginning," Simon says. "What did you see as you looked in here that night?"

A pair of silver eyes lined with kohl catch mine from down the street. I freeze, but they're gone before I can fully focus on them.

"Catrin."

Simon's face is close to mine, the flaw in his eye standing out like a dark knot in a plank of oak. I jump. "What?"

"Is something wrong?"

The person is gone—if they were ever there. "No, nothing," I say quickly.

Simon wears the expression I recognize as not quite believing what I've said. "Very well, then." He gestures into the alley. "What did you see that night?"

"Darkness," I answer simply.

"And you went in?"

"There was . . ." I pause, trying to put myself back in the moment. "There was moonlight on the wall, and muddy foot-prints leading out. The smell of blood was very strong."

Simon raises an eyebrow at me. "And you went in?" he repeats slowly.

I bristle. "Are you questioning my account?"

"I'm questioning your common sense," he mutters, walking into the alley. I follow warily, recalling the smothering sensation as I stepped into the shadows that night. Simon stops by the bloodstain on the wall, half washed away by the rain. "This is what you saw first?"

A shudder ripples through me. The first place I saw it was actually at the Sanctum. "Yes. The moon was shining right on it."

"Then what?"

"Well . . ." I hesitate, recalling the need to know if the wall felt as I impossibly remembered. "I thought those streaks looked like finger marks, and I reached out to touch them."

That was what I'd forgotten: I'd reached for the wall.

It was when my fingers crossed into the moonlight that I abruptly saw everything. And not just saw, I *heard* everything, *smelled* everything, *felt* everything with overwhelming intensity. I'd even heard Perrete's thoughts, like they were hanging in the air with the scent of her perfume—and blood. But until that instant, there was nothing.

All the other moments, too—hearing Perrete's scream, seeing her blood like it was mine, feeling my fingers drag across the rough wall, the clarity of the Selenae man's voice and the face of the woman in the window—all were in moonlight.

It was the moon. The moon had done something to me.

My arm is still outstretched, frozen as it had been that night. Simon puts a gentle hand on my elbow, startling me. There's pity in the wrinkle of his brow. "And that's when you saw her?" he asks.

I struggle to swallow. "Yes."

"How much could you see?"

"Everything." My arm drops back to my side. When Simon's pity turns to puzzlement, I grasp for an explanation. "There was lightning. It lit up the alley for a few seconds."

"Ah." Simon nods in understanding.

But it was for much longer than a few seconds, and the storm hadn't been close enough yet. And nothing about lightning could account for things I *heard*.

Magick. There is no other word for it.

"It's actually very easy to reconstruct what happened." Simon steps up to the wall, lifting his arms as though to hold on to an invisible person. "You can tell he cut her throat from behind. because there was nothing to block the blood as it sprayed out." One hand makes a fist as he pulls it across at neck height, left to right. "The scream you heard must have been just before," he continues softly. "She wouldn't have been able to make much noise after that."

I shudder, from the shock of both Simon's understanding and my own certainty that he's right. "But she still struggled," I whisper. I can't tell him I know what he said to Juliane about it that night.

"Yes. That was probably why he started stabbing her." Simon lowers his fist to his abdomen—a word I will never forget—and jabs a few times with an invisible knife, then points to a lower spot on the wall. "Panic, maybe. But it accounts for the blood there."

Again, something I know but can't admit.

Simon backs away, crouching with his arms curled, like he's carrying something heavy. "Then he dragged her here."

He stops at the dark stain in the packed dirt and stands straight. "But *why*?" His mouth has a frustrated angle and his eyes are far away—like he's trying to make this piece fit into some picture he sees. "There was plenty of room to do what he wanted right there. There's actually less here."

I understand though. "He was pulling her into a patch of moonlight."

Simon's face rises to mine, his jaw hanging slightly open. "Yes, that's it. He needed to see her." His voice drops to a whisper. "But then she could see him, too, and he didn't like that."

Of everything Simon has said so far, that last is the most chilling. "I thought you said she was dead when he took out her eyes."

I suddenly realize I've made a mistake. Simon doesn't know I was listening when he told Juliane that.

But he doesn't seem to notice. "She was." Simon raises a hand to his chin, the tendons on his wrist visibly twisting as he rubs his jaw. "He also smashed her face with something heavy, but I'm not sure what."

Sun and Sky, the hammer.

Perrete had the architect's hammer, and that's what the killer used. When it's found, it will lead straight to Magister Thomas. I stagger backward, looking around for a glint of gold in the muck, though surely it would have been discovered already.

Simon takes several running steps at me to grab my wrist. "Cat? Are you all right?"

He thinks I'm passing out. Maybe I am, given how light-headed I suddenly feel. His other hand catches me around the waist as my knees buckle, and he pulls my arm around his shoulder to half-drag, half-carry me out of the alley.

Faces turn to watch as we emerge, two pairs of eyes staring at us are lined with kohl. Or it's one and I'm seeing double. I blink, but the face—or faces—vanish as Simon swings me around to seat me on the nearby barrel.

He puts a palm to my cheek to keep my head tilted up. "Catrin?"

I grimace. "*Cat.*"

"Does that mean you haven't fainted?"

I can't tell Simon what I've just realized, but I also don't want him to think I'm weak. "I'm fine."

"You don't seem fine." But Simon stands straight, taking the support of his hands away. "I'm sorry. I got so involved in picturing what happened that I forgot how . . . awful it can be."

If he wants to think that's what made me dizzy, I'll let him. "What makes a person do that to another?"

It strikes me as an unanswerable question, but Simon responds without hesitation. "Rage, mostly. Perrete angered him, but she's not the true target. He can't get to the woman he needs revenge on—either because he's afraid of her or she's unreachable."

I want to know how Simon understands all this, but a more important question pushes its way to my lips. "If murdering Perrete won't satisfy his need for revenge, what does that mean?"

Simon shakes his head. "It means this is only the beginning."

———   •   *   •   ———

We return to the architect's home, this time in silence. Every step of the way, Simon's words jar my bones to the marrow.

This is only the beginning.

Weaving into my thoughts is the connection I made between what I heard and saw and moonlight. The farther we get from the alley, the more outlandish it seems.

When we arrive at the magister's house, Simon bows his head. "Thank you for your help today, Miss—Cat. Again, I'm sorry for causing your distress."

"Wait." I grab his arm before he can leave. "Did you really mean that about the killer? Will there be more of this?"

Simon nods, and there's something old and weary beyond a mere nineteen years in his eyes. "Yes. And it will be worse."

That's difficult for me to imagine, but somehow not, I'm sure, for him. "When?"

"Tonight, next week, next month." Simon shrugs tiredly. "Maybe next year. Maybe in another town. Maybe"—he bites his lower lip—"maybe this wasn't even the first time he's done this."

"How do you find someone like that? Catch him in the act?"

Simon exhales heavily. "Only if we're lucky or if I can predict his next move. Unfortunately, that's difficult to do with only one victim." He rubs his forehead. "And I hardly know where anything is in this city."

"The architect has maps of Collis," I offer. "I could bring them to you tomorrow. And I'd be more than willing to continue helping your investigation."

He smiles ruefully. "Are you sure you have the stomach for this?"

It's not just a desire to protect Magister Thomas that drives me. I struggle to put it into words. "I feel like . . . like I was the one meant to find Perrete. Because I was the only one who *could* hear her."

Simon sighs. "Very well. I'd appreciate the maps you offered. You can bring them the morning after tomorrow."

I look up. There's a spark of the earlier amiableness in the curve of his mouth. Does the prospect of my company account for it? "Why not tomorrow?"

His expression immediately darkens. "Juliane will be too tired. She isn't feeling well."

Of course he doesn't want to do too much work without her. She's written almost all his notes. Plus tomorrow is Sun Day. "I hope she recovers swiftly."

Simon opens his mouth to respond, then seems to think better of it. His head dips in a polite bow. "I look forward to seeing you again."

I watch him walk away. Despite the horror of the whole situation, I'm looking forward to it as well.

———— • ✳ • ————

"You're going to cause trouble with your meddling." Mistress la Fontaine slams my supper plate in front of me.

"I'm not meddling," I say. "The venatre asked for my help today."

"And then you offered to continue." The housekeeper ladles gravy over the slices of meat on our dishes, starting with Remi, who's been glowering at me since he came home.

Magister Thomas is silent, but he hasn't immediately taken a side, so I direct my appeal at him—he's the real authority in this house anyway. "I just showed him where I was and what I saw that night."

"You took him to Pleasure Road," Remi grumbles. "What did you offer the venatre there?"

I glare at him. He must have seen us walking around the square, but I can't imagine he truly thinks I was taking Simon there for other reasons. "That's where the murder was."

"Which means that's where *you* were that night."

"I was at the Sanctum," I grind out. "I had to inspect in the middle of the night because I was doing *your* work all day while you were taking your sweet time returning from Lutecia."

Remi pounds a fist on the table. "I have earned the right to manage my own time! I'm not at anyone's beck and call anymore!"

"You are if someone is paying your wages!" I shout back.

"Silence, both of you," says the architect in a low voice. Both Remi and I retreat and face Magister Thomas contritely.

"Remi, you are correct that your time is now your own. After years of hard work, you are entitled to take a day or two to celebrate your achievements. You should be proud of them."

Remi smirks. I want to stick my tongue out at him, but until he started with his ridiculous accusations, I hadn't really cared that he was late coming back. Sun knows he could use a little loosening up.

"But." Magister Thomas pauses sternly. "Your advancement doesn't give you any right to tell Catrin what to do or with whom she may associate. She is *my* assistant, not yours, and you will apologize for that disgusting insinuation."

It's my turn to smirk. Remi sinks into his shoulders and mumbles what almost sounds like "I'm sorry" into his food.

The architect isn't finished, though. "Moreover, you will not speak about her in such a manner to others. If I hear any rumors I can trace back to you, you will never work in Collis again. Not even shoveling ox manure."

Remi's ears turn redder than wine. Mistress la Fontaine clenches her jaw as tightly as the spoon in her fist and turns away to set the now-empty pot aside. I doubt the housekeeper would want to stay if her son left, so that's a double threat.

Magister Thomas focuses back on me. "Cat, I agree that perhaps today's assistance was necessary, but what more good can you do now?"

What he's really asking is if I remember his warning from earlier, but he doesn't know what I do about the missing hammer.

"Simon thinks there will be more murders like this one," I answer.

Remi snorts, but I can't tell if it's because of the venatre's opinion or because I referred to him by name.

"He also says Perrete may not have even been the killer's first victim."

The architect raises an eyebrow. "And how does 'Simon' know this?" Apparently he isn't comfortable with my familiar address.

"He knows what the killer was thinking and feeling and why he did those things to her body," I insist. "I don't understand how, but he knows."

"Maybe because he did it," Remi mutters.

"The venatre needs maps of the city," I say. "And I promised him some of your older ones. Lady Juliane and Lambert Mont-cuir are also helping him." With tomorrow as evidence, I add, "He wouldn't need me every day."

The architect sighs and gazes down at his plate. "You, too, have worked very hard, especially these past few weeks, and deserve free time. As long as your assigned inspections are per-formed, you may assist the venatre. Perrete deserves justice, and if we can help, we should."

I nod eagerly, but Magister Thomas isn't finished. "One additional condition: you must resume your weekly visits with Mother Agnes. She doesn't have much time left Under the Sun, and whatever has made you angry with her must be put aside. She deserves it after all she's done for you."

"Yes, Magister," I agree humbly. "Thank you."

He nods approvingly and turns to Remi. "Now, Remone, please tell me more about your new vault design."

Nothing cheers Remi up like being able to talk about ceilings. I listen with only one ear as I eat.

Much as I hated the idea, I'd already resolved to visit the pri-oress tomorrow. Few people are as widely traveled as Mother Agnes. If anyone can tell me about Simon's home of Mesanus, it's her.

CHAPTER 12

I walk along the sunny street, my feet unconsciously falling into the rhythm of the sisters' song drifting over the convent's eastern wall from the garden. Their chant and scents of overturned soil and freshly trimmed rosemary unearth a hundred bittersweet memories, and I brush my fingers along the regular stone and cement pattern as I stroll. Even recognizing the safety and security they offered parentless girls like me, I resented these walls.

One stone juts out a little farther than most. I tap both it and a nearby fist-size divot in the mortar. Countless times this secret ladder helped me return to the abbey without using the gate.

The last time I scaled the wall was the day Magister Thomas followed me after watching me climb the side of a three-story building to escape a street gang. I thought I was in trouble, that he was the man they had robbed, but instead he asked Mother Agnes if he could hire me.

I also know that somewhere on the other side of the wall, behind a shed, the fat purse of coins from that morning is buried. Having stolen it from pickpockets and with no idea who the true owner was, I felt no guilt in keeping it myself as resources

I would need when I left the convent for good. Working for the architect made such saving unnecessary, but the money is still there if I ever have need of it.

I turn right with the corner. The convent's main gate is on the south side—the sunniest wall, which is supposed to be symbolic. Across the street is the northern section of the wall surrounding the Selenae Quarter. I've often wondered whether the People of the Night originally settled on Collis's outskirts, or if Solis Abbey was built to stand between them and the rest of the city. Not even Mother Agnes knows, I think.

A tangle of vines covers the outer wall and most of the houses and windows facing the shaded north, while green arms arch across a few narrow avenues leading into their neighborhood. The delicate white and violet moonflowers only bloom at night, when Selenae confine themselves to the Quarter.

Flower of white, curled up tight,
In the day you hide from sight.
Selenae know, home to go
When your face begins to show.

I hum the melody without thinking as I ring the abbey's bronze bell. The nursery rhyme is often the first children of Collis learn, but I haven't thought of it in years. As I wait, I find myself searching window gaps in the heart-shaped leaves for signs the scarred man is watching me from within, continuing the tune like it will protect me somehow.

The woman shuffling to meet me little resembles the one who taught me that song. Three steps from the gate, a clawlike hand gropes to find it as foggy eyes stare past me. "Who is it?" she rasps.

"It's me, Mother," I say, unsure how she will react. Our last words were decidedly unpleasant.

Her wrinkled smile rises like the dawn and light comes to her eyes, though they remain unfocused. "Catrin?"

"Yes, I came to see you."

The matron's happy response is a surprise, but then sparse eyebrows lift and her mouth bends in skepticism. That's more like it.

"You want something," she says.

"Magister Thomas said you weren't well." When her expression doesn't change, I sigh. "And I wanted to apologize."

"Hmph." The prioress produces a ring of keys from under her gray wool mantle. She immediately selects the correct one, but it takes her several tries to insert it into the lock. "You must want whatever it is pretty badly."

The gate opens with a rusty screech, and I step inside the archway, blinking against the purple spots burned into my eyes by the sun. Mother Agnes closes and relocks the gate, then hooks the ring back on her belt. I decide humor might thaw the awkward moment.

"You're right about my motive," I say. "I could smell Sister Louise's ginger biscuits all the way from the Sanctum."

Mother's thin lips twitch as she leads the way through the gloomy passage. "Well, since you've come all this way, you might as well have tea." The prioress skims her fingers along the wall as I did outside, but she does it so she knows where to turn the corner and when she's reached the door to her sitting room.

A sister jumps up from a desk cluttered with ledgers and parchments as we enter. "Catrin!" she gasps, a hint of the once bubbly smile coming through.

I roll my eyes. "It's still just Cat. You gave me that nickname, remember?"

"Of course I do." Marguerite glances nervously at the prioress, and that's when I realize she's in the full garb of a Sister of

Light, her hair completely covered by a white cowl and a beaded necklace hanging to her waist.

"When did you take vows?" I ask.

Mother Agnes makes her way to a worn cushioned chair like she's not listening, but I know better.

"At midwinter," Marguerite answers. "You know that's traditional."

The ceremony takes place on the shortest day of the year, symbolizing how a sister is supposed to grow in the Light every day after. "And you didn't invite me?"

Marguerite twists her delicate hands as Mother Agnes answers. "I told her she had to issue the invitation in person." The prioress lowers herself into her seat. "You were never here to receive it."

My friend's blue eyes brim with tears, but Marguerite only ever cried for others. Quite often it was over my being punished, so nothing has changed. I sigh. "I'm sorry, Marga. I was just so—"

"Proud," finishes Mother Agnes.

I scowl. "I was going to say angry." And rightfully so.

The prioress sits back, unconcerned. "Anger is a form of pride."

I don't know if she's right, and I honestly don't care. I'm just sorry Marguerite suffered for it.

"You cut your hair, then?" I ask her. The thought brings a pang of loss. I'd envied Marguerite's glorious tresses all my life, and not just because their glossy near-black color made mine look like shades of pigsty.

She laughs softly. "No, actually. I was given a dispensation to keep it until the fall so it can grow a little more."

"The fall?" I ask. "Why—oh." Collis's massive trading fair. People of all professions arrive from every corner of Gallia—

including wigmakers. "You'll be able to auction it among several buyers."

Mother Agnes nods. "The money will buy a new weaving loom, which will increase our output."

The abbey is self-sufficient, and even turns a profit from selling cloth the sisters and novices make, but the loom they use is older than the prioress herself.

"I'm happy to make the contribution," Marguerite says. Of course she is.

"Sister," says the prioress. "You'll have to catch up with Catrin on her next visit. Could you bring us some tea while we discuss her current business?"

I snort. She acts like we'll be haggling over the price of wool. "And some ginger biscuits, please," I add, taking a seat on the long, hard couch to her right.

"How is the Sanctum expansion coming along?" Mother Agnes asks as the door closes.

There will only be small talk until Marguerite has come and gone again. "We'll start vaulting the ceiling in a few weeks," I say. "The masons spent all winter shaping stones for the arches."

I'm still describing how they will be installed under the peaked roof when Marguerite returns bearing a tray. She spends extra time arranging the cup, saucer, and biscuits in a precise way in front of the prioress, then pours the tea and sweet cream. Then she sets the honey by me, knowing I prefer it, and leaves an extra stack of cookies for me with a wink. All the while, I'm debating how to bring up what I want to know.

Each of Mother Agnes's three husbands lived in a different country, so she's likely seen more of the continent than even Magister Thomas. When the last died, her accumulated fortune—and lack of heirs—attracted the attention of the king himself. He already had a queen, however that didn't mean he couldn't tie the rich widow to someone beholden to him.

She was summoned to the royal court, but after stopping to rest at Solis Abbey, Lady Agnes decided never to leave. Writing the king a very lovely letter, she described how the Sun had called to her in a dream, commanding her to stay and serve as a Sister of Light. Her properties, therefore, now belonged to the religious superiors of Collis. She was also immediately elected prioress, a position ordained until death. Not even a royal order could undo it.

Over the next four decades, Mother Agnes expanded the abbey from a prayer commune of a dozen sisters to a center of religious education, producing more vocations than any on the continent. Most of that came from establishing a home and school for foundling girls, the majority of whom went straight from the classroom to the cloister.

Shrewd recruitment motivations aside, the fact is life offers orphan girls like Marguerite and me few better options.

"I heard there was a murder," says Mother Agnes as soon as the door closes again. "And that you were involved."

I've never figured out where her information comes from, but it's always accurate.

"Tell me," she says, raising her cup to her lips. "Why did the provost bother assigning a venatre over the death of this poor girl?"

"Two reasons," I answer. "The crime was rather horrific, and Oudin Montcuir admitted to, um, being in her company that night."

The prioress nods sagely. "And that's why neither the comte nor his older son leads the investigation."

"Exactly. Though Lambert Montcuir has been assisting." I tap the side of my cup. "The venatre, Simon, is a distant relative of theirs but he's dedicated to solving the crime and is very knowledgeable. I've been helping him, being that I found the body."

Mother Agnes's expression grows serious. "Catrin, what were you doing on the streets in the middle of the night?"

"Inspecting at the Sanctum," I say. She never liked my climbing habits, even before they took me away from the abbey. "We were behind, and I can see plenty well by moonlight."

"*How* well?"

Something in her tone makes the hair on the back of my neck stand on end. "Enough to do my job."

For several seconds, the only sound is the wheeze of air going in and out of her nose. "You shouldn't be out at night," the prioress says finally. "It's not safe, as that murder proves. I have a mind to write Magister Thomas just what I think about how he lets you work."

She sent him a scathing letter every week for the first year after I left, so I doubt it will matter.

Mother Agnes buries her nose in her cup. "So tell me about this Simon."

"What about him?" I ask, caught off guard.

Her lashless eyes stare at me, unblinking. "Come now, Catrin, I may be blind, but I'm not deaf. He's caught your fancy."

I reel in my memory, trying to recall what I'd said. He's dedicated to finding the murderer, and he's intelligent. Both admirable qualities. But thinking of his hesitant smile and his concern for my well-being brings an unexpected warmth to my core. How in the world did she sense that?

"Is he handsome?" she asks, reveling in my sudden discomfort.

"He's well enough," I mutter. When I realize she's still waiting,

I sigh. "Blond hair. Taller than average." My descriptions come in small bursts. "Not overly lean, but not an ounce of extra flesh on him anywhere, either. Fair in color. Two years older than me."

"And his eyes?"

"Light blue, like Sister Alix's." I don't mention the brown flaw.

"Basically the opposite of you." There's a lilt of humor in her tone.

"I'm not short," I counter. Even without the heeled slippers I'm wearing today with my Sun Day clothes, I tower over most women I know—and a good number of men. "And his hair is curly, too."

The prioress snorts. "I take it back, you sound like twins. However." She blinks away her amusement. "Have his looks distracted you from what's most important—his character?"

My face grows hot. "He seems honest."

"That's a start."

I sigh. How does one explain Simon? I've spent several hours in his presence, and I'm not sure I understand him any more than when I first laid eyes on him. "He's kind, but guarded. I don't think he likes being dependent on the Montcuirs."

"Will I ever get to meet him?"

I cringe at the idea. "I think you're imagining more between us than there is. I hardly know him." Now is my opening. "He's from Mesanus. Have you ever heard of it?"

"Of course." The prioress scoops up a ginger biscuit, then sits back to dip it in her tea. "It's a village with a famous luminary shrine on the coast of Prezia."

Remi was right about the location, but shrines need miracles attributed to them to earn the description luminary. "Who died there?"

"A princess fleeing from the island west of Brinsulli, several hundred years ago." Mother Agnes pauses to test the cookie with what few teeth she has left, then dunks it back into her cup. "Her father tracked her to Mesanus, but she refused to return with him, and he killed her."

Obedience to parents is one of the Ten Pillars of a faithful life, so that's a complete surprise. "A shrine that honors a runaway?"

"She left for the right reason. Her father had ordered her to marry him."

For a second I think I missed the name of some prince she was betrothed to. Then I recoil into the hard back of the couch. "He wanted to wed his own daughter?"

"Her mother had died, and the king was mad with grief." Mother brings the biscuit back to her mouth and gums a bit of it off. "Apparently, Princess Dimah looked much like her."

"Still . . . ," I say. The idea is disgusting. Luminaries, however, grant heavenly miracles in accordance with their life or death. "Are there that many fleeing incestuous marriages who call for her help?"

Mother Agnes swallows and gives me a scolding look. "Her tomb became a pilgrimage site for those afflicted with sickness of the mind, everything from babes damaged from birth, to those who see and hear things that aren't there, to murderers who eat the flesh of their victims." The other piece of biscuit goes into her mouth.

Imagining what the prioress describes turns my stomach. "Are there really those mad enough to eat human flesh?"

"It's rare, but yes."

"Why wouldn't someone like that just be executed?"

Mother Agnes extends her cup to me for more tea, and I pour it. "Our Faith frowns upon punishing those who aren't aware of the gravity of their crime."

I snort. "You mean punishment is meaningless unless they know *why* they're suffering." She continues holding her cup, and I add enough cream to match what Marguerite gave her earlier.

She ignores my hostility. "Families are often desperate for assurance it wasn't their loved one who did such a terrible thing, but something possessing them." Mother Agnes leans back in her chair and straightens her habit before taking a drink from her refreshed cup. "That's often the easiest explanation for the masses, especially when what's in here"—she taps her temple—"is so little understood by the wisest scholars. Three religious orders and hospitals are dedicated to helping pilgrims, but villagers take many into their own homes. Not violent ones, of course. Just those who can't take care of themselves. Many physicians spend time in Mesanus observing and speaking with the most disturbed minds, trying to understand them and bring balance to their humors."

Simon isn't a physician, but it's obvious he spent a lot of time around them. "So are the miracle cures due to their efforts or the blessings of this Dimah?" I ask.

Mother Agnes shrugs. "Your guess is as good as mine, but she wouldn't have been added to the Litany of Holies without good reason."

I'm more concerned with a vision of Simon's life before coming to Collis. The question is, was he born and raised in Mesanus, or was he there for a cure of his own?

CHAPTER 13

The call to afternoon prayers rings out from the convent's bell tower. I stand, grabbing the untouched ginger cookies to take with me. "I'd better go. It won't be so long before my next visit, I promise."

Magister Thomas is right. It probably won't be much longer before I can't visit her at all.

Mother Agnes accompanies me back to the gate. My parents—the subject of our argument from months ago—remain unmentioned. She lets me outside without a word, and I shade my eyes with my hand as she replaces the keys on her belt. I'm wondering if she's even going to say goodbye when the prioress suddenly leans forward, her nose pushing out between the bars.

"Catrin."

"Yes?"

She exhales heavily as if bracing herself for whatever she has to say.

"Your parents are dead. That was always true. But they loved each other, and you were very much wanted."

My heart creeps upward in my chest as I wait for her to

continue, but she doesn't say anything more. "That's it?" I finally burst out. "That's all you'll tell me?"

She shifts back, withdrawing like a battle is over. "Those are the only things that matter."

Not a word about why the rest of my family abandoned me while I still had the cord knotted at my stomach. No explanation for the hissed warning to Magister Thomas the morning he escorted me from the abbey that there would be consequences if "they" perceived I was mistreated. Almost as if she believed they would want me back someday.

The biscuits dissolve into crumbs in my clenched hand. "Maybe those are the only things that matter to you," I manage through gritted teeth.

Mother Agnes shakes her head. "Your family truly believed you belonged in the Light."

"Well, I don't," I snap. "I don't belong behind high walls and locked gates. I don't belong in a cage."

"We all live in cages, Catrin. Only those of us who are lucky get to choose which one."

The prioress turns away and heads in the direction of the chapel, humming the prayer song the sisters have already begun singing.

——— • ✳ • ———

Anger and bright sunshine combine to plant the seed of a headache which rapidly grows to wrap my temples with tight vines. By the time I reach home, pain is in full bloom, and I go straight to my room and lie down. My window faces south and slightly east, and over the next few hours, noise from the Sanctum gradually fades as workers finish their tasks for the day. First will be the blacksmiths, who cease pounding out chains and nails and iron frames. Then they brush soot from the day's creations and argue with craftsmen over whose needs are greatest tomorrow. Stonemasons and carvers are next, putting aside their chisels to finesse the precise edges of blocks and statues with sandcloth. Laborers raising and placing stones high on the walls complete their last load. Finally, the carts roll away—hawkers and tool sharpeners pulling theirs by hand while oxen ease wagons down the hill one last time.

The city sighs and relaxes. Smoke from hearth fires wraps the buildings with its woodsy scent, punctuated by a thousand pipes being lit after the evening meal. Mistress la Fontaine knocks and peeks in to announce supper. I pretend to be asleep, and she goes back downstairs. Bells from the Sanctum and numerous chapels throughout Collis call the religious to evening prayers. Mother Agnes will lead the sisters, half her mind listening for missing voices. Later those who skipped the liturgy will be polishing chalices and candlesticks. I did a lot of that.

Many girls at Solis Abbey were children of prostitutes—often women who'd left the convent only a few years before. Others were the result of infidelity—young noblewomen who allowed themselves to be seduced or servant girls who succumbed to the wiles of rich men. Saying my parents loved each other takes me out of the former category. I don't know if it puts me in the second or in another entirely, like Marguerite.

Your family truly believed you belonged to the Light.

My jaw tightens at the idea. They had no right to make that choice for me.

Wait. Mother Agnes said they believed I belonged *in* the Light, not to it. Is that difference significant? The prioress never said *when* my parents died, either. Was it they who left me at the abbey, or someone else? And then there was the bit about everyone living in cages. Was she saying they believed the convent was a better cage than the one they lived in?

I roll over to watch the deep blue-violet sky stretch up from the horizon. With the darkness, the tension behind my eyes finally begins to ease. Remi comes up the stairs and continues to the third floor and his room. Mistress la Fontaine isn't far behind, but I hear no sign the magister is going to bed yet. Perhaps he's piecing together another stained glass window. By the time the moon rises high enough to cast a shaft of pure silver on the floor, my headache is only a memory, and now I'm thinking of something else entirely.

What had the moonlight done to me that night in the alley?

The further I got from the realization that day with Simon, the more ridiculous it seemed, so much that I had forced the idea of moonlight and magick from my mind. Now it comes back to me whispering, *What if it was real?*

Over a thousand years ago, people of the Hadrian Empire considered the moon cursed, believing its constant changes meant it had something to hide. The fullest moon rises at dusk and sets at dawn because it cannot face the Blessed Sun, which is why Selenae—who keep the same hours as the moon—are often considered heretics. Modern Gallians know the moon is harmless, and the high altum preaches the same, but many hold on to the old notions.

It's only superstitious people who fear magick, describing it as something blasphemous and unnatural that can only be done in darkness. Until recently, I considered the entire idea nonsense.

The rectangle of moonlight glides slowly across the room, shrinking until it reaches its peak, then stretching longer again. Another hour and it will be gone. I order myself to move, sitting up in bed and placing my stocking-clad feet on the floor. A board sighs with my weight, but no more than what could be the house settling. I hesitate, chewing on the ragged edge of my nail. It's the one which had caught the splinter, mostly healed but for a circular bruise which spreads out from where it bled.

I drop my hand and tiptoe through the darkness to the window and stand just outside the light, partly because that's how I was in the alley that night, and partly because of a strange hunger which wells up as I approach. Hunger isn't the right word, though. The urge is so much deeper, spreading out from my very core to my skin in tingles of anticipation. I don't know what I expect to happen, but I *want* something, and that worries me a bit.

If magick *is* real, maybe I'm risking my soul. After all, if magick was good, wouldn't it come from the Sun?

Taking a deep breath, I stretch my left hand out, cupping it as though to catch a stream of falling water.

The world explodes into color and light and sound. Things I only vaguely sensed before wash over me like ocean waves.

I hear Remi shifting in his bed above and see dust motes drifting down from the ceiling. A wisp of pungent smoke comes through a crack between the floorboards at my feet, and I can smell that it belongs to the burning leaves in the magister's pipe and not the hearth. I'm wearing thick wool socks, and not only do I feel the tight weave of Mistress la Fontaine's knitting, I'm aware of the grain of the wood I'm standing on and the small knot beneath my big toe.

It's more than I can comprehend at once. Even the air in my chest is so heavy with scents I have the urge to expel it. I'm drowning.

I jerk back out of the moonbeam like it's made of fire, and to my relief—and agony—everything looks normal again. Almost. I can see and hear much better than before, but not nearly as well as when my hand was in direct moonlight. Overwhelming as those moments were, there had been something . . . *wonderful* about them. Powerful.

I want more.

There must be a way to ease into it. I cover my ears with my hands and close my eyes to cut those elements off. Then I exhale until there is nothing left in my lungs and step fully into the light.

Three. Two. One.

I inhale slowly and deliberately, savoring individual scents as they pass through my nose: the scratchy, dense fibers of wool from my skirt, the arid dust from the ceiling dancing with the fresh, floral pollens of spring. An unpleasant sourness from the barrel of food scraps Mistress la Fontaine places where street urchins can dig through it. That last one is muffled. The lid hasn't been raised yet by searching hands.

Once I've identified everything I can distinguish, I shift my attention to what I can feel. The moonlit air caresses my skin like silk. Below my feet, the floorboards bow a hair's breadth with my weight. If I concentrate, I can sense the eight-legged treading of a spider until it crosses the gap to the next plank of wood. My skirt sits low on my hips, pulling on my waist enough that the bruises from the other night feel fresh.

Now sound. I ease my hands away from my ears.

Wind brushes across the window frame as loudly as a broom. Remi snores—no, Mistress la Fontaine in the room across from his does. I turn my focus to the night outside and discern the rapid fluttering of moth wings and the leathery rustle of a bat diving toward it with a high-pitched shriek I've never been able to perceive before.

There are the steps of the watchman patrolling one block away, alternating with the rusty squeak of his lantern. Drawing back in, closer, I hear the scrabbling of rats in the attic of the home behind ours, the drip of water from a gutter.

The heartbeat of the man standing in the alley below.

CHAPTER 14

Someone is outside Magister Thomas's house, standing next to the kitchen door.

I step back out of the light, opening my eyes, and the sound of his pulse vanishes. My own heartbeat pounds so loudly in my ears I almost don't hear the soft knocking.

Golden light spills into the alley as the door opens. Whoever the man is, he must have been expected, because Magister Thomas—the only one still awake besides me—lets him in. Wondering if I could hear them, I kneel to place one ear to the floor.

Words are muffled, but the tone of their conversation is friendly. I would've been able to hear them a few seconds ago. Moonlight shines on the windowsill, and I reach up to put my hand in it. Just as I hoped, the instant my fingers are illuminated, the effect returns. With a tight grip on the window frame, I press my ear over a crack in the floorboards and close my eyes, listening.

"—have been doubled. It's risky for you to be out," Magister Thomas is saying. "And you do know that you were seen that night, yes?"

"By a *skonia* addict," the man replies. A wooden creak and

the stranger's grunt tells me he's taking a seat by the fire. "As for the watch, those Sun-lovers can't see beyond their lamps."

Sun-lovers. Only a Person of the Night would speak so disparagingly. And to be seen "that night" can only mean the evening of Perrete's murder. Even without those clues, I knew instantly who the man was by his voice. I can picture the shadows cast across his scarred face and the firelight reflecting in the silver of his eyes. The bigger shock is that Magister Thomas knows the Selenae man. Why didn't he tell me that?

"You realize why I've come, don't you?" the man asks.

A cork squeals as it's twisted from the neck of a glass bottle, and liquid is poured into two goblets. "You assured me this would never happen," says the architect.

"It gives me no pleasure to be wrong," the Selenae man replies. "And for my error, I am sorry. You have no idea how much."

Magister Thomas downs his cup in one gulp, then coughs and wipes his mouth. "I was the one who sent her out into the night. I am also to blame."

They must be talking about Perrete. My heart is torn in half to know the architect believes himself even partly responsible for her death.

"It is only proof that we cannot hide from fate," says the Selenae man quietly. "Any more than we can prevent the moon from rising."

"Still." Magister Thomas sets the bottle on the table and drops heavily into another chair. "I promised to care for her, and I failed. It's only a matter of time before it happens again."

"Yes," agrees the man. "It's like pure *skonia*. Once tasted, it will always be craved."

Like Simon, they understand the killer will strike again. That his rage and the need for revenge will never be satisfied.

"You managed to master it," says Magister Thomas.

"As we all must. But that is why we willingly keep to the Quarter at night—for the protection of others as well as ourselves." The stranger sips his drink. "But you have always been welcome to join us."

"Join you in what? Howling at the moon?"

The man chuckles ruefully, but his words are lost. Frustrated, I open my eyes to find the moonlight has shifted off my fingers. Worse, it won't be shining on my window much longer. I move my hand a few inches to put it back in the light and press my ear to the floor again, but I've missed part of their exchange.

"—you must trust me in this matter," says the man. "It is something you cannot understand as I do."

Magister Thomas sighs. "By when?"

"After the new moon, but before the full."

Simon had also predicted another murder, but this man seems certain it will be within a month.

"How do I protect Catrin in the meantime?" the magister asks. "She's involved herself in the venatre's investigation and wants to continue."

The stranger takes a long, slow drink from his glass before answering. "Hadrians and Selenae alike are ruled by instincts we barely understand. Have you considered that perhaps she was *meant* to find that girl?"

Magister Thomas's chair scrapes across the stone floor as he jumps to his feet. "Listen to yourself, Gregor! No wonder people think the moon makes people insane. She's—"

My hearing vanishes. Gritting my teeth, I stretch my fingers out of the window until it returns.

"—moon doesn't cause madness," the Selenae man is saying. "But it does make madness believe it's safe to come out."

The architect huffs in frustration like he does when he runs a hand through one of the gray streaks in his hair. When he speaks, it's too muffled to understand. I sit up, searching for the moonlight. None is within reach while keeping my head where it needs to be. Suppressing a groan of frustration, I pivot to lean against the wall under the window. A few minutes later the Selenae man—*Gregor*, I repeat to myself—leaves the same way he came.

I've heard enough to understand both men know more murders are coming—and sooner rather than later, but then the conversation had turned to me.

Have you considered that perhaps she was meant *to find that girl?*

That was almost exactly what I'd told Simon yesterday. Gregor called it instinct, but I know it's something more because I heard Perrete scream when she was unable to make a sound. Her *blood* called to me across the moonlit air. If that's not magick, I don't know what is.

Magister Thomas doesn't believe in magick, however, and trying to tell him or Simon that blood speaks to me through moonlight will have them thinking I belong in Mesanus.

I'm still fully clothed, so I undress as quietly as I can. Magister Thomas remains in the kitchen, and it's easy to imagine him smoking his pipe and staring into the hearth fire as he does when he's troubled. Just before I pull my nightdress down, I pause to study the bruises on my stomach, which have faded from blue-black to deep purple. There's a line across my middle from the safety rope but also seven distinct ovals spread out at random. No wonder it hurts to wear a skirt.

As I crawl back into bed, I can't help thinking of Gregor's assertion that while moonlight doesn't cause madness, it does make it believe it's safe to come out.

CHAPTER 15

I arrive at the Montcuir home late enough in the morning that everyone can be expected to be awake, carrying two older charts of city streets from the architect. The housekeeper lets me in again, and rather than escort me upstairs, she just points. Voices come from Simon's room on the third floor, but the door is open, so I step inside as I knock.

Simon straightens from where he stands over Juliane's shoulder. From his smile it's clear he's not just glad I've brought the promised maps, he's happy to see me.

Mother Agnes's assertion that he's caught my fancy has nothing to do with my freshly cleaned skirt or my neatly braided hair. Nothing at all.

Worried my own face might reveal some unseemly eagerness to be here, I stride to the table. "I've brought these. I hope they help. One is the area around the Sanctum and one is the city as a whole. They're a little outdated, but I made corrections. I, um, hope they help."

Apparently, I should have been more concerned about my words than my expression. I clamp my mouth shut before I can embarrass myself further.

Juliane looks up from her notes, the hollows under her eyes giving her an owlish appearance, especially as she blinks slowly.

"Thank you." Simon takes the rolled parchments. "This is just what I needed, so . . . uh, thank you."

Juliane's gaze shifts to him, her thin lips quirking in amusement.

Simon immediately spreads one map open on the table and beckons to Oudin. "Come here, Cousin, and show me where you saw the Selenae man that night."

Gregor.

Oudin grunts irritably from his slouch against the wall before obeying. He leans across the table and points. "There."

Simon makes a small *S* with a wax pencil. "And where were you?"

Oudin slides his finger an inch. "About there." He stands straight again and waits for Simon to mark the spot with an *O*.

Impatient to help, I also start to point. "I was—"

Simon almost slaps my hand away. "Not yet."

I withdraw, mortified, and he continues questioning Oudin. "Where did you and your friend part ways before that?"

A companion? Oudin points again. "He got me from the tavern to the square, then headed down this road."

Simon makes an *F* where indicated and an arrow to the minor street, which connects to Pleasure Road near Perrete's alley. This friend is an obvious person to investigate, but Simon seems unconcerned. He adds a dashed line connecting the *F* to the *O* to indicate the path Oudin traveled. "Is that where Lambert found you?" he asks.

Oudin's brother had been pacing by the window over the street, but he stops to listen when his name is mentioned.

"Pretty much," Oudin replies. "I was too spooked to go anywhere until the Selenae man left, and then the rain started so I took shelter."

"Is there anything else you want to tell me about that night?"

"No."

Simon studies Oudin for several seconds, like he's reading invisible words written on his face. Finally he nods. "Very well, you're dismissed."

Oudin bows mockingly. "Yes, Venatre." Then he addresses Lambert across the room. "Are you ready to face the lions, then?"

I realize both brothers are dressed in clothes normally reserved for Sanctum worship services. Lambert presses his gloves between each of his fingers to settle them lower, his face a pasty shade of white.

Juliane notices my puzzlement. "Lambert's bonding is today, for his wedding in the fall."

Oudin grins as he walks over to his older brother. "He's finally going to meet the girl." He throws an arm over his brother's shoulder, but Lambert is several inches taller, so the move pulls him down on one side. "You don't have to prove your manhood, yet. Relax."

Lambert angrily throws him off. "Day's end, Oudin! There are women present!"

Unconcerned, Oudin smooths his velvet-trimmed jacket and winks at me. "Only one is worth teasing, though."

The polished leather squeaks as Lambert balls his hands into fists, but Simon moves between them with his arms out like he's ready to hold them back. "Cousins, you'll be late." He lowers his voice and addresses Lambert. "You know he's only trying to upset you."

Oudin chuckles as he struts to the door. Despite his behavior, it's Simon's curt brushing aside from earlier that's hurt me more, but I manage a smile for Lambert. "Lady Genevieve is a lucky woman."

Lambert's flush of anger changes to pleased embarrassment. Simon gives me a nod of thanks as he pats his cousin on the shoulder. "That she is. Oudin's only jealous."

It's hard to imagine Oudin caring what a woman thinks, but the idea works on Lambert. He braces his shoulders and follows his brother without another word, smiling shyly at me as he passes.

Simon returns to studying the map of the Sanctum area. I'm reluctant to speak, given what happened last time I tried to contribute, but once the sound of the brothers on the stairs fades, he glances up. "I'm sorry I snapped at you earlier, Cat. Where you were that night isn't something I wanted him aware of yet." He raises a hand to me in appeal. There's ink all over the tips of his thumb and the first two fingers. "Will you please show me now?"

Of course. I should have realized that might cause Oudin to change his account. Still embarrassed, I step forward and lay my index finger on the southeast corner of the Sanctum.

"And which direction were you facing?"

I indicate, and he marks the spot with an arrow pointing south rather than with a letter C. We continue, tracing my path to Perrete's body and the location of the alley itself. Then Simon labels Perrete's home, Madame Emeline's, and the tavern where Oudin was drinking ale and consuming *skonia*. Juliane notes the same places on the other chart which depicts the whole city on a different scale.

When Simon asks about the man I now know was Gregor, my answers are more vague. The architect seemed confident in his intentions, and I suspect he was watching me only because of their friendship. To move away from the subject, I ask about someone who bothers me far more. "Who is this friend of Oudin's?"

"Remone la Fontaine." Simon tosses down his pencil and stands up, stretching. "Everything he's said corroborates with Oudin's statements."

That can't be correct. "*Remi?* But he wasn't even in Collis," I protest. "He returned from Lutecia late the next morning."

Simon cocks his head. "He told me he arrived in Collis in the evening and went to the tavern where he met Oudin."

"Then why didn't he come home that night?"

He shrugs. "That's something you'll have to ask Remone, but several people saw him."

"*Who?*" I demand. "And where did you see him?"

Simon shifts uncomfortably. "He was leaving Madame Emeline's when I arrived to examine Perrete's body. According to, um, witnesses, he arrived around the time of the murder but in no condition to have done it."

I fold my arms across my chest and stare at the map. The *F* doesn't stand for "friend," it stands for Fontaine. I wonder if he used *skonia*, too. Anything that impairs the mind would anger the magister. It would be grounds for losing his position.

But, I remind myself, that's *if* Remi was doing it. He never has before to my knowledge, though apparently he does other things I wasn't aware of. I'm not jealous, but I am disgusted to learn he's no better than Oudin.

Clearing my throat, I glance away from Simon. "How do you plan to proceed from here?"

He relaxes, like he's glad to move on. "We continue gathering as many facts and details as we can, then use them to paint a clear portrait of the killer."

I consider that for a moment. "When you say details, do you include the condition of Perrete's body and what was done to her?"

"Especially that, Cat," he answers. The brown spot on his left eye adds a disquieting intensity. "Our actions tell the world who we are. As repulsive as we may find them, those messages are the key to understanding and finding this killer."

Juliane watches our conversation, her widely dilated eyes moving back and forth between us. Unnerved and not wanting to leave her out of the discussion, I turn to her. "What about you, Lady Juliane?" I ask. "Do you have the stomach for this?"

"Of course," she replies, blinking in surprise. "I've killed lots of people, but then so has Simon."

My mouth falls open. "You've . . . what?"

Simon places a hand on his cousin's shoulder without taking his eyes off me. "No, you haven't. We haven't."

She looks up at him, distressed. "I'm sorry, I couldn't help it. I was startled."

"It's all right," he tells her, though his focus remains on my face. "I just don't think Cat here understands our private little game." Simon's smile is forced, unlike the other day when it just seemed unfamiliar. "How we like to talk nonsense just so we can correct it."

There's a silent plea in his expression for me to simply agree. The smile I return is as strained as his own. "Of course. Remi loves to tell outrageous tales just to see if I'll believe him."

Like that he wasn't in Collis until three mornings ago.

Simon nods his thanks, and Juliane slumps in what can only be relief. He asks for my help in nailing both maps to the plaster wall. As we work, Juliane goes back to pushing papers around on the table, organizing them into stacks.

But I can't help staring at how carefully she sorts and arranges all the pages, despite the fact that every single one of them is blank.

CHAPTER 16

For the next hour, I study the pictures Simon pins to the wall alongside the city map. His drawings of Perrete and the alley are discomforting, but I'd seen the reality.

The sketches he made from his visit to Madame Emeline's are much harder to take. He covered her breasts and lower parts with cloths—or at least depicted them covered, but I suspect if those areas had contained clues, he would not have done so. His talent for rendering such gruesome images on paper is also somewhat disturbing. Despite the ache from my bruises, I hug my arms over my middle as he points out the injuries and mutilations he cataloged in his examination.

"Seven stab wounds in her lower abdomen." Simon taps each one in the picture with an ink-stained finger. Like the blood on the wall, I can't shake the feeling that I've seen that pattern, but that it's somehow off. I must be remembering what I saw that night, except that rather than finger marks making it messier, the damage has been cleaned.

"Cuts on the insides of two fingers," Simon continues, his voice as emotionless as if he were listing geography facts. "She grabbed at her stomach when he began stabbing her, and one or more strikes went between. The wounds match up, making it probable he used a blade with two edges, like a dagger, rather than, say, a carving knife. Damage to her eye sockets also supports that."

The porridge Mistress la Fontaine insisted I eat at breakfast surges upward. I swallow it back down with effort.

Juliane's pen flies across the paper, recording his words. He pauses to let her catch up, though I suspect it's not necessary. "Scraped fingertips and torn nails from grabbing at the wall," he says, and I make a fist against the phantom throbbing in my own. "Once she stopped struggling, he dragged her over here and laid her down." Simon points to a sketch of the alley from above, resembling an architectural drawing. "As Cat pointed out, that was so she was lying in moonlight, where he could see."

My thrill from his acknowledgment is short lived.

"He smashed her face next. Whatever he used was heavy and likely awkward to carry around, so it may have been lying nearby. A stone, perhaps, or a brick."

Or a hammer. But Simon has no reason to suspect one was there.

"But nothing left behind could have done that," Simon continues. "Which means he took it with him."

A sweat breaks out on my forehead that has as much to do with my revulsion as with my fear of what that may mean for Magister Thomas.

Simon crosses his arms, still facing the drawing. "The removal of her eyes was messy, but he'll learn."

"Are you saying he'll get better at it?" I ask.

He nods. "His methods will improve every time."

What a thing to become skilled at, like it was a profession:

apprentice, journeyman, tradesman, master. Was this the work of a mere beginner?

Simon rubs his chin, leaving a purple smudge of ink. "These wounds on her stomach appear chaotic, maybe due to her resistance, but it's also evidence of his limited experience. He's right-handed though. You can tell from the angles and the wound in her neck which hand was holding the knife."

"You keep saying 'he,'" says Juliane. "Could it not have been a woman who did this?"

Simon shakes his head, his focus on some point beyond the wall in front of him. "No, this was a man."

"You don't think women are capable of violence?" I ask.

He turns to look at me. "Capable? Yes. But this kind of violence, this type of rage . . ." Simon shakes his head again. "It's masculine. I can't explain it other than to say it feels like . . ."

"Revenge," I finish. "Against a woman. I remember you said that."

"Yes." From his troubled expression, Simon's mind is back in the alley.

"But not necessarily against Perrete."

Simon purses his lips thoughtfully, making the blue-violet stain on his jaw more visible. "He might have a general feeling that women judge him, but it likely stems from one in particular. The first."

I grit my teeth. "Are you blaming this on a woman for rejecting him?"

"No." Simon's attention comes flying back to me, his answer absolute. "He may use twisted logic to justify murder, and there may be a woman who deliberately exercises some sort of perverted power over him, but the killer's actions are his own. Driven by madness, perhaps, but always his own."

Somewhat mollified, I ask, "But if it's madness, doesn't that make him *less* responsible for his actions?"

"There are several types of insanity." Simon pauses, glancing at Juliane. "You needn't write any of this down," he tells her. She continues nonetheless, her face blank, almost as if she's rendering what she hears without understanding, like a mockingbird.

Simon gestures to the gruesome drawings. "The killer knows when and how he must hide. He knows what he's doing is wrong but doesn't care. In fact, he revels in the fear he creates."

His eyes glaze over, and his voice drops to a whisper. "He's a monster who *allows* his impulses to be caged because he knows at some point they will be released again."

A shiver ripples through me. When Mother Agnes said all people live in cages, I doubt this was what she imagined. "But if none of that is visible from the outside, is there anything about the killer we can know for certain?" I ask.

Simon exhales, shrinking, and walks back to the table. He sits on the bench next to Juliane, facing outward, and leans his elbows on his thighs. "Tall and physically strong, more than average intelligence, between the ages of twenty and thirty but immature. Poor relationships with women."

Juliane's quill scratches across the page. When she stops and Simon doesn't continue, I gape at him.

"That's it? That's all you can say?" I'm not sure what I expected him to divine, but even I could have guessed that.

"That's all I can say with confidence," Simon says to his hands. "Until I have more to work with."

Until the monster is freed from his cage again.

CHAPTER 17

Rather than admit I spent too long at Simon's to inspect the new scaffolding before dinner, I imply my work is done by telling Magister Thomas I'll go over what I've found with him tomorrow at the site since I can't show him on the model. The architect, weary from his late-night visit from Gregor, agrees, going to bed as supper plates are cleared. Remi says he's meeting a friend and disappears soon after. I keep knowledge of his lies to myself for now, but I plan to confront him soon enough.

Meanwhile, I have more than work planned for tonight.

Once Mistress la Fontaine has lumbered up to the third floor, I dress in my skirted breeches and creep downstairs to let myself out the back door, locking it behind me with one of the keys we all have. I want to be deliberate with how I begin, so I avoid stepping through patches of moonlight on my way to the Sanctum Square. When I can get no closer without leaving the shadows, I pause to observe everything one last time.

This is what the world looks like to other people.

I think the air is quivering until I realize it's me who is shaking. Mindful of how overwhelming it was last night, I step into the moonlight with my eyes closed.

A waterfall of awareness gushes over me. I gasp, flooding my nose and lungs with a dozen scents, and immediately slap a hand over my mouth to help me hold my breath. Sound echoes from stone surfaces all around me, like ripples bouncing off the edge of a pool of water. The cacophony is worse than daytime with hundreds of people working and shouting to each other, but after several seconds, I find I can sort what's important and tolerate it the same way. A series of high-pitched screams in the air above me is terrifying until I recall the bat from last night. Who knew the creatures were constantly screeching?

Cautiously, I inhale through my nose to filter out some of the stone and wood dust until I no longer need to breathe deeply. Keeping my head down, I slowly open my eyes. If I thought the ground would be dull to start with, I was wrong. The stones at my feet are riddled with spellbinding patterns of cracks and ribbons of density. I could study them all day, but I force my gaze up.

What I see takes my breath away.

The Sanctum glitters with an infinite number of rainbows, struck from thousands of tiny reflective facets in the limestone walls. Any lingering question that this moon-given power was something to be feared vanishes in the face of such beauty. Impulsively, I run the length of the building, delighting in the breeze on my face, the texture of the stone through my boots, and the brilliance of my surroundings.

It's intoxicating.

Work now, play later. I'm out of breath when I reach the transept arm extending south at a right angle from the long nave. Beyond it is the eastern section being expanded, where the scaffolding had to be replaced. New supports mean new stresses, so I weave through stacks of wood and stone carving stations to the base of the structure and start climbing. I can see and feel the grain of the wood and easily smell the difference between aged and new, poles of oak and poles of ash. The lingering odor of iron, leather, and sweat in one spot tells me where a blacksmith took a nap in the shade that day.

Wood creaks and sings with my weight, but nothing carries the telltale sound of splintering or sliding. When I do hear a noise that makes me stop, it's a single lashing reed that's split—not worth fixing. On the third level I spot a hole bored by some insect that's created a hairline crack. It, too, probably doesn't merit addressing, but I pull a blue ribbon from my jacket to tie it on the frame to mark it for sealing with tar later. I have to wet one end of the ribbon with my tongue to push it through a tiny gap in the reeds like the eye of a needle.

Bitterness from the indigo dye has me immediately spitting. Of course I should've expected taste to be as enhanced as my other senses. Curious, I touch a red ribbon to my tongue and find it was colored with a combination of strawberry and beetroot.

I continue, inspecting each section faster and more confidently than I've ever been able to before. When I reach the top level, I pause to look out over the city. The open center of the Selenae Quarter glows as it did several nights ago, and the melody which drifts toward me is hauntingly familiar. Likely one I heard while living at the convent. If I had Juliane's perfect memory, I would know for sure. I can distinguish a number of deep baritones and wonder if Gregor's voice is among them.

The light coming from the Quarter seems to increase, the song also growing louder until they both peak and then begin to fade. Glancing up, I see the three-quarter moon has reached its highest point for the night, reminding me how late it is. Back to work.

I complete the last area quickly and make my way back down. The angles of moonlight are now such that I move in and out of shadow, and it's amusing—though somewhat dizzying—to experience the changes in my senses over and over.

The sound of footsteps on stone causes me to freeze, one leg dangling midreach to the next platform, my back to the square. The tread is slow and deliberate but definitely someone larger than me. I pull my leg back as quietly as possible as I swing around to look. Though the move takes me out of the moonlight, I can still see fairly well. More importantly, it would be difficult for anyone to find me in the shadows. Unless they already know where I am.

A cloaked figure appears around the corner, carrying a low lantern. The man is at least as tall as the one I saw four nights ago, but his hood is down and moonlight reflects off silver waves of hair. I can't see his face as he focuses on the ground, maneuvering steadily closer to me around blocks of stone and piles of wood. A night watchman? Magister Thomas did say the number of guards was doubled, but this man carries no visible weapon.

He stops and raises his lantern, like he's searching for something, before moving out of my line of sight below. His cloak lands on the ground with a soft *whump*. A few seconds later, he boosts himself up to the first level with a grunt of effort. He can't have realized I'm here or he wouldn't be so casual.

I back deeper into my corner as a ghostly white hand reaches up to set the lantern across from me on the woven platform. A small knife on my belt is all I have to defend myself with, and I grip the hilt with a sweaty hand. I don't want to get close enough to use it, but I may need to get past him.

The man hoists his upper half over the edge with a low groan. This is the moment when he's least able to react, and I have the best chance of getting away. I lunge forward, grabbing the side of the platform to swing around and down just as the lantern casts light on the man's face, and I recognize him.

Simon of Mesanus.

CHAPTER 18

Simon's eyes widen in panic, and he leans backward too far to hold on. I have just enough time to change my direction to go straight at him. My shoulder hits the lantern and sends it flying as I seize his wrist. Glass shatters as what little light the lamp provided vanishes. He swings around and slams against the pole below me but manages to grab on to it, relieving me of having to support his full weight.

"Sky on fire!" Simon gasps. "Is that you, Cat?"

"Yes," I answer, my heart beating so hard my chest pounds into the platform under me. "Can I let go now?"

"Yes. Please."

I release him and scoot up to peer over the edge as he grips the pole and looks up at me. "What in the Light are you doing up there?" he asks.

"I work here, remember? Why are *you* here?"

Simon lowers himself to a squat and hops back to the ground. "I was doing *my* job." He flexes his wrist and glances up again with a frown. "Trying to get a feel for what the city was like that night."

I swing my legs over to climb down. "You know there are easier ways to get to the top of the Sanctum." I land lightly in front of him and deliberately dust off my hands.

Simon's grimace deepens. "Hell Beyond, woman, you're like a cat."

His annoyance only makes me grin. "If the high altum heard you cursing like that in the Sanctum, you'd be chanting penance till sunrise."

"Good thing I'm not in the Sanctum." Simon heaves a sigh and nudges what's left of his lantern with his toe. "How can you see *anything*, let alone well enough to do an inspection?"

I shrug against the sudden tension in my shoulders. "There's plenty of moonlight up high." I bite my lip, knowing just how well I'll be able to see. "Do you want me to take you up there?"

"That depends." There's a touch of a smile in his voice. "Is the way you mentioned truly easier, or is it designed to humble me?"

I chuckle. "That depends. Do you enjoy stairs more than ladders?"

Simon kicks the shattered lamp aside and bends over to pick up his cloak. "Stairs I can handle. Lead on."

The Sanctum doors are locked, but I know which windows can be opened. I gesture for Simon to follow me. While I have no problem wending my way through the shadows without a lantern, he keeps tripping and stubbing his toes. Eventually, I grab his hand to guide him along.

It's a long walk to the western end of the Sanctum, and I'm aware of every second. I stop when we reach the carved stone blocks piled against the back side of the facade towers for later use. When I release his hand, Simon immediately wipes it on his trousers. Mortified, I turn my back on him without a word and climb up the stack to the ledge about eight feet off the ground. It's barely wide enough to walk on, and I wouldn't want to do it in a skirt—or while holding a cloak. "I suggest you drop that here," I tell him, and he does.

Our destination is a tall, peaked window facing east. Few realize it pivots around the center, and, after pushing it open a few inches, one only has to slide their fingers up the edge to pop the latch. I explain this to Simon as I rotate it and slide through. He quickly follows, though he has to suck in his breath to squeeze between the panes and the iron frame.

"I can't see a thing," Simon murmurs as I reclose the window. "Where are we?"

"On the stairs in one of the front towers," I whisper back. "We'll go partway up from here."

Simon grabs my hand before I can get too far away, which is reassuring but probably so he doesn't trip over his own feet. The stairs turn with the wall until we reach the landing which opens to overlook the Sanctum interior. Simon pauses to peer up into the darkness of the tower. "Do these stairs go all the way to the top?"

I nod, then remember he can't see it. "Yes. Once you get above the main roof, the tower is open to the air, and there's a spiral stair tucked into one of the corners."

He looks down at me. "Have you ever been up there?"

"Of course," I answer. "It's beautiful when the sky is clear, like lying in a cradle among the stars."

"You go at night?"

"Sometimes. When I want to think or be alone."

The best nights for the stars are moonless. Now I wonder if I might have discovered my strange abilities sooner if I'd gone up there at other times.

"You'll have to lead again." Simon squeezes my fingers. "I have no idea where I'm going."

The colored glass windows along the nave mute the light inside to wavy shades of blue and violet, like being underwater. Simon can probably see well enough to let go of my hand, but he doesn't this time. I tug him along the gallery level balcony which runs the whole length of the Sanctum. A part of me knows the darkness makes this even more inappropriate than it would be in daylight. The other part doesn't care.

Simon halts when we reach the center, mesmerized by the altar and the silent crown of light it wears. High above it sits a short, square tower with windows so this place—the holiest—is never in complete shadow. It's something I never tire of admiring, so I readily pause for him.

"In a place like this, I could almost believe," he whispers.

"You don't believe in the Sun?"

He huffs humorlessly. "I believe the Sun exists. Only a fool would not. As for the Power that gave it to us, not so much."

Blaspheme. I should recoil from someone saying such things, but he sounds lost, like he wishes he *could* believe. "Why not?"

Simon shakes his head. "If It were there, and It was truly good, why does It allow such misery and suffering in the world? Why does It allow people to act as they do?"

It was obvious days ago that Perrete's murder wasn't the first he's seen, nor the worst. His cynicism is understandable. "Mother Agnes says our lives are like the Sun: a gift," I tell him. "Once bestowed, the giver has no say in how it's used or misused, otherwise it wouldn't be a true gift."

"That freedom is dangerous when it can destroy the lives of others," he says.

"Yes," I admit. "But it's also necessary. You can't truly be good unless you have the choice not to be."

Simon's mouth tilts up on one side. "I didn't realize you were a solosopher."

"It comes from being raised in a convent."

His only response is to twist his hand and lace his fingers with mine. Though I doubt he can see my blush, I turn away quickly and lead the way to the next set of stairs. The floor of the south tower's first open level is crisscrossed with dusty footprints and dotted with bird droppings from the pigeons snoring contentedly in the rafters two stories above. Moonlight slants through the high, arched windows unblocked by glass or shutters.

Though I'm a little practiced in moving in and out of moonlight now, I hold my breath and narrow my eyes as I step directly into it. I immediately feel Simon's pulse through his palm and fingers, strong and rapid from climbing the stairs, and it jumps when he sees I'm leading him to the slanting edge of the roof.

"Is that safe?"

"Perfectly," I answer. The stone gutter is several inches high on the right side and scaffolds run along the entire length. "When it rains, all the water from the roof drains into this, which is why it's so wide."

"Wide?" Simon mutters. "It's not broad enough for a child's pull wagon."

"That's why we don't let them up here," I say lightly. He frowns at my joke. "Just don't look down. And lean a bit to the left, toward the roof."

Though he's shown no sign of wanting to let go, I squeeze his hand to let him know he can hold on to me. Then I step out, angling my left arm behind me. Simon pivots to a walk leading with his right, which makes him face the roof. That's probably best.

Pierre's silhouette crouches at the far end. Even without seeing so well, this place is familiar enough that I could walk it blindfolded, and I have to consciously make myself move slower than I'd like.

"What are these stone arms that arch out?" Simon asks as we pass the third.

"Flying buttresses," I answer. "They channel the pressure of the building's weight to the ground. Using them allows for thinner walls and bigger windows, which makes it brighter inside."

"They look like giant spider legs."

I nod in agreement. "That may have actually been the inspiration. Nature's designs are often perfect."

"You know a lot about architecture," Simon says.

I grin. Much as I complain about showing patrons and high-ranking visitors around the Sanctum, I enjoy every second of it. "You have no idea. I could probably spend an hour describing the mathematical aesthetics of the triforium arches along the nave."

"The what?"

"Exactly."

Simon chuckles. "I wouldn't necessarily mind that someday. Or anything else you'd like to tell me." He pauses, then rushes the next words. "I mean anything about, um, architecture and the Sanctum."

His embarrassment is so amusing, I'm glad I'm facing forward. I'm not sure I could keep a straight face.

"Then here is your first lesson," I say. We've reached Pierre and the wider area around him. "These full-bodied statues are called chimera. Gargoyles are only heads or partial bodies and are for draining water. But these"—I rest my free hand on the stone back—"are purely decoration."

Simon takes in the chimera's full height, made greater by the upright wings. "I didn't realize how big it was." He releases my hand to place his own on the statue. "And how hideous."

I hide my disappointment at losing his touch by pretending to be insulted. "He doesn't mean that, Pierre." I pat the muscled neck like it's a dog's. "You're beautiful."

"You gave it a human name?"

"What should I call him?"

"I don't know." He grins shakily. "Bat-dog-lion . . . thing." Tense as he is from being so high, something about him is more relaxed than I've ever seen, though I remind myself I've known Simon less than five days. He shakes his head. "Why put such a frightening statue on such a beautiful building?"

That I can answer readily. "According to Mother Agnes, they're meant to frighten away any real demons that might seek to roost on the Sanctum. They declare"—here I lower my voice menacingly: "'I have this watch, Brother Demon, and I am much more fearsome than you, so do not challenge me.'"

My eight-year-old self asked if that would really work, because wouldn't lady demons seek out strong mates like that to make smaller devils with? That question earned me two months of scrubbing pots in the kitchen, and I still don't know the answer.

Simon watches me like he knows my mind has wandered, but he's not irritated. "And this is where you were when you saw the man?"

"Yes, I was like this." I turn to face south. Simon steps up behind me, his clothes brushing mine at the back. His heartbeat echoes across the narrow gap between us. It's slowed some, now that we've rested from our climb.

Without thinking, I place my hand on Pierre's wing like I did that night and find Simon's is already there. Quickly, I shift it to be next to his but not quite touching. His loose sleeve has fallen down to his elbow, his exposed forearm parallel to mine. The veins beneath the surface of his pale skin extend like blue vines along his arm, tangling with all their divides under his wrist. My skin is as golden as his is silver, making the corresponding blood vessels a shade of green. The difference is fascinating.

"Where—?" Simon's voice cracks, and he clears his throat. "Where did the man come from?"

I lean back slightly to point. "Over there."

Simon's cheek skims against the crown of my head as he lowers his chin to almost rest on my shoulder. "Ah, yes, I see."

His voice in my ear rolls over me like gentle thunder, and I find myself swaying. Simon's right hand comes to my waist in a protective instinct. "Are you all right?" he whispers, and my hair catches the wind of his breath.

Sight is only a distraction. I close my eyes as I nod, making my ear brush along his nose and lips.

Oh my Shining Sun.

Simon's hand moves to cover mine on the statue. His wrist on my skin sends the shiver of his pulse through my arm as the heat of his breath drifts lower, to my neck. I sink into his warmth behind me, and his heartbeat speeds up again like he's climbing stairs, but so does mine.

Is it only like this because of moonlight or because I've never been this close to a man before? I know Simon can't possibly sense everything as I do, but does he feel something more than ordinary?

I open my eyes and turn to face him, my back to Pierre's solid form. Simon's left hand remains against the wing, his right still at my waist. His eyes are crystal clear except for that one spot. They search my face until his gaze settles on my mouth, telling me exactly what is on his mind. I've never been kissed except by Remi that one time. This would be different, though, and not just because I was wanting and expecting it.

Simon leans closer, then hesitates, like he's giving me a chance to move away, though I have no desire to do so. Instead, I take a deep breath, inhaling the scents I've ignored until now. He smells of sweat and lantern oil, lamb stew with rosemary, ale, and . . . blood.

I blink, looking for the source. "What happened to your neck?"

Three long scratches run from Simon's left ear to his collarbone. The marks aren't deep, but thin lines have scabbed over on each where the skin was broken.

He stands straight, his right hand going to the opposite side of his neck. "It's not what you think."

Is he saying they aren't fingernail marks? Because that's the only thing I can imagine doing that. "What is it, then?"

"Nothing." The spell of whatever had captured us is broken, and he abruptly turns away. "Thank you for showing me this place, but it's late. We should go."

Simon barely waits for me as we retrace our path back to the window in silence.

Though the lower moon makes everything darker, and I often make it easy for him to do so, he never takes my hand again.

CHAPTER 19

The magister is long gone by the time I come downstairs in the morning, but somehow I beat Remi to breakfast. When he finally appears and stumbles to his chair, I wrinkle my nose.

"You smell like the floor of an alehouse," I say as his mother puts a plate in front of him.

He scowls. "If I'm not allowed to have any say as to what you do with your time, you have no right to comment on how I spend mine."

Magister Thomas won't appreciate Remi arriving for work in a foul mood. I offer him a buttered roll. "My concern is purely for your safety. There's a killer wandering the streets."

He takes the bread, his expression easing into a dismissive frown. "You didn't seem worried for yourself."

Mistress la Fontaine turns around from the hearth, one hand on her hip. "Did you go out last night, Cat?" she scolds.

Curse you, Remi. I grit my teeth under a false smile. "Just to check something at the Sanctum. And I wasn't alone."

"Who were you with?" she demands.

"Someone close enough to merit holding hands," says Remi sourly.

If Remi had been where he could see us, how had I not heard him? I must have been distracted by Simon. Nothing untoward happened, though, and I have nothing to hide.

"I took the venatre to where I was when I saw the man running across the square," I say calmly, refusing to be cowed by Remi's accusing stare. "I was holding on to him as we walked along the roof because he was nervous being so high."

The housekeeper snorts as she returns to her pot. "Any normal person would be."

Remi's green eyes narrow. "You both left rather suddenly."

"How long were you watching us, Remi?" I growl.

He grins maliciously, his full lips parting just enough to see his teeth. "Long enough to know the Montcuirs wouldn't like it if they saw what I did."

I shove back from the table and jump to my feet. "You will mind your tongue and not start vicious gossip, Remone la Fontaine!"

The housekeeper swings around like she's ready to pull us apart, but Remi only raises his eyebrows as he looks up at me, surprised and a little hurt. "Relax, Kitten. You know I'd never do anything to ruin your reputation."

"Wouldn't you?"

"No, I wouldn't," he says seriously. "But that doesn't mean you can't ruin it on your own."

I have half a mind to reveal what I know about Remi's true whereabouts the night Perrete was killed. It wouldn't help his reputation, that's for sure.

A knock on the front door interrupts. I yank my skirt around my knees as I turn on my heel and stomp to the model room. Juliane Montcuir stands on the street outside with Oudin behind her.

"I'm here to collect you," she says before I can ask. "There's been another murder."

——— • ✳ • ———

"Simon asked me to bring you," Juliane explains as she guides me along the street, her arm in mine like we're friends out for a stroll. "But he'll have been there for over an hour already."

"Who was it?" I ask.

"Another woman from Pleasure Road," Oudin says quietly from where he walks behind us. His eyes dart between passing faces, though none appear to be paying us attention. "Her name was Ysabel."

I don't ask if he knew her as he did Perrete.

We navigate our way across the Sanctum Square, and my neck grows hot as we pass the place where I first took Simon's hand. I wonder if Remi is right that his family would object if something developed between us. Juliane is holding my arm now like I'm an equal rather than an orphan of questionable parentage.

But then, Simon had pulled away last night, acting like touching me, even innocently, was a mistake. Maybe *he* objects.

We angle away from the Pathway of Prayer, passing the tavern Simon marked as the one where Oudin—and Remi—had been the night of Perrete's murder. A grassy area with a few trees and a walking path lies beyond the block of houses. It's a popular place for courting couples, especially in twilight hours.

Oudin pales as the park comes into view. "Lambert brought Lady Genevieve here after the bonding ceremony," he says. "It was my idea."

"I doubt anyone will be promenading here for a long time," Juliane murmurs as we approach the crowd that's gathered on the street. City watchmen stand at intervals to keep people out, and Lambert paces behind them like a restless lion in a menagerie. As soon as he sees us, he waves for us to come to his way.

A chain hanging from short posts is meant to keep people

from entering the park except via the paths, but Oudin steps over it, then helps Juliane do the same. Though I'm also wearing a skirt, it's several inches shorter than hers, and I don't need assistance. Lambert rushes up, however, so I let him hold my elbow as I half-step, half-hop over the barrier.

"Simon is waiting for you over there." He points to a grove of trees in the middle of the park. Before Oudin can take a step in that direction, Lambert catches his arm. "Not us, Brother. We're to observe the crowd, noting anyone who seems overly interested."

Oudin leans around Lambert, searching the area where Simon stands with some distress. "But Ysabel—"

"Has already been taken away," says Lambert, not unkindly. "This is what Simon needs us to do."

Oudin's mouth twists into an ugly scowl as he shrugs his brother off. "Well, if that's what the venatre needs." With one last glare in Simon's direction, he turns away.

Lambert sighs and frowns at his sister and me. "I don't know why he insists on involving the two of you in this vile business." He follows Oudin, shaking his head.

Juliane and I cross the low-cropped lawn. Goats scatter out of our way as we approach Simon, who stands under an oak tree, gazing at the ground.

The body is gone, as Lambert said. Only a wide area of dirt matted with dark crimson blood remains. Morbidly, I wonder if the trees' roots will drink the wetness like rainwater and what that will do to their leaves.

"I had her removed as soon as possible," says Simon quietly. "There were . . . certain elements I felt neither of you needed to see."

"You'll have to tell us what was done to her if we're going to help," Juliane points out. I agree, but part of me is relieved. The drawings later will be bad enough.

"She was on her back." Simon gestures with his hands to show the direction she lay in. "The same as Perrete."

"Was she stabbed, too?" I ask.

"No, but her throat was cut." He points to a patch of ground so soaked it's black. "She was positioned so she would bleed directly on the ground when he did it. He's learned. Perrete's murder was too messy. Probably got blood all over himself that night and had to dispose of everything he was wearing."

Juliane cocks her head to the side. "You're certain this was the same killer? Were there other similarities?"

Simon nods. "This woman's eyes were removed with a little more expertise. Then her face was crushed by a single blow from a heavy object."

"I remember you saying it meant he didn't want to be looked at," says Juliane, and I nod. Though I don't possess her perfect memory, it's not something I'll ever forget.

"And the improved technique could mean this murder was to correct what went wrong in the alley," he continues. "It would explain why he struck again so soon."

I feel like he's leaving something out. "Was anything else consistent with last time?"

Simon looks up. His eyes are guarded and his posture stiff, so unlike last night—at least until the end. "Yes," he says quietly.

Before I can ask what, he suddenly tilts his head to look behind me. Without thinking, I turn to follow his line of sight. A goat placidly munches on grass several yards away, a dark, stringy gruff swinging from its chin as it moves in a continuous circular motion. I blink. Has someone braided the goat's beard?

Simon sprints past me, and I expect he would have tackled the animal if it didn't bleat and drop what it was chewing on before fleeing. Simon snatches up a long braid of what can only be human hair.

"Catrin," he gasps. "Perrete's hair was black, wasn't it?"

"Not naturally, but yes," I answer.

The braid is stiff with dried blood, but the color isn't in question. Simon turns it over in his hand. "Ysabel was blond. The killer either dropped this or left it on purpose. Either way, this definitely connects the two."

"Did you have any doubts?"

He shakes his head. "No. There are too many similarities." Simon clenches the hair in his fist. "Curse it! And now she's buried."

"Who?" I ask. "This victim? Already?" That's only ever done after sunset.

"No, Perrete," Simon explains. "Madame Emeline found a small braid of hair tucked in her dress. We didn't know whose it was, but it felt safe to assume it was a keepsake of some kind, so I let them bury it with her. What if . . . Cat, what if it was actually from someone he'd killed before?"

I roll the idea through my mind. "You think he leaves hair from a previous victim and takes hair from the next one? Was Perrete's cut off?"

Simon exhales heavily. "I honestly didn't look for that. Her hair was rinsed and lying back against her head and her face seemed like the only part worth studying." He tucks the braid in his tunic. "Madame Emeline took this body, too. I'll make sure to note if her hair was cut off when I go there later."

I suppress a shiver. "What other things will you look for?"

"I'll do some measurements to confirm what was used to crush her head was the same as what was used on Perrete." He heads back to where Juliane waits, watching and listening. "I'm already quite sure it was, though."

I turn as he passes, a sick suspicion tightening my chest. "How could you tell?"

He motions with his hands, approximating size and form. "It was unusual—flat and squarish and very heavy. Like a shaped stone. A brick perhaps."

I can't tell him, but I know it wasn't either of those.

It was a hammer.

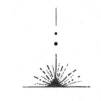

CHAPTER 20

We all walk back to the Montcuir home together. Juliane and her brothers turn off at the second floor, going to their bedrooms to freshen up. I continue to the next level with Simon. Being alone with him, even for those few minutes, doesn't feel proper, especially after last night. Perhaps because Magister Thomas always made such a point that Remi was never permitted in my room—nor I in his.

But what did happen last night? Did I read more into it than was written? Had he only held my hand and stood close for guidance and then withdrew once he realized he was sending me the wrong message? Then I remember how his pulse had raced and the flush rose to his cheeks as he'd focused on my mouth and leaned closer. His true thoughts and feelings were unmistakable, even if he felt he needed to hide them.

Simon is only a poor, distant relation of the Montcuirs. If he hadn't come to them for help, I'm sure they wouldn't care what he did with his life. Juliane appears to like me personally, but Remi seems to think the family would disapprove of any deeper connection I might make with Simon. I shake my head. I'll never understand why birth is so important to some people.

If it weren't, the parentless girls living at Solis Abbey would have more options in life than the cloister or Pleasure Road.

Oblivious to my inner turmoil, Simon goes about marking the place Ysabel was found on both maps. I move to the opposite side of the table and set out paper and ink for Juliane to take notes when she joins us, which thankfully is only a few minutes later.

She pauses in the doorway, cocking her head to the side as she looks at Simon before frowning and taking a few steps toward him. A frail hand comes up to touch the scratches on his neck. "Is that—?"

Simon twists away, though much gentler than he did with me last night. "It's nothing," he tells her.

"But—"

"Don't worry about it." He makes a grotesque effort to smile.

Juliane balls her hand into a fist and pulls it back, blinking rapidly. Simon turns to face me like nothing is amiss. "I never did thank you for coming, Cat. I value your insight."

I avoid his eyes by readying the ink bottle. "I didn't have much to offer this morning."

"Maybe not this time," he says. "But you help me think."

That's not the same as contributing. I keep my eyes low. "Will Lambert go with you to examine Ysabel's body?"

Simon shakes his head. "I don't think so. He didn't do so well last time."

"He had nightmares," Juliane tells me. "I haven't heard him moan and sob like that since Mother died. When will you go?" The last is for Simon.

"Around noon, when the light is best," Simon answers. "Madame Emeline didn't know the girl well, but she's seeking out those who did and will hopefully have some information by then. In the meantime, I should make some sketches."

He moves to the end of the table closest to the open window and sits down, setting the thin braid of Perrete's hair next to the blank page I've lain out. His ink pen flies across the paper with broad and short strokes, but otherwise he's silent.

Juliane settles on the bench and sorts her notes, apparently content, but my presence feels pointless. Almost to remind them that I'm here, I ask, "Why would a murderer take something from the victim?"

Simon stops and looks up. The image of a woman lying on her back is already taking shape on his paper. "Acts like these give the killer a sense of power he can't get any other way," he says. "By taking some sort of memento, he can relive the memory, which usually sustains his need for a while."

"It feeds the monster in the cage," I say, referring to what he'd described yesterday.

"Yes, but it will always hunger for more eventually."

I think about this for a few seconds. "You seemed surprised that he acted again so soon."

Simon folds his hands together over the sketch. "It's usually a much longer time between first and second victims, because everything is thrilling the first time you do it. The euphoria lasts longer. A space of only four days made me think he must have lost whatever item he took, which made him eager to procure another, but now I'm not so sure. Something left behind twice feels deliberate. Why would he give up his keepsake?"

"Out with the old and in with the new," I say, and he stares at me, almost stunned. I shuffle my feet in embarrassment. "Sorry. I didn't mean to make light of it."

"No, Cat," he says. "That's exactly right. I just can't decide if that's a fastidious and tidy mindset or one that embraces new ideas readily. Maybe both."

"Being fussy and neat is usually a feminine trait," Juliane

points out. If Mistress la Fontaine is any example, I concur. "Men are more often fascinated with new things."

I agree there, too. Magister Thomas and Remi can—and do—talk for hours about new construction methods and materials.

"But this killer obviously has trouble with women." Simon holds up a finger to emphasize his point. "The root of that is often in parents, and that kind of mother is the most overbearing. They're impossible to please." He shrugs. "In my experience at least."

So Simon did have a mother. At least for a while.

"And the hair isn't all the killer took," continues Simon. "He still has whatever heavy object he used. Something that big is harder to hide, which makes it more likely we'll find it."

I don't want Simon thinking about the hammer more than necessary. "If there was hair with Perrete, can we connect it to an earlier victim, then?" I ask.

He shakes his head in frustration. "We'd have to dig her up to retrieve it, and I doubt we could find the connection, unless it was very recent."

"I can't recall a similar murder," I say. "Not in the last few years."

Simon shrugs. "It's also possible the killer recently arrived in Collis or he was in prison for other reasons. Murder isn't usually the first display of violence."

Neither idea is comforting. "If he's not from Collis, then what's to stop him from moving on to another city and doing the same there?"

"Nothing," says Simon. "But he's more likely to stay if he doesn't think he'll be caught, which is a safe assumption with this investigation as it is. It's hard to draw conclusions with so little information."

"So *little*?" I protest. "Yesterday you said another body would give you more to work with."

"And it does," Simon insists, going back to his sketch. "Before it was really only a theory that he didn't like being judged or looked at, and now I'm almost positive that's the case."

"Maybe that hair is also only a fraction of what he took," says Juliane. "It's barely the width of a finger. When Mother died, Father gave all of us small braids of her hair as a keepsake. The murderer may still have some from all his victims."

Simon doesn't look up from his drawing. "I'd already thought that."

I watch him sketch. He's quite talented, actually. His proportions are correct—and I know proportions, though in buildings more than bodies. The woman—Ysabel—was laid out on the grass, almost like she was on display.

"No one saw Perrete," I murmur.

Simon looks up, and Juliane stops sorting her pages. "What did you say?" he asks.

I chew the inside of my cheek for a second. "I was just thinking that one difference was that Ysabel was left in a place where people could see her, but Perrete wasn't. Maybe that was the reason he felt the need to kill again so soon. He's trying to conquer something which tortures him, but so few were able to view his triumph the first time."

Simon nods to Juliane. "Excellent thought. Write that down."

I wish I could feel glad to have made a contribution—twice—but it's not exactly comforting to know I understand the motivations of a madman.

CHAPTER 21

The citizens of Collis soon fall into one of three reaction categories. The first kind live in the wealthier neighborhoods and assume such terrible things will never happen to them, and they are likely correct. So far the victims have been poor women known to sell themselves. If there's any concern, it's from the men who frequent the seedier side of town to indulge in its pleasures, like Oudin, who worry about being falsely accused.

The women who have buried two of their own are stricken with fear. Via Madame Emeline, Simon urges them to be cautious about whom they serve, and where, yet most live on the edge of destitution. They don't have the option of foregoing the employment which enables them to eat.

Lastly are those who love the drama. I hear no other topic on the lips of Sanctum workers. Rumors spread like fire in a dry wheat field and change direction just as fast. I suspect much is said in my earshot in hopes I will confirm or deny the gory details. Simon warns me not to correct anything I hear, though I don't fully understand why until four mornings later, when Remi brings us a note.

"Your killer has struck again," he says, waving a scrap of

parchment as soon as the Montcuir's housekeeper delivers him to Simon's room. Remi drops the page just before Simon can take it from him.

Simon examines the tear at the top of the parchment. "This was ripped from something." He glances sharply at Remi. "Where was it found?"

"Nailed to the Sanctum door." Remi looks pointedly at Simon's bed in the corner of the room and then to me with eyebrows as high as they'll go, as if to say, *Really? Here?*

"Which door?" Simon demands. "Where's the nail?"

Remi takes a step back at Simon's harsh tone before regaining his condescending attitude. "The one on the transept, facing south. Still in the door as far as I know."

Simon pivots to Lambert. "I need that nail. Disturb the head as little as possible." Lambert hesitates, obviously wanting to see what the note contains, but then runs out, yanking his gloves on as he goes. Simon returns to studying the parchment. "When was it found?" he asks Remi.

"It was there when workers arrived this morning, but most can't read so no one bothered to look at it until me." Remi folds his arms. "You're welcome."

"Next time I'll thank you for sending for me rather than removing it."

I step up beside Simon, and he angles the page to show me. The words are poorly spelled and barely legible.

It hass ben 4 days and you hav naught cougt me and so I am forc'd to kill againe

"Just what I was afraid of," Simon murmurs. Juliane appears on my other side, and he leans further to allow her to see, squishing me between them.

"I've never seen parchment so rough," Juliane says.

I rub a thumb and forefinger on the corner. "It's been freshly scraped, and not very well, nor was it pressed and smoothed afterward."

"Which means it was written on before?" Simon asks.

"Most likely," I tell him.

Simon moves to the window and holds the note to the light, squinting. "Yes, there's something there, but I can't read it."

I join him in looking, tilting my head against his shoulder to get the right angle, but I can't see anything either. "Do you think it's real?" I ask. "Is it from the killer?"

"Yes, but no."

What in the Gifted Sun does he mean by that? I turn back to Remi. "Has a body been found?"

His jaw is clenched so hard it's twitching. "Not yet."

"It's only a matter of time." Simon folds the page in half and shoves it into his pocket. "Let's go."

"What about Lambert?" I ask. "He's halfway to the Sanctum by now."

"That's where we're going. He'll expect to find me there."

I don't think he means Lambert is the one who expects him. We all follow Simon, Remi included, double-timing our steps to keep up with his lanky strides. Lambert is fetching a clawed lever to pry the nail from the wooden door when we arrive. While Simon waits, he pulls out the note and holds it up to the Sun again. "Too bright," he mutters.

He continues angling the parchment different ways against the Sun, but gives up with a sigh as Lambert returns. "I still can't read it. Maybe focused candlelight would work."

The moon. I look around, finding the half-circle hanging midway in the western sky. It seems crazy in broad daylight, but I have nothing to lose by trying. "May I see it?" I ask Simon.

He hands me the page without a word, and I hold it up to the moon, my back to the Sun. Words appear as plainly as the nose on Remi's face, but I pretend it's more difficult than it is. "B-A-R-L . . . E-Y." I pause. "And the number forty and what's probably a unit of weight." I leave it at that, though above it is written *Oats, 32 stones.*

I lower it before Simon can look himself, offering it back to him with a shrug. "Maybe an inventory or shipment list."

Simon holds it up as I did, tilting his head in frustration. "I don't see anything at all now. What kind of magick did you use?"

The comment is almost certainly in jest, and I laugh, the sound pitching higher than I intend. Fortunately, Lambert has the nail nearly out, and Simon stuffs the parchment back in his jacket with one hand while the other catches the piece of metal as it falls from the door.

"Thank you, Cousin." He steps back into full sunlight again. "Someone get me a blacksmith." When none of us move, Remi heaves a sigh and walks off.

Simon studies the nail. "Driven in by a metal hammer, I think."

My heart clenches. "How can you tell?"

"This flat part here." Simon points, and I shade my eyes to see. "If it was wood, the head would still be more rounded, and if a rock had been used, it would be rough with traces of stone in the scratches." He rolls it over his fingers. "Otherwise unused."

Craftsmen of any kind aren't far away at the Sanctum site, and Remi returns shortly with a blacksmith. The man's face and head are clean shaven, but a sooty cloth is tied around his forehead to keep sweat from dripping into his eyes. Simon hands him the nail and asks for his opinion on what was used to drive it in, and he confirms Simon's theory: a flat, metal-headed hammer. Few people possess that kind of tool—either by lack of need or coin to purchase one.

Simon doesn't seem excited by the narrowing of suspects, however. "What is a nail like this used for?" he asks the smith.

"This length and width?" The blacksmith turns it over in his hand. "Carts and wagons mostly."

"How do you know that?" Remi demands.

The man glowers back. "Because I make these cursed things all the time."

"Yes, but—"Remi begins.

"It's far too large for crates or barrels," interrupts the smith. "Too short and thin for the beams in a building, and too long for horseshoes or window shutters. There are other things these can be used for, but it's new." He drops the nail back into Simon's hand, ignoring Remi, who's silent with embarrassment. "Anyone who owes his livelihood to a horse and wagon has a ready supply of these for repairs, unless he's a fool."

Simon nods. "Thank you."

As soon as the man is gone, Remi recovers his confidence. "So our killer owns a wagon or a cart." He waves his hand at the sellers setting up for the day. "Where should we start? The flower peddler looks threatening."

To my surprise, Simon agrees. "Question anyone who will talk. I just want it known that I'm here."

"Don't you have a body to find?" asks Remi.

"Yes, we do." Simon heads to the nearest merchant. "But he'll come to me."

I have a hundred questions, but Remi grabs me by the elbow and steers me toward the flower cart.

"What is wrong with you?" I snap, yanking my arm away. "Why were you so rude to the smith? You don't know anything about nails."

"I know a far sight more than the venatre does, Cat," he growls. "And the blacksmith can't even read. I'm an architect. I'm *educated*."

"You're an ass is what you are. He was able to tell us exactly what we needed to know."

Remi looks down on me. "And what if I told you we have a dozen nails like that at home, and *no wagon*?"

"I'd say you're telling me we should consider you suspect."

He shakes his head, incredulous. "Are you really too blind to see where all the trails are leading?"

I gape at him. "You can't be serious. You think because Magister Thomas—*a master architect*—has a box of nails that he's the killer?"

"Shhh-sh!" Remi waves his hands at me. "Not so loud!" He plasters a smile on his face as he glances around. When his eyes stop on someone over my shoulder, I turn to look. Lambert is watching us, but I don't think he heard everything. Remi pulls me farther away, whispering rapidly. "The nail is the least of it, Cat. You know what Perrete did that night. How could he not have been angry with her?"

"But angry enough to kill her?"

Remi closes his eyes and fidgets for a few seconds before grinding out his next words. "I saw Perrete. Her face was smashed with a hammer. You know very well which one."

"The one she stole," I spit back. "And while we're on the subject, where exactly *did* you see her body?"

He knows I know. Remi lowers his head to avoid my eyes. "Madame Emeline's. The morning after. I got to Collis that evening and spent the night there."

"You are such a lying sack of—"

"I'm trying to be honest now, all right?" he says. "I'm trying to do the right thing."

I push my face up into his. "How is implicating Magister Thomas the right thing?"

He raises an eyebrow. "How is not telling the venatre everything you know about that night any better?"

"Magister Thomas is innocent," I hiss. "That would only waste Simon's time."

Remi snorts. "Your precious Simon would have us question a man who probably cried the last time he stepped on a lady beetle." He gestures to the flower seller, who wears more lace and ribbons on his sleeves than any lady.

"You're just jealous," I accuse. When Remi rolls his eyes, I press my point. "Simon knows things. He understands this murderer in a way that's almost . . . almost . . ."

"Unnatural," Remi finishes.

I scowl. "I was going to say instinctive."

He narrows his gaze on me. "Aren't you curious how he has that instinct?"

Before I can think of a good answer, a commotion erupts as three city guards approach, half-carrying a man wearing nightclothes and wooden clogs. As soon as he sees Simon, he bursts into sobs. "Venatre!" he cries. "My wife has been murdered!"

I wish I could say Simon looks surprised, but he doesn't.

CHAPTER 22

The man is a well-known grain merchant.

"We argued last night," he explains to Simon through his tears. "Sun forgive me, I said things I never should have, and she left." He wipes his eyes. "She left and I didn't think about the danger until she didn't come back. I know that madman killed her. What else could have happened?"

Remi leans closer to whisper in my ear. "Did he think to check her mother or sister's house?"

I don't want to agree with Remi on principle, but he's right. It does seems like quite an assumption. "Who else knows about the parchment?" I murmur back.

"No one. It was pointed out by someone who thought it was for me, but nobody around could read it. I brought it straight to you."

A shadow cast by the architect falls over us. "And now you're back, Remi," he says sternly. "I've been waiting half an hour."

"I'm helping the venatre," Remi replies.

Magister Thomas's gray eyes shift between us. "I've already lost Catrin's assistance to the inquiry this morning, I can't also spare you." He cuts Remi off before his mouth can fully open.

"For someone who begs for more authority, you're very eager to shirk the responsibilities you already have." He pivots away and leaves without waiting for a response.

I know the expression on Remi's face. He's holding back tears. I put my hand on his arm. "Thank you for bringing us the note so quickly."

He turns on me, green eyes blazing. "You know why the magister lets you help the venatre, don't you?" Remi clenches his teeth. "It's because he knows you'll protect him."

"It's because he wants Perrete's murder solved," I retort, my earlier empathy dissolving.

"Keep telling yourself that, Kitten."

"Very well," says Simon loudly. "Lead me to your house, and I'll see what I can find."

Thanking Simon profusely, the man beckons him to a road leading south from the square. Lambert and Juliane pause to look at me expectantly before following. Remi has already vanished, so I rush to fall in behind them. A small crowd follows, winding up the street like a funeral procession. Occasionally, I see Simon through the gap between the siblings. He walks alongside the babbling man, tension in every step. I can feel it building in my own shoulders.

Remi is right that I'll do anything to protect Magister Thomas. He should be willing to do the same.

Our destination is a prosperous neighborhood. The man opens the door of his home, but Simon ignores the invitation and looks around. On one side of the house is a large shed with chains across the door, which he points to. "I assume in there is your horse, wagon, and stores."

"Aye." The grain merchant shifts his feet, clogs scraping across the stone threshold. "She's not in there. I looked."

"I didn't think she was." Simon sweeps his gaze up and down

the street, then strides back the way he came, passing Lambert, Juliane, and me. For a second, I think he's leaving, but he stops outside an alley several houses away. The distraught husband runs to his side, panic and confusion on his face.

"Cousin," calls Simon to Lambert. "Will you please stay with Master Merchant?" Without a word, Lambert steps forward and takes the man's arm.

Simon motions to Juliane and me, then he turns and walks into the shadowed gap between buildings. Juliane and I are right behind him, but several steps inside he suddenly throws his arm out to make us stop. "There," he says. "What do you see?"

I follow his line of sight to the ground. "Footprints." Some are heavier than others, but I can't make much sense of them.

"Those are of no real consequence," Simon replies. "What else?"

"Two lines in the dirt," says Juliane, pointing. "Tracks of something being dragged."

"Good." He looks over his shoulder at me with his flawed eye. "What could have made those, Cat?"

It feels like a chance to redeem my unimportant observation about the footprints. "Two . . . ," I begin and stop. Two what? Suddenly I remember Simon talking about what happened to Perrete after she'd been stabbed. "Two heeled shoes. A person was dragged backward down this alley. Someone unconscious."

"Excellent." Simon lowers his arm and continues, stepping so as not to disturb the two lines, and Juliane and I follow suit. This alley has a dead end, with piles of trash against the walls. The parallel tracks lead to a person-size lump with flies buzzing over and around it. Though it's faint, the scent of decay hanging in the air is unmistakable. Simon pauses to let us brace ourselves. Juliane gives him a slight nod, and he bends down and flings the dingy canvas aside. I cover my mouth and nose with one hand just in time.

I'll never get used to seeing this. Ever.

Simon squats next to the corpse's feet, which are shod in sturdy women's boots with high wooden heels, and tests the movement of her leg. "She's been dead since about midnight, give or take an hour."

"The killer grabbed her as soon as she left her home?" I ask through my hand.

Simon shakes his head. "What's wrong with this one, Cat?"

Besides the fact that she's stiff and cold?

When I don't answer, he glances to Juliane. "What's different?"

"She's lying on her side, up against the wall," she says. "And she was covered."

"Yes." Simon moves sideways up to the woman's torso, lifting loose hair away from her face.

"She still has her hair and eyes," I say before Juliane can answer. "And her throat is cut, but there's not very much blood."

"Bruises," adds Juliane. "All around her neck." They blossom against the waxy white of the woman's skin, like a gruesome row of violets.

Without touching the dead woman, Simon extends his fingers over the purple marks to show how they match the shape of his hand, though not the size. "These happened before she died, which means she was strangled."

He rises to his feet. "Her throat was cut after death, that's why there's almost no blood." He pauses. "Conclusion?"

None of it quite matches the other two. This woman was strangled, dragged here, and then had her throat cut. Her body was covered, as though to hide what had been done or prevent discovery—unlike how Perrete and Ysabel were left. "We're meant to think this is our murderer," I say. "But it isn't."

"Very good." Simon doesn't smile, but the sentiment is genuine. "Now. Who did this?"

Juliane frowns. "You already know it was her husband."

"Yes, but we must be able to prove it," replies Simon.

"His hands," I say, thinking how Simon's didn't quite line up. "They'll match the marks on her neck."

Simon holds up his own hand. "Show me yours. Put it against mine."

I press my palm to his and align our fingers. It's the first time we've deliberately touched since that night on the Sanctum. Heat spreads up my arm from the contact, meeting a similar warmth expanding from my middle. Simon bends the tips of his fingers slightly over mine. "Your hands are about the same size as the ones that killed this woman," he says.

Embarrassed for more than one reason, I drop my arm.

Simon clears his throat and looks away. "Hand size can eliminate suspects, but it won't be enough to absolutely connect someone to her murder. What else?"

"He's a grain merchant," I say, twisting my fingers in my skirt as I avoid Juliane's eyes. "That parchment previously had a list of grains on it, and it was hurriedly scraped. That's evidence that he wrote the note left on the Sanctum."

Simon nods in approval. "Another good connection, but one that could also be argued as mere coincidence."

"The handwriting on the note may match the merchant's," says Juliane.

"Maybe, but I doubt it. He's not that stupid." Simon pauses thoughtfully. "Though it's obvious he thinks the real killer must be, to have written it as he did."

"The man immediately claimed his wife was murdered," I say, remembering how Remi had scoffed that the merchant should've checked her mother's or sister's houses. "That's quite an assumption, especially considering the other two were prostitutes from Pleasure Road."

My insides warm further when Simon smiles. "These are excellent thoughts, but not actual evidence. We need something that shows *he* was the one who killed and dragged her here."

"The cover she was under?" Juliane asks, and I kick myself for not saying that very thing. "Can we prove it belonged to him?"

Simon shakes his head. "It looks like it's been in this alley since at least the last time it rained, and even if we could connect it to him, all he has to do is say he threw it out. But." He holds up a finger. "That she *was* covered is significant. The murderer was ashamed or regretful about what he'd done. As Cat pointed out the other day, our killer is definitely not trying to hide. This one is." He nods at me. "Let's keep thinking."

I feel like I'm failing him as I reexamine the body and its surroundings. The tracks don't go all the way back to the house, so that doesn't help. Any signs of struggle in the home itself will have been cleaned up by now. The couple's neighbors may have heard them fighting, but the man has already admitted that. Maybe we could trace the knife that cut her throat to one the merchant has. But knives are common. So are nails, as Remi pointed out.

Then I see it. "Her shoes."

Simon studies the woman's feet. "What's wrong with them?"

"They're laced tight at the top but loose along the bottom," I say eagerly. "She would have rolled an ankle trying to walk in those. Someone put her shoes on her feet but only tied them enough to keep them from falling off."

"Which could only logically have been him," Simon finishes. We turn to look at the commotion brewing on the street. It's apparent what we've found, and the husband is wailing pitifully and making an effort to get to his wife, but Lambert has an iron grip on him. "Add that to all the circumstances, and no judge would find him innocent. He may have killed her in a fit of rage, or he may have planned it. Either way, he tried to take advantage of the other two murders."

"But he didn't know all the details," Juliane says. "That's why we didn't correct rumors." Simon nods.

One thing still baffles me, however. "How did you know she would be *here*?" I ask.

Simon shrugs as though I'd asked him why the sky is blue. "He couldn't have taken her far without being noticed, and he wasn't likely to have risked crossing the street. I wasn't sure at first, but it was logical, and when I saw his face as I stopped, it was obvious."

This man wanted it assumed she was the third victim, and everyone will want to believe it. "You know as soon as he's arrested, he'll also be blamed for Perrete and Ysabel," I say. "He'd hang tomorrow if it weren't Sun Day."

"Yes." Simon re-covers the woman's body. "But that also means the real killer will probably feel safe staying here in Collis."

He doesn't say whether he considers that good or bad news.

CHAPTER 23

"The inquiry is closed."

"What?" Simon stands before his uncle, stunned. "I thought you wanted me to stop this madman."

"He has been stopped, and well done to you," says Comte de Montcuir without looking up from his seat behind a wide, polished desk. "The grain merchant confessed to killing all three women."

"Because you tortured him!"

Juliane and I stand behind and to one side of him in the Chamber of Judgment. It's been three days since the grain merchant's arrest, and his trial was held yesterday. This morning came word that the investigation of Perrete's and Ysabel's murders were officially concluded, and Simon had marched straight to the Palace of Justice.

"You persuaded me the man was guilty." The comte signs his name on the order of execution with a flourish. "Your testimony was quite compelling, and he admitted killing his wife once he heard the evidence against him. I don't understand the problem."

Simon squeezes his eyes shut as he exhales through clenched teeth. After a long, deep breath he opens his eyes and speaks. "That evidence was also meant to convince you that we knew he'd killed his wife precisely *because* his mindset and method were so different from that of the other cases."

The provost sets the page and quill aside and meets Simon's glare with his own. "I seem to recall you didn't want to have anything to do with this investigation. Now you're complaining that it's finished."

"I won't deny I didn't want to be involved," replies Simon. "But since I am, it will be done right. This isn't our man. This isn't over."

Comte de Montcuir leans back in his chair, lacing his fingers over his stomach. "People are scared, Simon. They need to see us act. They need resolution."

"Hanging this man—justly—is action, Father," says Juliane. "But saying this is resolved when it obviously isn't will only damage your authority."

The comte's brown eyes switch to his daughter. "I tolerated your participation in this inquiry, but do not lecture me on how to perform my office, Child."

He also glances at me, but I don't dare say a word or attract his attention, lest his ire turn on me and the Sanctum by association.

"Besides"—the provost turns back to Simon—"if there is, indeed, a second killer out there, he's likely to have brought himself under control. He hasn't acted in over a week, according to you."

Simon throws his hands in the air. "That we know of! He could be in another town or out in the countryside, letting his compulsion free where we can't see it."

"All the more reason not to worry," says the comte placidly, though his jaw twitches. "He's moved outside our jurisdiction."

"That's *if*," snaps Simon. "He could easily be here in Collis, laughing as we congratulate ourselves." When his uncle is unmoved, Simon shakes his head in disbelief. "This is about freeing Oudin from suspicion, isn't it? That's all this was ever about."

"You said yourself you didn't believe it was him." The comte points out.

"I could be wrong!" Simon spits back. "But what disgusts me is how your first impulse isn't justice, it's to shield your own."

My skin grows cold at Simon's accusation. Remi had used different words but thrown the exact same sentiment at me. Not without cause, either.

Simon leans his knuckles on the table between him and his uncle. "It's only a matter of time before this man slaughters some woman in the street again, and in worse ways. And her blood will be on your conscience!"

Comte de Montcuir surges forward, slamming a fist down on his desk, then raises it, pointing his index finger at Simon. "If you speak to anyone about your insane conjecture, I will have you arrested!" he shouts. "This inquiry is closed! That's an order."

Simon grips the edge of the table. For a heartbeat, I think he's going to flip it over on his uncle. Instead, he wheels around and storms out the door. Juliane gestures for me to follow so she can be the last to leave. The two of us have to run to keep up with him, but Simon doesn't slow down until we're outside the Palace of Justice. Then his shoulders drop, and he shortens his stride—abruptly halting when he catches sight of the gallows being erected out front. I'm shading my eyes against the change of light and nearly run into him from behind.

Juliane stops beside me. "At least the grain merchant's wife will get justice," she tries to soothe.

Simon shakes his head. "I should've seen this coming," he mutters. "I should've known how your father would be eager to blame everything on him. He wants to believe this is over." He turns to face us. "I was showing off. I wanted people to see I was competent, that they could trust me to find the killer. I was too proud to let him get away with it."

I gape at him. "Are you saying you wish you'd let the grain merchant go free?"

"I am." Simon's voice is hollow with shame. "At least for a while. He wasn't likely to do anything like this again, especially if I hinted that he was suspect. And now more people will die because of it."

* * *

Simon doesn't object as Juliane and I follow him upstairs to his room. Lambert is there, staring at the maps and sketches on the wall.

The final drawings of Ysabel make me glad I hadn't seen her body in reality. I understand the expression Juliane's brother wears as he studies them. I, too, can hardly bear to look at the pictures, but neither can I look away. What I can't understand is how one human being could do that to another.

Lambert turns to face us, his lips white from being pressed together. "It's over, then?"

Simon collapses in the chair at the far end of the table, his wrath spent. "Your father thinks so."

"But you don't agree."

He closes his eyes and leans his head against the carved back. "No. I don't."

Juliane sits on the bench and begins gathering the papers strewn across the table. No one pays any attention to me. "I guess this is where I take my leave," I say, curtsying awkwardly. "You can keep the maps if you like."

"Whyever would you go?" Juliane pauses in her actions to cock her head at me. "You should know."

"Know what?" I ask.

She tosses her head like I'm being silly. "Simon isn't done. Not till he's found the one."

Simon's eyes snap open at her words. Juliane drops the page she's holding and wrings her hands. "I'm sorry," she mumbles.

Leaning forward, Simon puts one hand on her arm, but rather than look at him Juliane focuses on the table. "You need rest," he says gently. I almost feel like he's handing her something.

"Yes, yes, that's best," she says, rocking back and forth. "But Cat should stay."

Simon pats her arm. "Not today."

"Today stay," Juliane mutters. "Stay today."

I glance at Lambert. He's working his jaw back and forth as he stares at them.

Is this another "game" their family plays, like the one where they speak nonsense? Simon looks up at his cousin and smiles, but it's as fake as a dramatic mask worn in a play. "The past few days have been exhausting, and the execution is this afternoon. We can start again tomorrow."

"You're not quitting?" I blurt out, though Juliane had said as much.

Simon's gaze shifts to me. "No, I'm not. We'll just have to be smart how we go about it."

"We?" I ask.

Juliane's rhythmic motion had slowed, but now she stops to watch us. Simon hesitates for a handful of seconds, pressing his lips back together, his eyes pleading. "You're free to go, Cat, of course, but . . . I would hope you'd choose to continue helping us."

Magister Thomas still needs me to watch out for him, but he's not the biggest reason I promise to come back.

CHAPTER 24

Both Magister Thomas and Remi are glad the inquiry is over. Construction at the Sanctum progresses with the reinforcement of platforms inside to support lifting loads of stone for building the inner ceiling arches beneath the wooden roof. I explain there are a few matters the venatre wants to tie up, but I have no idea how I'll make excuses after today.

I arrive to find Simon pulling the last of his drawings off the wall. "Are you concerned your uncle will discover you're still working?" I ask.

Simon stacks the sketches together. "I'm leaving for Mesanus within the hour," he says, pausing to study one. "I want to consult with one of the physicians there."

"How long do you expect to be gone?"

"Ten days."

Ten days? It's been eight days since Ysabel, and there were only four between her and Perrete. "What if there's a murder while you're gone?" I ask.

He shakes his head and continues sorting the pages. "I don't think there will be one for a while. I'm almost certain Ysabel was so soon after Perrete to correct mistakes he felt he'd made."

I move to stand across the table from him. "You don't think he's eager to let everyone know how foolish they are to believe he's been caught?"

Suddenly I have Simon's full attention. He lowers the drawings. "I never said that."

"But it's logical," I insist. "Wouldn't you agree?"

"Yes." Simon regards me carefully. "And I thought of it, though I said nothing. Interesting that you concluded the same." He almost sounds pleased.

"I've just been paying attention to you, that's all." Heat spreads down my neck when I realize how forward that sounds.

"I know. You and Juliane were a great help with your observations about the grain merchant." He smiles reassuringly. "I have complete confidence that *if* there's trouble while I'm gone, the two of you are equal to it."

I shake my head vigorously. "We never could've done it without you."

"Only observations are necessary," he says. "We can discuss and draw conclusions from them when I return."

"And what makes you think the comte will let us anywhere near a body or crime scene?"

Simon arches the brow over his flawed eye. "Because Madame Emeline has promised to tell you and Juliane first if possible, and keep the body for you if not."

I fold my arms over my chest. "I still think this is a mistake. If something *does* happen, people will blame you for leaving when you were most needed."

He chews on his lower lip for several seconds, like he's debating inside his head. Finally, Simon gestures to the bench. "Sit, please. I want to explain how you're right, but also wrong."

I'm right but I'm wrong? I step over the bench and lower myself down as he does.

Simon folds his hands and takes a deep breath. "I *was* afraid the killer would strike last night, after the execution, but he didn't. That tells me he can hold his impulses in check and is probably savoring the false sense of security that Collis now rests in."

I purse my lips. "You'll be gone over a week, though. What makes you believe he'll be able to keep the monster caged for that long?"

Simon glances down at the table. "If I show you something, you must promise not to tell anyone, not even Juliane."

My mouth goes completely dry. "I promise."

He reaches under his tunic and pulls out a scrap of parchment. "I received this last night."

I unfold the torn page as I take it. The handwriting is strikingly similar to the grain merchant's note, but the parchment was smoothed after scraping, and the grammar is better.

You may know <u>what</u> I am, but I know <u>who</u> you are.

"It's from him," Simon whispers. "The killer."

I stare at it, disbelieving. "How do you know this is real?"

Simon slides the false note from the bottom of his stack. "Because it's the other half of this page." He puts it next to the one I'm holding, lining up the ripped sides. Parchment, particularly the cheaply made kind, doesn't tear evenly. These edges match perfectly. "In the right light, you can still read the rest of the grain inventory," he says quietly.

"You mean to say the killer went into the grain merchant's house and stole this, knowing you'd be able to tell where it came from?"

"That's *exactly* what I'm saying. And he took the time to scrape and press it properly, just to show me his level of patience." Simon pauses. "What do you think that means?"

This is a threat, obviously, but there's more to it. "It's a challenge," I whisper. "He's taunting you by saying he's aware of everything you know and do."

"Yes." Simon pushes the false note under the stack and refolds the true one before placing it back in his pocket. "He's in complete control, or thinks he is. It's very unlikely he'll strike while I'm gone because watching me flounder is much more entertaining. And . . ."

"And *what*, Simon?"

He hesitates. "It would also eliminate me from suspicion."

I digest that for several seconds. No one's accused Simon of anything, but even I'm uneasy at the level of horror he's comfortable with, or at least able to tolerate. The only other person I can imagine having such a tolerance is the killer himself. It won't be long before others make a similar connection. Remi already has. "So he'll wait for you to return," I murmur.

There's a mix of pride and pity in the way he looks at me. "Yes."

"Which means while you're gone, he'll have to restrain himself," I add, and Simon nods. Another thought occurs to me. "How long do you really need for this trip to Mesanus?"

"Probably only a week or so," he admits. "But we're telling everyone else a fortnight."

Now I understand. "You said he *thinks* he's in control, but the longer you're gone, the harder it will be to stay in control," I say. "You're taunting *him*."

Simon continues watching me silently.

"When you return earlier than expected, the killer will let himself loose before he's ready," I say.

"And he'll be more likely to make a mistake," finishes Simon, looking pleased.

I'm not smiling. "You're just going to let someone else die?" I shout, leaping to my feet so violently that the bench falls over backward. "You're not even going to try to stop it?"

He blinks up at me. "I don't know what else you think I can do."

"Before you said you wouldn't have enough to complete your picture without another victim," I snap. "Now you're saying you need a third!"

"You came to the same conclusion," he says calmly.

"What I concluded is that you think of this monster as more of a human being than the women he butchers!"

I'm out the door and halfway to the stairs before Simon catches up to me. He grabs my arm, pleading. "No, Cat, wait! I need you!"

"Why?" I spin around to face him. "You had all of this figured out on your own. What do you need me for?"

Simon's other hand clasps my elbow to keep me from turning away again. "It's more than that. I . . ." He drops his chin to his chest and sighs heavily. "This is why I need you. I need someone to hold me accountable. To remind me what is really at stake. That the cost of my failure is real lives."

We're suddenly as close as we were that night on the Sanctum. My anger wavers at the agony in his eyes. "Simon, I can believe some others might forget that, but how could you?"

"I don't want to, Cat," he says softly. "But if I let the horror of all this get to me, if I can't think dispassionately, the victims will never get justice."

That's how Simon endures what he sees. "You lock it away," I whisper. "Keep it separate."

"Yes." His hold on me relaxes, but we don't move apart. "And the longer it's removed from my thoughts, the easier it is to avoid going back to it." Simon's lip begins to quiver. "That's why you're so important. I don't think I can do this and stay human without you."

I shake my head. "Simon, you hardly know me."

He retreats a few inches. "I know I . . ."

When he doesn't continue, I use what's left of my own breath to ask, "You what?"

Rather than speak, Simon brings one hand up to my face. Slowly, he leans lower, until his blond curls brush my hairline. "I know I can trust you," he whispers. "You're the only one in all this with nothing to hide."

Those words flood me with guilt, but I shove it aside in favor of what I want in this moment. I want him to lift my chin, aligning my mouth with his. I want to taste the mint I can smell on his warm breath.

I want to let him know I'll think of him every day he's gone.

"Simon?" Juliane's voice echoes up the stairwell. His head snaps up, looking behind me, but she's on the floor below.

The stairs creak as she begins to ascend, and Simon puts a finger to his lips and pulls me quietly back into the room. Inside, he gestures for me to put the bench upright and heads to the wardrobe in the corner.

"In here, Juliane," he calls, then opens the cabinet door and leans inside, hiding his flushed face from view.

I've just resettled the bench when she appears in the doorway, looking much better than she had when I left yesterday. "The palfrey is saddled and ready. Are you packed?"

"Almost." Simon's voice is muffled by the wardrobe.

Juliane notices me and frowns. "I didn't know you were here, Cat."

"Just saying goodbye." I wonder how Juliane feels about

Simon going to Mesanus, given that she doesn't know the reason he's confident nothing will happen while he's gone.

"Spread the word that I'll return in two weeks." Simon steps away from the cabinet, his face calm and detached, and tosses a satchel on the table, scattering his neat stack. "But expect me in no more than ten days."

Juliane purses her lips, a move that makes me pull my own between my teeth self-consciously. "What should we do in that time?" she asks. "You said you had a task for us."

Simon hadn't told me anything about that, but I hope that's because we got distracted more than anything else. Though I'm privy to Simon's darkest conclusions, I feel a pang of jealousy that Juliane knows something I don't. To hide my expression, I busy myself gathering the sketches back together, though not in the order I'm sure he wanted.

"Yes." Simon pulls another bag from the wardrobe and shakes it out, inspecting it for holes. "I want you to look into possible victims before Perrete."

He's mentioned the idea before. "Where do we start?" I ask.

"My father's records," says Juliane confidently. "They're at the Palace of Justice."

I frown. At the grain merchant's trial, we all saw how little information was recorded about the murders of the past two weeks—only who died and where and one word on how. "Stabbing" or "bleeding" leaves much to the imagination, and the women's occupation was never listed. "Do you think there will be enough details to determine that?"

"Just note everything that has possibility, and ask around." Satisfied with the bag's condition, Simon begins stuffing items of clothing inside. Knowing how few people wanted to talk to us about the night Perrete died, I'm not sure that will garner much information. "But don't involve Lambert yet," he adds. "I don't think he'll be able to hide anything from my uncle. And commit nothing to paper."

He means Juliane should memorize what we learn. I don't think she's able to do otherwise—she only writes things down for the rest of us. No doubt she could do everything alone.

That suspicion seems correct when Juliane turns to me. "It will be faster if I go through the records by myself." Before I can object, she smiles and adds, "I'll come to your house tomorrow morning, and we can get started. I'm glad we'll be working together."

It feels sincere. "I as well, Lady Juliane."

Simon ties his packed bag closed and sets it on the table. I'm holding all of his drawings, one of Perrete's nearly exposed body on top. As he gathers pencils, a quill, and a bottle of ink, I wait to hand the pages to him, wishing desperately that Juliane would leave and give us another few moments alone. Perhaps he wants the same thing, because he pauses to address her. "Do you happen to know where my cloak is?"

"Hanging in the kitchen," she answers, turning back to the door. "I'll fetch it while you finish saying goodbye to Cat."

I could have sworn she smiled a little.

When she's gone, my heart quickens, hoping Simon might intend to finish what was interrupted, but he focuses on packing the satchel. "Thank you for agreeing to help Juliane while I'm gone."

Disappointment makes me clutch the pages harder. "I don't think she needs me at all."

"She does." He throws the strap over his head and shoulder so the bag rests across his front. "Juliane can collect and hold the pieces of this puzzle, but it's you who puts them together."

I don't care about Juliane right now. I want to talk about what's between us and whether it's the beginning of something—or the end. "Simon, I—"

"Catrin," he interrupts. Then he sighs. "I don't know." He smiles tentatively. "But I'll miss you."

I look down. "And I you."

Simon holds out his hand for the sketches, and I start to extend them automatically, then freeze. The drawing of Perrete is upside down—an orientation I've not looked at before.

Likely mistaking my hesitation for the overwhelming awkwardness of the last few minutes, Simon takes the pages just as they're slipping from my grip in shock.

Now I realize where I've seen the pattern of her seven stab wounds—across my own stomach. I just never made the connection because I only ever saw mine from above.

My breath strains against the waist of my skirt, pressing the bruises against them. *Don't you remember?* They seem to whisper as I follow Simon downstairs. *You were there.* Outside, Lambert holds the bridle of a small riding horse, a sturdy breed that can travel at a swift pace for several hours without resting. He smiles and makes small talk with me as Simon settles his bags and mounts, but I answer only with nods and half smiles.

Juliane joins us, offering Simon his cloak, and he folds it over the front of his saddle. The number of clouds in the sky has doubled in the last hour, so he'll probably need it soon. Lambert offers his hand. "Safe journey, Cousin."

Simon grips it firmly. "Thank you. Watch over Juliane while I'm gone."

A flicker of annoyance crosses Lambert's face. I imagine I'd feel the same if a new worker at the Sanctum instructed me to do something I'd done for years. "I will" is all he says.

When Simon looks at me again, I hold my breath. "Remember what I told you."

"Which part?" I can't help asking.

"All of it." Simon nudges the palfrey around. Just before he turns away, he adds, "But especially the last."

That should make me happy, yet all I can think about is how he believes I have nothing to hide when I have more to conceal than anyone.

CHAPTER 25

"Goodness, what a mess!" Juliane stands at the workroom's window open to the street. Lambert hovers behind her.

I dust my hands as I walk around to meet them. "It looks much better than it did a few days ago." My plan was to appear busy repairing the model so Magister Thomas wouldn't task me with anything this morning, leaving me free to go with Juliane when she arrived, but she's earlier than I expected, and he hasn't left for the Sanctum yet.

Lambert leans closer and squints to see into the room, lingering on the torn and wrinkled parchment of names below where the golden hammer used to hang. "What happened?"

"The table collapsed and dumped it on the floor," I explain. "Some of the mortar was so old that it crumbled like a stale cake." My laugh is a little forced. "But you needn't worry about the real Sanctum. We use much better materials for it."

Magister Thomas comes down the stairs, Remi right behind him. "I thought I heard visitors," the architect says cheerfully, though I detect some tension in his voice. "To what do we owe this honor, and so early in the day?"

"The inquiry put us behind in preparing for Lambert's wedding,"

Juliane says brightly. "I've come to value Catrin's opinion, and I'd be most pleased if she could accompany me in some shopping today."

Remi rolls his eyes, but the architect narrows his. He knows I've never enjoyed such things, and he also listened as I complained how Simon believed the grain merchant wasn't guilty of all three murders. "Where is the good venatre?" Magister Thomas asks with a sidelong glance at me. "I've wanted to congratulate him for successfully completing his inquiry."

There's a slight emphasis on the word *completing*. He's not a fool.

"He's visiting some old friends," Juliane replies. "He'll return in a fortnight."

Remi smiles sourly. "Those two weeks of work certainly earned him two weeks of leisure."

I clench my fists. Why does he have to be so nasty when it comes to Simon?

Juliane appeals to Magister Thomas. "Can you spare Catrin today, sir?"

He wouldn't dare refuse the daughter of his greatest patron, but he knows something is not quite as she says. "Of course, my lady. Since she will be out, Catrin can do Mistress la Fontaine's shopping as well."

I suppress a groan, but Juliane only smiles. "Thank you kindly, Magister."

After he and Remi are gone and I have a long list of items from the housekeeper, Juliane tells her brother he can leave us. When he hesitates, she leans closer to him and lowers her voice. "We'll be shopping for underclothes, Lambert."

Suddenly he's unable to look directly at either of us. "Yes, I think it's better if I leave that to you."

Juliane watches him go with a smile. "You do realize you were the reason he wanted to accompany me, Catrin," she says.

"Me?"

She nods. "Lambert has admired you for years, but he was always too timid to approach you—or any girl for that matter. Father had to arrange things with Lady Genevieve's family."

Strange to think the heir to the highest title in the region and the governorship of a large city would be attracted to me, and stranger still that someone so powerful would lack confidence. "The comte probably would've discouraged it anyway," I say, embarrassed. "Seeing as I'm not of noble blood."

"Neither was our mother," Juliane replies. "At least that we know of. She grew up in the same convent as you, under the prioress."

I'd never heard about that. Mother Agnes probably hid the story from us, not wanting girls to nurture the unrealistic hope of marrying a rich nobleman.

"Father was even engaged to another girl when they eloped," Juliane continues. "And Lambert always thought it was such a romantic story."

"I don't mean to cause him any confusion," I mumble. Juliane doesn't sound like she's trying to discourage the idea, but it's not her brother I'm thinking about, it's Simon.

Juliane half-snorts. "Honestly, I'm glad to see Lambert pay attention to anyone but me. Ever since our mother died, he's been annoyingly protective."

I join her on the street, and we set off together. Since she's brought up the subject, I ask, "What happened to your mother? She was ill for quite a long time, wasn't she?"

"She was unwell all my life." Juliane stares blankly ahead. "But that wasn't what killed her."

It's obvious she doesn't want to talk about it. "The memory must be painful," I say. "I'm sorry for asking."

Juliane nods curtly, and I'm content not to pry further. Though I don't know where we're going, I'm surprised when she directs our path to a shopping district.

"I thought it prudent to be seen walking here," she explains, politely acknowledging a few merchants as we pass. "Since this is where we said we'd be."

"Of course." The morning sun is blinding until we turn west and put it at our backs. We emerge from the avenue of shops and displays of goods to the open circle around the city's Temple of the Sun, ancient but for the statue of a Gallian solosopher on its lawn, posed to gaze at the Sun as it sets. The circular stone building was settled here so the bell tower created a sundial which could be seen from the hilltop above. Though maintained by only a chosen handful of brethren today, it's still a holy place, connected to the Sanctum by the Pathway of Prayer. The irony of what the street has become—a row of *skonia* lodges and houses of prostitution—is never lost on me. To my discomfort, Pleasure Road is where Juliane heads.

"I figure Madame Emeline is the best place to start," she says. "She'll probably know most if not all the names on my list."

I should have thought of that, or at least realized it.

Just before we move into the shadow of the first houses, I glimpse a pair of kohl-lined eyes watching me. Even without the plain black clothes among the colorful awnings and booths, the scarred face would have stood out in any crowd.

Gregor.

Selenae aren't uncommon in daytime, especially in the marketplace, but seeing him sends a chill up my spine. He told Magister Thomas I should be allowed to follow my instincts with regard to Perrete's murder. What about my instincts are so important? Am I following them now?

Like the previous times I've spotted him since that night, he disappears the instant I try to focus on him. My hesitation causes Juliane to get several steps ahead of me, and I run to catch up.

Rather than knock on Madame Emeline's front door, Juliane goes down the alley at the end of the block and raps four times on a side door. An old woman lets us into a kitchen with a large table and tells us to wait. As soon as she's gone, I consider asking Juliane how she knew about this entrance, but I remember Simon was here to look over Perrete's body. This must have been another matter he discussed with her but not with me. I have to swallow a surge of jealousy and remind myself he trusts me with more important matters.

Emeline comes in and shoos her hands at us to sit down. Both of us select chairs and accept her offer of tea. If it weren't for her garish red-orange hair, I might not have recognized the madam with her face unpainted and her plain dressing gown. Ironically, she appears younger, though I have no idea how old she is.

"I—we are here on behalf of Simon," begins Juliane. "He asked us to search for evidence that Perrete wasn't the killer's first victim."

Emeline raises thin, unenhanced eyebrows. "I see."

"I have a list of women from the last five years," Juliane continues. "Their causes of death are vague, but we thought you might know more."

"You'll have to read the list to me," says Emeline, lifting her cup to pale lips. "I can't."

"It's in my head," says Juliane. "Are you ready?" At the madam's nod, she closes her eyes and recites them one at a time, including the date they were found and where. Emeline considers each carefully. Many she recalls had died in accidents or childbirth—*bleeding* seems to be the choice phrase for recording the latter—and several were known to be suffering from some kind of ailment. Three were suicides.

What I can't get over is how many Emeline describes as murders.

Some perpetrators were caught and punished, but an astounding number were left unsolved. I begin to wonder if Perrete and Ysabel really matter. Even if we can connect more women to this killer, they're two small apples in a barrel full of others no one cared enough to investigate. Perrete's death would almost certainly have been as forgotten if it weren't for Oudin being under suspicion.

It's three hours and as many cups of tea before Juliane comes to the end of the list. I've lost track of which names were potential victims of this killer, but I know Juliane has them. I can also see how weary she's become.

"Thank you," she tells Emeline, rising to her feet. "We may have more questions for you later."

The madam also stands. "Simon's been the only official who's truly cared. Any help I can give, I will." She lets us out of the side door and back into the alley, and as soon as the door is shut, Juliane's eyelids droop, and she puts a thin hand to her temple.

"Are you well?" I ask, poised to steady her at the first sign of need.

"Shadows," Juliane mumbles. "So many shadows."

I glance around. It's just past noon, making this alley about as bright as it can be. The change from the dim kitchen makes my eyes water. "Do you need my help getting to the street?"

"Yes, thank you." She holds out an arm. "Keep them away, please. They want to talk to me but I can't. Not now."

There's no one in sight. I'm not sure who or what she wants me to ward off, but I guide Juliane to the mouth of the alley.

Before we step out into the street, I check for anyone we'd rather not notice where we're coming from, but this is the least busy hour for Madame Emeline's establishment and others. "Is that better?" I ask as we move into full sunlight.

"For now," she says. "But they follow, they're hollow." Juliane drops her hand from her face and looks at me with frightened eyes. "Cat, I must go home. Can't roam."

Remembering how Simon responded to her rhyming last time, I take her arm more firmly. "It's going to be fine," I tell her. "We'll go together."

"Weather," she says like she can't help it, then shakes her head. "Need something better."

We move up the street, toward the Sanctum. Though Juliane readily accepts my lead, I've never felt more inept. Something is terribly wrong, but I don't understand how to help. "What can I do?" I ask.

"Who? You?" Juliane takes a deep breath, her upper body swaying. "Walk with me. Talk with me."

Something about her behavior reminds me of a worker at the Sanctum who counts his steps wherever he goes. The architect tasks him only with stacking and moving stones in wheelbarrows—which he does without complaint, but always in groups of four, giving him the nickname Four-Block Jacques. Magister Thomas calls the number four his "anchor," because it somehow keeps him from floating away, and the more tired he is, the more important counting becomes to him.

Rhymes are Juliane's anchor. Simon had soothed her nerves by helping her make them.

"What do you want to talk about?" I ask.

I immediately want to kick myself for not setting up an easy rhyme, but Juliane responds without hesitation. "Out. I just have to let it. Get it."

"We can do that," I say. We continue, strolling up the hill, arm in arm, like close friends. Though our words make little actual sense, our conversation becomes a sort of game, and I manage to relax a little, making me painfully aware of how repulsed I was at first. But what was I supposed to feel? What's happening in Juliane's mind is not normal. Yet normal doesn't always mean better. Her memory is a rare gift, but no one would describe it as "normal."

We step into the square, and the area of sky we can see increases tenfold. A sliver of moon hangs in the west. I can think of many words to describe my own abilities: amazing, frightening, awesome, powerful, and—above all—magick. "Normal" is not one of them. It's also something I must conceal at all costs. In those respects, Juliane and I are very alike.

I wave cheerfully to Remi on the high scaffolds as we pass, hoping he hasn't noticed what road we entered the square from. To avoid the chance he might try to come down and talk to us, I turn around the north side of the Sanctum. Once there, I stay in the shade, though the sweat trickling down my spine has little to do with the heat.

What am I going to say when we reach Juliane's? Lambert has seen her like this, so he'll probably know what to do. As the Montcuir home finally comes into view, I ask, "Who should I fetch when we get to your house? Your father, or another?"

My words are chosen to allow her to say something about her brother, but Juliane goes in an unexpected direction.

"No, no, I'm Mother. She is me, and I am her. Or were." A spring comes into her step, and her mood flashes into something resembling delight, like she's sharing a secret with me. "We're the same, you know. We could both kill with a thought. Hundreds, thousands. All dead. That's why he had to kill her."

The rhymes are suddenly gone, replaced with statements

which are horrifying, and clearly impossible. I stop walking to stare at her. "Killed who? Your mother?"

"Yes," she answers solemnly. "But she killed him. Every day."

Nothing she says makes sense. "Who killed her?"

"Oudin. Father. They're always trying to kill me now, but I kill them first, every time. It's fun, isn't it?" She smiles brightly. "Simon's very good at killing people. We should go see him."

"I wish we could," I mutter, taking Juliane's arm again, thanking the Sun we have only a block to go. I prefer her rhyming to whatever this is.

Juliane's old governess, Madame Denise, answers the door. She takes one look at her former charge and pales.

"Hello," Juliane chirps. "I'm here to kill you, but we can wait until after tea."

"How long has she been like this?" The housekeeper demands as we help Juliane inside.

"I'm not sure," I say. "Perhaps twenty minutes. It came on quickly."

As soon as we've gotten Juliane to sit at the table in the front room, she hugs her arms across her chest and starts to rock back and forth. Madame Denise prods me in the direction of the door. "You need to leave, now."

"But I want to help her," I protest, though, honestly, I'm not sure I do.

The housekeeper pushes me over the threshold and out to the street. "You've done enough."

I can't tell if that's gratitude or accusation. Maybe both.

CHAPTER 26

It's not until I return home that I remember the errands I was supposed to do for Mistress la Fontaine. My mind is too muddled to recall everything she wanted, and I have to ask her to list what she needs for me again. She not only adds a significant number of new items, she insists I write it all down, which gives me no excuse to "forget" turnips. All the best vegetables have been picked over by afternoon, forcing me to visit twice as many produce sellers to find everything.

Everyone is in a foul temper at dinner. Remi and the magister quarreled on the site again, and neither is happy that I did no work today. The housekeeper grouses that the turnips I brought back were unsuitable for putting in the stew. I pretend that hurts my feelings, though I went to eight different stands to find ones that rotten. We all go to bed right after eating.

I want to check on Juliane first thing in the morning, but I don't dare turn my back on my work at the Sanctum. It also occurs to me if—like Four-Block Jacques—Juliane's confusions happen when she's tired, then she needs rest more than anything else. The previous times she'd begun to speak oddly, Simon called for the inquiry to halt for a day.

Simon. It's been only two days since he left for Mesanus. Has he even arrived yet? Does he think of me as often as I think of him?

Before I can start my lengthy inspection of the scaffolds inside, Magister Thomas tasks me with rechecking the braces under the next series of outer buttresses he wants done before starting the ceiling. Apparently, that's what Remi and the architect are arguing over—as the arch stones are ready to assemble, Remi wants to set the cross-ribs, but the magister worries the inner parts will advance before there's sufficient support from the sides.

"The arches can handle the load!" Remi shouts, drawing the attention of half the workers. "You want it to look like you're the only one making progress!"

Magister Thomas's answer is much quieter. "There are a dozen reasons the buttresses could be delayed, especially in the spring when cold and wet makes the mortar set more slowly," he says calmly. "I've promised you a free hand in vaulting the ceiling, *when the time comes*. Not before. This isn't a race."

I'm willing to bet Remi will make it one as soon as he's allowed to start, and that's precisely why the magister is holding him back.

"But—"

"Journeyman la Fontaine," the architect cuts him off. "My decision is final. If you disagree, you are free to leave my employment."

Remi's cheeks go crimson as stained glass roses, and he stomps away. Magister Thomas rounds on me. "Why are you just standing there?" he barks. "You're behind in your work. Remi would be right to direct some of his anger at you." Whirling away so quickly his master's robes spiral around him, he adds over his shoulder, "And wear your safety rope, Catrin."

Ugh. I wish I hadn't paused to watch the argument, but I'd

been unable to look away. Slinging the loops over my head so they angle from my shoulder to my hip, I go back to my inspection. The bruises from two weeks ago have spread from their original pattern into purple fading to yellow across my whole stomach, but they're still sore, and I don't like to put pressure on them.

I also don't like thinking about how they looked exactly like Perrete's wounds.

For the next two days, I'm the go-between for Remi and Magister Thomas, who are barely speaking. People who think girls my age are petty should consider how stubborn and brooding two adult men can be when they're fighting over a project they both consider their own. The architect's possessiveness is understandable, given how long he's been in charge at the Sanctum, but he'll damage his beloved if he doesn't give his successor the tools to carry on his work.

And Remi. I grit my teeth every time he comes looking for me. He needs to recognize all the issues which demand the magister's attention and that he's ultimately accountable for everything. That and how I'm going to stop believing him when he describes what he needs from me as "critical."

Fortunately, the third day is the Sun's, and work is halted for Sanctum holy services. I spend the entire ceremony squinting at the gallery arches on the second level where the Montcuir family sits. The sunlight streaming through the colored windows dazzles me so much I'm unable to focus at this distance, but by the end, I'm certain Juliane isn't with them.

Construction will resume after the noon litany prayers, as many farmers offer a half day's labor for a blessing from the high altum at sunset. I have less than two hours before my presence will also be required, so when the Montcuirs leave, I follow them. Remembering what Juliane said about Lambert admiring me, I aim to cross his path as he descends the front steps.

Oudin sees me first. "Hello, Kitten."

I make a noise of disgust. "Remi is the only one who calls me that."

"Then I'm honored to be in such exclusive company." He chuckles. "You look lost. Your home is that way." Oudin points at the street angling southwest from the square.

Lambert is within earshot, but the comte has vanished, probably to the Palace of Justice to review the guard, so I sigh. "I wanted to inquire about Juliane. Is she feeling better?"

Oudin snorts. "She's sulking over Simon's absence and won't come out of her room."

That seems odd. I turn to Lambert, clasping my hands beneath my chin and looking up at him. "That sounds dreadful. May I pay her a visit?"

Lambert blushes. "I suppose it might do her some good." Oudin rolls his eyes, but I keep my smile on the older brother. Before I can take the arm he offers, however, Oudin elbows between us.

"Now, now, Brother," he scolds as he leads me away. "What would Lady Genevieve say if she saw you playing with kittens?"

I want to retch, but I focus on what's important: seeing Juliane. Lambert follows, the tendons in his neck as strained as pulley ropes. When we reach their home, Oudin puts his hand in the small of my back and guides me all the way to the stairs and up them. Their house is large enough for three rooms on either side of a passage running down the middle rather than just a pair of rooms like we have. Oudin ushers me to the second door on the left and knocks three times.

"Juliane!" he calls. "You have a visitor."

Out of the corner of my eye, Lambert enters the first room and shuts the door behind him. A few seconds later, Juliane opens hers.

Light of Day.

The smell of sweat, unclean body, human waste . . . and fear washes over me from her room. Juliane appears thinner than ever, and her eyes are black pits, ringed with purple. Her hair hangs in matted clumps around her gaunt cheeks, but she smiles when she recognizes me. "Cat!"

I take a half step back. Her breath is foul, too.

Oudin makes a disgusted face, then raises his eyebrows as if to say, *This is what you wanted to see*, and turns away.

Juliane yanks me into the room by my wrist, then closes and bolts the door. The light is so dim I can barely see. I'm afraid to move lest I trip over something—like the chamber pot I can smell clearly.

"I'm sorry you have to see me like this." Juliane's voice is surprisingly steady as she crosses to the window which is boarded shut and pulls down a piece of wood, then another, letting both light and fresh air inside.

I quickly move to stand closer to it, holding my breath until I can feel the coolness on my face. Then I take in the rest of the room, which is a mess of wadded papers and soiled clothing. "Lady Juliane, what's happened to you?"

She turns her hands palms up and indicates her surroundings. "This is my life without Simon."

At first I think Juliane is pining for him, but her tone is matter-of-fact, like she's saying this is what happens when it rains. "What do you mean?" I ask. "Are you trapped in here?"

"I used to be," she says. "Even on my good days. Until Simon. He got me out." Juliane waves her hands around. "Awful as this is, until he comes back, I'm better off staying in here, where they can't see."

Her fear is contagious. "Where who can't see what?"

"My father and Oudin mostly." She shakes her head. "Lambert, too, though that's to spare him. He saw enough with Mother."

"Lady Juliane, you're not making any sense." If I was being honest, though, I'd say she only makes sense half the time.

She sighs and turns away, combing her fingers through her hair in a vain attempt to smooth it. When she reaches the bed, she pivots abruptly to face me. "Listen, Catrin. I'll tell you this because Simon trusts you, and therefore I trust you." She takes a deep breath and clasps her hands. "It has to do with my mother and her illness."

"Your mother?" I repeat stupidly. The other day Juliane had said she'd been unwell all her life, but the woman is hard to picture. I think I only ever saw her once.

"Yes." Juliane nods. "In body, my mother was healthy. Her mind, however, was very confused. For many years she was kept out of sight, at home or in our estate in the country."

When she pauses, I feel like my reaction is being gauged. "What kind of confusion did she suffer?" I ask carefully.

Juliane clutches her thin fingers to minimize their tremor. "She heard voices and imagined terrible things. Strange ideas would take root in her head and grow into complicated delusions no one could persuade her weren't true. Every time she saw Oudin, she'd scream that he was a demon put in his place by someone who had stolen her real child." Juliane blinks back tears. "Lambert and I are old enough to remember better times, but Oudin hated her. Frankly, I don't blame him."

She takes another deep breath before continuing. "Father

couldn't bear to watch her decline and buried himself in governing Collis. When he sent me to the convent for schooling, the burden of Mother's care fell on Lambert. Eventually he was the only one of us she would let near her. Often she would harm herself if he left her side."

My heart goes out to Lambert, and I even feel sorry for Oudin. As for Juliane, her perfect memory is a curse. Not only is she unable to forget anything she watched or experienced, she recalls every detail with perfect clarity.

When her pause lengthens to an uncomfortable point I say, "That must have been terrible for all of you."

"It was. I don't know which was worse—the way things were, or having to pretend none of it was happening." She grimaces. "And we're still pretending."

It's easy to see why Oudin never cared about anyone but himself and how the comte became obsessed with appearances. The other day Juliane had described how after the comtesse's death, Lambert had turned all his energy to caring for his sister, and she felt smothered by it. I'd assumed Simon's arrival had relieved Juliane of having only one male relative she could depend on.

Now I realize it's much more complicated.

"When did you first start experiencing the same sickness as your mother?" I ask.

Juliane half smiles, like Simon does when he's pleased with a conclusion I've drawn. "I had small signs all my life," she says. "But I knew for sure when I was about sixteen. People started coming up to me on the street and speaking to me, especially when I was feeling weary. Often they would tell me things I wanted to know. But though I heard, saw, smelled, and sometimes even touched them, they weren't real."

I blink. "That sounds like *skonia* hallucinations."

"Ironically, *skonia* actually helps me." Juliane takes a cautious step forward, as though I'm a skittish animal. "But I went out in public less and less, and I was always afraid to talk to anyone when I did. I could never be sure they weren't purely in my mind."

The night Perrete was killed she'd snapped her fingers for Simon's attention. "When I first tried to speak to you, you acknowledged me only after Simon nodded," I say. "I thought he was giving you some sort of permission, but he was confirming to you that I was real."

"Yes."

And because Simon was from Mesanus, he understood Juliane's illness and knew ways to help her cope with her delusions. When she spoke in rhymes or made outlandish statements, he worked to soothe her nerves. Not only that, but he welcomed her in his presence, treated her like an equal, and valued her opinion. "Does Lambert know?" I ask.

Juliane shakes her head. "After what he went through with our mother, I don't want to burden him with it. I'm sure he suspects I have some of her madness, but I've managed to hide how far gone I am."

I'm not sure that's true. Lambert would have to be pretty blind not to see what's happening to his sister. "What did you mean when you said *skonia* helps?"

Her thin shoulders raise and lower in a weary shrug. "It was something Simon wanted to try. When mixed with valerian and other calming herbs, it often slows or stops my mind from building delusions, like bending or breaking a chain of thoughts." She sighs. "It doesn't always work, though. Sometimes it makes me worse before putting me to sleep, especially lately."

So many things are making sense now. "That was the tea Simon gave me."

"Yes, sorry." Juliane bites her lip. "He didn't realize how potent it became from sitting overnight."

It takes a long time to digest everything Juliane tells me. It's easy to dismiss a person with madness as less than human, but the woman before me is a better human being than most people I've met. Mother Agnes said in Mesanus, people like Juliane are brought into homes and cared for like family. It may be the one place in the world where maladies of the mind are treated like those of the body—with compassion and care. I wonder why Simon hasn't taken her there. "What can I do to help you?" I ask finally.

Juliane's eyes are bright with tears, and her smile is a little shaky. "You haven't immediately made an excuse to leave after listening to all this. That's more than enough."

CHAPTER 27

I do have to leave Juliane soon, however. The Sanctum bells rang at least a quarter hour ago, which means the noon prayers have started by now. I was supposed to call on Mother Agnes today, but I won't even have time for a cursory visit. I'll barely have enough minutes to change out of my Sun Day dress and get to the site soon enough to satisfy Magister Thomas.

"What did you learn from Emeline?" I ask Juliane. "Were there any possibilities for earlier victims?"

"Six, specifically," she replies. Once we were past the awkwardness of her confession, Juliane's manner changed to brisk efficiency. "As Simon doesn't want us to write any of them down yet, I think it best if I give you only three at a time to investigate further. Any more and you're likely to forget or mix details."

It must be strange for Juliane to watch other people struggle with memorizing. Does she find it frustrating that no one else can recall everything perfectly, or is it a relief when they forget what she wishes she could?

She gives me the names, dates, and locations of the first three women, then makes me repeat them twice. When she's satisfied that I'll remember them, she urges me to leave. "It's not pleasant in here."

I don't want to abandon her to this foul confinement. "What will you do if . . . you start to have problems again?"

"Madame Denise will take care of me," Juliane answers. "She always has."

Then the bells toll to signal the end of prayers and the beginning of work on the Sanctum, and I'm already late.

* * *

In the next few days, I manage to get in Remi's good graces by putting extra effort into inspecting the scaffolds assembled under his arching ceiling frames. When Magister Thomas finally allows him to start placing stones for the vault ribs over the wooden braces, he won't have to wait on me. The architect I please by verifying the drainage from the new buttresses before he asks. Fine weather allows better-than-average progress, and both their moods improve. With the execution of the grain merchant, the mood of the city also improves.

In quieter moments, I allow myself to dwell on Simon's absence, but the moon is waxing, one sliver at a time, rising and setting later every day. By the time he returns, I should be able to see the moon until around midnight.

Which means I could be the first to know when the killer strikes again.

I might even be able to stop him.

In the times I'm able to slip away from the Sanctum, I visit the places Juliane's three women were found—an alley, a drainage ditch, and a cellar. I'm fairly certain she gave me ones that were different so I could distinguish them in my memory. When I ask questions of people in the area, I get mixed responses. Some are eager to talk to me and demonstrate exactly how the bodies lay when they were found. Others only mutter that they can't remember. Two were verified to be prostitutes, but the third had actually just been married, and her husband immediately fled the city. That one I think we can eliminate.

Juliane agrees when I visit three days later. She still wears only a dressing gown, and her appearance is little improved. According to Lambert, who led me upstairs this time, she's been suffering from splitting headaches, but I think that's her ruse to be left alone. It's a relief to unload everything I've learned, knowing she won't forget.

"Simon will return the day after tomorrow, correct?" I ask, pretending I haven't kept meticulous track of the days.

"That was his plan," she says. "Do you think you can inquire about the next three women by then?"

"If this rain keeps up," I reply. It had started early that morning, which was why I was able to visit her. Much as I appreciate the free time it gives me, the clouds will block the moon tonight and any effects I might feel. I'd wanted to experiment with tracking a person through the streets at varying distances.

I'm only able to find information on two of the women the next day, but I bring what I know to Juliane, stalling until afternoon to increase the chance of seeing Simon.

He's not back yet.

Frustrated, I return home, wishing I'd waited a few more hours. My only consolation is that after two solid days of rain, the skies have begun to clear. From my window, I watch the nearly half-moon peak as the sun sinks toward the horizon. Its effects seem much greater when the sun is gone, but I do think my senses are a little better whenever it's visible in the sky.

A knock on my door makes me jump. Then I realize the sound came from downstairs, and I smile. Yes, I am hearing better.

Knowing the magister is dining late with a patron and Mistress la Fontaine went to bed an hour ago due to a head cold, I hurry down the steps to answer the door, hoping it's Simon.

It is.

I'm wearing work clothes—a plain skirt that goes to my knees, with an overtunic of sorts which helps keep it clean, but I'd put extra care into my appearance when hoping to see him earlier. The look on his face is worth every second spent teasing my hair into a flattering style in front of a tiny mirror.

"Cat," he whispers, blinking rapidly.

I smile shyly. "Simon. I'm glad to see you're back. Does Juliane know yet?"

He enters the workroom as I step aside for him. "Ah, yes. I've already spoken to her. I wanted to thank you for all the work you did while I was gone."

Of course he went home first. But did he come just to thank me, or could there be another reason? "You're welcome," I tell him as I close the door and lean on it. "You didn't have to walk all the way over here to tell me that, though."

"Oh, it wasn't any trouble," he says, pushing one side of his cloak over his shoulder, then tugging at the clasp which pulls at his neck as he avoids my eyes. "I was passing by."

I try not to let my disappointment show. "Oh, well then, you're welcome," I say again, like a fool. "Did any of them stand out to you?"

"Actually, yes." Now he looks at me, but it's all business. "The one found in the canal three years ago has the most potential, I think. I'm going to Madame Emeline's to ask her for more information."

I frown, wishing my memory was half as good as Juliane's. "Which one was she?" I ask hesitantly. "I thought that one was married, but I must have gotten them mixed up."

"No, that's the right one," he confirms.

The woman had been strangled, unlike Perrete and Ysabel, and her face bashed several times, but nothing had been done to her eyes. Simon anticipates my question. "These . . . things tend to escalate," he says. "But I also have a theory."

Simon presses his palms together as if in prayer. "He may have killed this woman in a rage, both strangling her and beating her with whatever was handy—a clay pitcher or a stone for example, or even a wall. First murders are often messy and confused, but very thrilling, and since then he's wanted to relive that, only planned out. Since there was nothing nearby that could have done the damage we saw with Perrete and Ysabel, he might have brought along his own weapon for them."

"What kind of weapon?" says a voice. We turn to see Remi standing at the bottom of the staircase, next to the re-nailed parchment and the naked pegs above it. He saunters closer, his wool cloak hanging over his forearm. "A hammer?"

Oh Clouded Sky. Don't, Remi. I beg him silently from behind Simon. *Please don't.*

"Perhaps," Simon agrees. "I don't know much about hammers."

"I do, though, and I saw what happened to Perrete," Remi says. "It would probably be bigger and heavier than most, used for larger jobs." He stops a few feet from us, his green eyes fixed on mine. "Could be a rather distinctive tool. Maybe he works at the Sanctum."

"Half the city does," I say tersely. "And your contribution is not needed, *Remone*."

Remi snorts. "So much for your claim that the inquiry was over, but at least I'm not the only person who doesn't get the whole truth from you." He gives me a mocking bow and makes to open the door. "If you'll excuse me."

"Where are you going?" I refuse to move out of his way. "It's nighttime."

He pauses with his hand on the latch, eyes narrowed. "You don't answer to me, Kitten, and I don't answer to you, remember?"

"I just want to have an answer when the magister asks," I snap.

Remi shrugs carelessly. "I was planning to go to Madame Emeline's, but it sounds like it might be crowded tonight." He directs the last part at Simon with a smirk, then forces me aside by opening the door and leaves without looking back.

I slam the door behind him, feeling sick. "He gossips as much as an old woman," I tell Simon. "And he doesn't like you."

"Then it's not bad he knows I'm back," Simon replies, unbothered. "If he talks about me at the tavern, the right ears might hear the news."

Yes, but will Remi get drunk and start talking about distinctive hammers?

"I'm sorry, though, for making you lie to the architect about this," says Simon.

My shoulders droop in relief at his assumption of who else I'm not truthful with. "He'll understand." I twist my hands. Maybe I should tell Simon about the missing hammer. I could act like I've only just made the connection.

Spiteful and condescending as he was, maybe that's what Remi was trying to give me a chance to do.

"Simon," I begin. "I've been thinking."

"I should go," he says abruptly. "It's getting late, and I need to get to . . . where I can get my questions answered."

It's silly, but I don't want to imagine him at Emeline's. He's only going for information. "I'll be awake for a while yet," I tell him. "You're welcome to stop back here on your way home and discuss what you've learned."

Maybe by then I'll have figured out how to tell him what I know.

Simon shakes his head. "Don't wait up for me. I'll probably be out for several hours, if I go home at all."

"Do you think the killer will strike tonight?" I ask, needing to convince myself that's the only reason he would stay out so late.

"I think he's eager to show me how powerless I am to stop him," answers Simon. "But don't worry. I won't just wait around for him to act."

That's in reference to our argument before he left. I wonder if he's thought about what almost happened afterward as often as I have. "Can I come with you?" I blurt out.

Simon smiles tensely. "I appreciate the offer, but skulking around Pleasure Road at night isn't good for my reputation, let alone yours." He's trying to make light of his refusal.

"I don't care."

"You may not, but I do, and"—Simon steps closer—"it could be dangerous." His eyes rove over my face, and the fake smile softens into something real. He raises a hand and traces a finger under my jaw. "I know that stubborn look. But you have to promise me you won't do anything foolish."

"Me?" I reply with forced humor. "Act sensibly?"

"Please," he says quietly. "If only because I can't act sensibly around you, and I need all my wits tonight."

He can't just say something like that and expect me to think rationally. "I won't do anything foolish," I whisper.

"Good, because I'd never forgive myself if something happened to you." Simon takes a deep breath, and I think for one glorious second that he's going to kiss me, but instead he exhales slowly and takes a step back. "I need to go."

I stand rooted to the spot as he lets himself out. Then I count to twenty before bolting the door and heading upstairs to my room.

I know I promised, but my definition of foolish is not the same as his, especially when I have certain skills which are very useful at night.

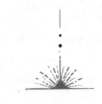

CHAPTER 28

Wanting to see the moon as long as I can, I climb the spiral stair-case of the transept tower I crossed with Simon to the second-highest level, which is even with the peak of the roof. I step into the shadow outside one of the three-story-high arched windows and place my left hand on the stone frame, pausing to calm my breathing before I move fully into the moonlight.

When I do, sounds and scents and the feel of the limestone at my fingertips are enhanced, but not as much as I'd hoped. The moon is less than half what it was the first time I tried to use magick. While it's better than being without, disappointment sits in my stomach like a lump of clay.

My sense of touch is distracting, so I lower my hand, but the breeze at my back makes me sway toward the sheer drop at my toes, and I begrudgingly brace my forearm against the limestone. Then I close my eyes again and concentrate.

The night is young, and men and women laugh and call to each other, claiming they're owed a pint from a previous night of drinking. Friends take leave from those they're visiting and return to their own homes. Among them will be Magister Thomas, but I don't hear anyone who is obviously him. In the direction of Pleasure Road, doors are knocked on, then opened and shut. Gradually, the noises decrease as more people turn in for the night.

One hour passes, and still I've heard nothing suspicious. I shift my aching feet and lean my shoulder on the beveled stone frame. Neither of the previous murders happened before midnight, and the moon will be gone by then. This quest is hopeless.

I sigh and open my eyes. The lower edge of the moon now dips below the horizon, taking with it my only chance to sense anything tonight.

What do you want?

Suddenly I'm pulled forward as though by an invisible safety rope around my waist. The world shifts around me as stone arching above changes shape, and a gargoyle jutting from the wall elongates to twice its length. I step back as the form of a man towers over me, unmoving, the moon hanging under his outstretched arm. There's grass under my feet and warmth at my back.

I'm somewhere else. I'm some*one* else.

I won't resist, please. Just please. I'll do anything you want.

A hard shove pushes me to the ground. I land on my hands and knees, but weight centered in my back presses me all the way down, until even the air is forced from my lungs.

Hands stroke my hair in its single braid, then my head is yanked back, bringing me high enough to catch a fraction of a breath. I've never been so scared in my life.

He's the one who killed Ysabel and Perrete. And he's going to kill me.

My hair is sliced away in one stroke, and the weight from my back is briefly lifted. I scrabble forward, away, until something heavy strikes me between my shoulder blades. There's pain for an instant before something inside me snaps, and I go down again.

Nothing holds me, but now my limbs won't move. Can't move. A hand grabs what's left of my hair and pulls my head up again.

What do you want? Though my lips move, I don't have enough strength to even whisper the words.

His hot breath hits my ear. "I want you to die."

Something cold and sharp presses against my exposed throat. Then there is warm wetness surging out of me, spilling down my chest. I gasp, but it's not air which pours into my lungs, it's blood. I'm drowning in it. Each attempt to draw breath is more futile than the last. Coldness spreads from the top of my head, flowing down my face like water. The edges of my vision darken.

I never thought it could be you.

Blackness sweeps inward until the only thing left is the bright moon setting on the hills in the distance. The last edge of it slips beneath the horizon, and I slide with it into hell.

I stumble backward and trip, landing on my rear with a jolt of pain, followed by my head hitting the ground with a thump that echoes in my skull. For several seconds I stare into darkness.

What just happened? Where am I?

Who am I?

A rustling coo above me is a pigeon flying from one perch to another, its ghostly form vanishing into the gloom. I curl my fingers, and they drag across what feels like stone. Levering myself up, I realize I'm in the south tower of the Sanctum, sitting on a floor sprinkled with bird droppings. The moon is gone, and only starlight comes through the high windows. Scrambling to my feet, I thank the Sun I fell backward and not forward.

While it makes no sense, I know I was someone else only seconds ago—someone who is now dead. But I saw what she saw. I heard what she heard and felt what she felt—until there was nothing left to feel. But where?

There was grass, and I could see the moon clearly. That narrows it down to a hillside area open to the west, of which there are several in Collis.

I look out over the rooftops, cursing the moon for setting when I needed it most. The dark shape of the gargoyle blocks part of my view, and I remember how it had transformed, becoming a statue. A man holding a scroll, his arm outstretched.

I know where that is.

Turning away, I dash down the stairs and out onto the gutter to leap onto the scaffolding. I slide down poles rather than climb, shaking so much I almost fall twice, but it takes less than a minute to reach the ground. Then I'm racing across the square to the Pathway of Prayer.

The street bends with the contour of the slope, but the spire of the ancient Temple of the Sun is visible in the distance. Shortly after the second turn, I pass the alley where Perrete was killed. At the last bend is a lamp next to a door that's opening to let someone in. Every second is precious, but I run to it, slamming into the wood before it can close.

"Simon!" I gasp. "I need Simon of Mesanus!"

A woman who isn't Madame Emeline bares her teeth at me. "He's not here." She pulls her customer deeper into the shadowed entry and blocks me from coming in. The sickly-sweet scent of her perfume washes over me as she leans close and hisses, "Leave before I call the guard."

She either can't or won't help me. Almost half a minute wasted. I pivot away and tear down the road. "Murder!" I scream as homes pass in a blur. "Murder! Come quickly! Help!"

The street ends at the temple, and I run around its curved walls and skid to a halt on the edge of a wide grassy area. A statue stands in the middle on a high pedestal, glowing gray in the starlight. Beneath it, a hulking silhouette slowly separates from a dark shape on the ground and rises to face me.

I may be about to die for the second time tonight. Even if I was skilled enough to fight a man his size, I'm paralyzed by the memory of what he's already done to her—to me. I take a deep breath to scream, the only defense I have.

The bell in the spire tower behind me suddenly rings out, not in alarm but to call the religious to midnight prayers. I look up at it reflexively, and when I bring my eyes back to the man, he's gone.

Gone where?

The temple itself is only a few yards away, and I dash to press my back against the stone wall, wanting a direction no one can come at me from. I look around wildly as ringing echoes off buildings, drowning all else out. Eventually, the sounds fade to where I feel safe enough to edge to where I can see the statue. The only shadow left is the one lying motionless in the grass. Without thinking, I push off the wall and run straight at it.

My feet have barely touched the grass when I'm tackled from behind.

CHAPTER 29

The side of my head hits the ground as I land, the impact briefly knocking every thought from my mind.

"Cursed Night! Are you trying to get yourself killed?" Simon breathes heavily against my neck, so much like what I'd felt in my vision that I screech and throw him off. He rolls away and sits up, pulling his cloak back and panting.

"He was here! I saw him!" I shriek. Everything in my sight doubles as I look around frantically. Two Simons lunge at me, but only one takes me in his arms and pulls me into his chest. His heartbeat pounds in my ear as he strokes my hair and lays his cheek on the top of my head.

"You're all right," he whispers over and over, though it feels more like he's assuring himself. "You're all right."

As my vision slowly merges into one picture, I focus on a man crouched on the edge of the grass, watching us. The shape of his eyes is strangely visible, hollow teardrops of black with the gleam of silver within. I shove Simon away. "Someone's out there."

"Where?" He releases me and looks around.

I don't even have time to point before the man vanishes.

A lantern light bobs up and down from a street leading north.

"It's the city guard," says Simon, lurching to his feet to wave his arm at the watchman, calling for him to come quickly. As the man runs toward us, Simon offers me a hand up. A moment of dizziness has me leaning on him for a second, and his lips graze my forehead, though I'm not sure it was on purpose. "What in the Sun's name are you doing out here, Catrin? You promised you would stay home."

I certainly did not promise that.

"Where were *you*?" I demand. "You said you were going to Emeline's"

"I *was* at Emeline's. We heard you at the front door. How do you think I got here so fast?"

The guard reaches us, gasping for air, and holds up the light. Simon squints and shields his face from the brightness, but not before the man identifies him. "Venatre! What's happened?"

"There's been another murder," Simon tells him. "Sound the alarm and wake the provost, but give me your lantern first."

The man relinquishes it and runs off, blowing on the horn he's pulled off his belt. Simon rubs his left eye with the palm of his free hand and turns around. "Let's look over the body before the crowds get here."

I balk, mumbling, "I can't."

Simon takes me by the elbow and drags me toward the shape on the ground. "You will. This is why you're out here after all, isn't it?"

I can't explain how looking at her will make me relive what happened. That I will know exactly which parts of his conjecture on the way she died are correct. But I understand his anger, too. Simon forces me closer without remorse as tears stream down my face.

He holds the lantern over the body. "Make your observations."

My hands shake as I wipe my cheeks. "She's lying on her back, but she was rolled over after her throat was cut. Her face was crushed . . ." I struggle to hold down what's risen to the back of my throat. "With something heavy."

Simon nods. "I don't see anything obvious around here that could have done it, so he must have taken it with him again." He glances at the people coming out of houses to see what the commotion is. We don't have much longer to do this without an audience. "What else?"

"Her eyes are torn out, like Ysabel's. And—and her shoulders look odd, like she was struck in the back. Maybe while trying to get away."

Simon bends over her body, trying to see what I'm describing. "I don't know what makes you think that, but maybe I'll agree after looking at her later." He pauses. "*What else*, Catrin?"

"Her skirts are pulled up to her waist," I choke. "Exposing . . . everything."

To my relief, Simon yanks her skirt back down to her knees. "Evidence of sexual invasion," he says.

"After she was dead?" I'd thought nothing could be worse than what happened before she died.

My knees give out as I spin around, retching, and I find myself in the same position the woman was right before she was pinned to the ground. When Simon kneels beside me and places a hand on the center of my back, I panic and twist away, putting my hand down in grass that's wet with blood.

I never thought it could be you.

The familiar thought sings through my mind. I gasp and grab at my throat to assure myself it isn't cut open, smearing blood on my neck.

Never thought . . . never thought . . .

Simon moves closer, his crystal blue eyes full of concern. "Cat?"

. . . it could be you.

Crawling back, I angle away from the bloody patch until I bump against the base of the statue. I turn and grab on to its squared edge like I'm falling off a cliff, pressing my cheek against the cool marble. Simon approaches again, this time slower, and puts a hand on my shoulder.

"What was done to her wasn't new, was it?" I ask. "He did the same thing to Perrete and Ysabel. You just didn't tell us."

Simon nods. "I'm sorry. There were some things I wasn't willing to put into words." He bends down and grasps my upper arm gently. "Come on. You need to get up. We're not done yet."

I allow him to pull me to my feet. A number of lanterns and candles gather at a distance. Several guards have arrived, some staring dumbly, others trying to herd people back like a flock of sheep eyeing a fresh pasture. Simon walks around the body, holding his light low to the ground, like he's searching for something.

"It's not here," he mutters after making a full circle. Then he kneels, careful to avoid the bloody ground, and tilts her misshapen head to the side. "Her hair is gone," he says softly enough that only I can hear.

"You were looking for Ysabel's," I say, understanding now.

Simon stands again and comes closer, keeping his voice low. "Yes. I think leaving hair from the last victim behind is something he feels he needs to do. Discarding the old as you said." He frowns, the narrowing of his brow exaggerated by the shadows cast from the lantern. "If that's true, it's very bad that it's not here now."

It's certainly not good, but I feel like I'm missing something. "Why?"

He gestures at the body. "You interrupted the killer before he could finish what he'd started."

My face tingles as I blanch with anxiety. "Do you think that means he'll kill again soon?"

Simon nods. "Maybe even tonight."

I slump against the marble pedestal. This is my fault. The woman lying here was already dead, but if I'd brought the guard here rather than run screaming myself, there was a chance we could've captured him. Instead, I've doomed another woman to this monster's sick need.

"We need to find out who she is," I say dully. "Madame Emeline will probably know."

"I agree." Simon calls for one of the guards to fetch her. Then he sets the lantern down and leans against the base of the statue next to me.

"Why did you come out tonight, Cat?" he asks quietly. "You of all people knew how dangerous it was."

How can I explain? He would never believe it. Sometimes I don't believe it, and I certainly don't understand it. "I wasn't looking for trouble," I whisper. "I was on the Sanctum."

"Inspecting?"

"No." I lean my head back against the pedestal and close my eyes. "Just looking at the moon."

To my relief, Simon doesn't ask any more questions. The minutes pass slowly, and the crowd gathering around the temple grows. After a time, Simon slides his hand across the marble to find mine. When I don't resist, he laces my fingers with his. It feels like an apology, but I'm not sure what for. Maybe forcing me to see the full horror of what this man—this monster—does, or for not telling me in the first place. Maybe for being angry when he found me here tonight.

The watchman is returning. Simon lets go of my hand and stands upright. I, too, push off the pedestal to meet them, but it's not Emeline who walks with the guard. It's Remi.

Simon frowns. "Where's Madame Emeline?"

Remi's shadowed eyes focus on me. "She's dead."

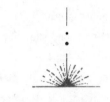

CHAPTER 30

Perrete. Ysabel. Nichole. Emeline.

I don't think Simon is aware of the coincidence as he nails a piece of paper to the wall, but he feels the same responsibility as the architect does for his own list, the same determination not to add any more names. The sketches are back up, too, surrounding the maps, and new drawings from last night have been added.

The inquiry has officially been reopened and Simon's position reinstated. At first the comte had tried blaming him for ending it in the first place, but Simon had given the high altum a sealed letter before he left, detailing his objections to ending the investigation. Between that and a signed recommendation from the altum of Mesanus, Collis's holy man had publicly sided with Simon, and the provost backed down.

Simon's hunch that the woman, Beatrez, had a history of prostitution before her marriage was the only topic he'd been able to discuss with Emeline. After leaving me at the architect's home, he'd spent the first couple hours visiting several taverns in an effort to make his return known. He'd only just sat down with Emeline when I came pounding on the door. When I asked why the woman at the door said he wasn't there, Simon shrugged and said that was probably what they told any woman searching for a man.

Unsurprisingly, Oudin was able to provide a few other details about Beatrez, such as her hair color being similar to the braid found with Perrete. Everyone assumed her husband had killed her, but he'd vanished. When it came to more personal knowledge of her, for once Oudin was more circumspect.

Juliane dutifully transcribes the night's interviews from her memory as Oudin paces back and forth in front of the wall. I suspect his presence is only tolerated because he was the one to identify the woman from last night as Nichole. That he's known every victim intimately has Oudin convinced someone is out to get him.

"Emeline's death doesn't match the others," he says. The last few hours have apparently made him an expert. He points to the drawing of her body as it was found in the kitchen of her home—the very room Juliane and I had sat in with her only days ago. "Her throat was cut and she was bludgeoned, but her tongue was removed rather than her eyes."

She also wasn't violated in the same way as the others, but only Simon and I know about that.

"Are you sure she was killed by the same man?" Oudin asks.

A blood-soaked coil of hair as thick as my little finger and as long as my forearm rests on a linen cloth in front of Simon. He draws a thin finger along the edge of it. "I'm sure," he says quietly. "He left it in Emeline's mouth as a message. He's telling me he's silenced the only one who could have given us answers."

Lambert shakes his head. "You're giving this madman too much credit for rational thought."

"On the contrary," replies Simon. "I haven't given him enough credit, which is why he's two steps ahead of me."

"Maybe that's because you're sitting here doing nothing," says Oudin.

Simon narrows his eyes. "I don't recall asking for your assistance."

"You plainly need it," snarls Oudin. "Half of your information has come from me. You wouldn't even know Nichole's name if I hadn't told you."

Rather than address that ridiculous claim, Simon pulls a stack of parchments covered in writing from his satchel and begins flipping through them. "Do you know why I went to Mesanus, Cousin?" he asks casually.

Oudin folds his arms. "You're assuming I noticed you were even gone."

Simon pulls a page from the bunch and studies it. "I wanted to consult with a man who has led many inquiries like this one." He pauses, but Oudin doesn't interject. "I shared the details of Perrete's and Ysabel's murders and asked for his opinions. He agreed with all of my theories."

"Am I supposed to be impressed?"

"He added a few things I should look for," continues Simon, as though Oudin hadn't spoken. "Namely that I should pay special attention to anyone who either involves himself in the investigation or watches it closely." He raises his eyes to his cousin. "So where exactly were you this evening?"

Oudin's ruddy cheeks go pale. "You saw me at the tavern yourself."

Simon doesn't blink. "I saw you an hour before the murder. Can anyone account for your whereabouts after I left?"

"Remi la Fontaine can."

"Then I'll be sure to ask him," says Simon calmly. "In the meantime, your assistance is not required."

Oudin glares at him and then Lambert before stomping out of the room, slamming the door behind him. When the sound of his heavy footsteps fades, the only noise in the room is the scratching of Juliane's pen and the buzzing flies now circling over the braid of hair. Simon brushes them away. "I suppose we ought to rinse this off before it fully dries."

Gruesome as that task is, I worry Simon may still be angry with me, so I offer to perform it. He gestures for me to go ahead. I pick it up by the linen cloth and carry it downstairs to the kitchen. Madame Denise provides a bowl of warm water as I peel the braid from the cloth where it's stuck.

I didn't expect to see you again so soon.

The husky voice makes me jump and look around. Madame Denise continues stirring a pot over the fire like she's heard nothing. I've dropped the hair into the bowl, splashing water on the table, which I hastily wipe away with a corner of the cloth. Then I prod the rest of the braid under the water with a finger.

. . . didn't   expect . . . you . . . soon . . . see   you . . . didn't expect . . .

This time the words spiral out and drift through my mind, strong in the beginning but dissolved by the end, fading like the blood in the water.

Like the blood is speaking to me.

Or maybe not *to* me. It feels like I'm overhearing a conversation or someone talking to themselves.

Hands shaking, I hold the braid under the surface of the water as I squeeze it, forcing threads of scarlet out, each one a whisper delicate as smoke in a voice that has the raspy quality of a *skonia* user. Madame Emeline's voice.

Hurriedly, I rinse as much blood away as I can. When the shade of the hair becomes apparent, at least enough for Simon's purpose, I pull it out and wring pink water from it, then pat it mostly dry with the cleaner parts of the cloth. I carry it back upstairs as the words continue to leak through the linen with the dampness, and I can't put it down soon enough.

Simon barely glances at it. "Blond," is all he says.

Juliane, who looks to have finished her recording, watches me rub my hands on my skirt. "What now?"

Simon stands and takes the quill from where she lay it on the table. "First things first." He goes to the list nailed to the wall and adds *Beatrez* to the top of it.

"Are you that certain?" I ask.

"I am." Simon turns around and tosses the quill onto the table. "The only real question is whether there are any between her and Perrete. Unfortunately, I don't think we can afford to investigate that. He's killing now at a frightening rate."

As if that was the most frightening thing about all this.

"That's not even the worst part," Simon continues, rotating back to the wall. "He got away with the first and Sun knows how many more, which makes him feel powerful, superior. Now he's reveling in this inquiry because it's a game, and he finally has an opponent to play against."

"But there he's wrong," Juliane says, gesturing to herself and then me and Lambert. "He has four opponents."

Simon glances at me. "After last night, I think he knows about Cat."

I face the wall in an attempt to hide my blush. Juliane and Lambert know that we found Nichole last night, but neither is aware of how Simon had hugged me when he realized I was safe, or that he'd held my hand as we'd waited for Emeline.

Simon shifts to address Juliane. "And he no doubt knows about you, too. That means both of you are in danger. You must

promise me never to go anywhere without Lambert or myself."
He turns his eyes on me. "Nor you, especially at night."

I cross my arms, conscious of how Oudin did the same. "I
have work to do."

And I doubt anyone could sneak up on me as long as the
moon is out.

"Then do it during the day, even if it means helping me less."

I pivot to face him. "You do realize I'm not a prostitute, right?
Every one of his victims has been."

"Of course." Simon flushes scarlet. "But he's going to change
the women he targets."

"How can you know that?" I ask.

"Because that's what I would do."

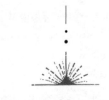

CHAPTER 31

The architect has a reserved place in the gallery but prefers to attend Sun Day ceremonies among the common people, choosing a different spot each week. Every corner of the Sanctum should be beautiful and inspiring, and these are opportunities to inspect his work. I like to watch the people, myself. Their awe at their surroundings is contagious.

Today we have clear view of the Montcuirs in their section overlooking the altar. Simon is next to Juliane. It's silly, but I'm jealous of her freedom to stand so close to him. If anyone knew I'd walked through that very area with him in the dark—and holding his hand—it would force Simon to state his intentions publicly.

Yet what are his intentions? After the morning he left for Mesanus and the night of Nichole's murder, it's obvious his *feelings* are more than just friendship or partnership in the inquiry, and he's worried about the killer targeting me, but what about when this is all over?

I know Simon wants to be free of dependence on the comte, yet I doubt he'd be comfortable being supported by me. Would he think it charity if the architect hired him or found him work?

I glance at Magister Thomas, whose gaze and dreamlike smile is focused on the south window with its flower petal–shaped frames arranged to create one giant wheel. The morning sunlight glows through the stained glass, casting patterns of color toward the front of the Sanctum. He hadn't designed that to occur—that would've been one or two masters before him—and I can see his admiration and envy.

And then, among the scattered hues near the altar, I see a familiar face.

A small number of Sisters of Light are tasked to launder the embroidered robes and altar linens, so they come every Sun Day with fresh ones and leave with those needing to be washed. It's not an easy job either, as I can testify. Often the cloths are splattered with candle wax and ashes of incense, and—in the summer especially—sweat from the altum and his assistants drench the underrobes. Marguerite has never been assigned to collect or return them, but she's here today.

I'm so eager to see her that when the final blessing is finished, I fight the tide of the departing crowd to get to her before she's swept away by duty. Marguerite must have been hoping to see me, too, because she lingers as the other sisters move to begin their work.

Her arms are up to embrace me long before we're close enough to touch. "Oh, Catrin, it's so good to see you!"

I squeeze her back tightly, feeling the thick hair under her cowl bonnet. It will be gone in a few months, but I'm comforted it's still there for now. "Don't tell me you've finally snuck away from Mother Agnes."

Marguerite pulls back, scandalized. "You don't really think I'd do that, do you?"

"Of course not," I tease. "I just can't imagine her letting you out of your cage now that you're her personal secretary."

She wrinkles her snub nose. "That's actually why I'm here. I have a message for the master architect from Mother Agnes."

"Oh, well, you can just give it to me," I say, holding out my hand.

Marguerite reaches beneath the plain smock covering her mantle but shakes her head. "No, I can only give it to the magister."

I glance around, but only Remi is paying any attention to us, and he's out of earshot. Since Nichole's murder, he's hardly let me out of his sight. Magister Thomas is speaking with the Comte de Montcuir while his family stands nearby. Simon's eyes briefly catch mine, then he goes back to feigning interest in his uncle's conversation.

"What's it about?" I ask. When Marguerite shrugs, I frown. "Don't be stubborn. I know you must have written it."

"No, truly. I didn't. But the thing is"—Marguerite lowers her voice—"I don't think she wrote it either."

Intriguing. "Who did, then?"

She fidgets under her habit. "I don't know, but I suppose it wouldn't hurt to show it to you." The outer rectangular paper is folded like an envelope around a note inside, which immediately tells me it's not from the abbey—they use only parchment. A mottled circle surrounded by flames is pressed into the wax seal. It looks like the moon. On fire.

It has to be from Gregor. But why would a Prioress of Light agree to pass on a message from a Person of the Night?

"Well, there's no better time to deliver it," I say, tugging her along to where the Montcuirs wait for their patriarch to finish his business. As we approach, Juliane peels away from the group and meets me with a smile. Her eyes dart nervously to Marguerite, probably worried she's a hallucination, so I quickly introduce her. "Lady Juliane, this is my closest friend from my years at the abbey, Sister Marguerite."

Juliane extends her hand, looking relieved. "Yes, I recall you from my own time there, finishing my education. It's a pleasure to see you again."

Marguerite curtsies as she grasps Juliane's fingers. "I'm surprised you would remember me, my lady. I think I was barely nine years old. Most of the older girls never paid us any mind."

I'm not surprised, of course. Juliane could no doubt list every day their paths crossed, the weather, and what they were both wearing, though in Marguerite's case, that last wouldn't be hard at all. The only difference between her outfit then and now is the hood which covers her hair.

Oudin glances over, but, seeing only me and a young woman he could never pursue, his attention quickly wanders again. I'd like to present her to Simon, but before I can catch his eye again, Remi inserts himself into our conversation. "Aren't you going to introduce me, Kitten?"

I roll my eyes. "Marguerite, this is Journeyman Remone la Fontaine. He also works for Magister Thomas."

Remi has to tilt his chin whiskers into his neck to look down on tiny Marguerite, who blinks up with wide blue eyes. In her cloistered life, she's probably never been this close to a man other than the abbey's ancient chaplain, but I have to admit Remi can be intimidating if you don't know him.

"I didn't think they made sisters so young," he says, flashing her a wide grin. "I thought they were born thirty years old with wrinkles and a double chin."

Marguerite flushes red as a rose apple, and I kick Remi in the shin.

"Ow!" he yelps. "Watch it, Kitten. We're on Holy Ground."

"Call me Kitten one more time," I say through gritted teeth, "and you'll feel my claws."

"Promise?" Remi sidesteps my attempt to stomp on his foot.

"So how did *you* escape the abbey, Sister Marguerite? You don't look like the climbing type."

Marguerite's answer is too soft to hear. Remi leans down so close his wiry black hair brushes against her hood. "What's that?"

She mumbles again, and he stands straight, apparently able to understand her this time. "I can take it to him." He snatches the envelope from her hand.

"Give it back, jackass!" I yell. "It's not for you!"

Remi raises the envelope up high, thinking it's beyond my reach, but he underestimates me. I not only leap high enough to grab it, I manage to put my knee into his stomach as I do. My heavy skirt reduces the effect, however, and he barely grunts before grabbing me around the waist with his free arm. I wriggle in his grasp as he laughs.

"*Children*," says a quiet, angry voice. The pair of us jump apart and face the architect, shame-faced. Well, Remi has no shame. "What in the Sun's name are you doing in this hallowed place?"

I hold up the note before Remi can say anything. "This is for you, Magister. Sister Marguerite brought it for you and you only, but Remi thinks he deserves to know your business."

Sighing in exasperation, Magister Thomas holds out his hand. To emphasize Remi's wrongness, I pass the note back to Marguerite. She scurries up to the architect and gives it to him. "Thank you, Sister," he says kindly. "Please refrain from telling Mother Agnes about Catrin's behavior—"

The architect breaks off as he focuses on the wax seal.

The comte, Lambert, Simon, and even Oudin all strain to get a look at what's caused him to stop so abruptly, but Magister Thomas shoves the note in the sleeve of his robe. "Where were we, gentlemen?"

Montcuir chuckles. "I think I've occupied enough of your time today, Magister. It looks like you have matters to attend to."

Juliane is wringing her hands and muttering. Though I'd been focused mostly on Remi, it hadn't escaped my attention that our argument had affected her. The stress of this investigation and all these unpredictable situations always have, now that I think on it. She does best when her surroundings are tightly controlled, which was why she was so level-headed after spending days in her room. Our conflict, on top of being around hundreds of people and meeting Marguerite, may have tipped some delicate balance.

Simon notices it, too. He takes her arm, speaking softly as he leads her away with her family. The envy from before rises in my chest. Even if Juliane is getting the help she needs, I wish I could be as close to Simon as she is.

The architect glares at Remi and me, then makes a gesture with his finger that commands us to come with him. We follow contritely, as does Marguerite. She reaches for me, and we walk hand in hand like we used to ten years ago.

Once we're safely inside the house, Magister Thomas turns on us, his gray eyes dark as storm clouds. "I have never been more embarrassed than I was today, and in the Sanctum, in front of the provost and his entire family. There is no doubt the high altum will hear of it. Both of you have been behaving like children for the last few weeks and yet expect me to give you more freedom and responsibility than ever."

He pauses to take a deep breath, but neither Remi nor I dare interrupt. "Catrin, you will spend the rest of the day repairing the miniature of the south window, and you will not leave the house until it is finished to my satisfaction."

I only manage to stifle my groan because I suspect Remi's punishment will be worse. The architect pivots to him.

"Remone, your work on the ceiling is suspended for two full weeks, and your teams will be directed to other sections. If you disobey or I hear a single word of protest, I will remove the vaulting from your supervision entirely. Is that understood?"

"Yes, Magister," we chorus like naughty seven-year-olds.

The architect blinks, noticing Marguerite cowering behind me. "Why are you here, my dear?"

She steps out to face him, blue eyes brimming with tears—over my punishment, of course—and curtsies. "I wasn't to leave without your reply, Magister."

"Very well. Give me a moment please." He turns toward the kitchen as Remi heads for the stairs. "And Remi," Magister Thomas calls to him. "Be a man and stop pulling pigtails to show your feelings."

Remi hunches his shoulders and slinks away, and I'm left to pick my jaw up off the floor. The magister can't be serious. Remi acts the way he does because he's a brat, not out of some expression of puppy love. But at least now maybe he'll leave me alone.

"I'm sorry to have gotten you into trouble, Cat," whispers Marguerite.

I sigh. She would blame this on herself. "And I'm sorry I won't get to walk you home now."

A minute later, Magister Thomas returns to the workroom, holding the blank and creased sheet of paper which had been folded around the note itself, minus the wax seal. He hands me the page, saying, "No need to waste this," then addresses Marguerite. "Please tell Mother Agnes I will come tonight to discuss the next step."

The architect shuffles to the stairs, looking wearier than I've ever seen him. "You may escort Sister Marguerite back to the abbey, Catrin, if you don't dawdle."

That's for Marguerite's benefit and comfort, but I'm not going to complain. Before we leave, I grab a straw hat from a peg near the door to shade my eyes, then we stroll down the hill, holding hands again.

"I really missed you over the winter, Cat," Marguerite says. "So did Mother Agnes. I think it hurt more than she'd ever admit when you stopped coming to see her."

"Funny that she would lecture me on my pride, then," I reply dryly.

We walk almost a block before she speaks again. "What did you argue about?"

"I asked her about my parents, and she wouldn't tell me who they were."

Marguerite shakes her head. "But she doesn't know who any of our parents are."

Apparently, the prioress hasn't let her secretary know about the file tucked between holy books that lists every foundling in her care and their known or suspected origin. I'd snuck in to read it when we were eleven and received quite a shock at some of the secrets it contained. She certainly never treated any of us girls differently that I could tell—even Marguerite, who's the previous high altum's child by Sister Alix. Any favoritism my friend received was by her own merit, but I suspect Mother Agnes's knowledge was the reason the abbey received a massive grant to expand when we were young.

My name wasn't listed in the file, however. Not even with a blank spot next to it.

"She knows," I said. "I heard her talking to Magister Thomas the day he asked to hire me."

"Maybe you misunderstood."

I roll my eyes. "You'll never believe ill of anyone, will you? But no, I'm not mistaken. She said she still had hopes that my family would accept me."

"That doesn't mean she knows who they are, Cat."

"Except that she also warned they would hold him accountable for any harm that came to me," I say. "And how would she know that if they hadn't told her so?"

We turn the last corner as I'm speaking, and the vine-covered walls of the Selenae Quarter stretch out for several blocks in either direction. That's when it hits me: *They* have been watching me, even coming out of their neighborhood after dark to do so. Or perhaps just Gregor watches, but enough that he communicates with Magister Thomas. Because *he* is my family.

I'm Selenae.

CHAPTER 32

I have half a mind to confront Mother Agnes right then and there, but the bells toll for noon prayers, and she would never forgo those to talk to me, especially if she had an inkling about what I wanted. Waiting isn't an option, as Magister Thomas will be furious if I don't come straight home.

The architect knows, too. He's always known. I grit my teeth as Marguerite rushes to unlock the gate—she has her own keys now? "I'll tell Mother you can't have tea today," she says, swinging the gate shut. "Promise you'll visit again soon?"

I keep my lips sealed as I smile to avoid looking like a growling dog. "I promise. You can tell Mother Agnes that, too."

Maybe it's my imagination, but now I feel eyes watching me from the narrow streets leading into the Quarter, through every gap between vines growing over windows. I hurry home, checking often to see if I'm being followed. Both Magister Thomas and Remi are already gone, and after changing into work clothes, I reluctantly begin my task.

The rest of my day is spent hunched over the window ledge, sorting and arranging tiny bits of colored glass. To keep the unused pieces from getting too scattered, I set them in the paper envelope, whose folds contain them nicely. The sight of it makes me grind my teeth, however, and the tension in my jaw quickly leads to a headache.

I don't know much about Selenae, other than that they've been around as a people for over a thousand years. When the Hadrian Empire fell apart, it took a few centuries for Gallia to unite itself under a single ruler. The relatively recent explosion in trade brought a mixture of people and ideas together, ushering in a Golden Age of construction—both in cities and the massive Sanctums that sprung up. Gallians mingled with Taurans and Prezians and Brinsulli and others to the point that those of mixed parentage—like Remi—are as common as not.

The People of the Night held themselves apart through all of that, however—a preference made easier by the hours they keep. Non-Selenae are good enough to do business with when it suits them, but they treat outsiders with a sort of pity, as though they consider us misguided. No one joins their communities, and the few that leave seem to wither away like a vine severed from the main branch, often from *skonia* addiction.

Mother Agnes made a point of telling me my parents loved each other, so if they weren't wed, they likely wanted to be. That wasn't all she said, though.

Your family left you here because they truly believed you belonged in the Light.

They didn't think I was like them somehow.

The thought I've shoved aside a dozen times will no longer be denied. What I can do—what the moon does for me—must be a power every Selenae has. They gather at night to enjoy what I've only recently discovered. For some reason, they must have assumed I didn't have the same abilities, yet they continued watching over me, and Gregor has realized the truth.

As has Magister Thomas.

By sunset, my fingers are covered with cuts from handling tiny, sharp edges, and my face hurts from squinting in concentration. Remi comes home alone, and when I ask when Magister Thomas will return, he avoids my eyes and mutters that the architect said not to wait for him to eat dinner.

"You can start without me," I tell him. "I want to finish this section."

Remi only shrugs. "I'll save you some bread."

"Thank you."

I'm not mad at him anymore. There's too much going on in the world to be petty, and his punishment was more harsh than even I expected. It's not just being forced to stop his beloved work, it's having everyone know it.

Remi passes me again a while later with a quiet "Good night, Cat" just as I'm plucking the last piece of glass from the bent paper. My vision blurs as I fit it into place. The moon is already up, but maybe I should stay indoors tonight. I have a headache, and if I'm caught by the magister, there will be hell to pay. Still, my eyes are drawn to the silver light shining on the slate outside like those of a starving man attracted to the sideboard at a banquet.

No longer weighed down, the paper wavers with a breeze and starts to fly out the window. I grab it before it can go far and stand to let the shutter down when something on the page catches my eye. Writing. But not writing. I hold it up to the moonlight reflecting off the street. The paper has the impression of letters, like it was under a page that was written on. It's too faint to read, however. At least here and now.

Swiftly, I refold the sheet as it was, not wanting to add any more creases. I guess I will be going out tonight.

———　•　＊　•　———

My heart pounds as I climb to the window ledge in the front tower. The moon had already passed beyond where I could have seen it from my room, so I changed into my climbing clothes but didn't dare leave the house until Mistress la Fontaine finished setting tomorrow's bread to rise and went to bed. The Sanctum's facade is slightly shorter than the transept arms, but it's closer, and I have no desire to ever set foot in the south tower again.

I'm in such a hurry that I tear the elbow of my jacket on the double prong of the latch as I squeeze through. After pivoting the window back in place, I climb the stairs past the gallery up to the triforium that runs above it. The next level higher is the facade's tower, with an outdoor bridge of sorts to its twin on the opposite side, identical except that it houses the Sanctum bells. I could stop here, but I continue up the spiral staircase to the very top.

The moon greets me like a friend as soon as I step out of the round house and into the open air. A shiver of exhilaration goes through me as moonlight soaks into my skin, ending with the glorious sensation that I could fly if I wanted to.

Is this what using *skonia* feels like? And if this is barely more than a half-moon now, what will it be like in a few days?

Though I'm tempted to stretch out my senses, I came here with a purpose. I quickly unfold the paper and raise it to the moonlight. The impression of writing becomes visible on the page, almost as clearly as if the words were written in ink. Some letters weren't pressed quite strong enough—often the last of a word or an E appears to be missing—until the final sentence, which was written with a heavy hand and underlined.

Y u promis action by th n xt ful moon. Ther are only 6 day lef .

<u>*Katarene needs guidance*</u>.

Magister Thomas had told Marguerite he would come tonight to discuss the next step, but he's not meeting with Mother Agnes. He's in the Selenae Quarter, talking to Gregor. About me.

I am Katarene.

Now swirling beneath the tumultuous idea that I have Selenae abilities that need guidance is the hope that every foundling child carries in their heart against all odds: I have a family and they want me back.

Mother Agnes isn't standing in the way of the Selenae reaching out to me, either. In fact, she's facilitating it. Her emphasizing that my family truly believed I belonged in the Light was a preemptive urge to forgive their decision to leave me in her care. I'm tempted to march down to the Quarter right now and demand answers from them. Then again, knowing that would be my first impulse was probably why the prioress never told me who left me at her door.

And because of that abandonment, I was raised to be a Child of Light, even if I rebelled against Mother Agnes's vision of vows and a habit. Instead of prayers and charity, I offer my talent and labor to the Sun by building the Sanctum.

I run my hand along the limestone rail, savoring the subtle texture and the beauty of its lines and curves. I love everything about this building inside and out—its statues and arched ceilings, its colorful glass windows and ornate marble floors, even the smoky wisps of incense and the echoes of voices raised in song. Standing here now, I'm more at home than anywhere else.

Is this the world I truly belong in, or is it simply the only one I know?

My eyes are closed and my hands on the stone, which is probably the reason I can both hear and feel the latch on the window below being opened.

CHAPTER 33

There's a soft grunt as a man squeezes between the frame and the glass panes. Once through, he rotates the window back into place and pauses, feeling around in the pitch blackness. Then he ascends slowly, and doesn't stop at the first or second landing. He's coming all the way to the tower.

When he reaches the spiral stairs, I open my eyes and back into the shadows behind the round house in the corner, my movement thunderously loud in my ears until I'm out of the moonlight. Then I feel uncomfortably blind and deaf, but being seen is more dangerous right now.

The man's footsteps are so soft, it's his heavy breathing that tells me when he's almost to my level. He emerges slowly, arms outstretched, his face too shadowed to make out. "Cat?" he calls softly.

It's Simon.

I slide one hand out to the left, putting my fingers in the light. Now I can see him plain as day, from the worried lines on his forehead to the trembling of his legs. His heavy pulse echoes through the air, while the light breeze carries the scent of his sweat soaking into the starched linen of his shirt. There's blood, too, from two fresh scratches on the back of his hand.

Simon takes another step away from the shelter. "Cat?" he says again quietly, though he might as well be shouting as far as I'm concerned. "Are you up here?"

"Behind you."

Simon spins around, putting one hand to his heart, which jumps to a rhythm fast and loud as a running horse. "Holy Sun!" he gasps as I move out of the shadows. "Why didn't you say something sooner?"

"I didn't know who you were or what you wanted," I reply. "You scared *me*."

He laughs a little and drops his hand from his chest. "I suppose that's fair."

We fall silent for several moments. "What are you doing up here?" I finally ask.

Simon clears his throat. "I wanted to talk to you. I went to your house first, but you weren't there." He shrugs sheepishly. "And I remembered you said you come up here sometimes to think."

Oh no. "Who answered the door?"

He shuffles his feet. "I didn't knock. I, um, went around back and tossed a few rocks in your window."

Romantic. Or desperate. "What is it you wanted?"

"I owe you an explanation." He swallows and looks down as he runs a hand through his blond curls. "After some things I've said . . . and done."

Suddenly I dread what he will say. "You don't owe me anything, Simon."

"Yes, I do." He raises his eyes to mine. His legs are shaking, but not from climbing the stairs. "Please. It took a lot for me to get up the courage to do this."

"To talk to me, or to come up this high?"

"Both."

Alone again with Simon in the moonlight. Last time I was helping him, but this time will definitely be different. "All right. Let's talk."

Simon grabs my arm. "Here?"

"It's perfectly safe." I gesture to the evenly spaced columns around the perimeter. "You'd have a hard time fitting more than your head through the gaps."

"I'll take your word for it," Simon mutters, looking up at the open sky.

I also take a moment to appreciate the stars, which are breathtaking in my sight. The cloudy glow of previous nights is dotted with thousands more points of light than I've ever been able to see before. Simon moves to stand beside me, his upper arm pressing against mine, a contact which thrills me more than is proper.

"Can we sit, though?" he asks. "It's a bit dizzying."

I tear my eyes away from the banner of diamonds above. He's more than just dizzy—he's positively green. I smile indulgently and turn my face back up to the sky. "As long as you admit it *is* beautiful up here."

"Yes, yes," he mumbles, plopping to the stone at our feet. After a half minute of calming himself, he tugs my hand. "I've truly never seen anything lovelier, but I'm not sure how much time we have."

I lower myself to sit near his bent legs, facing him and the moon. "Why would you throw rocks in my window rather than knock on the door like a normal person?"

A flush replaces the sickly shade. "I didn't want to risk Remone answering. He seems rather jealous of you."

"And getting caught at my window would have been so much better." I shake my head. "Between that and climbing up here in the middle of the night, this must be important."

"Important, yes," he says. "But also . . . personal." Simon

takes my left hand in his and turns it over, pausing to study a number of small cuts. "What happened to your fingers?"

"Handling tiny pieces of glass. Repairing the windows of the Sanctum model was my punishment for what happened today." I don't want to discuss it, though. "What happened to *your* hand?"

Simon frowns at the two oozing scratches from the back of his knuckles to his wrist. "Not sure. Maybe climbing in the window."

"They're like the ones on your neck the other night," I say. "Except there were three."

Simon reaches for his throat, though it's healed. "Juliane did that. Surely you've noticed she's not well, though maybe not in what way."

"She told me of her mother's illness," I admit. "And that she thinks the same thing is happening to her."

"It is."

"How do you know that?"

In my vivid sight, the brown flaw in Simon's eye appears like strands of yarn bunched within a circle of blue ones. "Because I've seen it," he says quietly. "All my life."

"In Mesanus," I breathe.

"Yes." He tilts his head to the side. "You know of it?"

"A little. Mother Agnes said there's a shrine to a Holy One who cures sickness of the mind, and that the people there often open their own homes to care for those who are ill."

"Did she tell you why that's necessary?" The tremble of his chin leaks into his voice. "That many pilgrims are abandoned to the mercy of strangers by their own flesh and blood when their miracle doesn't come?"

I pull his scratched hand into my lap, curling my fingers around his. "Did someone leave you there?" I ask softly.

Simon nods numbly. "My mother. Or rather, she abandoned my father and I refused to. So she just left me there, her only son." His mouth twists up like he's in pain. "I was eight."

"I'm sorry."

"I don't want your pity," says Simon abruptly. "I just want . . . to explain." He keeps his eyes low. "A family took us in, but I couldn't stand the idea of living off charity when there was nothing wrong with me yet."

Yet?

He takes a deep breath. "Mesanus is mostly a fishing village, where people have little need for schooling. Since I was one of the few who could read and write, I found employment recording notes for physicians." Simon smiles ironically. "I was never as good a scribe as Juliane, of course."

I squeeze his hand. "No one is."

Simon's expression fades to blankness again as he continues. "When I was fourteen, I was hired by Altum Ferris, who studied the violently insane. The pay was enough for me to support my father in a small home of our own." To my dismay, he pulls his hand from mine and tucks his forearms under his legs, rocking himself like Juliane does. "I sat through countless hours of people describing the vilest impulses and actions, often involving children." He squeezes his eyes tight as tears glitter in his blond lashes. "The killer we're chasing is nothing compared to what else I've seen, what I've heard. It was hard to believe they were human." He shakes his head as though trying to rid himself of terrible thoughts. "After a while, you can't help wondering if you're capable of the same thing."

"Simon," I say firmly. "You're not insane."

Now he looks at me. "That's just it, Cat. Most of them knew exactly what they were doing, and that it was wrong. They weren't insane, not in a way that separates someone from reality and deserves pity, not like . . ."

"Like Juliane?"

"I was going to say my father, but yes. She's very much like he was in the beginning."

I swallow. "Was he dangerous?"

What I really want to know is, is she?

Simon shakes his head. "He was more of a risk to himself. Once he tried to bore a hole into his head, attempting to let the bad thoughts out." Simon's hand goes to his neck again. "Juliane scratched me when I stopped her from jumping out of her window. She was convinced she could fly. I don't know if that was her illness or the *skonia* in the tea I'd given her."

I shiver. That's why boards had been nailed across her window, though she knew how to pull at least two down. "Juliane told me sometimes the tea makes her worse before making her sleep."

Simon nods. "*Skonia* acts on what's already in the mind, which is why it's also used to get someone to tell the truth—it breaks down the walls around what someone is trying to hide. Unfortunately, many like Juliane build vast, complex misapprehensions around things they observe."

"Like what?"

He sits back as he crosses his arms over his chest, pulling away once more. "She believes Oudin or her father killed her mother, which makes her fear they will do the same to her. That's why she hid herself away for the past few years, trying not to let them know that her mind was suffering the same way. She doesn't conceal it as well as she thinks."

The dark, wretched room she hid in while he was gone. *This is my life without Simon.*

"You understand her from living with your father," I say, and he nods. I reach for his hand again. "It was noble of you not to abandon him."

Simon snorts. "I regretted that noble foolishness for nine and a half of those ten years. I resented him for what he couldn't be, and I hated my mother for letting me stay with him." He grimaces, speaking through gritted teeth. "Do you want to know how he died?"

My stomach flutters. "You said he was sick. Sicker than Juliane."

"He was, but that wasn't what killed him." Simon forces his words out a few at a time. "I got careless. I left the house one night without putting out the lantern. I just needed to get away, a few moments of peace. And in that time he set the house on fire."

"That was an accident," I insist. "You didn't want it to happen."

"Maybe not," he whispers. "But I was relieved when it did. For the first time in my life, I felt free." He chuckles ruefully. "Dirt poor and completely alone, but free."

"That doesn't make you a bad person." I tentatively touch his arm and am relieved when he doesn't recoil. "And you're not alone anymore, Simon."

"But I have to be," he says. "That's what I really came up here to talk to you about."

My throat clenches so tight I can hardly breathe. "All right."

Simon's eyes go unfocused as he returns to the dark thoughts he recalled earlier. "I've never conducted an investigation on my own, and I'm terrified of misreading the evidence or some clue and sentencing another woman to death with my mistake. Altum Ferris has been doing this for much longer."

That must have been who he went to consult. "You shouldn't have to take all of this on yourself," I say. "Perhaps he could come here to help."

"No," whispers Simon. "He can never leave Mesanus."

Suspicion dawns on me. "Does he suffer madness, too?"

"He does now. Most of the time Ferris is lucid and rational. Other times he stares at the walls of his room, not reacting to anything, hardly eating or drinking. All his digging in the most poisonous minds has taken him to places he can never return from. Yet he still does it, saying the more we understand about these killers, the better able we'll be to stop them. He considers his own sanity a price worth paying."

Simon is afraid he's on the same path, but he doesn't have to follow it—or does he? Not only has Simon been ordered to conduct this investigation, the only home he has depends on him obeying.

"When this is over," I say, and my heart clenches at the next thought. "You can leave Collis and go somewhere your uncle can't force you to do this kind of thing ever again. Altum Ferris's fate doesn't have to be yours."

"It may be too late. Do you know what the altum said when I visited him?" The moonlight shines on all his lashes individually as Simon turns his face to the stars. "He told me I understood this killer perfectly. That I was better at this than he was after decades of study. That I should trust my instincts." He shudders. "What kind of person has understanding and instincts like this?"

I don't dare let him know the same thought has occurred to me. "But you hate doing this. Don't you think that says something about you?"

"That's just it, Cat," Simon whispers. "I *don't* hate it. I actually enjoy it."

"You enjoy bringing violence to an end and saving the lives of innocents," I insist. "As anyone should."

"No." Simon shakes his head. "I was thrilled when the killer sent me that note. It meant he considered me worthy of his attention."

"Simon, it meant that you were doing things right! That you understand him!"

"Which means I'm drinking the same poison. It's only a matter of time before it sickens me as it did Altum Ferris. Until I'm drifting in and out of sanity."

I have no answer for that.

"But you . . ." Simon hesitates and swallows. "You've been like an anchor. More than once you—or the thought of you—has kept me from drifting too far."

"Then why do you push me away?"

"Because that's too much to ask of anyone, especially when I have so little to offer," he says bitterly. "I have nothing. I *am* nothing. I was fine with that until I met you and started wanting things I could never have."

"Simon, I can help you," I say. "I *want* to help you."

He shakes his head ruefully. "I was my father's anchor for ten years, Cat. Now I'm Juliane's. It's a prison I accept, but I refuse to sentence anyone else to it, least of all you. It's not a weight you can simply put down when it becomes too much, not without consequences."

"Are you worried I'd abandon you in Mesanus?" I demand.

"No." Simon focuses on his knees. "I know you never would. You're too stubborn and loyal." He finally raises his head to look at me again. "I worry that someday you'll wish you could."

Like he wanted to leave his father.

I pivot around to sit next to him, our backs to the moon. "Do you know what Mother Agnes once told me?" I wait for him to blink before continuing. "She said we all live in cages. It's only the lucky ones among us who get to choose which one."

Simon furrows his brow. "Are you saying I've chosen my own cage?"

"You said that yourself."

"That doesn't mean you should be caged with me."

"No." I grasp his shirt and pull him closer. "But it does mean it's my choice."

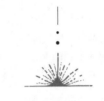

CHAPTER 34

I'm not prepared for how it feels to kiss Simon in the moonlight.

The whole time we talked, I'd focused on his voice and his face, occasionally distracted by the scent of his clothes or skin or the silver light on his hair and eyelashes as he moved. Whenever I'd touched him, the shock of that sense was quickly lost in the conversation. On some level, I believed I'd gotten used to all of it.

That assumption shatters the instant our lips touch. Small as it is, the contact blossoms in my mind like the reddest rose. His mouth yields in surprise, then immediately seeks to meet mine, filling the gaps between us with soft yearning.

Until Simon eases away.

He doesn't go far, though, holding himself near enough that I can feel his breath curling through the air with warm tendrils. "And what if I drag you Beyond the Moon and to the Gates of Hell itself?"

"Then we'll find our way back." Painful as it is to resist, I know I can't kiss him again. If this is going to continue—and in this moment I would give up all my magick to make it do so—it has to be his choice. "Simon, for once in your life, consider that you might be worth saving."

One hand comes up to my cheek, and I feel his pulse—quick and erratic—through his fingertips and then his palm. "Is that what you believe?"

"I do." I skim my own fingers up Simon's arm to the tendons at his wrist and settle them between the ridges of his knuckles. "But it only matters if you believe it, too."

He shivers and tenses, bringing me a fraction of an inch closer. "I think I'd believe the Sun was the moon if you said so." Simon leans in, his nose grazing mine. "Thank the Light you're too honest to take advantage of my trust."

I think he was trying to make me smile, but his words slice through me so deeply that I flinch right as he moves to close the gap between us again.

Simon freezes. "I thought you wanted . . . I'm sorry—"

My hand on his shirt keeps him from moving away again. "No," I say, shoving my guilt aside and following the heat of his breath back to his lips. "It's exactly right."

And it is.

It's the soft molding of his mouth to mine, the sharp tickle of short whiskers on my upper lip. It's Simon's other arm slipping around my waist to pull me against his chest until his heartbeat echoes through me like a Sanctum bell. It's his shuddering inhalation between kisses that never quite end as the next begins.

It's warmth and color and light flowing through my veins to every inch of me, inside and out.

I don't realize I've been holding my breath until a different dizziness forces me to stop. Gasping, I open my eyes to see the half-moon staring at me through the narrow stone columns, so bright I immediately squint.

"Is something wrong?" Simon asks, and I can tell he desperately doesn't want it to be him.

"The moon," I mumble without thinking, the fresh air in my lungs slowly unfogging my mind.

Simon gently pulls me into the shadows cast by the railing, cutting off the cascade of sensations. He lowers me down to the stone beneath us, which is warm from the heat of his body, and holds himself just out of reach. "Better?"

Strangely, it is. Now there's nothing to distract me from the places we press against each other or the wonder and concern in his eyes as he looks down on me. Out of moonlight, the harsh lines of his face are reduced from those like a stained glass window portrait to a painting so achingly lovely I want to touch it. I raise my hand to his cheek and trace the softened contours with my fingertips, making him blink so slowly I think he's closed his eyes. When he reopens them, I smile.

"It's perfect," I whisper, and pull him back down to me.

———— • ✳ • ————

An hour. A week. A month.

I have no idea how long we stay up there. The night is cold enough to see the mist of our breath, and the stone floor hard and unyielding, yet I feel nothing but warmth and softness. My body fits perfectly against Simon's as his lips move as gently as feathers up my jawline to my ears and down my neck and back to my mouth.

"The first time I saw you," he whispers. "*Really* saw you, was the day I came to the workshop to apologize. I think I stared at you for ten minutes."

"Is that so?"

He nudges the hollow at the base of my throat with his nose.

"You were so lovely, so peaceful, so at one with what you were doing I could have watched you all day." Simon shakes his head, making his curls brush across my nose. They smell of cedar from the headboard of his bed, a thought that would warm my cheeks if I wasn't already flushed. "I envied what you had—a skill and a place in life. A purpose."

Simon raises up to look at me again. "That was the first time I yearned for something more than what I'd settled for. I wanted to be a part of the world you lived in."

That world is much more complicated than he realizes, but there's no need to explain that right now, and I'm not certain I could if I wanted to.

Though . . .

Simon leans down to kiss my ear, and I turn my head to the silver light spilled across the stone next to me, lengthened by the lowering moon. Soon it will be gone. This could be my last chance to feel its effects like this for a while. I take my hand off Simon's shoulder and stretch it out to the side.

"Help me," Simon pleads. "I can't . . ."

I pull my hand back so I can focus on him. "Can't what?"

He pushes up on his elbow to look down on me. "What did you say?"

"I asked what *you* said." I frown when Simon only looks puzzled. "You said 'help me,' and then 'I can't,' but you never finished."

Simon shakes his head. "I didn't say any of that." He sits up higher and peers at the tower door. "Did you hear someone else?"

When the moonlight strikes the top of his hair, I realize what must have happened. Throwing my left arm out, I reach for the last traces of light on the floor. As soon as the faint voice tickles my mind, I close my eyes to concentrate.

"Cat?" asks Simon.

"Shhh!" I strain to hear more, though what muscles and parts I'm using are a mystery.

Help me. I can't . . .

It's a woman, her physical pain clamping against my own skull like a vice. How am I supposed to know who she is, or where? How can I find her in a city so—

Help Mother . . . please . . . I can't . . . It hurts . . .

My eyes fly open. I know this voice better than any in the world.

It's Marguerite.

CHAPTER 35

Simon can't keep up with me.

"*Cat!*" he shouts as I reach the bottom of the spiral stairs. "Where are you going?"

I don't answer, just run for the steps and down again, feeling my way blindly along the wall. At the first landing I run smack into the religious brother on his way to the bell tower to ring midnight prayers. His lantern crashes to the ground and extinguishes, a metallic clatter ricocheting off bare marble floors. I scramble back to my feet, realizing if he's up, then the side door is unlocked and that will be faster than squeezing through the window and climbing down.

Simon is right behind me as I race along the gallery level. The elderly brother follows, shouting between wheezes and quickly falling behind. Simon's legs are longer than mine, and halfway along the nave he manages to grab my arm. "What is it? What's happened?"

"He's going after her!" I scream, throwing him off. "He's going to kill Marguerite and Mother Agnes!"

"What? How could you know that?"

I'm already a dozen steps away.

This time when Simon catches up, he keeps pace rather than try to stop me. "How do you know?" he gasps. "What did you hear?"

There's no way I can tell him, even if I had the breath to try. Down another set of stairs and out the door into the square—and the moonlight. I stop and close my eyes to listen, though I only expect the same whisper as before.

There is nothing.

I reopen my eyes. The moon is sinking below the rooftops. Simon starts to ask questions again, but I dash for the road heading south, toward the abbey. It's not a direct route, though it's the fastest, and every turn on dark streets feels like an obstacle. By the time the corner of the high wall comes into view, I think my lungs will burst, but I don't stop until I reach my climbing spot.

Simon finally intervenes, pulling me down before I get more than a few feet off the ground. "What in the Light of Day are you doing, Cat?" he demands.

I struggle against him for a few seconds before it hits me. If I heard Marguerite's thoughts, it means she's already dead. I'm too late. I collapse against Simon, painfully aware how only a few minutes ago I was in his arms and everything was perfect—and I didn't know my best friend was dying. "Marguerite's dead!" I sob into his chest. "And Mother Agnes!"

"Who?" Simon asks, baffled. "That sister you were talking to today? You think the killer went after her?"

I look up at him. "I know he did. Please, Simon. You have to trust me."

His answer is so quiet his lips don't even move. "There's no one I trust more."

My hand is on Simon's wrist, and I step back and pull him with me to the wall. "This is the fastest way inside."

When I release him and reach for the finger-size divots in the mortar between stones, I notice a crimson smear on my palm. Blood? Simon steps up behind me, his arm over mine, and I realize it came from the scratches on the back of his hand. I hoist myself up to the top of the wall, then move aside to make room for Simon, wiping my hand on my breeches as he climbs. Then I show him how to hop onto the roof of the shed and down to the ground, and we run through the garden and around the corner of the kitchen.

Why haven't the bells sounded for prayers yet? The faint light of a lantern glows from the chapel tower where a sister waits for the Sanctum to start the call to wake everyone. I must have delayed it when I ran into the bell ringer up there.

Paved paths radiate from the fountain in the center of the abbey. I creep around the curved stone as the water laps gently against the edge. No direct moonlight shines on the prioress's flower garden. The covered walkway leading to Mother Agnes's private quarters and those of her assistant—Marguerite—casts the building next to it in complete shadow. Beyond it, the door to the sitting room lies open, which would've told me something was wrong even if I didn't feel it to the marrow of my bones.

Simon puts a gentle hand on my back. *I'm here*, I can almost hear him say.

"That door shouldn't be open," I whisper.

"Which one?"

I don't know if he can't see it or if he just doesn't know where to look. Rising from my crouch, I sprint down the slate path and across the corner, where hundreds of feet have already worn away the grass in the same shortcut. I stop in the doorway, overwhelmed by the smell of blood even without magick. My hand rises to cover my mouth and nose, to stifle both the scent and the sob which fill my chest.

The shutters are closed, making it pitch-black inside. Bending over to feel my way to the furniture, it's only a few shuffling steps before I trip on a soft lump too large to be Marguerite. I drop to my knees, fumbling over the body until my fingers plunge into something warm and wet.

"I always knew this day would come," Mother Agnes says sadly.

"What?" I cry, unable to believe what I'm hearing. "Mother, it's me, Catrin! Are you all right? Where are you hurt?"

I always knew this day would come, her voice says again, and this time I realize it's inside my head.

And from what I'm feeling, she's definitely dead.

Still, I press my fingers to her neck, feeling for a pulse, then lower my bloody hand to the center of her chest where I find a braid of hair. It can only be Emeline's.

Simon's silhouette hovers in the doorway, a black shape against an only slightly lighter background. "Where are you, Cat? Did you find anyone?"

"It's Mother Agnes," I moan. "She's dead."

"What about the killer?" he asks. "Where did he go?"

I reach for the cord tied around Mother's waist and immediately find her ring of keys. "The gate is still locked! He might be in the abbey!"

The shadow that is Simon vanishes.

Suddenly I'm alone in the darkness. What if the killer hasn't left this room?

Terrifying as that thought is, a second quickly makes me forget it: Where is Marguerite?

I sit up on my knees, looking around, though I can see nothing. "Marga?" I use her childhood nickname without thinking. "Marga, where are you?"

I knew I knew I knew this day would come, repeats Mother

Agnes. Her blood won't stop talking to me; I wipe my hands clean on her habit until it's barely a whisper.

"Marga, please answer me!" I crawl around the room, knowing she can't hear me but unable to stop calling her name. "Marga, it's me, Cat! Please! Marga!"

The bell in the chapel rings out, not with the gentle call to prayer, but in a loud, urgent rhythm of alarm. Simon probably scared the life out of the sister up there.

I still can't find Marguerite. What good is being able to see and hear so much better in moonlight when the moon is gone?

Understanding hits me like lightning. I heard Marguerite from the Sanctum because she was in moonlight. She's outside.

I jump to my feet and run for the door, tripping on the leg of a chair and lurching outside. The ringing bell echoes off walls, making it sound like a second has joined it. Sisters are stirring. Many were probably already awake out of habit. Moonlight streams almost horizontally through trees outside of reach but after the darkness of the sitting room, it's bright enough to see by.

Not twenty feet away is a shapeless pile of wool with two bare feet sticking out of it, reminding me sickeningly of the night I found Perrete. She's lying on her side, where she either crawled or was dragged from the covered walkway. I scream and throw myself at Marguerite's body and roll her onto her back.

She still has her eyes, but the left side of her head is bloody and misshapen. What remains of her hair sticks to the red and black mess at odd angles. As I cradle her limp form, Marguerite's lips move almost like she's speaking.

I know what will happen if I touch her blood, that it will only be my friend's last, terrified thought I hear, but I can't fight the need to hear her voice while I still can. My fingers tremble as I place a hand on the side of her face, then slide them gently back into the wet, matted hair.

Cat.

She thought of me?

Cat. Help me. Help Mother.

She heard me outside? Was she still alive as I ran past her, focused on the door?

"Marga," I sob. "I'm sorry. I didn't know what was happening until it was too late."

Where are you? Everything is so dark.

It's more than I've ever gotten from anyone else, but somehow it's worse. I press my forehead to hers and let the tears fall on her face. "I'm sorry, I'm so sorry! I love you, Marga."

I love you, too, Cat.

I flinch away. That was too much like an answer.

"Marga?" I whisper. "Can you hear me?"

Yes, but I can't see, and my head hurts. Her voice fades a little. *I'm sleepy . . . so sleepy.*

Slowly, like I'm in a dream, I pull my bloody hand down to her neck. A weak, unsteady pulse pushes against my fingertips.

Grace of Day, she's still alive.

CHAPTER 36

I'm screaming for someone to help Marguerite, and Remi appears at my side. I don't question why he's there, just beg him to find a physician. When he returns shortly, a middle-aged woman in plain black clothes gently nudges me aside and begins examining my friend. As she bends over, a silver chain slips out of her shirt and dangles an iridescent, polished stone from her throat.

As soon as I'm not touching Marga, I lose our connection, but her last response to my imploring her to stay awake echoes in my mind. *I'm trying, Cat. I'm trying.*

I know she can still hear me, though. "Marga, someone's here to help you," I call as Remi pulls me farther out of the woman's way. "And I'm right here, too. Just stay awake, please."

The physician looks up at me, her kohl-lined eyes narrowed. Threads of gray follow the curls in her dark hair from her temples to where it's bound at the nape of her neck. "Were you talking to her?" she asks sharply. "Did she respond at all?"

"Catrin!" The architect swoops down next to me, robes flying. "What are you doing here? What happened?" He searches for the source of the blood that's all over my hand.

"None of it's mine," I tell him. He starts to wipe it off with his sleeve, but I make a fist, unwilling to let go of Marguerite's voice. *I'm trying, Cat.*

Magister Thomas stops dabbing at me and looks around, taking in the Selenae woman tending Marguerite and the wailing Sisters of Light. The sitting room is now lit by candles and lanterns, making the shape on the floor visible. "Is that—?"

"Mother Agnes," I affirm, my voice cracking.

Remi squats down in front of me. "Cat, where did the venatre go?"

"Simon?" I haven't seen him since he left to raise the alarm. "He went to the chapel to ring the bell."

Remi stands. "I'm going to find him. Stay here. Both of you."

As if I would leave Marguerite. The architect pulls me against his shoulder as we watch the physician. She keeps one hand on Marguerite's neck while gently probing the wound on the side of her head with the other, murmuring.

"Yes, she's still here." The woman speaks to Marguerite as though she's conscious. "Can you remember anything?" She pauses. "That's all right."

"Can you hear her, too?" I blurt out.

The physician glances up at me. "Could you?" Her silver gaze moves to Magister Thomas. "You never told us that."

"I have no idea what you're talking about," he replies.

Frowning, the woman goes back to Marguerite. "I don't know, my dear, but I'll do my best." Then she sighs. "The old woman? She is Beyond the Sun. I'm sorry."

Marguerite was asking about Mother Agnes. The physician looks up again. "I need to move her to a place where I can better care for her."

Several sisters move forward. "We'll take her to the sickroom."

"No," says the woman. "She'll need constant watch and likely surgical draining to relieve pressure on her brain. I can do much more for her in the Quarter."

The sisters gasp in unison. "That's impossible," one hisses. "We cannot allow it."

"Then she will almost certainly die."

"So be it," declares Sister Berta. I remember her from years ago, and I disliked her then. "If it is the Will of the Sun."

I jump to my feet. "Don't you dare forbid it!" I shout at her. "Mother Agnes would have allowed it!"

Berta crosses her arms. "We cannot afford the price they will demand."

"Then I will pay it," says Magister Thomas, rising to stand beside me.

While Berta protests weakly, several more Selenae arrive, carrying a rigid cot. The physician instructs them how to lift Marguerite, keeping contact with the bloody side of her head throughout, even as they walk away, though she pauses to address me. "She wants you to know it will be all right, and she loves you." The woman's eyes shift to the architect. "And we will have a great deal to discuss later, Sun-lover."

"What is she talking about?" I ask Magister Thomas as soon as they're gone.

In response, he hugs me. "Oh, Cat, I don't know where to begin, and I don't understand half of it."

Remi has returned with Simon, who's carrying a lantern he probably got from the sister in the bell tower. "I found him in the orchard."

Simon nods, oblivious to Remi's scowl. "I searched the perimeter of the abbey," he says. "There were fresh, muddy marks on the orchard wall, like someone climbed out there."

Magister Thomas blinks. "Where did you come from, Remone?"

Remi folds his arms and glares at Simon. "I followed Cat and the good venatre here. They climbed the wall to get in, but I went around to the gate like a normal person. When Cat started screaming, I broke it down to get inside."

"Why were you out tonight?" I demand, though I know.

He only raises an eyebrow. "Why were you?"

Simon holds his lantern over the blood-soaked grass. "Was there a body here?"

"Sister Marguerite," I say. "But she was still alive."

"Really?" Simon's eyes widen. "Did she say anything?"

My hand clenches reflexively, and her blood silently whispers, *I'm trying.* I shake my head. "She was unconscious. They took her away."

"I'll want to speak to her if she wakes." Simon looks past us to the sitting room. "And the prioress is in there? Dead?"

I choke. "Yes."

He turns kind eyes on me. "You don't have to accompany me if you don't feel you can."

Despite his offer, I follow him to the door, as do Remi and Magister Thomas.

Simon stops just inside to take in the room. Someone covered Mother Agnes with a sheet, which I know frustrates him as it likely means the body isn't lying as the killer left it. "By the authority granted me as Venatre of Collis," he says, his voice carrying a gravity I've never heard before, "I order everyone to leave now so I may investigate this crime."

The sisters are nothing if not obedient, and they file past him silently, leaving several candles behind. Magister Thomas squeezes my hand and eases away. "I'll go check on Sister Marguerite."

I join Simon inside, but Remi remains in the doorway, arms crossed, watching me with an unreadable expression.

Simon rubs his face, sounding again like the man I'm used to.

"I'm sorry about this, Cat. I know she meant a lot to you." He exhales heavily. "You knew her and the abbey well, what do you think happened? How do you think he got in?"

I look around the room. The only disturbed furniture is the chair I tripped on. Mother Agnes's feet are not covered by the sheet, allowing me to see her sandals. She also had her keys on her belt under her mantle, like she expected to use them. *I always knew this day would come.* "She was fully dressed," I say. "And not far from the door. I think—I think she let the killer in herself."

"Are you saying she knew him?" Remi asks.

"She was blind," I snap. "She could easily have been fooled, especially if she was expecting someone."

I pray Marguerite is the only other person who knew the prioress anticipated a possible visit from Magister Thomas.

Simon lifts the sheet to look at the body. "Same type of weapon," he says softly to himself. "But she still has her eyes and hair." He raises the cover higher. "Did anyone find—ah." Simon reaches under and pulls out the braid which had fallen to the side. In the light it's the dyed orange shade of Emeline's hair. "I guess this settles it, though I'm not sure why he didn't do anything else."

"M-maybe Sister Marguerite surprised him," I stammer. "She was outside like she was crawling away. He took her hair."

Simon's eyes dart to Remi and back. "Was anything else done to her?" he asks in a low voice.

"No, no." I shake my head. "She was just hit in the side of the head." It could have been the complete darkness of the room and the surprise of Marguerite's arrival that changed his actions. "Why do you think he didn't . . ." I choke.

"I don't know yet," says Simon. He lowers the cover and stands, absentmindedly scratching the dried scab on the back of his hand. "This could be another murderer trying to copy what ours has been doing. Maybe word of the hair got out."

"You said he'd change the type of victims he would go after," I say.

He nods. "Yes, and given the similar weapon used, I'm almost certain this is his work. I just wish I knew what he was using."

"Perhaps it was that."

Both of us turn to look at Remi, who nods in the direction of Mother Agnes's desk.

On top of the piles of papers and accounting books lies a familiar object. It's covered in blood and gore—even the handle—but I can still see the glint of gold.

Gifted Sun and Hell Beyond, not that.

Simon hands me the braid as he walks eagerly to the desk. "Cat, make a mental note of how this lies," he says, studying the hammer from several angles.

I suspect I'll be able to remember it as well as Juliane would.

He nudges it. "Even heavier than I thought," he mutters. Carefully he lifts it to carry into better light. "It looks like it's plated in . . . gold?" Simon rotates it to study every angle. "I've never seen anything like this, but the dimensions are right. This could've been used in all the murders, maybe even on Beatrez."

Remi leans against the doorframe, his green eyes locked on me. I look back at him, pleading for him to do or say something that will stop this nightmare, but his lips move silently in a phrase the architect has uttered countless times. *You harvest what you plant.*

What's about to happen is my own doing.

"There's something engraved on this side." Simon raises it to show me, sounding almost excited. "Observe all this, Cat. Juliane isn't here so our combined recollection will have to do.

And you"—he nods to Remi—"are also witness to the condition of this hammer."

I can't nod, but Remi does—stiffly, just once—and Simon moves to the pitcher of water on a small table against the wall. There's just enough in it for him to pour over the golden head. Then he sets the ewer down and wipes the blood away with his sleeve. All of it takes much longer than it should, like time itself has slowed.

Simon tilts the hammer into the candlelight, and I close my eyes, not wanting to see his face. "Presented to . . . ," he begins, then stops.

Presented to Magister Thomas of Iscano, the 6th Master Architect of the Holy Sanctum of Collis. May his work be Blessed by the Hallowed Sun.

Simon doesn't read any of it out loud, however. And in the unbroken silence, my heart shatters in my chest.

CHAPTER 37

I press my lips together and lower my head, eyes still firmly shut.

"Do either of you recognize this hammer?" Simon finally asks.

My jaw is clenched too tightly to answer.

"Yes, Venatre," says Remi, using the title with respect for the first time. "We know it."

A silence of at least a dozen heartbeats follows. "Do you have any idea how it got here?"

"It's been missing," Remi answers. "It was stolen from the architect."

"*When?*" Simon demands. "Under what circumstances?"

Tears flood my eyes as I look up at Remi. *Please*, I beg him wordlessly. *Don't say it. Don't tell him.*

"I wasn't there that night." Remi walks into the room, toward me. "You'll have to ask someone who was."

He may think he's giving me the chance to redeem myself, but it feels like betrayal.

Simon focuses on me. "Catrin?"

Slowly, I turn to face him. The pain in his eyes thrusts a dagger into my already fractured heart. Remi steps up beside me and puts a hand on the small of my back. "I wasn't there either," I rasp.

It's the truth, even if it feels like a lie. Simon isn't fooled.

"Cat," he says quietly. "What aren't you telling me?"

I press my lips together, unwilling to destroy the two most important people left in the world to me.

Remi finally breaks the silence. "Perrete stole it," he says. My only consolation is the torture in his own voice. "She visited Magister Thomas the night she died, and they quarreled. She used the hammer to smash the model of the Sanctum. Then she left, taking it with her." Remi stops to take a breath before finishing. "That's what I was told."

Simon never takes his eyes off me. "I see." The hammer in his hands drips bloody water onto the floor that immediately slips into a crack between the stones. "Did you know this, Cat?"

I nod, wanting to hate Remi, but also grateful he was strong enough to tell the truth when I couldn't.

"From the beginning?" Simon demands. "Since Perrete?"

"Yes," I force out.

"You knew I was looking for something like this, and . . . you didn't tell me about it?"

I'm so afraid he'll interrupt me that my words come in a rush. "Only because it would've led you in the wrong direction. It wasn't Magister Thomas who killed her."

"You didn't trust me to have determined that for myself?" Simon lowers the hammer and stalks toward me. "You didn't think I would've had the sense to put him under a quiet watch so that when the next murder happened, he could immediately have been eliminated from suspicion?"

As he advances, Remi moves behind me to add support—or keep me from running out the door. Simon stops barely a foot away and glowers down on me. "Don't you understand that withholding information is the same as lying?"

The tears I've been desperately holding back stream down my cheeks. "Simon, I'm sorry. I didn't know you. I didn't know if I could trust you."

He backs away, disgust twisting his mouth. "Save your apologies for the dead."

"This is the last thing Cat wanted and you know it," says Remi. "Don't be so hard on her."

Simon raises an eyebrow. "I recommend not saying another word, Remone la Fontaine. Both of you are lucky you're not headed to the gaol right now."

He turns and marches to the door, where several sisters have moved closer to watch. One already holds a stack of linen towels. Simon asks her for one and wraps it around the bloody hammer. Then he nods his thanks and sympathy to her. "I'm very sorry. For everything."

He strides away, carrying the hammer within its bundling under one arm. Remi gently prods me to follow, but I can't leave without saying goodbye to Mother Agnes. I drop to my knees and put my arms around her as best I can. "I'm sorry, Mother," I tell her, as though she can hear me. "For all the times I disappointed you or made you worry."

Tears drop like rain onto the sheet as I pull one hand out from under it and hold it against my cheek. Her skin is already cold as I kiss her fingers. "I know you loved me. I just hope you know I loved you, too."

Remi gently pulls the prioress's hand away and lays it on her chest. "We need to go, Cat. Now."

He helps me to my feet and half-carries me out the door, past the sisters and down the passage to the gate. My mind is numb to everything around me as we step outside, facing an arc of people attracted by the commotion. A few Selenae watch from one of the entrances to the Quarter, but none steps beyond the moonflower vines. Comte de Montcuir and Lambert are already here, speaking to Magister Thomas. The architect sees us and rushes to my side and puts an arm around me.

"Marguerite woke for a few seconds but is unconscious again," he whispers in my ear. "They'll tell us if anything changes, and I'll bring you back to see her tomorrow afternoon." He strokes my wet cheek. "It will be all right."

No. No, it won't. Simon is speaking in a low voice with his uncle, and I strain to hear his words.

". . . certain this murder is connected to those I'm investigating," he says.

The provost tugs on his mustache. "I'm getting the impression that you aren't up to the task of finding this man."

Simon's free hand closes into a fist, but he maintains his composure. "If I hadn't been forbidden from continuing the inquiry for almost two weeks, I assure you I would be much closer to stopping him."

That doesn't please the comte, but he waves his hand carelessly. "Very well, but my son will continue to assist you and keep me fully informed on your progress." He raises his bushy eyebrows and gestures for Lambert to come forward. "I want no further mistakes."

Lambert steps up, looking uncomfortable. "I will obey your order, sir."

I know what's coming next. I grab the magister's robes. "We need to leave, now," I whisper, but he shakes his head, as engrossed in what's happening as everyone else.

"Do you have any persons of suspicion, Venatre?" the comte asks patronizingly.

"Magister, please," I hiss. "We need to go."

"I do, Your Grace." Simon rotates to face us, his expression as flat and emotionless as the first time I saw him. The vulnerable young man who barely an hour ago whispered how much he needed me to stay sane has vanished; only the venatre with terrible responsibility remains. "Magister Thomas of Iscano, can you account for your location on this night and name witnesses?" he asks.

The people murmuring around us fall silent. *Say something,* I beg the architect with my eyes. *Tell him where you were and who you were with. Prove your innocence.*

But the architect's eyes are not on the venatre. I follow his gaze to a figure beyond Simon, standing just inside the shelter of a narrow street framed by purple and white moonflowers. Even outside the glow of torches, lanterns, and candles, Gregor's scarred face is unmistakable.

Magister Thomas then turns to look at me, his gray eyes full of resolve as he slowly shakes his head. "No, Venatre. I cannot."

The crowd bursts into exclamations of shock, and I can barely hear the comte ordering his arrest. Magister Thomas pushes me into Remi's arms—"Take care of her," he says, "of your mother, of the Sanctum"—and I'm screaming and clawing at the guards as Remi hauls me back. The architect is marched away, men around him using pikes to restrain the crowd that shouts and spits at him.

When at last almost everyone has left, either following to the prison or heading back to their homes, I'm left facing Simon across the street. Remi holds me upright, blessedly not saying anything.

"Simon," I plead hoarsely. "It's not him. You have to believe me."

He shakes his head, refusing to answer. "You should take her home," he tells Remi. "And keep her there for a while. The next few days will not be pleasant."

Then he turns and walks away, the instrument of my betrayal under his arm, leaving me with the knowledge that I've only succeeded in ushering in everything I'd tried to prevent.

CHAPTER 38

I don't know whether Remi gets any sleep that night, but I don't. At first I thought I'd be able to cry myself into at least a restless doze. Failing that, I stare at the ceiling, seeing the faces of Simon and Magister Thomas in the shadows over my bed. One is cold and accusing, the other calm and accepting of his fate. But when I close my eyes all I can envision are Marguerite's and Mother Agnes's terror.

Scattered on the floor of my room are four small stones—ones that Simon must have thrown in the window trying to get my attention last night after I was gone. Now they're the only evidence I have that Simon cared for me. As the sky outside fades from black to violet to gray, Mistress la Fontaine rises from her creaking bed and ambles downstairs to start breakfast. Remi stirs above me, preparing for what will have to be a full day of work at the Sanctum.

In the magister's absence, he's in charge.

No doubt he'll spend the day reveling in the role he's always coveted, everyone answering to him, needing his approval. Rather than go straight downstairs, Remi stops outside my room.

"Cat," he says in a raspy voice, pushing the door open several inches. "I'll need your help today."

I roll over and turn my back on him. "I'm sure you'll do fine on your own."

He exhales in exasperation. "I didn't want this to happen. You know that."

Throwing the covers aside, I swing around to sit up facing him. "Then why did you betray the magister?"

"*Me?*" Remi yells. "You want to blame this on *me?*"

"What you told the venatre got him arrested, so yes, I blame you."

He opens the door wider but still won't set foot in my room. Doing so was the one thing Magister Thomas would have sent him packing for, no questions or excuses. "Of course," he says sourly. "It couldn't be your fault for not telling the venatre the truth in the first place. Nor could it be the magister's, who refuses to explain where he was last night."

I know he must have been in the Selenae Quarter. Why wouldn't he just say so? And why did Gregor—the man Magister Thomas considers a friend—only watch as he was marched away like a criminal?

Remi lowers his voice to almost a whisper. "Have you ever considered it might be him?"

"No. Never." If Remi knew the details of what was done to Perrete and the others, he would side with me. "Simon thinks the killer has a troubled and violent past, that he wants revenge on a woman other than the ones he's slaughtering because it's someone he can't get to. Does *that* sound like Magister Thomas?"

"Actually it does, Cat."

I blink at him. "He's hardly ever raised his voice to either of us, not even yesterday or with you goading him the way you have in the past two weeks."

Remi slouches against the doorframe and looks me over, eyes softening a little. "Do you want to go down to the kitchen and discuss this over breakfast?"

I cross my arms. "I'm not feeling well."

He sighs. "I won't make you work today, but a cup of tea might make you feel better."

"You can explain what you're talking about from right there."

"Fine." Remi runs a hand through his tangled black hair, making it stand on end. "Did you ever wonder why he left Brinsulli? Why he never returns to visit his family?"

Though I've traveled across Gallia and Doitchlend with the architect as he consulted with other masters during winter months, the island nation across the channel is a mystery to me. All I know of it and his hometown of Iscano comes from a map of Mother Agnes's. "He was hired here," I answer feebly. "He fell in love with his work."

Remi snorts. "How right you are." He raises his eyes to the ceiling. "Magister Thomas fled Brinsulli before he could be arrested for beating his own master half to death. It seems they had a disagreement on the construction of the Grand Sanctum in Londunium." He looks back down at me, brows arched. "Sound familiar?"

"Not really, considering he hasn't thrashed you when you've deserved it."

Has Remi been *trying* to get the architect to lose his temper?

He ignores my jab. "Did you know he was married?"

My mouth drops open. I'd always thought of the magister as wed to the Sanctum.

"You were too young to remember, and trapped in that convent," says Remi. "I can barely recall it. But she came with him from Brinsulli, and one day she disappeared."

I stare at him. "Are you saying she died?"

"Cat, I'm saying nobody knows what happened to her. She just vanished." He shifts against the wood. "The magister claimed she went back to be with her family. Maybe she did. But the fact is no one ever saw her again."

My heart pounds so loudly in my ears I can hear nothing else. "No." I reject the possibility outright. "I refuse to believe it's him."

Remi sighs. "I'm not going to argue with you because I honestly don't know. What matters now is that Magister Thomas asked me to carry on at the Sanctum and to care for you and my mother."

I jump down from the bed. "When did he say that?"

"Last night, while you were too wrapped up in your own agony and guilt to notice." Remi stands straight. "I never understood why, but you've always trusted Simon to find this killer, so trust him now. And if you want to honor the faith the magister has in me, then you'll do your job." He turns away from the door. "It's all I can do."

His footsteps move down the passage to the stairs, and I stand in the middle of my room, thinking.

It pains me to admit it, but Remi is right. I'm no good to the architect if I neglect what was most important to him. Yet I can't live with myself if I don't do everything in my power to save him. I look out the window. Only a handful of stars are still visible with the approaching dawn. The moon rises and sets later every day as it grows in fullness, giving me more hours and stronger magick.

I'll go back to work like Remi asked. I'll spend my days answering to him as I answered to Magister Thomas. The three of us were always a team, and now Remi is the leader.

My days belong to Remi and the Sanctum.

But the nights belong to me.

CHAPTER 39

Before I go to the Sanctum, there's something I must do. I splash cold water on my face and step into my working skirt. Remi won't need me for climbing today. I've finished all the inspections and signed off on the supports for building the ceiling, though that work was delayed by Magister Thomas.

I lace my boots quickly, then let myself out the front door without bothering to eat whatever it smells like Mistress la Fontaine burned. A light rain has begun to fall, the sky indicating it will last for several hours at least. The streets are nearly deserted at this early hour, and I'm halfway to the Montcuir home before I see another soul.

Simon's third-story shutters face the street, open enough to see shadows moving within. I doubt he ever went to bed.

The other windows of the house are dark, indicating no one else is up. I lean against the front of the house, cursing myself for not having thought this through. I'll have to return at a more reasonable hour.

"Miss Catrin?"

I whirl around, coming face-to-face with Lambert Montcuir.

He ducks his head in apology. "I'm sorry to startle you. Are you looking for something?"

His kindness gives me courage. "I was hoping I could talk to Simon," I admit. "I need to tell him I'm sorry, among other things."

Lambert frowns. "I'm not certain that's a good idea. He's . . . not in a forgiving mood."

"I know," I say. "But I have to try. Even if he won't listen, I have something important to give him."

He glances up and down, as though trying to see what I've brought, before tilting his head toward the house. "Then please allow me to facilitate that."

To my surprise, the front door is unlocked. In explanation, Lambert holds up several sheets of paper covered in writing. "I was only gone for a few minutes. Simon sent me to the Palace of Justice to fetch these."

I enter first at Lambert's polite gesture. Once he bolts the door, he indicates he'll follow me up the stairs. I'm a little self-conscious about putting my backside at his eye level but relieved it's not Oudin behind me.

My hands are trembling with anxiety by the time we reach the third floor. Lambert takes the lead and enters the room after a quick knock, but I hesitate just outside. Though I know Simon has a temper, and I've seen signs he's capable of violence, I've never been afraid of him until this moment.

"I found what you asked for, Venatre," Lambert says. "And I've brought someone who needs to speak with you."

He steps aside, sweeping his arm out in presentation. His support gives me enough resolve to move forward into the room. Lambert offers me a small, sympathetic smile before turning to the table and setting down the pages he brought.

The entire wall around the city maps is covered with sketches now that drawings of Mother Agnes and her sitting room have been added. On the table lies the architect's hammer, dried blood flaking off in places. I can see the engraved words from where I stand. Oudin is here, too, and he pivots from where he stands next to the gruesome wall papering.

Simon looks like he's aged ten years in a few hours. Pale skin stretches across angular cheekbones, emphasizing the purple rings under his eyes. Uneven splotches of color darken his face as he gapes at me. "What are you doing here, Cat?"

I pull Madame Emeline's braid of hair from the pocket of my skirt. "When I got home, I realized I still had this." I set it on the table and step back, twisting my hands. "But mostly I wanted to . . ." My voice fails. *Apologize* sounds pathetic, so I finish with, "explain some things."

After a long moment, Oudin crosses between us and grabs Lambert by the upper arm, urging him toward the door. As he passes, I catch a whiff of alcohol.

"Let's let them sort this without an audience, Brother," he says. Then, because he's Oudin and he's disgusting, he leers at Simon. "After all, we'll be able to hear from my room below if things get really interesting."

Lambert yanks away, reminding me of the night Perrete died, when their roles were reversed, but Simon sighs and nods. "That's enough for now, Cousin, get some rest. Thank you for your help."

With obvious reluctance, Lambert follows his brother. I don't speak until the noise of them going down the stairs fades. "Have you drawn any conclusions about what happened?"

Simon's gaze bores a hole right through me. "That is something you no longer have the right to know."

"Has my assistance been replaced by Lambert's?" He was present before, but more often as an enforcer of Simon's orders, not an investigator. "And Oudin's?"

"Again, not your concern."

"Where is Juliane?" I push out. "That I ask as a friend." *Friend* might be assuming too much, but I care about her.

Simon sighs before answering. "Not likely to wake for a few hours. She's been having more and more problems. I may have to forgo her help as well as yours."

I doubt learning what I'd withheld will do her mental state any good, either. "Please, Simon . . . ," I begin, raising my hands in appeal. "You have to understand."

"I don't want to hear it, Cat," he says coldly. "You lied to me. You lied and Nichole and Emeline and Ysabel and Mother Agnes and Sister Marguerite paid the price."

"That's not true," I insist. "Magister Thomas isn't the killer. The other attacks would have happened even if you'd locked him away after Perrete's murder."

Simon appears to choose his next words carefully, though the tension in his neck and jaw never eases. "I believe you genuinely think he's innocent, but I haven't had a chance to properly research the magister's past or interview him." He nods at the stack of pages brought by Lambert. "Though apparently my uncle had a file on him." Simon raises his eyebrows. "You wouldn't happen to know what in the architect's past could merit six pages in the provost's records, would you?"

My stomach rolls over as I remember what Remi told me. "I've only heard rumors," I manage to say. "It was all before I knew him, but Mother Agnes would never have let me live with him if she thought him capable of harming me."

That's not entirely true because she *didn't* allow it—I ran away to accept his offer of employment, and partly because of what I overheard her say about my family. But she would have put up much more of a fuss if she thought I was in danger. Or maybe she did. My eyes drift to the documents on the table. Are there complaints from her in there? Then I shake my head to dismiss that thought. In five years, she never once indicated to me that I should fear Magister Thomas.

"And I would never have accepted your help if I'd known why you wanted to be involved," says Simon.

"It wasn't only about protecting Magister Thomas, Simon. You have to believe that."

"Believe what?" He waves a hand at the horrible sketches. "That you forced your way into this inquiry because of your concern for these women?"

"No," I admit. "It wasn't that at first. I'm not sure when it changed, but it did. It became for them and for you and for Juliane."

"And yet never enough for you to tell me about *that*." Simon jabs a finger at the architect's hammer.

The gore on the handle reminds me of other details. "You act like I'm the only one who withheld information," I say. "I might have been more forthcoming if I'd understood just how depraved this killer is."

"I doubt it." He folds his arms across his chest. "You drew solid conclusions without that knowledge."

"And you did the same without the cursed hammer!"

Simon's mouth remains set at its skeptical angle. "Do you know what the worst part of all this is?" His voice changes, becoming fragile as an eggshell. "How you came at me from my most vulnerable side." He smiles, but it's a wretched, humorless, ironic expression, which only becomes worse when it crumples like a wad of parchment. "I actually . . ."

Without thinking, I step toward him, reaching out. "No, Simon, it was never like that—"

He jumps back before I can get too close. "Don't touch me," he snarls. "Don't ever touch me again."

My arm drops like it's made of lead. Whatever we had, whatever we were, is gone.

"You need to go," he says.

"May I visit Magister Thomas?" I whisper.

"No. That would interfere with the investigation."

"Simon, please!" I struggle to keep my voice down. "He's all I have left!"

"Then you have more than I do."

I spin around and run out and down the passage to the stairs, careless of how much noise I make. At the bottom of the steps, I stumble to the front door and throw the series of bolts open and burst out onto the street. My footsteps echo off the slate like someone is following, but I don't stop until I'm in my room again, where I can let the sobs out.

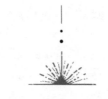

CHAPTER 40

Though it feels like sacrilege, work continues that morning on the Sanctum. Remi forbids gossip about Magister Thomas's arrest, addressing the issue before work begins for the day. He declares his complete confidence the architect will be found innocent of the charges, but until then, the best everyone can do is make him proud of what is accomplished in the meantime. It is the only thing he does which I agree with.

Using the magister's absence as an excuse, Remi pushes ahead on the new ceiling. As he tells it, the smart thing to do is advance the areas that he knows best. He orders the first stones of the ribs to be set on the floor in preparation for raising them to scaffolding across the top of the new section.

Oudin Montcuir comes by shortly before the noon break, and Remi proudly describes his intentions for the crisscrossing arches to support the vaulting. I've shown Oudin around with his father on several occasions, but he has more questions for his friend than he ever did for me. As they walk along the scaffolding platform itself, over fifty feet overhead, I catch sight of Lambert. He shuffles his feet and glances in my direction often enough that I decide he might want to speak with me.

Lambert's face lights up as I approach, though his brow is creased and his eyes are fixed in teardrop shapes of worry. "Miss Catrin," he says, "you left in such a hurry this morning that I wanted to ensure you were all right. Simon wouldn't say a word about what happened."

I stop about arm's length away, warmed by his concern. "I was upset," I admit. "But I assure you Simon wasn't cruel."

No more than I deserved.

Remi's and Oudin's heads appear over the edge of a high platform, looking down. I doubt they can hear us, but they're obviously watching.

Lambert sighs. "I don't know why Simon is so angry with you, but I'm certain he's being unjust. His . . . past creates barriers I fear are impossible to overcome."

"Yes, I've learned that myself." Last night I'd come so close to breaking them down.

He traces a toe on the marble floor design before looking up shyly. "I just want you to know that I would listen to you where he would not, Miss Catrin."

Juliane said before that Lambert fancied me. Maybe he still does, and I can use that to my advantage.

"Cat, please." I take his arm, though it wasn't offered, and guide him out of sight of our audience overhead. "That's what my friends call me." I lower my voice, forcing Lambert to lean down to hear me. "It's just that Simon won't allow me to visit Magister Thomas. Not even to bring him something to eat."

"That does sound a little unreasonable," Lambert admits. "Even the grain merchant was allowed visitors."

"Yes, exactly!" I stop to turn to face him, focusing on his chest in front of me. "I just—I just wish . . ." I bite my lip but it's not difficult to bring moisture to my eyes. "I'm sorry. It's not fair of me to ask."

"Perhaps it's not fair of him to forbid you." Lambert ducks his head to catch my eye. "And the venatre may have ordered his arrest, but he's not the authority in the gaol. That's the provost's office."

I act as though that thought hadn't occurred to me, allowing myself a look of hope before dropping my gaze and letting my shoulders sag. "But he'll be furious when he learns."

"Then he needn't find out."

— • ✳ • —

Lambert agrees I should meet him at the Palace of Justice after stopping at home. Mistress la Fontaine is dishing warmed stew from last night into a wide-mouthed jug for Magister Thomas as Remi arrives for his own lunch. His mother slathers a loaf of bread with fresh butter as he pulls me away to stand by the fireplace.

"I'm not sure this is a good idea," he says quietly. "I'm amazed the venatre is allowing it."

"All prisoners have the right to receive visitors," I reply, settling my rain cloak around my shoulders.

He raises eyebrows. "Have you considered this might be a trap?"

"A trap?" I stare at him. "To lock *me* in the gaol?"

"Not necessarily, but maybe the venatre is only letting you in so he can listen to what the magister says to you."

I wave my hand in dismissal of the idea, neglecting to correct him on who is authorizing this. "All the more reason to go—we have nothing to hide."

"That you know of," Remi says darkly. Then he sighs. "Don't stay too long. We have work to do." He drops heavily into his chair at the table.

"Do you have any messages you'd like me to pass along?" I ask as I take the jug of stew and wrapped bundle of bread from the housekeeper.

Remi stares at his bowl like he's not hungry. "Just tell him I have everything under control."

——— • ✳ • ———

Lambert waits for me around the corner from the Palace of Justice, but so does Oudin. "I'm sorry," Lambert says quietly after taking my burdens from me. "I couldn't convince him to go home. Fortunately, he's more than glad to keep our secret from Simon."

Or to have blackmail material, I'm sure. But I'm committed to this.

I follow Lambert into a side door of the palace and through several twisting corridors and stairways, each level down getting cooler and more damp until the walls glisten with perpetual moisture. My breath fogs in the air in front of me, making me glad I bothered with the cloak though the rain had stopped. Just before what Lambert indicates is the last passage, a guard catches up to us with a summons.

"The provost wants you, sir. Says it's urgent."

Lambert clenches his jaw. Oudin takes the jug of stew with a wink at me. "Good thing I came along after all. I can escort Miss Catrin." The way he says my name makes it sound almost like "Kitten."

"Will you be all right?" Lambert asks me as he hands the key he wore on a steel chain around his neck to his brother. "We can come another time if you want."

I'll endure a hundred hours in Oudin's presence if it means seeing Magister Thomas for five minutes. "I'll be fine," I assure Lambert. "Thank you for everything." On impulse, I stand on my toes and kiss his cheek.

"Careful, there," says Oudin as soon as Lambert's gone. "He gets jealous easily."

I yank the bread from his hand. "And you don't?"

"Not really, no," he says, unlocking the last door.

The narrow passage beyond is lit by a single torch on the wall. I count ten doors with bars across the middle lining either side. "Not sure which he's in," says Oudin.

I'm not eager to look into any of the wrong ones. "Magister?" I call.

Chains stir behind several doors, but a familiar voice comes from the one on the far end. "Catrin?"

I run past eyes gathering to watch and fall to my knees in front of the last door. "It's me," I gasp, dropping the wrapped bread to clutch the rusty bars. "I'm here, Magister."

The fingers which cover mine are cold as ice. "Light and Mercy," he says. "Are you well?"

"Am *I* well?" I shake my head. Oudin strolls up behind me and sets the jug down next to the bread. "You're worried about me?"

The white streaks in the architect's beard move with his smile. "Of course. About you and Remi and his mother, and poor Sister Marguerite as well. Have you heard anything about her?"

I shake my head and switch my hands to fold around his, willing warmth to flow from my fingers to his. "This is all my fault, Magister. I'm so sorry."

"Did you take that hammer?" he asks gently. "Did you leave it with Mother Agnes?"

"No, of course not." I lean my head against the bars. "But I knew it must have been used in Perrete's murder, and then later in the others, but I never told Simon."

"Is that the true reason you joined the inquiry, Cat?" Magister Thomas whispers. "To protect me?"

"Yes." My tears fall onto our joined hands. "But I failed."

He sighs and kisses my forehead. "Oh, my dear."

I sit back to look at him. "There has to be a way to prove your innocence."

Magister Thomas glances up at Oudin. "Would you mind giving us a little privacy, sir?"

Oudin shrugs and saunters away. The architect refocuses on me. "Catrin, that's not how justice works. It's not innocence that must be proved, it's guilt."

"That's how it's *supposed* to work," I say. "But they already hanged a man falsely for two of these murders."

"He was guilty of the one, however," the magister points out. "And that one was proved beyond doubt."

How can he be so serene? Doesn't he understand how well he already fits into the mold Simon has created? "Why wouldn't you tell the venatre where you were that night?"

The architect leans closer and lowers his voice. "I was in the Quarter."

Since I shouldn't know that, I try to look shocked. "But why?"

"That's something I need to explain to you, but not here," he says. "It's not safe. The walls have ears."

Remi had warned of the same.

I know it must have to do with me and the magick I can use. "The reason doesn't matter," I insist. "Just that your whereabouts are accounted for. Why won't you tell anyone?"

Magister Thomas shakes his head. "You know the high altum has wanted to replace me for a long time. I've taken several cuts in pay to keep him from hiring someone younger but with less experience. It doesn't matter what he says from the pulpit about Selenae being harmless, they're considered heretics. If my friendship with . . ."

Gregor, I fill in silently.

He sighs. "It's complicated, but that would be the last excuse the altum needs. You, Remi, and Mistress la Fontaine would be left with nothing."

"*That* is your concern?" I ask. "You're willing to sacrifice your life so we can keep our *jobs*?"

"It would destroy everything Remi has worked his whole life to achieve," Magister Thomas says. "If I'm executed for an unrelated crime, he can take over. If I'm banned as a heretic, so is my assistant. So are you. Either way I'm lost, but this way everything I care about is safe."

"I'd rather you were found innocent and came home."

"As would I."

This is the man Remi described as having a violent past? Whatever drove him from Brinsulli must have been a false accusation. "Magister?" I whisper. "May I ask you a personal question?"

He wrinkles his brow. "If you think this is really the time for it."

It's not, but I have to know. "What happened to your wife?"

Magister Thomas sits back into the shadows with a long sigh. "She left me." For several seconds I don't think he's going to say anything more, then he murmurs, "Maybe it would be more accurate to say I left her."

The question is difficult to ask, but I suspect I don't have much more time, so I force the words out. "Was there another woman?"

"You could say that." He smiles without humor.

"But . . . who?"

"Not who, Catrin," he corrects me. "What. What do you think came between us?"

"The Sanctum," I breathe.

Magister Thomas nods. "I wanted to be the youngest master architect on the continent and build the most beautiful home for the Sun that ever existed. When ambition that great is in your heart, there's room for little else." He looks down. "We had a daughter. A tiny thing with blond curls and the bluest eyes, but then came the plague. She didn't have a chance."

I sniff and rub my cheek on my shoulder, unwilling to let go of his hands. "What was she called?"

"Therese." Magister Thomas pauses for several heartbeats. "I haven't said her name in years. She deserves better than that." He clears his throat before continuing. "But the head architect also died, and I was named to replace him. Just when Eleanor needed me most, I wasn't there." He shakes his head sadly. "I came home one day and realized she was gone. There was a note, saying she went back to Londunium, but it was dated twenty-nine days earlier. She'd been gone for nearly a month, and I hadn't noticed."

"Why didn't you go after her?"

"A number of reasons. The plague had passed, but it still existed in other towns. Collis refused to let anyone in for over a year. If I'd left, I wouldn't have been able to return. I'd already lost what was most precious. The Sanctum was all I had left."

"It's only a building," I say through gritted teeth.

"Catrin, you know it's more than that," he scolds, beginning the lecture I've heard a hundred times. "You, me, Mistress la Fontaine, Remi—even Mother Agnes—our lives are as short and fleeting as phases of the moon, but what lies Beyond the Sun is forever. That's why we need a Sanctum like ours—to bring the divine to where we can experience it. Life is full of suffering. Nothing is more important than to give people a place of hope and beauty and meaning so they may endure it. And there is no greater privilege than to create that." He pauses. "Can you honestly tell me a part of you wouldn't die if it was taken away from you?"

I'd asked myself that very question last night. "No, it would be like losing an eye or a limb," I admit. "But I would still live," I add defiantly.

Magister Thomas smiles. "I know you would. You have so much yet to live for. But I . . ." He sighs. "By the time I realized I'd sacrificed the wrong thing it was too late. Now the Sanctum is all I have left."

"You have *me*!"

"Yes, I do." He switches his hands to cover mine. "It has been my honor to be your guardian. You gave me back a piece of what I lost."

He's acting like this is goodbye. I shake my head. "Stop talking like this!"

Oudin appears at my side. "Simon is coming. We need to leave, now." He starts to lift me by my elbow.

"No! No!" I grip the bars harder, and rust flakes off, digging into my skin.

Magister Thomas gently peels my fingers loose. "You have to go now, Catrin. We'll see each other again. If not here, then Beyond the Sun."

"No! Please!" I struggle against Oudin as he hauls me away.

"Curse it, Girl," he mutters in my ear. "I'm not ending up in here myself just for doing you a favor."

"Catrin," booms the architect in a voice no one could help but obey, and I cease fighting. "You're better than this."

I wipe my face on my sleeve. "Yes, Magister."

He nods. "Now stand up straight and walk out of here."

I do as he says, but I walk backward, letting Oudin lead me. When we reach the door, Magister Thomas calls out to me one last time.

"I love you, Catrin."

Though he's never said those words before, it was something I'd never doubted.

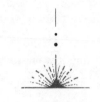

CHAPTER 41

I tilt my face up as soon as I'm outside, letting the soft rain wash away the evidence of my tears. Oudin sags against the wall next to the side door, looking relieved to have escaped the gaol without being discovered by Simon. I wonder just how much trouble he and his brother could have gotten into for helping me.

"Catrin?" I spin around, clutching my chest. Lambert's russet eyes are anxious. "Were you able to see him?"

I nod, wiping my face on my sleeve again. "I can't thank you enough, Sir."

Oudin rolls his eyes. "I did all the work."

Lambert ignores his brother and waits as I pull myself back together piece by piece. "I think, given time, Simon's anger will fade," he says. "I can try to smooth it over for you. Perhaps get him to let you rejoin the inquiry."

Oudin stands straight. "Or maybe you should leave it alone before someone else gets hurt, Brother. It's obvious the prioress and that sister were attacked because they were connected to Catrin."

Lambert glances back at him dismissively. "Yes, I heard your rant this morning."

"If this madman would go after women like them to hurt her, do you think he'd hesitate to target Juliane?" Oudin demands.

"She never goes out alone," counters Lambert. "Simon isn't worried about her safety."

Oudin folds his arms across his chest. "He should be. He is the one that got her involved in the first place."

"I'm not going to argue about this in the middle of the street, Brother, and certainly not in front of Miss Catrin, given what she's been through." Lambert turns his attention on me. "Would you allow me to escort you to the Sanctum? I'm sure you're eager to get back to work."

I don't think "eager" is the right word, but Remi had asked me not to linger. "Thank you, Sir, I would be grateful for your company."

Oudin scowls as I take Lambert's offered arm. As we set off, he calls to my back, "You're welcome, Kitten."

For a second I'd felt guilty for not acknowledging his role in sneaking me in to see Magister Thomas, but when he called me by that detestable name the feeling vanished.

Lambert and I take a slightly longer route to avoid the Mont-cuir home and the possibility of running into Simon, one which gives us a beautiful view of the Sanctum. The clouds hang low enough today that the tops of the square towers disappear into them, which in some ways makes the building look more holy than when the Sun shines on it, at least in my opinion.

Our lives are as short and fleeting as phases of the moon, the architect had said. *Nothing is more important than to give people a place of hope and beauty and meaning.*

The Sanctum will outlive him, outlive us all. Magister Thomas sacrificed his family to contribute to that ideal. His life's work was, to quote Mother Agnes, the cage he chose for himself, a concept the prioress was undoubtedly familiar with. After a lifetime of moving from cage to cage—for marriage *is* a cage of sorts, even when willingly entered—she, too, had opted for one of her own choosing.

And this killer, who keeps his internal monster caged when necessary, what outer cage constrains him?

I stop in my tracks. The killer and the monster exist within the same cage.

Lambert is forced to halt when I do. "Is something wrong, Miss?"

My mind races. That's the essence of Simon's method—he's observing what constrains the monster and trying to match it to a person.

But the methods have changed. The targets have changed.

The killer wants something he can't get.

Does he want something different, or is he just going after the same thing in a new way?

"Catrin?"

I jump at Lambert's face right in front of mine. "Are you well?" he asks, all concern.

"Yes." I shake my head. "Yes, I'm fine. I was just thinking."

"You do know Simon is making every effort to delay the magister's trial," says Lambert, and I notice he avoids adding anything about execution. "He told my father this morning that no one as smart as the architect would have left something so easily traceable to him. He considers it false evidence."

Simon is saying that? Not just for my sake—or Magister Thomas's, I'm certain. For the victims who are yet to come. And because it's true. But perhaps the hammer wasn't left behind just to throw suspicion on someone else. What if the architect—or possibly what he represents—stands between the killer and what he wants?

"That's—that's a great relief to hear," I stammer.

Lambert's cheeks turn pink at my gratitude. "I'm glad to be able to ease your fear somewhat."

We continue uphill, and Lambert walks a little taller than before. I worry my earlier emotional appeal—I will *not* call it flirting—may have had more effect than I intended. Oudin's assertion that his brother was more jealous than him flies straight in the face of his own behavior, but Juliane understands Lambert quite well. He likes the idea of a woman he can rescue.

Flattering as his attention is, I've never thought of myself as a damsel in distress. It's not a comfortable image.

Lambert clears his throat. "I expect you'll want to attend the prioress's funeral this evening."

My thoughts had been so completely occupied I'd forgotten about that. In Gallian tradition the soul is believed to follow the Sun into the Beyond with the first sunset after death. To discourage the soul from wandering away until that time, the deceased is never left alone until the funeral that evening. "Yes," I answer. "Magister Thomas would want me to go."

"It's only proper," Lambert agrees. "I, ah . . . my father has already ordered me to represent the family, and Simon wants me to observe who else is there."

That means Simon isn't coming himself. Does he hope his absence will embolden the killer to revisit the scene, or does he want to avoid seeing me? Suddenly I realize Lambert has asked a question. "What?"

His face is beet red. "I said, may I have the honor of escorting you there?"

Oh Sun, this is not something I want to encourage. "I worry that may not sit well with Lady Genevieve's family," I say to remind him of his betrothed. "Perhaps if you also brought

Juliane? She would be perfect for remembering who's there, and her presence would be a great comfort to me."

Lambert's lower lip trembles. "I don't think that's possible. She's not well. You know how."

He's so distraught I can't help patting his arm in sympathy. "I'm sorry," I say, careful not to reveal what I know about their mother. "It must be very difficult to watch."

"It is." He blinks away his emotions. "But you're right, Miss Catrin, in how it might look to be seen walking the streets in the evening hours with you. Thank you for your consideration."

"And I thank you for your concern for my welfare." We've reached the north part of the Sanctum Square, which is much smaller than the other side due to the shape of the hill. There are far fewer people around, which allows me to pick out Remi's face among those looking down on us from the roof. "I'd better get back to work. Thank you again for helping me today."

Lambert leaves me with a polite bow and the promise to visit me again tomorrow—if that's all right.

After what he's risked for me, I don't have the heart to tell him no.

That and because he's my only connection to Magister Thomas.

· * ·

Though the rain eases and the skies clear shortly after noon, Remi calls off work early and over dinner declares he will accompany me to the abbey. I should've known he'd insist on that. As we pass the vine-covered walls of the Quarter, I try to look into the windows, wondering which house Marguerite is in, but it's unlikely to be one of the few I can see.

Selenae don't allow outsiders into their neighborhood, especially at night, except by special invitation. Anyone who tries to sneak in—usually drunks or adolescent boys with something to prove—are always caught within a block and escorted out. I wonder what they'd do if I simply walked in, demanding to see Marguerite.

The waxing moon has risen above the rooftops, and already I can hear the ghostly songs drifting out of the alleys in praise of its light. Remi doesn't seem to notice. He's tense and sweating as we enter the abbey gate. It's not yet repaired from him breaking it down last night. "Do you think they cover her face?" he whispers to me.

I shudder. "Merciful Sun, I hope so."

Fortunately, the sisters have completely wrapped Mother Agnes in a clean shroud of embroidered silk. I hear a few murmurs from bystanders on the strange extravagance of that, but I know the fabric came from a trunk in her private cell. More than once I'd sneaked in to sift through its contents and marvel at the riches she'd kept from her marriages, wondering if she'd held on to them for financial emergencies or out of emotional attachment.

My heart seizes with a thousand other memories. I never got to say goodbye, to thank the prioress for giving me a childhood home so safe and secure. Magister Thomas had scolded me about her having little time left, but somehow I believed she'd live forever.

Lambert is already in the back of the chapel, scanning every face that enters, and he nods gravely as we pass. Beside him stands Oudin, whose expression is much less pleasant. I ignore him.

As the sun sets, everyone moves outside to the garden to watch, singing the hymn of farewell. The melody rising from the Selenae Quarter mixes between the notes in a perfect harmony, but no one seems to mind the blasphemous blend of songs. In fact, no one else appears to even notice it.

No one, that is, but the man standing on the edge of the crowd in a gray cloak. He sings the other tune in his soft baritone. As the sun slips beyond the horizon and the song reaches its crescendo, Gregor turns his eyes to meet mine from across the open area. Now that the moon is the only source of light, he addresses me, his scarred lips moving in a whisper I know only I can hear.

"Stay behind. The little sister needs your help."

CHAPTER 42

"I'll be fine," I assure Remi. "You have hours of work to do with the architect's logs before you can turn in, so you ought to go ahead."

Remi hesitates. "It's not safe. Perhaps I can get Oudin to wait for you." Both the comte's sons had volunteered to close Mother Agnes's casket and were now carrying it to the cemetery on the far side of the compound.

I tilt my head to the chapel, where the sisters' evening prayers drift out of the open doors. "Sunset liturgy has only just started, and I think I'd like to stay for it and the next one tonight." When Remi's frown deepens, I gesture to several city watchmen assigned to patrol the convent. "I'll ask a guard to escort me home afterward, will that satisfy you?"

He agrees, though reluctantly, and joins the crowd filing out of the broken gate. Oudin and Lambert leave shortly after, brushing dirt from their hands. I hide in the shadows of the chapel as they pass. Though Lambert would undoubtedly be concerned for my safety, I don't think the killer will strike tonight. He'll want to revel in the atmosphere of terror he's created for a little while.

I wait for the streets to clear, listening to the sisters sing without Mother Agnes for the first time in nearly forty years. Most of them have never known life without her, myself included. No matter how capable her successor is, Solis Abbey will never be the same.

At last I'm satisfied that it's quiet enough, though there's still a pair of watchmen outside. I'd rather they didn't see me go into the Quarter, so I might have to come up with a diversion. Both guards nod politely as I pass through the broken gate, just as Gregor steps out of an alley across the street in full view.

The men don't react. I wait a few seconds but they continue as if they don't see him.

I frown. How is that possible? Gregor isn't a small man by any standard, and it's fairly light out. The sun isn't that far gone yet, and the moon is bright enough that I'm casting a faint shadow.

Gregor catches my confused look and smiles, his white teeth glowing in the moonlight. It's not a pleasant expression, however. More like taunting.

"Come on then, Little Cat," he whispers, though the sound is nearly drowned out by the singing from both the abbey and the Quarter. "Your friend is waiting."

Taking a deep breath, I walk casually down the street, toward the wall of moonflower vines. When I reach Gregor, he holds up a hand to tell me to stop. Then, after a glance at the watchmen, he silently glides two steps forward to block their view of me.

We wait a few seconds until one of the guards speaks. "Well, wasn't she in a hurry. Already gone."

The other chuckles. "Girls wouldn't run from you if you'd bathe more than once a month."

They still can't see Gregor—and now me. Baffled, I look down at the ground and realize he casts no shadow.

Nor do I. Or rather, my shadow ends at his feet.

Gregor raises one arm and the cloak with it, indicating I should go into the alley. I slip past him through the opening and he quickly follows.

It's so dark I stumble several times, unable to see where I'm going, but Gregor doesn't seem to have any problems. Once we exit onto a proper street, my guide moves past me, signaling that I should follow, which I do, slowly, taking in my surroundings.

The first row of houses is as covered with vines as the Quarter's outer walls. Five-petaled blossoms glow among the leaves like the night sky sprinkled with stars. Many are fully open to face the moon the way other flowers open to the sun, exposing the veins of purple at the center of the hornlike shape.

Selenae know, home to go

When your face begins to show

I touch a curled head as we pass. The next one I cross is fully open, and I pause to put my nose in the funnel, curious about its scent.

"I wouldn't do that if I were you." Gregor's silver-ringed eyes shine with amusement. "If you want to be in any condition to help your friend."

I frown. "You speak like it will steal my senses."

"Where do you think *skonia* comes from?"

I jump back, then rush to catch up with Gregor, who's resumed walking. Now that I've spoken, more questions come tumbling out. "How could the guards not see you? Or me?"

He glances over his shoulder and holds the edge of his gray cloak out like the wing of a bat. "Moonweave. Spun and woven under the full moon." He smiles coldly. "Invisible as the dark side of the moon to Hadrians."

Hadrians. I'd overheard him use that word in Magister Thomas's kitchen. Modern people refer to themselves by nation—Gallian, Prezian, Tauran, Brinsulli, Doitch—but they're all descended from the old Hadrian Empire which spanned the continent and lands across distant seas. Do Selenae come from somewhere beyond those boundaries?

Gregor drops his arm and continues down the road. Voices float up the cobblestone streets to us from several directions, and I catch glimpses of people going about their business as though it were daytime.

So far the streets don't look different from many areas of Collis, though perhaps cleaner. The houses are smaller—two stories maximum, with greenery hanging from almost every window, though no more moonflowers.

"There you are, Uncle!" The physician from last night comes rushing toward us, wiry gray hairs springing loose from her braid. "I've been begging him to bring you here all day," she says to me. "Your friend has been fading since this morning."

I round on Gregor. "She's *dying*?"

He shrugs. "If I truly thought you could help, I would've fetched you long ago."

The physician snorts. "I am the expert in such matters." She takes my arm and pulls me in the direction she came from. "This way, Cousin."

"Cousin?" Her address confirms my theory that Gregor is somehow related to me, but it's still a shock. "Is he also my uncle?" I ask her.

"Yes." She throws a harsh glance at Gregor as he falls into step behind us. "Apparently, he didn't bother to explain anything."

"Did you know me . . . before?"

"As much as one can know an infant." She smiles a little. "As a matter of fact, you were the first baby I delivered on my own. I was barely your age."

That means she can tell me about my parents, or at least my mother. "What's your name?"

"Athene." Her eyes gleam as they meet mine. "And you are Katarene."

"Catrin."

"If you wish."

Her flat tone makes me wonder if my insistence is an insult, but I can't help holding on to the person Mother Agnes and Magister Thomas raised me to be. "You can call me Cat."

Athene's cheek tightens in a half smile. "Very well, Cat."

We stop at a green door with a white circle painted at eye level. A thick vertical line through the middle of the circle has a snake wrapped around it. "The mark of a physician," Athene explains. "The family trade."

"Does that mean you're a physician, too?" I ask Gregor.

He chuckles deeply in his chest. "No, my brother had the skill for that, but I got the good looks."

I assume he's making a joke about his appearance. "Your brother?"

"My twin brother, actually."

My father?

Athene opens the door and gestures for us to follow her inside. Stairs go up to the left, but she walks down the passage leading to the back of the house. At the end, a door on the right opens to a kitchen, with dried herbs hanging from the ceiling. Opposite is a sickroom, unlike any I've ever seen.

Though there are no windows, the air is fresh, almost with a breeze. Soft light comes from apple-size spheres of polished stone sitting on what in Gallian homes would be candlesticks. Their glow provides just the right amount of brightness—easy on the eyes, but enough to see a pale, motionless form on the bed.

"Marguerite!" I rush to her side to kneel and take her cold hand in mine. Her head is wrapped in clean bandages, but the misshapenness is still evident. "Can she hear me?" I ask.

"She hears almost everything." Athene moves a stool next to me, which I gratefully sit on. "If you wish to hear her, you must do more."

"I have to touch her blood, right?" For once, I'm eager to do it. Gregor's eyes narrow. "How did you know that?"

"Because I've done it," I say. "Not intentionally, though."

Athene smiles smugly at Gregor. "I told you."

He shakes his head. "Not possible. It's rare even in Selenae. Diluted blood should be even weaker."

"I have a theory about that, but we have work to do first." Athene turns Marguerite's hand over and places a metallic stone in the center of her palm. "Contact with blood isn't necessary if you use this," she tells me. "Take her hand again."

I obey, pressing the stone between our hands. *Marga?* I plea silently. *Can you hear me?*

"No, she can't." Athene has one finger on the stone as she nudges it into a secure position. "You have to speak out loud."

That means both Athene and Gregor will be listening to at least half the conversation. I take a deep breath. "Marga?"

Catrin? Cat?

I lean forward, wrapping my left hand around our joined ones. "I'm here, Marga!"

Marguerite's relief floods into me with her voice. *I'm so glad to see you. Or hear you. I can't see anything.*

"I'm sorry I didn't come sooner."

You're here now. That's what matters.

"Very good," says Athene. "Ask her if she has any pain she can identify."

Who is that?

"The physician who is caring for you," I tell her.

Selenae? Fear ripples through our connection. *Sister Berta's influence.*

I won't lie, even if Marguerite might never know otherwise. "Yes. She's doing everything she can to help you."

I will trust her if you do. Marguerite pauses. *I have some pain on the back of my body, but not bad. More like a pressing ache.*

I repeat that for Athene, who nods. "That's from lying flat and motionless, but feeling it means there is less damage in the brain."

"Do you remember anything from last night?" I ask Marguerite. "Did you see the man who hurt you?"

There's a pause, like she's thinking. *Mother said she expected a late visitor, and I heard her let him in. There was a crash, like she fell, so I left my cell and called out to her.* Marguerite's stress rises. *A man came out of her sitting room. I screamed and turned to run when something threw me into the wall.*

"Did you recognize him?" I ask.

No, he was just a dark shape. Wearing a cloak. I'm sorry. Her thoughts grow weak with misery.

"Don't worry about that," I tell her.

"Enough," Athene interrupts. "If you don't guide her back to consciousness soon, we could lose her forever."

I clench Marguerite's hand tighter, as though that will keep her from slipping away. "How do I do that?"

"The mind is like a forest with many paths," Athene explains. "She is essentially lost in the wilderness between. You must enter that forest and lead her back to the known paths."

Her analogy is concerning. "Can I get lost in this . . . forest?"

Athene shakes her head. "You can only walk in your own, but your forests overlap where you have shared memories. If you can get her on strong paths for long enough, hopefully she will reach a point where she can continue on her own."

I ease my grip, worried I may be hurting her. "Did you hear that, Marga? Do you understand what we need to do?"

Yes. I understand. But it's so dark. The thoughts are almost sluggish, like she's dozing off.

"Remind her of something you used to do together," Athene prompts. "A memory she will have recalled several times over the years. Well-worn paths are easier to find."

I close my eyes and think of the days we shared a room. "Do you remember sewing doll clothes together?" I ask. "Using fabric scraps from the weaving room?"

My dolls were always dressed as sisters.

"Yes, but we made colorful outfits for mine."

I remember. There's a pause, then her voice is stronger. Indignant. *You put bright undergarments on my dolls.*

I bite my lip to hold back a grin. "I did that for a year before you noticed."

She's as scandalized now as she was then. *Of course I didn't! There was no reason to look under their clothes.*

It's not long before I notice Marguerite's responses become more solid if I bring forth a memory and let her complete it. We continue, recalling pulling weeds and shelling peas and making a tangled mess in our first weaving lesson.

Athene's voice is suddenly in my ear. "Ask her a simple question, and let go of her hand, quickly."

I say the first thing which pops in my head. "What is my favorite kind of biscuit?"

Our hands separate just in time for me to hear Marguerite's answer, which comes from her own lips.

"Ginger."

CHAPTER 43

Marguerite is awake. Athene nudges me aside, holding a small glowing stone as she lifts Marguerite's eyelids to study her pupils. "Very good," she murmurs. "The damage isn't as great as I feared."

"She's all right?" I gasp. "She'll recover now?"

Athene leans back. "There are no guarantees," she cautions, "but I'm optimistic." She nods to me as she stands, and her eyes dart to Gregor in the doorway. "You did well, Cat, especially considering you've had no training."

Marguerite's blue eyes shift around without focusing. "It's so dark in here."

Light of Day, she's blind. I sit forward. "I'm right here, Marga."

As soon as I'm in front of her, she smiles. "There you are."

"Can you see me?"

"Yes, a little now that you're in the light coming from the door."

I frown in confusion. "But the whole room is lit."

"It isn't for her," says Gregor, and I look over my shoulder at him. "Hadrians can't use moon magick." He takes a few steps into the room and rests his hand on one of the spherical stones sitting atop a candlestick. "This is a moonstone," he says. "It absorbs moonlight and recasts it back out. These are fading, though. They only last a few weeks."

"That you can see by them means you've passed the basic Selenae test," Athene adds.

He grunts. "There are others."

Athene smiles with grim triumph. "She will exceed in them all."

The metallic stone is still in my hand, and I offer it back to my cousin. It doesn't glow like the moonstones, but it seems to hum with an unseen energy. "What is this?"

"We call it bloodstone because it conducts magick as well as blood does." As soon as she takes it, my fingers tingle like I've hit my elbow. "They absorb and store magick like a moonstone, but release it in invisible ways. If you put them close to a wound, it will heal much quicker, though it works better on Selenae than Hadrians."

The rumors that Selenae physicians use unnatural methods aren't unfounded. I shake the numbness from my hand. "Are you using them to help Marguerite?"

"The swelling must go down first," says Athene. "I'll also need to move the bone into a better place before encouraging it to mend. She should be ready for them in a few days."

Marguerite whimpers. "I don't want healing with magick."

Athene rolls her eyes, but I reassure my friend. "Marga, do you believe I'm a good person? Do you trust me?"

"Yes," she answers swiftly. "But the moon is the thief of the Sun's light. Anything from it is corrupted."

"The Moon is not a thief," rumbles Gregor. "It's gifted the same Light as everything else. The difference is it blesses others with what it has received."

Marguerite cringes from his hostile tone. I scowl at my uncle as I take her hand again. "If moon magick is corrupt, then so am I, Marga. Because I am Selenae." Or at least partly so, as my blood is apparently diluted. "These people are my family."

"You have their magick?" she whispers.

"I do. And Mother Agnes knew it."

Marguerite is silent for a long time. Tears leak from her eyes back into the bandages. Finally she whispers, "I will trust them for your sake."

"Good, thank you." Her forehead is wrapped, so I kiss her cheek. "It will be all right. I promise."

Athene takes my elbow and urges me up. "My assistant will be back with some broth, Little Sister," she says. "Don't go to sleep yet."

"I'll see you soon," I call as my cousin herds me from the room.

Gregor has vanished, but I hear him going upstairs as Athene propels me into the kitchen. "Take off your cloak," she says. "Stay a while."

I unclasp it and lay it over the back of the chair by the fireplace as I look around. A young woman chops vegetables at a counter, her face obscured by dark waves of hair flowing over her shoulders, much like my own.

"The Hadrian sister is awake, Hira," Athene says to her. "Please take her some broth."

Hira obeys without a word, quickly ladling steaming liquid into a bowl from a pot over the fire. "Is that your daughter?" I ask as soon as she's gone.

"She might as well be." Athene ties an apron around her waist and resumes the work Hira left. "She's one of many orphans from the trouble surrounding your birth. Hira was only three, and her parents were murdered right in front of her. She's never said a word since."

Athene speaks of the violence like it was my fault, though there's no resentment in her tone. If there is something to what she says, I can imagine other Selenae may not feel so generous, however.

"My mother took her in," Athene continues, "convinced she could get Hira to talk again, though she never succeeded. The girl doesn't even have a whisper of blood magick, so we couldn't train her as a physician, but she's a fine nurse, even without speaking."

Hira didn't take a light with her, so I assume she can see by moonstones. That means blood magick is something different—and Gregor doesn't have it.

"Was my father the physician Gregor spoke of?" I ask.

She nods. "They were twins. The Hadrians couldn't tell the difference between him and your father that night. Not that it matters. They beat so many of our men within an inch of death that we couldn't waste bloodstones on injuries that would heal on their own. In the end, Gregor's scars were advantageous. He could no longer be mistaken for his brother."

"But my father died that night?"

"Yes." She glances at the doorway, but Gregor hasn't returned. "Do you really know nothing of what happened?"

"No, nothing," I say. "Though I'm guessing my mother was Gallian, or Hadrian, as you say."

"Yes." Athene focuses on cutting vegetables, I suspect to avoid looking at me. "She came from a wealthy family. During the plague, your father was kept busy with Hadrians crying for physicians at all hours. When he finally made it to your mother's bedside, there was little hope she would survive, but she did. That was when they fell in love."

I walk around to face Athene, but she keeps her eyes on the counter. "How did they manage to . . . be together?"

"Her family had fled to their country estate, basically leaving her in Collis to die. When she didn't, she was still too weak to go anywhere for a long time, so she recovered at the convent."

Mother Agnes made a significant amount of money housing female travelers, many of whom actually came to give birth to an inconvenient baby in secret. At least half the foundlings I grew up with had those origins.

"Your father used to visit her at night, and they'd walk through the orchard," Athene says. "After about a month, she told the prioress she was well enough to leave, but instead of going to her family, she came here. They were married for two seasons before anyone realized where she was. By then your mother was nearly eight months pregnant." My cousin's mouth tightens. "Things got ugly very fast."

The knife comes down hard on a piece of carrot, and one half of it jumps off the counter. I stoop to pick it up as she goes on. "It was she who wanted to stay, but her family spread the rumor that we refused to return her until the physician's bill was paid. It was a pretense, of course, to hide the shame of her elopement, but many in town were in debt to us after the plague, and we were hated. It wasn't difficult for them to gather a mob to go after your father."

And the brawl that followed killed and maimed dozens. I don't want to make Athene relive the event, but there are still questions I need answered. "How did my mother die?"

"You came that night, mostly due to stress, but she'd never fully regained her health after the illness." Athene sweeps the chunks of carrot into a pot. "The birth wasn't difficult, seeing as you were early and rather small, but she left the childbed too quickly, determined to get to your father's side before he died. She wanted to show you to him."

The lump in my throat is hard to speak around. "Did she make it?"

"His face was too swollen to see you, but he passed Beyond the Sun with you in his arms. He was happy. I know because one thing a physician does is listen to last thoughts of the dead or dying."

Athene pauses to clear her throat. "He named Gregor as your moonparent, not knowing his brother was almost as close to death as he was. In all the chaos, we didn't realize how badly your mother was bleeding until it was too late. Her last thought was of love for both of you."

They loved each other, and you were very much wanted . . . Those are the only things that matter.

"Romantic fools, both of them," says Gregor from the door-way, startling us. His voice is gruff, but he blinks several times. He holds up a leather pouch. "We only have one hour of good moon left, Katarene, and many important matters must be explained in its light. Please come with me now."

He turns and walks to the front door without waiting for a response. Athene nods encouragingly. "Go with him, Catrin," she says. "Once your little sister is resting again, I will join you."

I hesitate, her use of my Hadrian name bringing up another question. "May I ask one more thing?"

Athene carries the pot of water and vegetables to the fire. "If it's short."

"Does the name Katarene mean something to Selenae that it was chosen for me?"

She snorts. "Our uncle was right when he described your parents as romantic fools." Then Athene's face softens a little, and she smiles as she hangs the pot on the spit hook.

"It means pure."

CHAPTER 44

I walk outside to meet my uncle—my moonparent, as Athene said he was named. Gallian children have sunmothers and sunfathers who perform the roles of guides in spiritual matters, as well as guardians should something happen to their parents. Moonparent must be the Selenae equivalent.

With that responsibility, it would have been Gregor's decision to leave me with Mother Agnes. In which case, I've made a decision of my own.

"My name is Catrin," I tell him before he can say anything. "You gave up the right to call me by a Selenae name when you put me in the Hadrian world."

Gregor raises his eyebrows. "It was my foolish brother and his Hadrian wife who named you Katarene."

"Then they may call me that when I see them Beyond the Sun," I say. "You may not. If Catrin is distasteful, you can call me Cat."

My uncle shrugs like it doesn't matter, but there's a glimmer of hurt in his eyes. "As you wish, little Cat."

At least it's not Kitten.

He steps out into the street and a patch of moonlight. The

sight of it fills me with the desire to feel it on my own skin, a hunger as strong as I imagine an addict has for *skonia*.

The analogy makes me pause. Gregor had said something similar to the architect. At the time, I'd thought he was referring to Perrete's murder and the killer's lust for blood. Now I realize the entire conversation had been about me and my taste of magick, and how the craving was something all Selenae had to master.

That is why we willingly keep to the Quarter at night—for our protection as much as for that of others.

Would my using magick somehow threaten Magister Thomas and Remi and Mistress la Fontaine? Had I already endangered Marguerite? Simon?

"Come along then." Gregor moves away.

I swallow my unease and trail behind him through the winding streets. Every time the moon peeks from between rooftops, I'm showered with sounds and scents from all directions.

We see a few people going about their business, and to my surprise, the clothes they wear look completely different in the moonlight. What appears as monochromatic blue-black during the day is now many shades of indigo and violet with elaborate embroidery flowing down sleeves and around collars. The most common designs are moonflowers and phases of the moon.

"Not as plain as you pretend to be," I murmur.

Gregor smiles over his shoulder. "The truth is we have nothing against finery, it's just that when you can see as well as we do, a little goes a long way."

I eye his moonweave cloak, apparently invisible to Hadrians. "Do Selenae come out of the Quarter at night more than everyone believes?"

"Yes, though it's still rare. When we are, we're never seen, except by each other."

I frown. "That's not true. Oudin Montcuir saw you watching me on the Sanctum."

Gregor raises his eyebrows, but not in surprise. "That's because the provost's son had taken a large amount of *skonia* that night."

"So?"

"So moonflowers bloom under the moon, absorbing the same magick we carry in our blood." He tilts his head as though waiting for me to understand, which I don't. "*Skonia* enhances the senses to the level we have by nature. Hadrians simply cannot handle it."

"And if I took it?"

Gregor's mouth twitches. "You'd begin to hallucinate as they do."

"But Selenae make the drug."

"Yes. Aside from healing, it's our primary source of income."

His casual admission turns my stomach. "Doesn't that strike you as wrong?"

"To profit from Hadrian weakness? Not really."

If *skonia* gives Hadrians the same senses as Selenae—though they're unable to process them—then the euphoria it also creates must be like what moonlight gives me. Apparently, comparing magick to a drug addiction is accurate.

We turn one last corner and Gregor stops inside the edge of a shadow, facing an open space bright with moonlight. Like many plazas throughout the city, this one is set lower in the ground and ringed with three steps, but it's much larger than any I've seen. Selenae gather within like it's a park on a sunny afternoon, some spreading blankets for picnics. On the far side, a group of mostly women work looms and spinning wheels. They sit in full moonlight, singing as they weave silver-gray fabric that shimmers like ripples on water. Moonweave. Others stir boiling vats of violet dye. The cloth they lift out to examine is as dark as the night sky.

In the very center of everything lies a shallow pool. Most neighborhoods in Collis are built around a communal well or fountain, but this is too small to be a water supply. The textured black stone bottom is only a few inches below the surface. Round patterns under the water mirror those on the face of the moon, which I should have expected. The edge is a halo of golden flames.

I shiver as I realize the crown of fire represents a solar eclipse. They've covered the Blessed Sun with the moon. Blaspheme.

Gregor watches me take it all in, saying nothing. Aside from a few infants snuggling in parents' arms, there are no children younger than twelve. A half dozen young people near my age sit in a circle, passing an object from hand to hand, each taking several seconds to hold it. "At what age are Selenae introduced to moon magick?" I ask.

"At the first crescent after their fourteenth birthday," he answers. "It can be overwhelming, so we start when power is weaker and introduce them gradually over two weeks as the moon waxes and lasts longer, then celebrate their first full moon."

There's a long pause before he continues. "A young person's initiation is usually done by their moonparent. Blood must be exposed to moonlight to wake the magick within, so the skin is cut. The first time leaves a distinctive scar."

Gregor opens his right hand to show me. In the center of his palm is a raised purple mark in the shape of a crescent, no larger than a pea. "Only a drop is required," he explains. "Once the moonlight touches it, the magick conducts through the whole body."

I study his scar, puzzled. "That was never done to me."

"Sometimes it happens by accident." My uncle takes my left hand and raises it, pointing to my middle finger, where a violet spot sits half under the nail—the place I got a splinter that night on the Sanctum. "I could see it from the street as you stood by the statue," he says. "I realized then that not only did you have moon magick, but that it was fully awake."

I stare at the mark, remembering how sharp the blood had tasted in my mouth and Perrete's scream reaching me from an impossible distance. And then I fell, and the moon flashed through my vision and for an awful second I *was* her—just like with Nichole.

Gregor drops my hand. "The moon works in mysterious ways. Though I've always watched over you from a distance, that night I felt compelled to find you. I can only think it was calling me to be with you in that moment."

I smile in spite of all the horror of that night. "I'm not sure I would've been receptive had you tried to speak to me."

His scarred lips twist up, yet the sadness remains in his shining eyes. "Perhaps not, but the result was you discovered much on your own, without guidance."

I gaze out into the plaza, the need to join them surging through me. "I'm here now."

Gregor clears his throat. "Yes, Catrin, you are. And while your magick is already awake and the time is not traditional, I'd like to introduce you as I should have. As I would have if you were raised among us."

His use of my Hadrian name is deliberate, saying I can do this on my own terms. "All right."

He lifts the silver chain from around his neck over his head, cupping the glowing teardrop-shaped pendant in his hand. "This is also when we test for blood magick, to see if thoughts can be heard through a moonstone."

"You already know I have it."

"True, but I'd still like to say something." Gregor takes my hand once more, holding his underneath with the moonstone between them, then stretches them out together into the silver light as though to catch it like falling rain.

The world becomes instantly clearer, as if I'm waking up from a deep sleep or coming out from underwater, suddenly able to breathe and see again. Like I'm finally home after a long journey.

My uncle says nothing, but I hear his voice in my head as I heard Marguerite's, coming through the stone against my hand.

The night welcomes you.

CHAPTER 45

The thrill of magick is quickly replaced by the familiar sensation of drowning. Before, I had always started in a quiet place with very little to smell or see, and even then it was paralyzing. Here I'm surrounded by dozens of conversations and many more faces, not to mention foods and flowers—some of which I don't recognize. Even the vibrations of people walking over stones halfway across the plaza are distracting. I close my eyes and pull my hand from Gregor's to cover my ears, but not wanting to look weak, I only allow myself a few seconds to adjust.

When I force my eyes open again, he's watching me. He puts the silver chain over his head so the moonstone hangs from his neck again. It rests against his chest, glowing brighter than a candle. "You look overwhelmed," he says, not a little smugly.

"There's so much to see and hear." My gaze drops to the paving stones, yet even those are brilliant in their clarity. "But it's bearable if I focus on one sense at a time."

The patronizing tone vanishes. "You can do that? How?"

I shrug. "I don't know. I just concentrate. But it's easy to be distracted."

Gregor frowns. "We'll discuss that later. In the meantime, you can control your senses another way." He upends a small leather bag to drop a shiny black stone into his hand. "With this."

Unlike the moonstones, which cast a welcome glow, or the bloodstone that radiated some invisible force, this one seems to pull light and energy into it, like a hole in the air. I don't want to touch it.

"We call it voidstone," Gregor explains, holding it up. "Born deep in the earth in a place no light reaches. It absorbs magick."

He offers it to me, but I instinctively shy away. "It's harmless against skin," he insists. "Only taking what you give it."

I cautiously accept the stone. "Why would I want to give up my magick?"

"Think of it as only lighting the rooms you're using in a house." Gregor gestures to a pair of women working a loom. "The weavers need to see and feel well for their task, but other senses aren't as helpful, so they extinguish them."

I turn the voidstone over in my fingers, feeling the beveled edges I strangely cannot see. Though it reminds me of glass more than anything else, I've never seen any so dark and opaque. "But in this case," I say, "every candle in the house is lit, and you're putting out the ones you don't want."

"Yes." He smiles, amused. "Except only Hadrians use fire for light."

I ignore his disdain. "Can you move the light from one room to another, or must you relight them all to change senses?" My metaphors are mixing, but Gregor understands.

"The latter." He motions to the sky. "But you need only look at the moon to regain them. Your eyes are like windows which let the light back in."

A couple hurries past us, giggling and holding hands, pausing to kiss in the doorway of a house. I flush as the woman opens the door and drags the young man inside with her. Gregor further embarrasses me by saying, "I imagine they've shed everything but touch."

What would it have been like to have kissed Simon like that? I face the reflecting pool, certain no one would need magick to see my flaming cheeks. "Doesn't it go away as soon as they're in shadow?"

Gregor taps the moonstone under his throat. "As long as you have one of these, you're in moonlight." He tucks the pendant back under his shirt. "And like moonlight, you must be touching the stone for it to provide more than just illumination. Silver conducts magick as well as blood, so most Selenae wear it as some kind of jewelry."

That explains why Gregor saw just fine in the pitch-black alley. I thrill at the idea of never having to be in the dark. "So with it, you always have the senses you would in moonlight?"

"Not quite, but well enough. And a stone's power fades over time."

The one in my hand creates a question. "What happens if you touch a moonstone to a voidstone?"

"Just what you'd expect—all the magick is immediately drained from the moonstone. That's why we carry them in different places." Gregor pulls up a sleeve to reveal a thumbnail-size voidstone set in a silver bracelet. "Some swear completely emptying a moonstone before refilling it makes it last longer."

"I've done experiments," says Athene as she approaches us from behind. "But they were inconclusive." She nods to me. "Your friend is sleeping now."

"Thank you. I'll make sure you're paid as the architect promised."

"Unnecessary." She waves her hand dismissively. "We owe him a debt for your care over the last few years."

"The moonstone," Gregor says impatiently.

I turn back to him. "Yes, you were saying they can be refilled with magick. How do you do that? Put them in moonlight?"

Gregor nods. "That works, but setting them in the pond is faster."

"Something about the water bending the light to fill it from all sides," adds Athene. She plainly thinks deeper on the hows and whys of magick. "Bloodstones are basically the same, though the veins of iron within somehow hold the magick close." She raises her eyebrows at Gregor. "Has she passed all your tests?"

He shakes his head. "We haven't even begun to try controlling the magick itself."

"Hmph," says Athene. "She must be doing something. Usually a freshmoon is cowering in shadow after less than a minute. Some even vomit."

"She says she's able to focus through it," says Gregor. "Which implies she's not as strong as you believe."

Athene rolls her eyes. "Or she's simply a natural at using it. The ancients used voidstones as weapons, not tools for managing themselves. It's also not a full moon."

"You only see what you want to see in her," Gregor grumbles.

"And you refuse to see what's there, Uncle," she replies smoothly. "My theories are yet to be disproved."

I'm tired of being talked across. "Excuse me. What exactly are these theories you keep mentioning?"

Athene motions to the plaza. "Would you rather sit to discuss this?"

I agree, and we walk around the open area to a table with chairs in front of what smells like a bakery. Such outdoor places are common in wealthier areas of Collis, where people can afford to spend daylight hours drinking tea and eating cakes. I suppose to Selenae, this is like a pleasant afternoon. Gregor follows, his face set in stone. Athene requests three cups of tea, and the server hurries away.

Without the need to focus on anything, the cacophony of senses is starting to give me a headache, which I admit to Athene.

"Use the voidstone, then," she replies. "Focus on one particular sense and push it into the stone with your mind until what's left is bearable."

Smell seems like the easiest to try first, so I close my eyes and turn my mind to the dizzying bouquet of scents—maple wood from the table, the floral soap in Athene's clothing, smoke from the nearby fire under the boiling vat of dye—and imagine all their vapors flowing into the stone in my hand. Suddenly I can't smell a thing.

I reopen my eyes and confess I went too far and lost my sense of smell completely.

Athene shakes her head. "You can't go lower than normal Hadrian senses." She snaps a narrow leaf off the plant in the decorative pot on the table and holds it up to my nose. Lavender.

I look up to the moon to refresh my magick and try again. Putting all of something in the stone is easy. Putting an exact fraction in is less so. It takes several more attempts for me to achieve anything resembling success. Then, self-conscious at how closely I'm being watched, I do a messy job with the other senses, leaving them all at different but bearable levels before dropping the stone on the table, glad to not be touching it anymore.

Athene smirks at Gregor as the server places our tea in front of us. "See? She's a natural."

I wipe sweat from my upper lip and reach for my cup. "I don't know. That took a lot more effort than you implied."

"It will become second nature with practice," Athene assures me.

I sip the tea, which is a burst of orange and clove on my

tongue. Taste had been difficult to judge with nothing in my mouth. "So why do you need to touch a moonstone or moonlight if the magick is already in your—*our*—blood?"

Athene sets her cup down. "Simply put, it's contained. The moonlight—or a moonstone—on your skin connects it to the outside world." She pauses. "It's like putting hot water into a cup. You can warm your hands on it, but only if you touch it."

"I think I understand." My fingers dance on the edge of the glazed earthenware, letting the heat seep into my skin as she described. "Why doesn't it work when the sun is present?"

"Sunlight essentially washes it out," replies Gregor, slurping his drink. "Which is why eclipses are our most sacred days." His teacup has pink flowers on it, which contrasts rather comically with his rugged features.

"You look uncomfortable," says Athene when I don't say anything for half a minute.

I grimace. "I've been told all my life that the moon is cursed. Using its magick feels . . . wrong, especially when you tell me the Sun washes it away." I may have told Marguerite the opposite, but it's hard to ignore seventeen years of solosophy lessons and sermons.

Athene chuckles. "Would it help if I told you moonlight is only sunlight reflecting off the face of the Moon?"

Gregor said something like that to Marguerite: that the Moon was gifted the same light as everything else, but chose to give it back. "Does that mean magick actually comes from the Sun?" I ask, and she nods. "Why do you only use the reflection then, and not the source?"

"Magick from the Sun is too intense," Athene answers. "Its radiance overwhelms." She leans forward. "What happens to bright dyes and paints that are in the Sun too long?"

I get a sense of what she means. "They fade."

Athene nods. "And what happens to dough or meat in a pan set too close to a fire?"

That I know from experience. "It burns."

"Exactly." Athene sits back. "The Moon is like an unpolished mirror, reflecting light in a form gentle enough to use." She points to the thick black lines around her eyes. "That's why we use this. We're overly sensitive to light, and the kohl absorbs some of the Sun's glare."

Now I understand why the Sun has been giving me headaches and making my eyes water. Even so, I'm not ready to wear kohl and rise with the moon rather than the Sun. "How long have Selenae been able to use magick?"

"Our ancestors used it to build an empire over two thousand years ago," Athene replies. "Selenic warriors were never limited by night, easily conquering those who could only see in daylight hours."

She falls silent for a few seconds before smiling ironically. "Back then, blood magick was common. Our historians don't mention it, but I imagine it was most useful in interrogating prisoners. Crime within the Selenic Empire was almost nonexistent, because transgressions could never stay hidden. People may lie, but blood never does."

When Athene stops this time, she doesn't continue, just stares at the half-full cup in front of her. "What happened?" I ask. "How did the empire fall?"

For it must have.

"The magick began to fail," she says quietly. "Blood magick slowly became rare, and moon magick grew more and more difficult to handle, as if we became smaller vessels, and it was overflowing, drowning us." Athene looks to Gregor. "We learned to manage it with voidstones and other methods. In an attempt to preserve what we had, consorting with non-Selenae became grounds for being cast out of communities. But blood magick continued to dwindle, even as we kept ourselves separate from the Hadrian Empire which rose to take our place."

Our uncle folds his arms across his chest. "My niece believes if we mingled with Hadrians, it might somehow unlock the magick within our blood."

He plainly doesn't see merit in the idea. "Did my father agree?" I ask.

Gregor snorts. "Your father fell in love with a pretty face. It just happened to belong to a Hadrian. He would have been voided if physicians weren't so rare and needed."

Voided? I don't like the sound of that.

"There's logic in the idea," Athene insists. "Pure metals are rarely as strong as alloys. Bronze is made from copper and tin, steel from iron and charcoal, brass from copper and cadmia. Even gold holds its shape better with some impurities. Meanwhile, the Selenae rust like cast iron."

"And if you're wrong," Gregor challenges, "we lose what little we have."

Athene sets her mouth. "At this point we have nothing to lose. Catrin is evidence I may be right. She not only has blood magick, it's stronger than mine and probably her father's, and that she's discovered, used, and somewhat mastered moon magick completely on her own speaks for itself."

I flush. "You overestimate me."

"Do I?" Athene raises her eyebrows. "When did you first hear the blood of that woman in the alley? When did it call to you?"

"It was at the Sanctum," I say. "I heard her, but . . . I don't think she actually screamed. Her throat was cut."

Gregor scowls. "That's impossible."

That he thinks so is unsettling. I'd accepted the things I could see and do as magick, yes, but as something all Selenae were capable of. Now I'm being told I can do far more.

Athene holds up a hand to tell Gregor to remain silent. "Did you have any other connections with her?" she asks me.

I hesitate. "Bruises. Across my middle. At first I thought they were from my safety rope, but there were seven of them. They matched the knife wounds on Perrete's stomach. I never told anyone."

Even Athene looks startled by that. "Were there any other times you saw or felt something from a distance?"

My fingers tremble so violently the cup rattles in its saucer, and I pull my hands to my lap. "The night the third girl died. By the statue."

"What did you see, Cat?" My cousin leans over to cover my hands with one of hers. She's in awe, but sympathetic.

I take a deep breath. "I was watching the moon set, then suddenly I *was* her. I saw and felt everything she did as he killed her." I choke, remembering her terror and the sensation of blood pouring down my chest, the inability to breathe. "Is that—is that normal among Selenae?"

"No," Athene says quietly. "It's not." Keeping her hand on mine, she eyes Gregor. "Have you ever heard of that happening, Uncle?"

I can tell she knows the answer. "There are legends," he murmurs. "Ancient as the empire, describing how warrior kings and queens could cross a bridge of moonlight to the mind of another person. No one believes they're actually true. Just stories."

"Apparently not," Athene says. She comes out of her chair to wrap her arms around me as I sob.

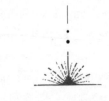

CHAPTER 46

It can't be comfortable for Athene to hold me as she does, bent over my chair as I cry into her moonweave vest. Gregor is silent, watching us. Eventually I pull away, not wanting to ruin her clothes with my runny nose.

"Sorry," I mumble, wiping my face with my hands and sleeve.

Athene backs into her seat with a smile. "It's not the first time you've cried in my arms. You're just a little bigger now."

I look around, realizing we've been overheard by at least a dozen Selenae, who are all staring. Perhaps this wasn't a conversation we should've had in public on a moonlit night. "Does everyone in the Quarter know who I am?" I ask, keeping my voice low, though I know the effort is pointless.

"Most everyone over twenty years does," answers Athene.

"Because of what happened when I was born," I say, and she nods. I chew the inside of my cheek. "Do many of them have the same hopes for me as you did?"

Athene glances at the people overtly eavesdropping. "To be honest, hardly anyone thought of you at all. Selenae don't tend to concern themselves with magick-less outsiders." She sighs. "As for any 'hopes,' I really only wanted you to have enough magick to prove that pure blood wasn't necessary to preserve it. I never dreamed . . ." She gestures vaguely at me as her voice drifts off.

"One problem I foresee now," Athene continues after clearing her throat, "is that you may give our people grand expectations but be something that will never be repeated. The combination of parents' features in their children is by chance, which is why siblings can vary in looks and ability. We could spend generations trying to 'create' another person with your gifts and never succeed. Even if we did, that's more power than any of us know what to do with." She pauses for a few seconds to look pointedly at our silent uncle. "But I firmly believe you and other mixed bloods may save our magick from extinction. At the very least, you're proof that there's no harm in allowing it."

"I disagree," rumbles Gregor. "Catrin is proof of the danger that mingling puts us in. Fifteen Selenae, including my brother, died at the hands of a mob." He gestures to his scarred face. "I was nearly killed for simply looking like him. All because of Hadrian shame over losing a daughter to heretics."

Athene doesn't have an answer for that. All I can think is how I don't want to be seen as any kind of symbol, and certainly not as the person meant to save everyone. My gifts are just that—not something I've earned or achieved. Worse, there is no one equal or superior I can look to for guidance.

Or is there?

Magister Thomas has a brilliant mind, far greater to anyone I've ever met. Remi comes closest, though I'd never tell him that. They could have turned their intelligence to dominating others, but instead they've used it to glorify the Sun and inspire thousands with the Sanctum's beauty, sacrificing their hearts and souls, and—in the architect's case—his family.

And Simon, with his terrible gift for understanding the inner workings of a monster, could easily surrender to the madness himself. He strives to use it in saving others, even at great cost to himself.

Where are my gifts needed the most? I suspect both Gregor and Athene would say that place is here, among people of my blood, but they'd be wrong.

I push back from the table and stand. "I need to go home."

Gregor jumps up, nodding. "Yes. You can stay with me—"

"Not there," I cut him off. "Nor with you, Cousin," I tell Athene, who also rises to her feet. "I mean to go back to the architect's home."

The diagonal scar across my uncle's cheek stretches down as his jaw drops. "No, Catrin, your place is here. With us. We're your family."

I shake my head. "I can't simply forget everything I was before tonight. People I care about have died. Others are fighting an evil bent on destroying more lives. If my magick can help, I'll use it."

"You intend to waste your Moon-given gifts on people who'd spit on you if they knew what you are?" Gregor demands. "The high altum would never let you set foot in your precious Sanctum again."

"Not everyone is so prejudiced, and you know it." I tilt my head in the direction of Solis Abbey. "Besides, those are the very people who raised and cared for me when you abandoned your role as my guardian."

Gregor leans his fists on the table as a vein bulges from his temple. "Do not seek to lecture me on matters you know nothing about."

"I know enough," I snap. "I know you sell *skonia* to the most wretched and miserable among us, profiting from their weakness while telling yourself they deserve it. That's not strength, that's cruelty. If you had any real power you'd be a tyrant." I meet his glare with my own. "Is that the real reason you want me back? Because you think I'll help you get revenge for past wrongs?"

"Get out of my Quarter," he growls. "Before I throw you out."

"You already did that seventeen years ago," I reply. "And as far as I'm concerned, it was the best thing you ever did for me." I reach for the voidstone, but Gregor slaps it off the table.

"That is not yours," he spits as it bounces across the cobblestones. "You will take nothing with you. You were never here."

I'm done arguing with him. Turning away, I head for Athene's, where I left my cloak. I half expect Gregor to follow to prevent me from staying longer than absolutely necessary, but he doesn't. Athene quickly catches up and walks by my side.

"That argument rose faster than a harvest moon," she says dryly.

"Our uncle is a hypocrite," I reply. "He abandons me for years only to welcome me back once he thinks I have magick worth acknowledging. Then he seeks to dictate how I use my gifts."

We reach Athene's door, and she opens it for me. "I didn't say you were wrong."

I step inside. "Thank you."

"Nor did I say you were right."

I stalk to the kitchen. "Then you also think I shouldn't use my abilities to help stop a killer and free an innocent man from prison?"

"If you'll stop putting words in my mouth, I'll tell you what I think." She stands in the doorway, crossing her arms over her chest.

I lift my cloak from the chair. The wool is toasty warm from being near the fire. "I'm listening."

Athene raises her chin. "Gregor has no right to expect you to turn your back on the only world you've known and the people you love, but you need to recognize that he's trying to correct what he sees as the biggest mistake of his life."

"Would that be giving me up or trying to bring me back?" I ask.

She rolls her eyes. "Dark of Night, you're just as stubborn as he is." Athene drops her arms and steps forward to straighten my cloak as I work the clasp. "As for your gifts, I believe you have the right to choose what to do with them, but you need guidance. You need us. And we need you, too."

I sigh. "Maybe I do. But there's a more urgent need for me to stop a killer and free the magister." My cousin is several inches shorter than me, and I look down on her. "And there are other matters I need to set right."

Like Simon.

"Then you should do those things." Athene unfolds the edge of my hood where it was turned inside out. "But like it or not, you are a bridge between Hadrians and Selenae. If you destroy that connection, you destroy yourself."

It may be too late. "Is Gregor truly angry enough to never allow me to return?"

Athene steps back and shrugs. "You've wounded him, but family is more important to him than anything else. Why else would he have watched over you for so many years?"

"Because he promised my father he would?"

She shakes her head. "Because barely an hour after you were gone he regretted leaving you at the convent. He's been waiting over seventeen years for an excuse to swoop in and bring you back, but neither the prioress nor the architect ever gave him one. That's why it cut him so deeply when you said giving you up was the best thing he ever did for you."

I never would have befriended Marguerite or worked for the

architect. I never would have met Simon. "I'm not sure it *was* a mistake."

"And that hurts him even more to admit."

I need to go before Gregor comes to make sure I've left. Wanting to say goodbye to Marguerite, I cross the kitchen and go into the sickroom, but she's asleep. Athene discourages me from waking her, so I just squeeze her hand and kiss her nose. Then my cousin walks with me through the streets. The moon is gone, and I'm not certain I could find my way in the dark alone.

At the vine-draped alley leading to the road separating the Quarter and the Abbey of Light, Athene gives me a quick hug, promising to send word if Marguerite's condition changes. Then she places something in my hand—the leather pouch with the voidstone.

"Gregor said I couldn't take this," I object, even as my heart beats faster with anticipation of practicing with it.

"He borrowed it from me, so it's none of his affair what I do with it." Athene nods at the small sack. "There's a moonstone in there, too, though it's almost spent. Be sure to keep them separate."

Something she said earlier flashes in my mind. "You said voidstones were once used as weapons. How so? Because they're sharp?"

Athene shakes her head. "A voidstone will absorb any magick you push into it through your skin." She pauses as though what she's about to say is awful. "But if it touches your blood, it will *take* your magick. All of it. In an instant."

I shiver imagining how it must feel. "Forever?"

"Thankfully, no. You can get the magick back by exposing your blood to moonlight again, like the first time, but it's . . . like dying." Athene shudders. "In the days of the Selenic Empire, thin arrowheads and blades of voidstone were designed to break off tiny pieces inside wounds, leaving the victim completely without magick. Those who weren't killed shortly after often wished they had been."

"Voided," I whisper, understanding the term Gregor used earlier. "Is that what you do to Selenae who are cast out of the community?"

She nods. "Several pieces are put under the skin to prevent them ever using magick again. Many go mad without it."

"Will Gregor try to do that to me?"

"It's what he's been trying to prevent," answers Athene. "By our rules, it should have been done when he left you with the prioress, just in case you had magick, but he convinced our elders that you did not. If your origins become known to Hadrians, you will have to choose whether to be part of us or part of them."

"And if I refuse to make that choice?"

"It will be made for you."

Now I know the reason Mother Agnes kept no written record of where I came from. Magister Thomas, too. He may have been truthful about shielding Remi and Mistress la Fontaine and the Sanctum by not saying he was in the Quarter that night, but he was also protecting me.

I don't know what else to say. "Thank you. For everything."

"Moon keep you, Catrin." The silver of her eyes gleams as Athene steps back into the shadow. "Until we meet again."

As her shape melts completely into the dark alley, I turn to face the Sanctum on the hilltop, which glows a ghostly white even in just starlight. For a long moment I stand there, in the no-man's-land between the People of the Sun and the People of the Moon.

Then I cross the divide and head home.

CHAPTER 47

A bank of cold, wet clouds rolls over Collis the next morning, shrouding the Sanctum towers in low-hanging fog. I drag myself out of bed two hours after Remi has already left. My climbing clothes are still damp from washing, so I put on my skirt, tucking the pouch with the two stones in the inner pocket where I keep my key to the back door. Though I won't have a chance to use them during the day, their presence gives me some comfort.

When I join him at the work site, Remi is too preoccupied to complain about my tardiness. The wet weather gives him the perfect excuse to shift work indoors and start raising the ceiling's rib stones to the platform. I consider telling him off for doing exactly what the magister had forbidden, but little can progress outside with so much rain coming down.

I opt to work outdoors despite the steady drizzle, seeing as it's the first time the newly aligned drainage system is truly being tested. Also, I want to be where Remi isn't. Even with the magister's old waterproofed jacket over my clothes, I'm soaked to the bone by noon, when a voice from the ground calls my name. I look down to see Lambert Montcuir waving at me. Since I'm wearing a long skirt, I walk along the edge of the roof to the south transept tower and take the stairs rather than climb down the scaffolds, and Lambert waits patiently just inside the door.

His cheeks are ruddy with more than the cold day. It's on the tip of my tongue to ask him for news of the magister or if, against all expectation, Simon has sent for me, but he's the son of a comte, and therefore always gets to set the topic of conversation.

"Good day, Catrin," Lambert begins. "Is there a problem that requires you to work outside today?"

Raindrops fly from the oiled cloth tied over my hair as I shake my head. I don't know why I bother. The moisture in the air has my hair springing out in every direction. If I'd let it get soaked, it would be too heavy to do anything but hang in clumps, but at least I wouldn't look like a wild bramble patch. "Just making sure there are no leaks and all the rain is flowing in the right direction, my lord," I say.

He frowns. "You insisted I call you Catrin yesterday. I'd hoped we were on friendly enough terms that you might just call me Lambert."

I'm not sure how to react. There's a world of difference between dropping Miss or Master for people of low rank like Simon and me and omitting the noble title of a superior. Remi is casual with Oudin because of their friendship, and when it comes to men and women, only siblings and engaged or married couples tend to have that closeness. I am none of those things to Lambert—nor do I want to be—but I suppose after yesterday's visit to the gaol, we share a secret of sorts, though so does Oudin. The thought of him makes me grimace.

Lambert misunderstands my expression. "Or that's not necessary," he says quickly.

"Oh, no!" I say. "I was just thinking of someone else."

"Do you mean Simon?" The soggy feather in his velvet cap droops down next to his face, making him look forlorn.

"No, no," I assure him. But I don't want him to believe I think about Oudin a lot, either. "Remi. I mean, Remone, the architect's assistant. We got into an argument over that topic, is all."

Of course, that was about my familiar address with *Simon*, not him.

"Remone la Fontaine." Lambert's voice is flat. "You've known him many years."

The last person Lambert ought to be jealous of is Remi. "Yes. He's like a brother," I say. "A big, annoying brother who makes you want to shove his face in a bowl of porridge."

Lambert smiles at that, and I relax.

"I don't want to take you from your work for too long," he says.

I push a wet spiral of hair off my forehead. "It's time to break for the noon meal anyway." I deliberately avoid using his name. "I was about to head home to eat. Would you care to accompany me?"

"Nothing would please me more," he says, offering his arm. I take it, and we walk outside. Mercifully, the rain has stopped for a few minutes, but he's still much drier than I am. Lambert clears his throat. "Don't take this as an insult, Catrin, but you don't look like you've slept well."

"I haven't," I reply. "I'm worried sick about the magister, but Simon won't tell me anything, and meanwhile work must continue here. In a way, having something to do is helpful, but it's difficult to concentrate."

Lambert stops. "Simon has managed to delay any kind of trial," he says. "The architect is in no immediate danger."

"Yes, but he's not young," I say. "His cell is cold and damp, and I can't imagine he's fed very well. He could easily become sick."

Lambert coils a finger around one of the curls which escaped my hair cover. "I hate to think of all the burdens you carry, with no one to share them with."

He's looking at me in an unmistakable way. Light of Day, this is my fault. Yesterday I hung on his arm and cried and kissed his cheek to get what I wanted, and somewhere in all of that I crossed a line and made him think I feel more for him than I do.

Lambert leans a little lower, dipping his head close to mine. I have no doubt he's one second away from kissing me—and in public where anyone could see. In fact, anyone on this side of the Sanctum has a full view. *Remi* might be watching us.

I take a quick step back, yanking my hair from his grasp, trying to think of something to say. Anything that will end this moment without hurting him. "Do you hear that?" I gasp.

He looks back at the Sanctum, eyes wide. To my surprise, there's a commotion on the roof. Workers are running and shouting where I was walking only a few minutes ago. As we watch, the whole structure groans and shudders. Lambert wears a stunned expression. "What's happening up there?"

Muffled cracks and pops are suddenly interrupted by the shattering of windows. As the noise of glass fades to a series of almost musical tinkles, the sound of splintering wood becomes louder. Through the openings I can see objects inside—one looks like a person—falling from the highest scaffolds, and I hear thuds and bangs as they hit the marble floor.

Light of Heaven, Remi, what have you done?

I'm already running back to the Sanctum with Lambert on my heels, my heavy, damp skirt clinging to my knees, as the last of the crashing noises echoes out and across the plain below the city.

CHAPTER 48

A rescue effort is underway by the time I get inside the Sanctum. Workers and bystanders dig through the wreckage, searching for survivors, calling the names of friends and loved ones. Heavy stone blocks rest where they landed. Parts of the marble floor are smashed, with cracks running out from the center of the impacts in a sickly imitation of the sun designs so carefully set in place last year. Wooden beams hewn from ancient forests lie broken like matchsticks. Shards of colored glass litter the ground inside and out. All the while, rain pours in from the windows and unknown holes in the roof, trailing in rivers through the wreckage.

The high altum and his assisting priests and brothers don't even pause for prayers, singing the evening liturgy from memory as they work, providing a haunting sense of hope and beauty in the devastation. Not a single eye is dry when they finish.

It could have been much worse. The rain meant fewer people were working today, and the slow collapse had allowed almost everyone time to run to safety. Almost.

At least three more names will be added to the list on the wall tonight. Two men may never walk again. A dozen others will need months to heal from their injuries.

Lambert is right beside me, feverishly pulling pieces of rubble aside, long scratches running up his arms from lifting splintered wood. At some point, my hair cover is used to bind a wound. Oudin is there, too. He works as hard as anyone I see, finding the first of the three bodies. I don't dare touch any of the dead. Their last thoughts will only haunt my dreams.

———— • ✳ • ————

Everyone trickles away from the Sanctum as night falls, many to mourn. There's no energy to start cleaning up the mess or cover the windows now empty of their colorful, intricate designs. The Montcuir brothers are the last to leave, and Oudin scowls as Lambert squeezes my hand in sympathy before slipping quietly away.

I find Remi in the middle of the wreckage, sitting on the remains of the great wheel used to raise heavy loads to the scaffolding platform sixty feet above. Marble and limestone dust coats his skin, making him look like he belongs on a high perch outside, glowering over the whole city with the rest of the statues.

The guilt he feels must be unbearable. I want to shout at him for doing exactly what the magister had told him not to, but what good would that do? Instead, I pick my way across the rubble until I'm within arm's reach. "Remi?" I whisper. "Let's go home."

He turns on me, his face contorted in wrath. "You have a lot of nerve speaking to me right now."

Blame is the last thing he needs to hear. "There's nothing more we can do tonight. I'm sure your mother's worried about you."

Remi clambers down from the broken wheel and faces me. "Why are you here, Cat?"

"I'm here because I care about you," I say. "Not to gloat. Even master architects make mistakes. You just have to learn from them."

His green eyes widen. "This is *my* fault?"

If he thinks he's going to turn this around on me like he did Magister Thomas's imprisonment, he'd better think again. I jab a finger at the stones for the vaulting arches, representing months of precise cutting and shaping, now cracked and broken and unusable. "This is exactly what the master architect forbade you from doing." Then I raise my arm to point at the splintered remains of the supports above. "And *that* is exactly why!"

Remi wrenches my arm down by the wrist, his expression cold. "There's something I need to show you."

He drags me to a side door as I trip and stumble on debris. Instead of going outside as I expect, he pulls me into the staircase leading up into the south tower. I know these steps well enough to tread them with my eyes closed, yet I continuously stub my toes as Remi yanks me relentlessly upward. When we reach the roof level, he leads me to the edge, facing east. The setting sun breaks through on the horizon behind us, painting the clouds with brilliant shades of orange and pink and violet. It would be beautiful, if it weren't for the destruction that lies under the roof.

"What do you see, Cat?" he spits. The grip on my arm is like an iron shackle while his other hand points to the outer wall.

"Flying buttresses," I retort. "Meant to support the weight of the ceiling by drawing it outward and down to the ground." I may not have Remi's extensive knowledge in building such things, but I understand how they work.

"Correct," Remi snaps. "Now tell me where it looks like they've failed."

I open my mouth to answer but realize the columns and stone arches are all perfectly straight and undamaged, as is the wall itself. Impossible.

"The other side is the same, before you ask," says Remi. "All the buttresses were set enough to bear the weight, that was never in question." He releases my wrist, and I turn to face him, my lips moving in silent confusion. His eyes are full of hurt. "Did you really think I would do something so dangerous?"

"But then what—"

"Made it collapse?" Remi cuts me off. "We were lifting vaulting stones to the platform, arranging them to assemble tomorrow. The wheel was raising the last load when everything began to fall apart. Not even the central beams supporting from above could hold it up. I can't even imagine how those might be damaged."

Until I saw the buttresses, I'd assumed Remi's actions had put strain on them too early, making the walls collapse outward, but they were intact, and he hadn't even started the arches that would put stress on them. I shake my head. "But what you're describing is weight the platform should have been able to hold."

Remi crosses his arms. "And there you have it. The internal support failed." He lets a long silence draw out before forcing me to acknowledge what he's saying. "Whose job is it to inspect the scaffolding, Cat?"

Though I've hardly eaten all day, I think I'm going to vomit. "Mine," I whisper.

"Who signed her name to the final schematic drawing, saying it was all in place and safe?" he demands.

"I did."

"Who told us her work was done enough to spend half her

time running around Pleasure Road chasing ghosts? Who spent the last two days flirting with the provost's son?"

That accusation is something I won't let pass. "I went to visit our master where he languishes in prison!"

"While I'm trying to hold his life's work together with no help from you!" he bellows.

"People are dying, Remi!" I shout back. "People I care about! I have to do something to stop it!"

I realize what I've said. Both my hands clap over my mouth, but it's too late.

Remi raises his eyebrows. "You're right about people dying."

Agony swells inside my chest, and I struggle to hold it in.

He leans down to put his eyes level with mine and twists the knife of guilt in my stomach. "As for the people you care about, I think it's obvious the killer chose them for exactly that reason, including framing the magister for their deaths."

My knees give out, and I land in a heap of soggy skirt. "Remi, please!" I sob into my hands as he stands over me. "You have to know I never meant for any of this to happen. I only thought of protecting Magister Thomas!"

Remi had defended me only two nights ago, but not now.

"Soup and apologies are no good to him, Cat," he says coldly. "He needed you *here*, doing what you were hired to do." Remi chokes. "*I* needed you here."

I have no answer, and he doesn't wait for one. Remi pivots away and stalks back to the stairs, disappearing from view at the same time as the sun.

⸺ • ✳ • ⸺

I stay where I collapsed long after Remi leaves. The rain begins again and falls on me through the open arches, but I don't move.

Bells in the facade tower call the brothers to midnight liturgy, and soon after their haunting chants echo out of the broken windows below. When the voices finally die away, the altum leads them back to bed. Two sets of footsteps walk through the Sanctum, sandals crunching over debris as they secure the doors for the night. Then they, too, are gone.

At last, I am completely alone, as I should be. Even the moon refuses my company, hiding behind thick clouds.

How had I let this happen? I've spent the last hours mentally climbing over and under and through the scaffolding which collapsed, trying to find the place I neglected. I'd done the work in a hurry, yes, but I'd found areas that needed to be addressed. Two were enough of a concern that I didn't sign Remi's sketch until they were fixed. I had been swift, but thorough. Or so I'd believed.

I need to understand where my mistake was. Joints and muscles scream as I lurch to my feet, and I'm nearly overcome by dizziness. When was the last time I ate? Bread rolls and cups of water had been passed around while we were searching, but I'd barely managed to eat one. Other than that, I'd choked down half a bowl of porridge this morning, and almost nothing yesterday. It's a miracle I can stand.

Despite that, I'm not leaving until I have answers. Without moonlight, I can barely see, but I have the moonstone in my pocket. I pull out the pouch and open it, finding the bag has a dividing part between the two stones to keep them separated. Carefully, I pour the one I want out into my palm, and it glows faintly, but my senses barely increase. Athene had warned me it was almost spent.

Still, I can see a little better. I limp across the tower and down the spiral stairs Remi had dragged me up so many hours ago. My sight is weak enough that I borrow a branch of candles burning near the altar as I pass. The Sun won't begrudge them, and the altum doesn't need to know. Even with the extra light, I can't see how the scaffolding above is damaged, so I start with what's below.

According to Remi, the center of everything was the wooden wheel, and I begin there, visualizing how it was secured to the beam above. A few of the thick supports that had braced the roof itself lie about, one of the many reasons Remi dreads tomorrow. The impact of falling nearly a hundred feet caused fractures along their lengths, meaning they can't be reused. They came from forests many hundreds of miles away, and replacing them will be costly in both time and money.

Spots bare of pitch tell me where beams leaned against each other at angles. Here they are cleanly sheared away, almost like they were cut. Not in every place—some are splintered as I expect. It's hard to judge what something this big breaking apart should look like, especially in the dark, but it feels wrong. Too many things had to have failed for this much damage.

Those parts were the last to fall, however. The critical weakness had to be in the scaffolding that extended up and inward from the wall, but nothing is lying on the ground in a place which tells me where it came from. Stones and lumber were thrown aside in the search for those buried underneath. I have to study the angles of pieces still attached to others for clues as to their position. Several poles and beams are split partially or completely, but it's impossible to see if any of those cracks existed before the collapse or happened during it—or as they landed.

After over an hour, I've found nothing that explains what occurred.

Clutching the moonstone, I sink to my knees next to a pile of rubble and look up to the black cavernous roof above, letting tears stream back into my hair. How did the master architect manage to continue after such a failure? I want to climb up to the highest point and let myself fall back down. A fitting end. What I deserve.

No. I close my eyes and rest my hands on my lap. That would kill Magister Thomas to hear. I can't do that to him. And if he can bear the weight of his past mistakes, so can I.

I will stand up and walk out of here as I did yesterday morning in the prison. That's what he would want.

Shaking from fatigue and hunger, I tuck the moonstone into its pouch and force myself back up to my feet, then bend over to pick up the branch of candles which are almost burned down. Something sticking out from under a pile of debris catches my eye. It looks like pitch-covered rope . . . or hair. Lunging forward, I fling several stones away, thinking I've found another person, but it soon becomes obvious that's not the case. A long braid is wound around a piece of wood more than once, like it was tied to it.

I hold the candles overhead with my left hand as I unwind the braid with my right until I have a length over three feet long of smooth, black hair.

Marguerite's hair.

A message. Left here to be found.

I don't know how the killer managed it, but the destruction around me isn't my doing.

It's his.

CHAPTER 49

Simon. I need to tell Simon.

Getting out of the Sanctum is complicated, though. All the doors are locked, so it's either the window at the far end or ascending the tower to the roof level where I was earlier, and down the scaffolds outside. I'm still in my working skirt, which is full enough that any way out will be awkward, especially in the dark. The broken gallery-level windows are low and wide. They seem like a good option, though I'll have to be careful.

Replacing the candles on the altar, I stuff the long braid between layers of clothing to free my hands. Then I run to the stairs I came down earlier. Just getting to the gallery makes me dizzy, though, and I pause on the landing to let my head stop spinning. As my breathing returns to normal, I hear the tinkle of glass falling to the floor.

Has Remi come looking for me? I step out into the gallery, where murky light streams through the shattered windows. Halfway to the end, a dark shape slides inside the Sanctum, glass crunching as it lands.

"Is that you, Remi?" I call.

The figure startles and turns to face me. Says nothing. Rainwater drips from the cloak covering him head to knees.

That's when I know who it is.

Simon always said the killer would be drawn back to the scene of the murders. On Simon's instructions, Lambert had repeatedly questioned the city guards about men who lingered in those areas. I'm the only one who knows the Sanctum is now one of those places.

I have to get away, outside. I know my way around the building with my eyes closed, but there are too many places to get cornered.

The shadow moves slightly, and metal hisses like it's being dragged across leather. The sound of a knife being drawn. He takes one step toward me, and the blade of a dagger pushes the cloak aside.

Next to me is a window, but not one I would've chosen to climb out. A dozen jagged pieces of glass remain in the frame, pointing inward like teeth. I can't see what's outside, but if there's no scaffold there, it's several feet down to the arcade roof. The killer takes another, faster step, and I have no choice. I leap at the knee-high ledge and launch myself through the dark opening, shielding my face with my arms and praying something is there for me to land on.

Sharp edges catch in my hair and across my skirt as fabric tears. There's scaffolding—thank the Light—but it's a few inches higher than the bottom of the window, and my toe catches on it, dumping me face-first on a platform of woven reeds. I barely have time to realize how I've landed when a gloved hand grabs my ankle. Screaming, I kick his fingers with the heel of my boot and get free enough to crawl out of his reach.

Ahead of me is a twenty-foot drop onto irregular blocks of stone. Just as I pull myself up, the killer comes crashing out of the window. I turn away from flying bits of glass and swing around the upright pole to the other side. My feet find the next horizontal support, and I move across it, gripping the one over my head.

Step-slide. Step-slide.

I open the distance between us to just out of reach as he lunges for me again. A fleeting wish for my moonstone's effects, weak as they would be, goes through my mind, but I would never be able to hold on to it. The poles are slippery with rain and cold enough to numb my fingers in seconds, and I need both my hands. Between darkness and water dripping into my eyes, I move almost entirely by feel. My toes bump into the next vertical strut, and I step around it. Here there's a diagonal pole, too, and I choose to go up rather than stay on this level. The killer follows, grunting, and I nearly fall as my hand reaches for a pole where I expect one but comes up empty. Watching his progress endangers me.

Just get away.

I focus on climbing the web of poles, going up when it seems easier, which is often. If I can get to the roof, I'll have a straight running path along the gutter. Rainwater drips into my left eye, and I take a precious second to wipe it away. My fingers come away dark with blood. I must have cut my scalp going through the window, but my thick hair probably saved me from a much deeper wound. I can't tell how much it's bleeding, though, or if the faintness I feel is from fear, hunger, or loss of blood. Probably all three.

After hauling myself up to the next reed platform, I have to pause until my dizziness subsides. Creaks and groans below tell me what gain I had is dwindling rapidly. I'm next to the clerestory, at the highest row of windows but still two levels below the roof. Here the glass is colorless to let in pure light. The end of a roof beam rests on the edge of my platform, having punched through the window, and if I could trust the scaffolding, I might have considered climbing inside. A narrow triangular fang of glass hangs from the top of the circular frame, and I stretch up to wrest it free.

The skin of my palm splits open against the broken edge, leaking blood on either side. Now I have a weapon, but I doubt my ability to use it effectively. What kind of man am I facing? Simon described him as intelligent, and to have known how to bring the scaffolding down in the short time since I inspected last week, he must be.

A gloved hand appears on the edge of the platform, and I scramble out of its reach. The pointed edge of my makeshift knife scratches across the woven platform, slicing deeper into my palm, but suddenly I have an idea.

Adjusting the glass in my hand, I keep moving backward, dragging the sharp edge along the reeds where they're lashed around the frame, pressing hard enough to cut through them.

Deeper into the shadows I move until my back is against a corner created by a thicker part of the Sanctum wall. A visible trail of blood leads to me, hopefully obscuring what I've done. The killer heaves his upper body over the far end of the platform. With the hood over his head I can still see nothing of his face, but he can see and hear me as I gasp and wheeze. I'm not trying to hide or get away anymore. I'm setting a trap.

As he brings a leg up, I worry he'll have a close look at what I've done, so I hurl the bloody piece of glass in his direction to distract him. He bats it away and rises to his feet. The effort of my throw puts me on the verge of passing out. The killer pauses, like he's savoring this moment, and draws his knife again.

Yes. Come toward me.

He takes one step forward, then another. Under his feet, the reeds sag, but don't break. Blackness creeps in from the margins of my already narrowed and dimming sight. If this isn't going to work, at least I'll be unconscious when he kills me.

But then there's a series of shredding cracks, each one coming more rapidly than the last, and the platform gives, tearing away from the edge like fabric. The killer falls, at first only to his waist, then the impact of his weight rips the remaining hold the reeds have on the frame, and the rest of him vanishes beneath, the last being the hand still holding the dagger.

I sag to the side, fighting the dark waves that seek to cover me, as the scaffolds shudder with every impact the killer makes on the way down. There's no work being performed below, so there are no more platforms, only poles at several angles. The hits are frequent enough that he never builds up any speed as he falls, but nor can he slow himself. Everything finally ends with a thud as he lands on the slanted roof of the arcade below.

It's not safe yet. I should get up and move away, but all I can think of is rest. Curling up on the tiny corner of the platform that remains attached, I close my eyes.

Just for a minute.

CHAPTER 50

It's still dark when I open my eyes, and too many clouds blanket the sky to give any hint as to the hour. My bloody right hand is cradled to my chest, making me aware of the thick, coiled braid between the layers of my clothes. As soon as I recall what happened, I sit up straight, wincing as a number of hairs rip out, glued to the platform by thickening blood. Then I fight a wave of nausea that eases only to leave a pounding headache in its wake.

Where is he?

Cautiously, I lean over the edge and peer down. The roof of the arcade where he would have landed is clear, and there's no movement on the scaffolds. Though I'm tempted to stay here until morning, my instincts tell me the killer has fled. I need to find Simon and tell him what I found.

Climbing down is slow and arduous, especially as I stop often to listen for signs the killer is still about. The cuts on my hand and fingers bleed freely again despite my efforts not to use them. Once my feet are on the ground, I want to run, but I don't have the strength to do more than hobble the length of the Sanctum and down the street leading to the Montcuir house. Not wanting to cause a scene, I limp around to the kitchen door, hoping at least one servant sleeps downstairs. I pound my good fist on the wood, but the sound is weak. "Help!" I croak. "Please! Somebody!"

Simon himself opens the door only a few seconds later, silhouetted by the golden light of a low fire. He had to have already been in the kitchen, but he blinks like he just woke up. "Cat?" His eyes widen as he takes in the sight of me. "Light of Day, what's happened?"

I open my hand to show him. "It's all my blood, but I'm all right."

"Like hell you are." Simon pulls me inside and shuts the door. Then he puts a finger to my lips and looks up at the ceiling for a few seconds. When we don't hear anyone stirring above, he leads me to a wooden chair between a table and the hearth. "Sit," he commands.

I obey. The seat is warm like he was in it before I arrived. Simon turns away to rummage in a cabinet. His blond curls are pressed flat on one side and the impression of wrinkled fabric is on the cheek below. "Were you sleeping here at the table?" I ask.

"Yes." He uncorks and sniffs several bottles and jars, setting some aside and putting others back. "It was a bad night for Juliane. Worse than usual."

A pot rests nearby on the table. I'm shivering with cold and shock and pain, and it looks heavenly. "Is that tea hot?" I ask, my teeth chattering. "Can I have some?"

"Grace and Light, no!" Simon swings around, balancing his chosen containers and a wad of linen bandages, and hastily drops it all on the table. He grabs the pot away and runs with it to the back door to dump it on the ground outside.

Shaking his head, Simon switches out the empty pot with a large wooden bowl on a shelf and brings that to the table. He fills it with steaming water from a kettle before bending over my head to study the cut in my scalp. I close my eyes as his long fingers comb through my hair. "Not very deep," he mutters. "I think it's done bleeding, but it'll still need to be cleaned." Simon kneels in front of me and gently opens my hand. "What happened, Cat?"

"There was a collapse at the Sanctum," I say, relieved he seems to have put aside my betrayal. "Three people were killed."

Simon hisses in sympathy, either over my wound or the news. "Lambert told us. I'm sorry." He dips a scrap of cloth in the bowl and begins wiping my hand. The water is warm but not hot. "These cuts happened within the last hour, though. What were you doing?"

"I was at the Sanctum, trying to discover what had caused it." I sniff and wipe my nose with my free hand. "It's my job to make sure these things don't happen."

Simon looks up sharply. "Did Remone blame you?"

"He had every reason to."

Simon tosses the bloody rag on the table. "If Remone was in charge at the site, that makes it his responsibility," he growls, angling my palm into the light. With his free hand, he opens a bottle and pours clear liquid onto a fresh cloth. The pungent fumes burn the inside of my nose. "This will sting," he warns before putting the wet linen on my palm.

Sting isn't the right word—it feels like I'm being slashed with a red-hot knife. I jerk away reflexively, but he holds on to my wrist. "Easy," he says softly. "It won't last long."

I writhe in the chair as the pain slowly recedes to a bearable level. When he lifts the cloth away, I expect my hand to have a hole burned through the middle, but it looks the same. "What was that?"

"Alcohol, more pure than anyone would sanely drink. It will prevent infection." Simon drops the bloodstained cloth onto the table and opens the lid of a clay jar, doing everything with his right hand. His left has never stopped holding mine.

"Are you still angry with me?" I ask timidly.

Simon scoops salve with two of his fingers and pauses to meet my eyes. "For lying about the hammer or for visiting the architect in the gaol?"

So he knows. I shift uncomfortably while he just raises his eyebrows and lets me fidget.

Finally, Simon looks back down and spreads ointment on my palm and fingers gentler than I expected him to. "The jug of stew you left was too wide to fit between the bars of his cell. It was still warm when I got there." He sighs. "I gave it to him."

"I'm sorry."

"No, you're not." Simon wipes his fingers clean, then pulls up a long strip of linen. Swiftly, he wraps my hand with the bandage while I struggle and fail to come up with an adequate reply. He finishes looping the end around and ties it to the beginning. "This needs to be sutured, but I can't do it. You'll have to find a real healer soon."

"Thank you," I whisper.

"You're welcome." Simon uses the table to lever himself to a stand. "You scared the Light out of me, banging on the door covered in blood." He soaks a fresh scrap in the water and angles my chin up to wipe the side of my face, studiously avoiding meeting my eyes. "So you were climbing around the Sanctum in the dark and what? You hit your head?"

For a few minutes, with Simon tending to me, I'd forgotten what happened. Now it comes crashing down on me like Sanctum scaffolds. "Simon, he was there."

Simon rinses the cloth and squeezes it out, still refusing to look me full in the face. "Who was there? Remone?"

I shake my head, tears leaking from my eyes. "No. *Him*. The killer."

He freezes with the cloth dripping water into my hair and finally meets my gaze, disbelief on his shadowed face. "What?"

Taking a shaky breath, I reach into my over-tunic with my left hand. "What happened today at the Sanctum wasn't my fault or Remi's." I pull the long braid out to show him. "And it wasn't an accident."

Even coated in dust, the ebony gloss shines through. Simon drops the sopping cloth and takes it from me. "Is this . . . ?"

"Marguerite's hair, yes, or some of it." I'm too exhausted to do anything but babble. "I found it wrapped around a broken piece of scaffolding. I don't know how or when, but he did it. He killed those people. He killed them because of me, like he killed Mother Agnes."

Simon comes to his knees in front of me again, anger radiating from his eyes. "No, Cat. *None* of this is your fault. It's his." He cups my cheek with his free hand. "It's *all* his. And mine. For failing to stop him."

Firelight throws shadows across his cheeks and the hollows under his eyes. I still haven't told him the worst part. "Simon," I whisper. "He came back to the Sanctum tonight. I saw him."

Comprehension dawns on him. Simon releases the braid to fall in my lap and takes my injured hand in his as the other slides into my hair. "*He* did this to you?"

I nod again and slowly tell him what happened, finishing with, "And when I looked down, he was gone."

Simon closes his eyes and lowers his head, shaking it as if in denial. His fingers tighten in my hair and around my bandaged hand, and the muscles in his arm tense, bringing me closer.

Then, without warning, he pulls my mouth to his.

The restraint he had before is gone, and he's kissing me—not with gentle agony like last time—but with urgent need, as if he desperately wants to tell me something before it's too late.

I'm sorry I'm sorry I'm sorry.

I'm not sure what he's apologizing for—for being angry with me, for what happened tonight, for not kissing me every time he wanted to—maybe all those things and more, but it's effortless to kiss him back. I want him to know how sorry I am, and that I never want to hurt him again.

I almost lost you.

I use my lips to tell him that he didn't. That I'm here.

Save me from myself, Cat. Please. You're the only one who can.

Wait. Something's not right.

It's almost physically painful to break away, but I place my unwrapped hand on Simon's chest and push him back. His heart beats like a drum against my fingers as he searches my face. Something about the firelight gives the brown flaw a reddish cast, like dried blood, and there's the beginning of a bruise on one cheek and a recent cut in the corner of his mouth. A tiny drop of blood emerges as he licks his lips.

"What happened?" I reach up to touch the spot, straining in anticipation to hear what it will say.

Simon leans back, covering his cheek with his hand. There are several small puncture wounds above his wrist I hadn't noticed earlier, with flowering blue-black spots beneath.

"Juliane," he says. "Lambert and I had to restrain her." Simon looks down at the fresh bruises on the back of his hand. "Lately it's harder and harder to talk her out of her delusions. Tonight she was convinced the shadows in her room would kill her."

My heart aches for her and for those watching her deteriorate. "Was your father like this?"

Simon nods wearily. "For years. And this is only the beginning with Juliane." He rubs his neck as he rises from his crouch. "My uncle found out we've been using *skonia* to calm her down, and he was furious, him being the provost and all. At least Oudin never used it in the house."

"I'm sorry."

He shrugs. "I think it was starting to do more harm than good. And the doses had grown dangerously large." Simon glances at the empty teapot, and I understand why he'd swept it away from me. "She's been asleep for the last few hours. Madame Denise is with her."

I stand, wincing with all the bruises and scrapes. "Is there some way I can help?"

Simon shakes his head. "They want to keep this quiet like they did with her mother. In the family."

"What about the inquiry?" I ask, my throat tightening with hope. "If Juliane can't help anymore, you need me—"

"Cat," Simon interrupts with gentle firmness. "You're too close to the magister to be objective. It's bad enough that I'm . . . close to you."

I step up to him. "Are you . . . close to me?" My bandaged hand settles on his chest again. "Am I forgiven?"

Simon's mouth quirks to the side, stretching the cut open wider. "Your actions weren't helpful, but you wanted to protect him." He leans down until his nose touches mine. "As for being close to you, I thought I made it obvious a couple minutes ago," he whispers. "I need you more than ever."

My good arm goes around his neck, and as Simon pulls me against him, I forget my injuries, my weariness, and my fear, focusing instead on the feel of my lips on his.

Will you protect me as you protected him?

"Yes," I whisper against his mouth. "I will."

For one minute, nothing else exists in the world.

For one minute everything is perfect.

Then the screaming starts.

CHAPTER 51

It's muffled at first. Distant.

Simon breaks from our kiss and looks up, still holding me against him, and stares at the ceiling as though he can see through it. A door upstairs bangs open, and the screaming becomes louder.

"Is it Juliane?" I ask. "Did she wake?"

Simon shakes his head, eyes wide. "No, that's Madame Denise."

Juliane's governess pounds on other doors above, her shrieks echoing down to us.

"She's dead! Lady Juliane is dead!"

Simon releases me and staggers back, his gaze going to the teapot on the shelf. "Holy Light, what have I done?"

I take a step forward. "Simon—"

"Cat, you have to leave, now." Simon spins me around by my shoulders and pushes me to the door. "No one can know you were here." Throwing the door open, he sweeps me outside. "Go! Now! Get somewhere safe!"

"Simon!"

The door slams shut. I stand on the stoop for a moment, dazed. Juliane is dead? I step back and my boot lands in a puddle.

The pungent scent of valerian root rises from the splashed liquid. The tea Simon poured out.

He thinks he killed her.

I'm not leaving. Even tired, bandaged, and wearing a skirt, I'm able to scale the wall into the garden behind the house. I tiptoe past a window until I'm under Juliane's room. Digging into my pocket, I find the moonstone and clench it in my unwrapped hand. Magick illuminates the world around me, and I close my eyes to listen.

The effect isn't very strong, but I'm too tired to concentrate beyond the mild distractions. I'm forced to switch the stone to my other hand and dip my left into the side of the pouch with the voidstone. Once I've clumsily pushed everything but what I hear into the pitch-black stone, I release it.

"Juliane! Wake up, please!" The bed creaks as Oudin collapses either on or against it, sobbing. "It was the *skonia*. We killed her."

"It was no more than we've given her before," insists Simon.

"Father will blame you, though," says Lambert. His heavy footsteps move around the room. It sounds like he's barefoot.

"Maybe he should," says Simon dully. I can barely hear their voices over Oudin's weeping—something I didn't expect from him.

"No," says Lambert firmly, then pauses. "Where's Father? Wasn't he in his bed?"

"He went to the Palace of Justice around midnight, remember?" says Simon.

"I thought I heard him come back a couple of hours ago." Lambert ends it like a question.

"That must have been me." Madame Denise's voice is muffled, like she's holding her apron over her face. "I went downstairs for a few minutes."

"What?" Lambert yelps. "You left her alone?"

The woman starts to cry. "She was asleep. I just needed to use the privy and stretch my legs. I was gone less than a quarter hour," she wails. "When I returned, it was a while before I realized how still she was. She must have passed while I was gone."

"Someone needs to fetch Father." Oudin sniffles.

I can't warn them he's already here, at the front door. A manservant is telling him what happened. Barely seconds pass before the comte pounds up the stairs and crashes into the room, shouting, "Where is she?"

There's silence as he takes in the scene. Then, "You killed her, you Prezian bastard."

"Father, no!" Lambert grunts like he's restraining him. "You saw what she was like tonight. We all tried to calm her down. He did no more than any of us."

"It was his *skonia* tea," the comte snarls.

"It was my *skonia*," says Oudin quickly.

Oudin is defending Simon?

"And I forced her to drink it," finishes Lambert.

My hearing isn't strong enough to discern the comte's reply, but from the sound of it, he stopped struggling.

"She's gone, Father," Oudin says. "But you know how much worse she was going to get. Her suffering is over. Maybe this is a blessing."

"We need to discuss this elsewhere," adds Lambert. "And let her spirit rest until it can leave."

Madame Denise steps forward, snuffling. "I'll stay with her."

"Simon will do that," growls the comte. "He has no say in our matters, especially now."

"I was going to volunteer to stay," Simon says quietly.

Footsteps move toward the door. "Madame Denise," says Lambert. I imagine him guiding her out. "Please fetch the tea we made for Lady Juliane so Father can see for himself how mild it was. We'll be in the study."

Simon is left alone, and I desperately want to talk to him. I step away from the house and study the wall. Several wooden beams are set at angles with plaster between them. Grand as it looks, rich people don't realize the decorative effect only makes it easier for someone to climb up to a second- or third-story window. I've just visualized the best way to get up to Juliane's room when light comes from the window facing the garden. I dodge out of sight and press myself against the wall next to it. Apparently that room is the study.

"I won't have it known I had *skonia* in my house," the comte is saying. "Nor that my own daughter was mad."

Oudin snorts. "It's always about appearances with you, isn't it, Father?"

The diamond-shaped panes of glass glow brighter as more candles are lit, and a chair creaks as someone—probably the comte—sits down. "You only think so because you care so little," he says. "I want Simon out of my house by sunrise. I haven't decided whether that's on his own or with an escort to the gaol."

"You can't imprison a venatre," Lambert insists.

"Simon botched the inquiry," the comte snaps. "I've got my master architect in prison on his orders, yet he insists the man isn't guilty. Meanwhile I've publicly hanged a man for crimes he didn't commit."

A shadow moves across the glass like Lambert is leaning down. "Trust me, Father, no one wants to stop the killer more than Simon."

"You will take over his investigation."

"I don't understand the things he does!" Lambert protests. "He knew exactly what had happened with the grain merchant's wife before we even found her! If it had been me, I would've made the same mistake you did. You should have listened to him!"

No matter what happens, I owe Lambert more than anything.

A knock on the door interrupts what anyone might have said next. Knowing they will all look away from the window, I take the chance to peek in. Madame Denise enters the room, but the glass distorts too much for me to tell what she's holding.

"Begging you pardon, Your Grace." She bobs a curtsy. "I've brought the pot as you wanted, but it's empty."

"Of course it is," grumbles the comte.

"And I brought this, too," she continues. "I don't know where it came from, but I thought it was strange."

"Is that hair?" the comte asks, rising to his feet.

Grace of Day, Marguerite's braid. We left it in the kitchen.

"It was on the floor." The distorted shape of Madame Denise sets something else on the desk. "But this was on the table."

Red on white is all I can distinguish. The rags Simon used to clean my hand.

"Is that blood?" says the comte. "Who was in the kitchen?"

"Simon," answers Oudin. "He came up the stairs rather than down."

I duck back from the window, my heart pounding. No. Not this.

"Is Simon injured somehow?" asks the comte.

"Not that I saw," Lambert answers. "But there has to be a logical explanation."

"You know exactly what it is, Brother," says Oudin. "Simon hasn't found the killer because he *is* the killer."

I bite my bandaged hand to keep from screaming. *No, no, no, no, NO!*

Shadows flicker as Lambert paces across the room. "That's not possible."

"It's the *only* possibility," Oudin snaps back. "That hair belongs to the little sister and you know it."

"Explain this to me," their father says. "Now."

Lambert doesn't answer. Oudin's shadow raises an arm, probably holding up the braid. "The killer always took the victim's hair and left at least part of it with the body of the next woman. That's how Simon knew they were all connected. The only person who could have this hair is the one who killed the prioress and the sister."

"The sister didn't die," Lambert says feebly.

There's a long pause. "There were also no deaths while he was in Mesanus," says the comte slowly.

"Simon isn't like that!" Lambert insists.

Oudin snorts. "Simon has spent his whole life surrounded by insane people, why is it so hard to believe that he didn't become one of them?"

The comte's shadow rises from its chair. "Do either of you have proof he didn't commit any of the murders?"

Another endless silence before Lambert answers, "No, Father." I can feel the pain being honest gives him.

"It's settled then," says the comte. "Call for the guard, Lambert."

"I won't."

"You always were a disappointment," Montcuir says flatly. "Oudin, go. Bring them back here. Quickly. Quietly."

"What about Juliane?" Oudin asks.

"She's dead." The comte moves closer to the window, and I back away. "She died in her sleep. That's all anyone needs to know."

"Yes, Father."

Oudin leaves the room. The moonstone is already back in my pocket, and I'm halfway up the wall, using both hands though it causes my wounds to bleed anew. I peer into Juliane's room before raising my head fully above the sill. A single candle lights the space. Simon sits in a chair near the door with his face in his hands. He looks up, startled, as I pull myself over the window ledge as quietly as possible.

"Cat?" he whispers, coming to his feet. "What are you doing here? Why didn't you go home?"

I rush to his side. "Simon, the comte is going to have you arrested."

His pale eyes drift to the body of his cousin on the bed. "Maybe he should."

"No!" I grab his shoulders and shake him. "Listen to me! They found Marguerite's braid in the kitchen. They're going to arrest you for the murder of all those women!"

Simon looks back to me, numb. "Does it even matter anymore?"

"It will matter when he kills again!"

"Just leave, Cat. Don't worry about me. My arrest will free the architect."

I want to slap him. "No. If you don't come with me now, I will stay here and explain exactly what I found at the Sanctum and why you're innocent. And I'll tell the whole city how Juliane died."

Simon's expression darkens, but at least it's not blank anymore. "Cat, my uncle will do whatever it takes to save face, even if it means throwing you in the gaol, too."

"I know. That's why you'd better come with me."

He shakes his head. "Cat, I'm not worth this kind of risk."

I drag him with me to the window. "That's my decision." The garden below is dark, meaning the study is empty again. Quietly, I point out the places Simon needs to put his hands and feet to climb down. "You first," I tell him. I won't risk him not following.

Making a noise of exasperation, he throws one leg over the sill, then the other, and feels for the toeholds I showed him. "How did you do this in a skirt?" he hisses.

"Years of practice." I help Simon ease down until he's at a height low enough to jump the rest of the way. He lands with a grunt.

I stand straight and look back at the room. We'll need all the time we can get, so I quickly cross to the door and bolt it from the inside. That will take a while to break through. Turning around, I catch sight of Juliane's sallow face. She lies on her back with her eyes half open, like the shutters of an empty, lifeless house. The coverlet has fallen to her waist, probably from Oudin shaking her, and one thin arm hangs over the side of the bed. I can't just leave her like that.

I tread quietly to her side and gently close her eyes with my fingers, then pull the blanket up higher. When I grab her cold hand to lay it across her chest, I feel something under the fabric, looped around her arm. The end of it peeks out of the sleeve at her wrist. It looks like twine until I look closer . . .

Oh Sun. It's impossible.

I pull on the end, and it comes out easily as it was only wrapped loosely. It's exactly what I thought it was.

Not possible. Not possible.

Hurriedly, I stuff it into my own sleeve and dash to the window. Simon looks up with panicked eyes. I don't even bother trying to climb down; I've jumped from much higher before. I land softly, taking the impact with bent knees. Simon seizes my arm. "What the hell took you so long?" he gasps. "I thought you were about to do something stupid."

"I'll tell you later. Let's go."

"I can't," Simon says. "I landed on a stone and twisted my ankle. It might be broken."

Gritting my teeth, I grab his arm and heave it over my shoulder. "You're not getting caught tonight, Venatre. *Now move.*"

We limp out of the garden by the gate and into the back street as I grope for the moonstone again. My hearing returns to my eavesdropping level, but there's no moon, and I can't regain the sight I put in the voidstone. It does, however, provide a tiny amount of light that no one else will be able to see.

Simon shifts his weight onto his good foot. "Where are we going?"

"The only place they'll never look for you," I answer. Resettling my shoulder into his armpit, I head south.

CHAPTER 52

I aim for the west of the abbey. The guards have been called out, searching for Simon, but they're still several blocks behind by the time we reach the relative shelter of the orchard wall. We creep along it in the twilight, Simon stumbling on roots that grow out under the barrier, until we come around to the far end of the Selenae Quarter. I choose the alley Athene had taken me to, though it's not the closest.

The moon has set, and it rained most of the night, so no Selenae are out. The dark streets are difficult to navigate in reverse, but I manage to find the circle sign with the dancing serpent after only one wrong turn. I pound on Athene's door until she answers, wearing a dressing gown over her nightclothes and pushing loose hair back from her temples. "It's me," I gasp. "My friend is hurt."

She ushers us inside and closes the door, looking us over. "I said you could probably come back one day, but this is rather soon," she says dryly.

Simon looks back and forth between us. "Who is this, Cat?"

"This is my cousin." I avoid deeper explanations for now.

"She's a physician." While I won't insist or try to force her to treat him, I beg her with my eyes to help.

Athene sighs and extends her arm, indicating I should go to the back of the house.

"Thank you," I say as I help Simon limp past her and down the passage.

I trip into the sickroom's moonstone glow, ready to set Simon onto the cot across from Marguerite when I realize the room is empty. Swerving around, I face my cousin. "Where is she?"

Athene's mouth tightens in anger. "We took her back to the abbey this afternoon."

"Why?"

"The sisters demanded her return," she says. "They threatened to go to the provost if we didn't."

I grind my teeth. "You mean Sister Berta demanded it."

Athene shrugs. "They all look the same to me, but the last thing we need now is trouble, though it appears you've brought it." She looks pointedly at Simon.

"His ankle is hurt," I say, turning back to the cot. "Maybe broken."

Simon is pale and sweating from the pain. Athene helps me lower him down. "Your Hadrian doesn't weigh more than a sack of flour," she mutters. "Has anyone been feeding him?"

My immediate concern is elsewhere. "Will the sisters allow you to continue tending Marguerite over there?"

"Doubtful." Athene kneels to pull Simon's boot off. "But I think she's past the most danger, thanks to you. As long as they keep her abed, she should continue to recover."

Simon winces as Athene prods his foot. "Do you intend to light a lantern?" he asks. "Or do you physicians work only by feel?"

I sigh. "Add it to the list of things I need to explain to you, but suffice to say both of us can see quite well."

He yelps as Athene rotates his ankle in a circle. "Quiet, Hadrian," she scolds. "I'm trying to hear if your bones are intact." Then she wrinkles her nose. "Where is the smell of blood coming from?"

"That's me." I hold up my bandaged hand.

Athene scowls but continues working on Simon, moving the joint back and forth as he struggles to stay silent. "Remind me to teach you that bleeding is more urgent than sprains."

"Not broken, then?" I ask.

She sets his foot down on the cot. "All the echoes are solid, though there's displacement from swelling. One ligament was strained beyond its length, but it isn't torn."

I gape. "You can tell all that just by listening?"

"And feeling." Athene stands to pull out a drawer of the cabinet. "I have no doubt you could do it, too, and more, with proper training."

From what she said about Hira, I know only those with blood magick can become a full physician, but somehow it never occurred to me that it was something I could do. Athene takes out a roll of tightly woven fabric and sits back down. "I'm going to bind this now, Hadrian, to keep the swelling down," she tells him.

He grits his teeth. "My name is Simon."

Athene pauses in her actions and looks up at me. "Simon of Mesanus? The venatre?"

I nod. "The comte thinks he's guilty of all the murders, and maybe even of his own daughter now. He has the whole guard looking for him."

She glares at me. "And you brought him *here*?"

"He's innocent." I cross my arms.

"I don't care if he's innocent," she snaps. "I care if the city guard is going to burn down my house looking for him."

"No one saw us or has reason to suspect this is where he went."

"So you believe." Athene turns back to Simon's foot and stretches the fabric over it, wrapping with brisk efficiency.

Visions of what I may have brought upon the Selenae—for the second time in my life—rise in my mind. "I'm sorry," I whisper. "I didn't know where else to go."

Athene sighs. "I suppose there was no other place."

There's a long silence until Simon clears his throat. "I'll leave if there's any danger of my being discovered."

"You won't get far on this ankle," my cousin mutters. She ties the ends to each other, then gestures to me. "Let's see your hand and whatever Hadrian grease has been slathered on it."

Simon frowns. "It's balm. And I did not 'slather' it on."

Athene snorts and slides the bandage over my fingers and off. "I'd be able to smell it from a block away on a sunny day." She holds my hand up to the moonstone. "Dark of Night, Catrin! What happened?"

Now that I'm not fighting for my life or Simon's, I'm too exhausted to tell the whole story. "I cut it on glass."

"She needs sutures," Simon adds. "Can you do that?"

"Sew it shut?" Athene twists her face in disgust. "Not unless she wants to look like our uncle the walking tapestry."

She pulls a clean scrap of silk from a pocket in her shirt and begins wiping the oily balm out of the cut. "What else did this Hadrian do in his bungling efforts?"

My face heats in his defense. "He put pure alcohol in the cuts. It burned worse than a branding iron."

"Really?" Athene glances at him. "That was actually good. Your Simon is forgiven."

The use of his name counters the sarcasm of her praise. She finishes cleaning the wounds and lays three round bloodstones across my palm before wrapping them down with clean gauze. "This will take six hours at least," she says.

I close my fingers around the stones, baffled that my sense of touch is only enhanced in a small area. "Don't they work the same as moonstones?" I ask. "I just feel it in my hand."

Athene puts everything away. "You touch on something we don't quite understand. Bloodstones release intense magick, but something about their veins of iron keeps it within a small radius. Our ancestors called the property *maegnetis*, which is to hold magick closely."

"That sounds like lodestone," says Simon, and Athene looks at him in pleasant surprise. "I don't believe in magick, but we had lodestones in Mesanus that could hold iron nails close and change their orientation without touching them. Some physicians think they can be used to realign the thoughts of a mad person, if applied correctly around the head."

My cousin nods. "Yes, they are the same—your Hadrian word comes from ours. I have doubts about bloodstones curing madness, however. As for magick, that's something I will let Catrin explain." She bends down and props Simon's twisted ankle on her cushioned stool, so it's higher than it would be on the cot. "Keep this raised for the next hour or so. And you"—she turns her attention on me—"you look like you haven't slept in days."

"I haven't."

"Then you should lie down, too," she says. "If trouble is coming, you'll face it better with some rest."

"I will," I promise. "But I need to talk to Simon first."

Athene yawns as she turns to leave. "I'm going back to bed. Don't wake me before noon unless the house is on fire."

I drag another stool next to the cot and sit down. Simon is silent, staring blankly at the ceiling. "I'm sorry about Juliane," I whisper.

He takes a shaky breath and blinks like he's holding back tears. "I failed her," he says. "I failed her like I failed my father. I should've let myself be arrested."

"Simon, you didn't fail her, just like I didn't fail the workers at the Sanctum." I reach into my sleeve and pull out a thin braid of hair which I press into his hand. "I found this wrapped around Juliane's wrist."

He sits bolt upright, feeling its length with both hands. "That's impossible."

"It's Marguerite's," I say. "The length and color are unmistakable. She kept her hair in two thick braids. This one must have been made from the other. He killed Juliane."

I take a deep breath. "It was Oudin. He's been the killer all along. And now he's convinced his father it's you."

———— • ✳ • ————

I wake with my head on Simon's chest. My lower half is pressed against the wall, and his right arm is behind my shoulders, cushioning my upper body from it. Long fingers trail in a soothing rhythm through the curls which have come loose from my leather hair tie. I have no memory of lying down, only that I started shivering with exhaustion and cold, and Simon pulled me to him. The cot definitely isn't big enough for two people, though it helps that his injured foot still rests on the stool. Most of my discomfort is from injuries.

"Are you awake?" Simon asks softly.

"Yes," I admit. "But I don't want to move."

Simon shrugs his other shoulder. "Don't then."

"Did you sleep at all?"

"Not really. Your cousin came in a little while ago to check on us. At least I think it was her. I still can't see a thing."

I smile against his shirt, though the prospect of explaining moon magick isn't pleasant. "Does that mean it's noon?"

"I think it's several hours past."

My heart skips. I wonder if Athene has told Gregor I'm here, and that I've brought a Hadrian fugitive with me. Probably not. He'd be here now if he knew, hurling us out of the Quarter. "What have you been thinking about?" I ask.

"Mostly that it doesn't matter who killed Juliane," he answers. "I failed her as I failed my father. I left them both alone with a monster. With him it was fire. With her it was Oudin."

I push up to look down on him. "Simon, you didn't want either of those to happen."

"Yet they did, because of me."

Athene's silhouette appears in the doorway. "Are you finally awake, then?" she asks. "I have some bread and stew ready." She sniffs and leaves again. "I'll prepare a bath, too."

We agree to postpone our discussion until after we've eaten. It's been so long since I've had a meal that I make myself count to ten between spoonfuls to keep my stomach from rebelling. Simon sits across from me at the table in the kitchen, eating equally slowly, though I think out of politeness or lack of appetite.

"Where is Hira today?" I ask Athene. I'm sure she helps with more than the kitchen and sickroom, but those are the only places I've seen her.

My cousin ladles more stew into my bowl. "I've sent her to a friend's home. Your arrival this morning frightened her, and I knew seeing a Hadrian would be even more upsetting."

I look down at my food. "I'm sorry. I didn't consider that."

"You didn't consider much, frankly." Athene puts the pot back on the hook near the fire. "For instance, what do you intend to tell Gregor?"

"Does he have to know I'm here?"

"Either you tell him, or I will," Athene says firmly. "He's a leader in the Quarter. He has to know, and he deserves to know."

I wipe my chin with a cloth napkin and avoid her eyes. "I'll think of something."

"Do. And what about your Hadrian?" she asks. Simon's eyes dart up to her, offended, and she smiles a little. "Are you going to explain anything to Simon here?"

I guess I should start with the most basic fact. "As it turns out, I'm half Selenae," I mumble.

Simon snorts. "I figured out that much on my own."

When he doesn't say anything more, it takes me several seconds to gather enough courage to peek at his reaction. Rather than the disgust or horror I expect, Simon looks as though he's waiting for me to continue. "Doesn't that . . . bother you?" I finally ask.

His brow creases. "Should it?"

He doesn't know what it means. "Probably."

Simon reaches across the table and places his hand on mine—gently, because it's the injured one. "Cat, none of us can choose our parents. Light of Day, do you think I would have chosen mine?"

"No," I admit.

He waits, but I don't say more. "I get the feeling this is something you only recently discovered," he says. "How long have you known?"

So much has happened I'm not even sure what day it is, but Athene answers. "Our uncle brought her here two nights ago to explain."

Has it really only been two nights?

"Your uncle," says Simon. "Is that the Gregor you mentioned?"

I nod. "It's a long story, but I had actually realized it before that." I hesitate before continuing. "There's more."

"I'm listening."

Simon is the most accepting person I know, but even he probably has his limits. "Do you know anything about Selenae?" I ask.

His eyes drift around the room, like he feels silly answering as he does. "I've heard stories that they can see in the dark and use magick to heal injuries and listen to secrets for blackmail purposes. I never had reason to believe any of that was true until last night. It was almost pitch-black in that room, but the two of you moved around like there was plenty of light. Now that I think of it, you've always seen very well at night."

I slide the bandage off my hand, letting the bloodstones fall to the table with a series of rapid taps. "There's more."

Simon's breath hitches as he sees the cuts across my palm and fingers are completely healed, leaving thin white lines, like month-old scars. "Tell me."

And I do.

CHAPTER 53

Athene moves between the kitchen and another room beyond used for washing, carrying water to a tub as I talk. I begin with my parents, telling Simon of their falling in love and marrying without her family knowing. Then I touch on how they died and why I was left at the Abbey of Light.

"Because they didn't think you could use Selenae magick." His emphasis on the word *magick* tells me it's not something he quite accepts. "But you can."

"Yes." I describe their ability to use the Light from the Moon, which is really a reflection of Sunlight, to enhance their senses. I show him the moonstone in my pocket and explain that it does the same, and how I used it to listen to his uncle and cousins and then guide us here in the dark.

I bring out the voidstone and say only that it's used to absorb unwanted magick before sliding it back in the pouch. Its capacity for consuming power makes me nervous, even if it was useful last night. Simon asks a few questions, which I answer as best I can, but I haven't even touched on blood magick yet.

A deep voice makes me turn to the doorway. "You realize that by telling a Hadrian all this, I may be forced to keep him in the Quarter for the rest of his life," says Gregor. He's calm, but I expect a storm to break at any second. His eyes narrow. "You're a wanted man, Simon of Mesanus, but you're not wanted here."

Simon raises his eyebrows. "I thought you just said you wouldn't let me leave."

"For the rest of your life," my uncle replies coolly. "That doesn't have to be a long time."

I stand to face him. "Are you going to throw me out again?"

The scars on Gregor's jaw tighten. "I haven't decided."

At least it's not an immediate yes. My eyes dart to Athene. "How did you know I was here?"

"A note from Mistress la Fontaine saying you never came home last night."

I wrinkle my brow. "I can't imagine the magister's housekeeper willingly writing to a moon worshipper."

"It takes a great deal of worry on your behalf." His cheek twitches as he looks over my bloody clothes and hair. "And it appears her concern was warranted."

"I'm fine."

Gregor snorts, then exhales in resignation. "What should I tell her?"

I think for a few seconds, catching sight of what must be Marguerite's wool dress hanging to dry in the washroom. Apparently Sister Berta didn't care about it or Marga's modesty when she dragged her back to the convent. "Tell her I'm at the abbey, tending to Marguerite."

"Very well." Gregor regards me silently for several heartbeats, then stands straight, tugging his jacket down. "Will you join us tonight?"

A hunger for the magick rises in me as strongly as my earlier desire for food. "That depends," I say. "May I bring Simon?"

When Gregor doesn't answer right away, I add, "He wouldn't be the first whose company you accepted."

"No," he says firmly. "Your Hadrian must stay hidden." With that, he turns away and disappears down the passage. The front door opens and closes.

Simon looks up at me from his seat. "I assume that was your uncle. We weren't properly introduced."

"Yes," I say wearily. "And there's still a great deal more I need to explain."

"Later," calls Athene from the washroom. "Your bath is getting cold, and if you go to the Moon Pool smelling as you do, everyone will pass out from holding their breath, even if they use voidstones."

I clean myself as fast as I can, though my hair is never a quick task, and it's matted with dried blood. Fortunately, the cut on my scalp is well into healing. Athene leaves to hunt down a Selenae outfit in my size. Her own clothes would be too short, and Hira's too tight. She's not back by the time I finish, so I put on Marguerite's dress. It doesn't fit that well either, but one almost can't tell, considering how shapeless it's meant to be. My calves are exposed by the short length, though.

Simon waits at the table with a fresh bowl of stew he must have limped across the kitchen to get for me. I'm hungry again, and it tastes almost as good as my first meal two hours earlier.

"I've been thinking," he says after I've eaten a few bites. "Maybe you're wrong about Oudin. There were reasons I dismissed him from suspicion in the beginning, and I don't see my way around them now. The probability of someone climbing in Juliane's window is remote, though, compared to it being someone in the house or close enough to the family or the provost's office to not be out of place. They were very private, especially as Juliane got worse."

Neither Juliane nor Lambert had friends I knew of. Outside prostitutes, Remi was the only person Oudin spent his free time with. "A servant, then," I say. "Or the Comte de Montcuir himself."

"He's not my first choice." Simon avoids my eyes. "But he is a possibility. Juliane told me several times that he killed her mother, but that's a common delusion in a mind like hers. Maybe she was right to be afraid of him." He taps his long fingers on the table. "He keeps a braid of his wife's hair in a prayer book by his bed, too. Lots of people do things like that, but it seems like an odd coincidence."

It's not difficult for me to come up with motivation, either. "The comte is obsessed with looking like a perfect family. Juliane endangered that image with her illness, as did her mother before her."

For some reason, Simon still won't look at me directly. "That's true, too."

I can tell his mind is somewhere else, but I continue my line of thought. "Lambert is now engaged, which his father arranged, but Oudin's behavior might have been making Lady Genevieve's family have second thoughts. So the comte sets out to eliminate the women Oudin is known to visit and also scare him into giving up his night life. That would match what you said about the killer not wanting them to look at him—they weren't worthy."

"That's possible." Simon pauses. "Why would he kill the prioress, though?"

"Because she knew things," I say. "Juliane's first signs of madness were years ago, perhaps while she was being educated at the abbey. And Lady Montcuir was raised there. If Mother Agnes knew of their condition—"

"Lady Montcuir was raised at Solis Abbey?" Simon interrupts. "Like you?"

I nod. "She was a foundling. You didn't know that?"

Simon shakes his head. "They rarely spoke of her. I only know she suffered as Juliane does—did, but no one would give me any details."

"It's rather a romantic story," I say. "The comte was engaged to another noblewoman, but he married his wife in secret, causing quite a scandal." When Simon doesn't say anything, I move on. "But my point is, Mother Agnes probably knew about her affliction and Juliane's, and that's something the comte didn't want to risk getting out."

Simon frowns. "Then why implicate the master architect?"

I shrug. "Once his work was done, he just needed someone to take the fall. The hammer was the perfect way to do it."

"That doesn't explain the destruction at the Sanctum or blaming me for Juliane's murder," Simon points out.

After a long quiet moment passes, I ask, "You said he wasn't your first choice. Who is?"

The evasive manner instantly returns. "Lambert," he says quietly.

"*Lambert?*" I would have suspected Madame Denise before him.

"He fits the picture," says Simon. "Intelligent, physically able, involved in the investigation, a somewhat strange attachment to his mother, an overbearing father, no friends, difficulty with women . . ."

"Half of it sounds like Oudin," I protest.

"But *all* of it sounds like Lambert."

I shake my head in disagreement. "Just because he doesn't visit Pleasure Road and had his father arrange his engagement doesn't mean he has trouble with women."

"No," Simon admits. "But he could be jealous of Oudin's relative ease."

Anyone could be as "successful" as Oudin if they had enough coin—which Lambert does. "Even if he was jealous, Lambert is engaged to Lady Genevieve," I say. "Any troubles he had were over."

"The timing might actually make sense," Simon insists. "Some sort of stressful event almost always pushes a killer from fantasy into action. One that is out of their control, like the loss of a loved one, or that forces their life in a drastically new direction, like getting married. But something significant changes their world before they act."

I shake my head. "You also said Beatrez was the first victim. She was three years ago."

Simon purses his lips stubbornly. "Maybe I was wrong."

I don't think he believes that. "What if Beatrez's murder was driven by Lady Montcuir's death?" I suggest. "The comte may have gone searching for consolation but then became disgusted with himself. Or—" I sit up straight with sudden inspiration. "Perhaps he was looking to replace her with another woman he could raise from terrible circumstances."

That makes Simon pause. Then he shakes his head. "Except that Lady Montcuir died two years before Beatrez."

"Unless Lady Montcuir was actually the first victim," I say. "In which case it couldn't be Lambert. He idolized his mother."

Whereas Oudin hated her.

Simon sighs in frustration. "And he also loved Juliane."

We lapse into silence, and the only sounds in the kitchen are the crackle of the fire in the hearth and the bubbles rising from water heating for Simon's bath. "How do you think he killed Juliane?" I ask quietly.

Simon thinks for a few seconds. "It might have been something added to the tea, but quick-acting poisons tend to have violent physical reactions, so I lean toward suffocation. He would have only had to cover her face with her pillow for several minutes. Without looking closer at the body, I can't say with any certainty, though I didn't see any obvious signs of violence. If it weren't for the braid, I would never have connected her death to him—but he wanted me to know it was him."

I imagine Juliane with her hands crossed on her chest and the blankets tucked up to her neck. Somehow that's worse than the other bodies I've seen. "Madame Denise said she thought Juliane was still sleeping. He must have taken care to make it look so," I murmur, and Simon cocks his head to look at me. "Not left on display like Perrete and the others, and not completely covered in shame and regret like the grain merchant's wife. Not left in a panic like Mother Agnes after Marguerite showed up."

Athene enters the kitchen, carrying a bundle of blue-black fabric and the sight of her interrupts my thoughts like a bolt of lightning.

I turn back to Simon. "Do you think Juliane woke up at all before she died?"

He blinks away whatever he was thinking. "Maybe. If she did, it was at the very end, when lack of air made her too weak to struggle much or for long."

But there's a chance.

I join my cousin at the counter as she sets the clothes down. "Athene," I ask quietly. "How long do thoughts stay in blood?"

"As long as the blood is still liquid, though they get more difficult to hear. Why?"

"How much time before the Moon gathering begins?"

"The Sun will set in about an hour, so another hour after that."

Plenty of time.

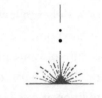

CHAPTER 54

Simon objects, of course, but I feel reasonably safe going to the Montcuir home right now, even if one of them is a murderer. With sunset coming, many mourners will be there to share in the moment the Sun carries Juliane's soul below the horizon.

Athene loans me her moonweave cloak. It's eerie to walk the streets with everyone looking right through me, and I'm relieved to duck into an alley near the house and turn the cloak inside out to the magick-less solid black lining. The evening is warm enough that the cloak is actually a little stuffy to continue wearing, but Marguerite's dress makes me feel almost naked. Normally a sister wears layers both under and over it.

I step back onto the street and join the noble and wealthy citizens arriving to pay their respects—to the comte, not his daughter. Juliane's coffin lies in the center of the room, no one within arm's length of it, while most people linger around the provost, wanting him to notice that they came. Her sallow and sunken face has people murmuring that she must have been unwell for a long time, and they lament how they would have done something if they'd only known.

For some reason that angers me. I doubt any of them would've offered their help if they'd understood her malady. Sicknesses of the mind are viewed with a shame not associated with illnesses of the body, but isn't the brain an organ like the heart or lungs? People will shun an insane person more than they would someone with plague, which is ironic. Madness isn't catching like a cough.

I'm also willing to bet more minor nervous complaints are fairly common. Maybe the shame would go away if people were just honest. Then mental affliction would be considered no stranger than swollen joints or digestion problems, and could be accommodated with the same compassion, as apparently it is in Mesanus.

As I look at Juliane, however, I realize how far that day may be. Her behavior had frightened and repulsed me, too. Had it not been for Simon's example, I likely would've avoided her like anyone else.

The open space around her coffin means anyone in the room will be able to see what I'm doing, but sunset is only minutes away, and then her body will be covered to encourage her spirit to leave it behind and follow the Light. I glance at the comte on the far side of the room, accepting a steady stream of condolences. He's not even looking at his daughter.

Taking a deep breath, I approach Juliane's casket. Athene's strongest bloodstone is in my right hand, almost numbing my fingers with its strange energy. I plan to act like I'm saying a prayer while I hold it to Juliane's skin, but I worry after so many hours her last thought will be too faint to hear, especially in a room full of people.

Before I can reach for Juliane's stiff hand, a gap in the crowd reveals Oudin sitting in a chair against the wall, bent over with his forearms on his thighs.

Staring at me.

I shift my cloak to hide Marguerite's thin dress from his blood-shot gaze. Oudin rises to his feet unsteadily and steps forward to stand across from me, Juliane between us. Even without magick, he reeks of alcohol and *skonia* from several feet away. "Thank you for coming," he says in a raspy voice.

Politeness was not what I expected. "I'm sorry for arriving so late."

"Remi was here earlier," he says, looking me over. "But he left to attend sunset service for the workers." Though their souls should have left yesterday, with so little time to prepare beforehand, their farewell gathering will be tonight. "He said he hadn't seen you since last night."

"I was at the abbey, sitting with my friend."

"The sister?" Oudin's accusing look changes to concern in a flash. "Did she wake up? Does she remember anything?"

"Unfortunately not." I don't dare admit Marguerite is awake, let alone lucid, even if she remembers nothing. I clear my throat. "I haven't seen Simon yet. Is he upstairs?"

"He's run away, that bastard," Oudin growls, rage flooding into his hollow black eyes. "You might want to reconsider your attachment to him."

His wrath makes me take an involuntary step backward into something solid. The impact to my elbow knocks the bloodstone from my loose grip, and it drops down the fabric of my dress to skip across the floorboards with an audible clatter.

Oh no.

"Miss Catrin," says the mass behind me, and I turn around to find Lambert. His eyes are red from weeping, but he manages a smile. "It's so good of you to have come."

I shuffle my feet modestly while also attempting to locate the stone but have no luck. "Juliane was very kind to me, and I felt I had to say goodbye."

Lambert looks me over as Oudin did and tilts his head to squint at my hairline. "What happened to your head? I don't recall seeing that during the rescue effort."

I reach for the scab without thinking, then make a fist to hide the fresh scars across my palm and fingers. "It happened after that. I stayed behind, trying to find out what caused the collapse, and I brushed against a piece of broken glass in the dark."

Oudin raises his eyebrows. "That must have bled a lot." He casts a significant look at Lambert. "I hope you got help somewhere, seeing as you didn't go home."

Though I hadn't anticipated having to explain my injury, I'm ready to lie about my whereabouts. "I did, thank you," I answer. "I went to the abbey because Remi was so angry with me I didn't want to go home. Then I stayed to help care for my friend. As I said earlier."

Lambert frowns. "Why is the magister's assistant angry with you? Surely he doesn't blame you for what happened."

The mist which rises in my eyes is genuine. "I told him the scaffolds were safe, but I was wrong."

He grimaces. "That doesn't matter, Catrin. *He* was in charge. Blaming you isn't just shirking his responsibility, it's immoral."

I want to tell him I know who is responsible, but that man is likely standing across from us or on the other side of the room. At least half the mourners have gone outside for sunset, and the comte has an unblocked view of our conversation. I clear my throat. "I was hoping to see Simon, too, but Oudin said something about him running away?"

Lambert hesitates, and Oudin leers at him from across Juliane's coffin. "Tell her, Brother. Tell Catrin all about how she helped a murderer."

He knows I'm responsible for Simon's escape. My hairline prickles with anxiety, but Lambert shakes his head. "We all helped him, Oudin—including you, and your assistance was never asked for."

I'm almost dizzy with relief that Oudin was referring to helping Simon with the investigation. "But what happened?"

Lambert takes my hands in his before answering. "It appears he may have been the killer all along, Miss Catrin. After Juliane died, we found some . . . things which we couldn't explain any other way."

I gasp. "I can hardly believe that!"

"Nor I," he says, glancing fiercely at Oudin. "I'm inclined to withhold my judgment until we find him and hear what he has to say."

I could kiss him for that. Even having failed to get Juliane's last thought, coming here was worth it to learn that Simon has at least one potential ally.

Their father suddenly appears at Juliane's feet, glaring at all of us, but mostly Lambert. "The send-off is beginning," he says. "I'm going outside. You take care of her."

The comte turns and walks off. Voices raised in the hymn of goodbye drift in the front door as he steps outside. Lambert sighs. "Go and sing, Oudin," he says. "I'll close the casket."

His brother steps back to obey, then—to my horror—bends over to retrieve the bloodstone by his feet and holds it out to me. "Don't forget your rock, Kitten."

I take it quickly, though my fingers can't help touching the stone while he does, sending a jolt of wordless anger into my mind before he releases it and walks away. Lambert cranes his neck to see. "What is that?"

"Blessing stone." I shove it in a pocket of Marguerite's dress meant for prayer beads. "None of the sisters could come, so they prayed on this stone so I could transfer the blessing to Lady Juliane."

Lambert blinks. "I've never heard of those."

Which is not a surprise because I just made them up.

"Have you used it yet?"

"No, actually," I say. "Your brother startled me, and I dropped it."

Lambert nods solemnly. "I need to get the lid to her coffin. I'd be honored if you would stay with her and give that blessing while I'm gone. You were one of her only true friends."

I flush with both excitement and embarrassment. "Thank you. I'm honored that she thought of me that highly."

"She's not the only one," he says, then hurriedly leaves to get what he needs.

I'm alone with Juliane.

I quickly pull the bloodstone from my pocket with one hand and lift her stiff arm with the other. Cringing at the macabre nature of what I'm doing, I close my eyes. I expect I'll need to concentrate to hear anything which remains in her blood, but the instant the stone is pressed between our palms, her voice comes to me as loud and furious as a hailstorm.

—*my Sun my Sun I know it was you and you killed Mother and the shadows have eaten your liver and left it lusting for blood*—

Her thoughts split in multiple directions like a thunderbolt across the sky, some fading into oblivion, others striking one place and moving immediately to another.

—*you can't kill me because I've already killed you a hundred times Simon I'll tell him I'll tell and Father will kill you like he killed her*—

There's no order. No rationality. No pause. It's like trying to drink from a waterfall pouring directly on my face.

—*my Sun I always knew it was you the shadows they tear at my eyes make me wise Simon Simon is the key Simon is the lock let me sleep let me weep soul to keep*—

I desperately want to let go of Juliane's hand, but I can't. Not when no one listened to her in life.

—you think I won't remember this but I will and I'll tell I'll tell my Sun my Sun I know it was you and you killed Mother—

The instant I realize her thoughts are repeating I practically fling her away. Grace and Light, was that what it was like to live inside her head? Could her madness have been caused by an inability to *stop* thinking?

Shuddering convulsively, I repocket the stone and rub my tingling hand on my sleeve. Juliane's stream of thought might finally be silent, but her despair and pain still echo in my own blood. Then the hair on the back of my neck rises, and I look up to see the Comte de Montcuir glowering at me through the doorway open to the street.

"Miss Catrin?"

I jump. Lambert stands across from me, where Oudin was a few minutes ago. In one hand he holds a hammer and his other props a polished piece of wood against the floor "Are you well?" he asks.

"Yes, thank you," I manage to say. "The blessing is finished. Do you want help?"

Lambert shakes his head. "No, thank you. I know you'll understand when I say I'd rather do this alone."

"I do." His father isn't visible anymore, but I'm sure he's waiting just outside. "Is there a back door? I'd rather avoid your brother if I can."

"Of course." Lambert nods to the kitchen as he puts the hammer down to set the lid on Juliane's casket. "Good night, Catrin."

"Good night . . . Lambert." I walk to the kitchen, pausing at the door to switch my cloak around to the moonweave side. Before letting myself out, I catch a glimpse of Lambert gazing at his sister's face for the last time.

CHAPTER 55

Simon is hobbling up and down the passage between Athene's front door and kitchen on a set of crutches when I return. He doesn't even wait for me to come all the way through the door before he seizes me in a hug, letting both supports fall to the floor.

"I've been waiting more than an hour," he says, pulling back to frame my face with his hands. I want him to kiss me but he doesn't.

"Did you get what you needed?" Athene asks, coming up behind him.

"Yes and no." I lean away from Simon, and he releases me. I still haven't explained blood magick to him. "It was too rapid and disjointed. She was thinking of Simon a lot, but like she needed to tell him something."

"Who needs to tell me something?" he asks.

I exhale heavily. "Juliane."

Simon blinks. "You're making it sound like you spoke to her."

"In a way, I did."

His eyes dart to Athene. "Is this another magick Selenae possess? Conversing with the dead?"

"Yes," I answer. "But not all Selenae have it, and that's not all it can do." The look on his face is slightly terrified. I'm not sure my explanations will make him any less so.

"This discussion can come later," Athene says. "Gregor is expecting us."

If I want peace with my uncle, I ought to make an effort, but I've decided I need to return home tonight, if only so I don't endanger the abbey should Oudin or the comte come looking for me. "I can't," I tell Athene. "Simon and I need to talk."

My cousin frowns. "What should I say when Gregor asks where you are?"

I bend down to pick up Simon's crutches for him. "Tell him I'm following my instincts, and he should let them play out."

Athene leaves with a sigh, and I walk Simon back to the kitchen. He lowers himself onto a chair, groaning softly. "I don't want to cause more conflict in your family."

"It has nothing to do with you," I tell him. "They sent me away. My return will be on my terms."

Simon shifts in his seat uncomfortably. "Are you going to tell me how you spoke to Juliane?"

I look down at my hands to avoid his stare. "It's less like talking and more like listening."

"I'm listening."

My fingers curl into fists. "Thoughts—mine, yours, everyone's—are carried in our blood. When a person dies, the last thought remains." Simon's lips part with the first of at least a dozen questions, but I continue before he can get a syllable out. "I can hear them, either by touching blood or using a bloodstone."

He closes his mouth and waits for me to elaborate.

"That's pretty much it," I say after a handful of seconds. "When it first started happening, I thought I was as mad as

Juliane, hearing the voices of dead women. I was afraid to say anything."

Simon smiles ironically. "I doubt I would've believed you."

"But you believe me now? You don't want a demonstration?"

The smile drops away. "You probably don't want to hear my thoughts."

I don't tell him I already have.

"Is that all you can do?" His voice tight with anticipation. "Or is there more?"

I bite my lower lip. "There's something else, but not even Gregor understands it. It's one of the reasons he's so eager to have me back."

"And one reason you're reluctant to return, I imagine." Simon takes a deep breath. "So you went to listen to Juliane. Her blood. What did she say?"

I describe the cascade of disjointed thoughts, Juliane's residual energy causing me to pace restlessly. "It's more than I heard from any other victims, but it makes less sense. I think it points to Oudin, though."

I can tell by his reaction that Simon disagrees. He avoids my eyes and scratches his cheek, where fine fuzz from not shaving has developed. "Cat, while you were gone, I spent some time thinking about Mother Agnes, Magister Thomas, and the Sanctum, trying to connect them to the earlier victims. And there's one thing Altum Ferris insisted was critical to remember: What the killer *needs* will never change. The way he tries to get it may."

Different methods, same madness.

"So what does he need?" I ask as I reach the doorway to the washroom.

He watches me pivot around again. "I'm sure the answer is in what the killer did to their bodies."

I stop and frown at him. "He was disgusted. They weren't worthy to even look at him."

"Exactly." Simon nods. "He feels very superior."

I resume pacing. "Which sounds exactly like Oudin."

Simon looks doubtful. "Oudin plays in the gutters, and he knows it. He has no illusions about himself."

"Fine." I don't want to argue. "Why did the killer switch to Sisters of Light and Sanctum workers and framing the master architect and you?"

"Because there is one thing all of them have in common." Simon waits for me to stop and meet his eyes. "You."

"*Me?*"

Simon holds his hand up to keep me from objecting further. "That doesn't mean you were the target. Before I left, he taunted me with that note, indicating this was now a game for him and he would defeat me. After Nichole, he must have realized the most effective way to hurt me was through you." Simon pauses and swallows. "He not only took away your family and your life's work, he managed to turn me against you."

"And then he came for me," I whisper.

"Yes." Simon shudders.

Why hadn't the killer finished the job then? Maybe he thought I was as good as dead. And he needed to deliver the masterstroke against his enemy: Juliane's murder and the blame for it.

I still feel like a critical piece is missing. "I'm with you, Simon, but you have to agree that all means it can't be Lambert. He loved Juliane more than anyone."

Simon slumps in his chair, his eyes dropping to the floor. "And I have a hard time believing he would hurt you, too. I just . . ." He stops and sighs. "You're right."

Something about his acceptance is off. "What would Altum Ferris say?"

"He would say to trust my instincts," Simon says to his hands.

"Then why aren't you doing that?"

"I am," he mumbles. "They're telling me Lambert has feelings for you. That's what's clouding my judgment."

I stare at him. "Are you saying you're *jealous*?"

Simon lifts his head, but only halfway. "I'm saying compared to him, I have nothing to offer."

I kneel to put my face level with his. "I don't care about that."

"But I do," Simon whispers. "Enough to step aside for someone who could take care of you as I could not."

I lean closer. "That's my choice, remember?"

Simon lifts his mouth just out of reach of mine, his eyes full of anguish. "It's also mine, Cat."

CHAPTER 56

Even in his martyrish mood, Simon dislikes the idea of my going home. I'm not willing to stay, however, as it could put the abbey in danger if the killer thinks I'm there.

Dawn is still two hours off when I let myself in the kitchen using the key that now shares a pocket with my voidstone and a fresher moonstone from Athene. As I turn the bolt back into the lock, Remi appears in the doorway to the workroom. His dark, wiry hair is stretched and pressed away from his face, as if he's been pulling on it with his hands. For several seconds he stares at me, like he's not sure I'm real. Then, without a word, he crosses the kitchen and takes me in his arms. I'm as surprised by his embrace as I am about how much I need it.

"I'm sorry," he says into my hair. There are no tears, but the swelling around his eyes tells me he's been crying. "I was upset. I said things I didn't mean, Cat. I'm so sorry."

My arms go around him, my big, stupid almost-brother who despite everything will always mean *safe* and *home*. "You had every right to think it was my fault," I murmur into his chest.

Remi leans back and puts calloused hands on either side of

my face, tilting it up to look me in the eyes. His own are made bright green by the bloodshot whites. "I didn't tell anyone," he says. "I *won't* tell anyone. Ever. No one has to know, not even Magister Thomas."

Even thinking I'm guilty, he wants to protect me. "But I wasn't to blame, Remi," I say. "Some of the beams were cut or the nails loosened."

"Why would anyone do that?" He frowns and lowers his hands to my shoulders. "And how do you know?"

Simon had always kept the killer's signature and other details a secret, but there should have been other ways to tell. "Did you find anything odd? Cut beams or severed joints?"

Remi blinks. "I didn't consider looking."

"Perhaps we can find some evidence today."

He shakes his head. "It's all been cleared and burned. You know the altum would never allow something cursed to remain in the Sanctum."

I remember that happening when the scaffolds collapsed years ago. It was a huge loss of materials that could have been reused, but the magister knew no one would ever trust them again. Still, that was fast. "Already?" I ask. "In one day?"

"Half the city turned out to help." Remi releases my shoulders and takes my hands, rubbing rough thumbs over the back of them. "But it doesn't matter. I'll never let anyone think you were at fault. Just . . . promise me you won't run off and join the Sisters of Light."

"Is that—" I stop and choose my words carefully. "You knew where I went?"

"Mum said you'd sent word you were going to the convent for a few days." He turns my palms over and looks at them. "She almost acted like you wouldn't be coming back."

I wonder if Gregor had hinted that last part, hoping I would stay in the Quarter permanently this time. "I just needed to think."

Remi's eyes widen as he notices the red-brown stains on my sleeves and tunic. "Is that *your* blood?"

I'm about to explain that I cut myself on glass—though not the circumstances—when I remember that my hand is healed. "I got it on me the day of the collapse. During the rescue."

"I don't recall seeing that much on you." Remi frowns at the white scar from the wound that was the source of most of the blood, like he knows it shouldn't be there.

All I can do is shrug. "I've bathed, but I need to change."

"Yes, yes. Of course." Remi moves to the front of the house, releasing only one of my hands and pulling me along. "Have you slept?" he asks. "I mean, will you want to rest today?"

"Maybe for a few hours." His kindness and concern are unusual, but I suppose he really was afraid I would never come home. "Have you had word of the magister?" I ask as we reach the stairs. "Is he well?"

Remi continues holding my hand as he leads the way up. "I bribed one of the guards yesterday for an update. Magister Thomas was in good health but saying very little when questioned."

We stop outside my room. Even now, Remi won't cross the doorframe. "Do you still believe he could be the murderer?" I sound more accusing than I mean to.

He looks down at our joined hands, mumbling, "I don't know, Cat. He won't say where he was that night, and I don't understand why, but . . ."

"But what, Remi?"

He bites his lip. "Mother Agnes's murder was to hurt *you*. And if you're right that somehow the collapse was by design, that was your part of the Sanctum. I can't imagine the magister ever hurting either of you." Remi sniffs. "He cared more for you both than he did for me, that's certain."

"That's not true," I tell him. "Magister Thomas knew one day he would have to hand the Sanctum over to someone, but *you* were his choice for that. He just had to make you as worthy as he could."

Remi raises his eyes to mine. "He said that about you, you know. Before he was arrested. 'You don't deserve her. Not yet.' Those were his words."

The back of my neck warms with embarrassment. "Are you sure he wasn't talking about the Sanctum?"

"Cat, I'm trying to tell you something important. I'm . . ." Remi exhales in exasperation. "I was stupid, all right? I swear I'll never go to Pleasure Road again. I'll never call you Kitten or say cruel things. I'll never try to tell you what to do. Just . . ." He hesitates and takes a deep breath. "Promise that you'll stay. Here. With me. Forever."

Oh.

It's several seconds before I'm able to say anything. "Remi . . . ," I begin gently, and his face crumples.

"Is it Simon?" he spits. "You know the provost is looking for him, right? They're saying he's the one who killed those women."

"Not everyone thinks he did."

"Then why did he run?" Remi demands. "Unless he had something to hide?"

"I don't know, Remi!" I snap. "Perhaps he saw how the magister was treated when he surrendered to his arrest."

Remi snorts. "Even if Simon is innocent, he wouldn't forgive you for not saying what you knew about the magister's hammer, but I understand why you wouldn't. I actually admire it."

"This has nothing to do with him." Simon's rejection only an hour ago is still raw, and I rub my temple against the tears gathering behind my eyes. "Things are just complicated right now. The magister is still in prison, a murderer is loose, and so much has to be done at the Sanctum . . ."

Hope springs in his eyes. "Then you're not saying no?"

I take a few seconds to imagine what kind of life it would be, and the vision isn't terrible. Only a month earlier, it might have even been ideal. But that was before Perrete and Simon and magick. I'm not the same person I was a few weeks ago. I don't know where I fit anymore, but Remi matters to me, and I don't want to hurt him.

Finally, I sigh. "I'm saying I don't know."

Remi exhales heavily. "All right," he says hoarsely. "I need to be at the work site by dawn. If—if you're up to it, I hope you'll come today. I've missed having you there. For more than one reason."

"I'll come."

My answer encourages him more than it should. He puts his free hand to my cheek and leans down. "In the meantime, I'll do everything I promised," he whispers. "I'll be worthy. You'll see."

I want to tell him that none of that matters, that my hesitation doesn't come from annoying nicknames and teasing, or even from his visits to Pleasure Road. But I can't because his lips are suddenly on mine.

A part of me craves the comfort and forgiveness he offers, but this isn't something I can allow; it's not fair to him. He ends the kiss before I can, however, and withdraws, vanishing up the stairs to his own room.

CHAPTER 57

When I arrive at the Sanctum shortly before noon, I busy myself inspecting the damage from the killer's chase and fall. The reed platform I slashed went unnoticed during yesterday's efforts to clear the wreckage inside, but I mostly search for places he may have sabotaged the outdoor scaffolds. My fear has me using a safety rope in almost every situation.

Remi lets me do whatever I want and even leaves me in charge while he goes to inspect a load of stone at the city gate before it's hauled up the hill. In some ways, it's a welcome change, but I almost miss the teasing and superior air that had defined our relationship until this morning. When the workday is over, I wind the rope around my waist several times and wear it like a belt before climbing to the top of the south tower.

I've seen neither Lambert nor Oudin near the Sanctum all day. Likely they're combing the city for Simon. Hopefully, there's no reason for them to search the Quarter, as tightly as Selenae control it. They'll think it more probable Simon left Collis than managed to gain sanctuary there.

I sit behind a column to shield myself from the setting sun as I watch the moon rise in the east. As long as I stay out of direct sunlight, I have my senses, and I stretch my hearing toward the Quarter, listening for any signs of disturbance. Few are moving at this early moon hour, however, just as many Gallians sleep an hour past dawn.

I feel the vibration of his steps and hear Remi long before I see him. "There you are," he calls when he reaches the top of the spiral stairs. "I've been looking for you."

"I inspected all the scaffolding that's still up," I tell him. "There's some incidental damage. Everything I found is marked."

"Yes, I saw." Remi plops down across from me in the window and leans on the opposite side, facing the sunset. The orange light brings out the reddish tones in his tawny complexion, and makes his eyes appear almost black under the reflected glare. His legs are so long he could tap my knee with the toe of his boot without stretching, but he keeps them folded. Giving me space. "Thank you."

How rarely he's thanked me before. "Just doing my job," I say. "But you're welcome." I pick at a loose thread on the knee of my breeches. "It felt good, so thank *you*, for letting me come back. I've lost so much over the past few days that I don't know what I would do if the Sanctum was taken away from me, too."

"I'm here, Cat. You haven't lost me."

I smile a little. "I can't get rid of you."

"Like a wart," he says cheerfully. "I'm under your skin." Remi hops up and offers me a hand. I take it, and he pulls me gently to my feet.

Something catches my eye as I rise. "What's that?" I ask, flicking what looks like a tiny tail hanging from his waist.

"Oh that." Remi flushes, and his heartbeat speeds up. "It's for luck, but I didn't have it the day of the accident." He unhooks a small ring from a notch on his belt and holds it up. A braid of hair loops around the metal, attached with some kind of resin. "Mum gave it to me when I left last fall. She said all her gray hair was from me, so this way I could take her worry and prayers with me."

I can almost hear her telling Remi that. Most of the hair matches Mistress la Fontaine's familiar shade, but it's not the only color in the braid. One of the three woven strands is dark brown. I trace my thumb along its curves. "What about this part?"

"That's yours," he says shyly. "I added it because . . . well, now you know why. I cared. Even back then. I just couldn't figure out how to tell you."

My stomach twists into a knot. "When did you take it?"

"Don't tell Magister Thomas, but I cut it while you were sleeping." He grimaces. "That is honest to Light the only time I've set foot in your room."

I fumble to think what a girl would say if a young man admitted such a thing to her. "I won't tell." My own voice sounds like it's echoing from the far end of the Sanctum. "But you could have just asked."

Remi takes the braid back and rehooks it to his belt. "I will next time. Are you ready to go home?"

"Yes." I suppress a shiver as I take the arm he offers. We go down the steps and through the Sanctum out to the square together. Every step jolts up my leg with what I've realized.

An attachment to his mother. Problems with women—or at least one woman. Highly intelligent. Physically fit. A stressful promotion and problems with his work. An employer who stood in his way. Hatred of Simon. Pushed himself into the investigation.

Unaccounted for on all the nights that mattered.

The killer isn't Lambert. It's not Oudin or the Comte de Montcuir or anyone in their household. Simon's picture of the killer perfectly describes the one person I never considered.

Remi.

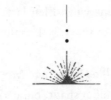

CHAPTER 58

Now I must sit through dinner with him. The food tastes like sawdust, so much that I voluntarily eat more fried turnips than I ever have, simply because I'm not paying attention to what's on my fork. I find myself looking at Mistress la Fontaine every few bites. Does she know what Remi is?

Or has she been covering for him?

Oudin arrives for Remi as we clear the dishes away. "Are you ready to go?" he asks.

I blanch at the thought of them on the streets tonight. Remi sees it and misunderstands. "It's not what you're thinking." He leans down to take my healed hand, fascinated once again by the white scar. "Simon of Mesanus still hasn't been found, and Oudin and I are meeting with a group of men to augment tonight's watch."

I must look frightened, because he bends down to put his lips to my ear. "I promise if we're the ones who find him, I'll give him a chance to explain himself before we take him to the provost."

He sounds earnest, but it's clearly a lie. "Will Oudin's brother be joining you?" I ask.

Remi shrugs like he hadn't thought of involving Lambert,

but there's a spark of jealousy in his eyes. "Will you stay home, tonight? Please?" he asks. "I just want you to be safe."

I'd planned on going to see Simon under the guise of visiting Marguerite, but I agree. Otherwise Remi might try to follow me.

"Thank you." He releases my hand. "Any chance I can borrow your knife? I've misplaced mine."

I have no excuse to say no. Without a word, I unhook the short dagger from my belt, realizing I've sat through all of dinner with my safety rope still looped around my waist. I offer the knife to Remi, trying to both smile and look worried. The latter is rather easy, and I stand on my toes to kiss his cheek. Maybe if he thinks he has no competition, he won't do anything terrible, at least tonight. "Be safe," I tell him.

Oudin raises his eyebrows but says nothing.

Remi backs away, a confidence in his stance unlike the juvenile swagger I'm used to. For the first time, it strikes me that he's a grown man.

But then, a child could never do the things he's done.

Once the door closes behind them, I collapse against the wall. I need to get to Simon as soon as possible, but there's no way we could bring Remi to the provost ourselves.

There's only one person I can think of to ask for help.

I feel guilty going to Lambert, especially considering Simon's earlier jealousy and suspicions, but he doesn't know about those. However, it's probably not safe to leave for at least an hour.

To pass the time, I help Mistress la Fontaine in the kitchen. She seems to think my sudden interest in domestic chores has something to do with Remi's proposal. Since she's pleased with the idea, I make no effort to dissuade her. Sun knows how much longer she'll be happy.

When she finally goes upstairs to bed, I force myself to wait another quarter hour. With only two minutes left, there's a gentle knock on the front door, and to my relief, it's Lambert himself. I let him into the workroom, telling him how glad I am to see him.

"Father has me looking for Oudin," he says grimly. "But he's not in any of the usual places. I was hoping you would know if he was with Remone."

"They're out together," I reply. "Helping patrol the city and looking for Simon."

He nods. "I imagine Simon is long gone from Collis by now, though."

I hesitate, unsure how to tell him I know that's not true. "The killer isn't Simon, it's Remi. I don't know how I didn't see it until now, but it's been him all along."

Lambert gapes at me. "Remi as in the man who's like a brother to you?" His voice rises. "Remi as in the man who's out in the dark right now with *my* brother?"

"Shhhh!" I wave my hands at him. "Yes, I'm sorry, I couldn't do anything to stop him from going out. If it helps, I see no reason why he'd harm Oudin. But I was about to come find you with what I realized."

Lambert exhales. "I suppose you're right." Then he blinks. "You were going to come to me?"

"Of course," I say. "Who else would I go to?"

He shrugs and avoids my eyes, the tips of his ears turning pink. "Simon, for one, but I guess you don't know where he is."

I bite my lip. Gregor will be furious if I bring another Hadrian into his Quarter, but this is a matter of life and death. "Do you trust me?"

Lambert wrinkles his brow. "Of course I do, Miss Catrin."

"*Cat.*"

He smiles a little. "Yes, I trust you, Cat."

"Then follow me."

As soon as we're outside, I find the moon, letting it soak into my skin and savoring the power that flows through my veins like lightning. The world is brighter and more colorful than a sunny day, and full of scents and sounds from all directions. It's like being everywhere the moonlight is. I'm both floating and thoroughly grounded.

"Are you ready?" I ask Lambert.

"Absolutely," he says. "Lead the way."

I turn and run through the streets with Lambert on my heels. It's no trouble to avoid the guard or anyone else who's out at this hour—I can hear and see them long before they're a concern. My pace has me straining to breathe against the rope still around my waist, but I don't slow. The convent comes into view, followed shortly by the vine-covered wall dotted with delicate flowers. A sense of *home* wells inside of me, similar to what I'd felt with Remi this morning. How many homes can a person have? Or does it feel this way now because my previous safe haven is gone?

The singing around the Moon Pool has already begun. As a child listening to it from my bed at the abbey, the melody had seemed to dance across my skin; now it fills me like water absorbed into a sea sponge, settling deep in my bones. The magick in my blood sings along, weaving the music together into a harmony, and I want nothing more than to be a part of it. My soul will have no rest until I've joined the song.

Not now, though. Tonight I must resist one world for the sake of the other.

Lambert hesitates when we reach the entrance to the Quarter. I doubt even his father the provost has ever been inside, and certainly not at night. "It's all right, Lambert," I say, extending my hand to him. "There's no need to be afraid."

Taking a deep breath, Lambert clasps my fingers and follows me through the moonflower vines.

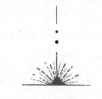

CHAPTER 59

With the nearly full moon, most Selenae must be gathered around the pond, but I can't believe we enter the Quarter unnoticed. Nevertheless, I try to be as quiet as possible.

Athene's door is unlocked. I lead Lambert inside, immediately feeling the loss of the moonlight, and call Simon's name. He appears at the end of the passage and hobbles forward to take me in his arms. It's more a gesture of relief than romance, but Lambert hangs back, embarrassed.

Simon leans away and holds me by the shoulders. "I was afraid something would keep you from coming. Have you—" He breaks off, eyes wide, realizing who I've brought with me.

"It's all right," I assure him. "Lambert and I have discovered who the killer is."

Simon takes a step backward, tensing like he wants to run. "Really."

I put my hand on his arm. "It's Remi. Everything you said last night fits him perfectly." I quickly explain my logic. The hardest part for me to believe is his destruction at the Sanctum, but now I see it as bringing me to a low point, leaving him as the only thing standing between me being completely alone in the world.

"And he has a braid of hair he carries with him. He says it's for luck."

"Whose hair?"

"Mine."

Simon's shoulders slump. "And I never suspected him," he whispers.

"Neither did I. And I knew him. Or thought I did."

It takes Simon another half a minute to absorb the idea. Then he shakes himself. "Come sit down. We'll discuss what to do now."

As he walks back to Athene's kitchen, I notice he's barely limping. "You look much better."

Simon glances down at his sprained ankle. "Your cousin rewrapped it this morning with bloodstones or lodestones or whatever. It barely hurts now. Most of my awkwardness is from having rocks in my sock." He grins weakly, but I can tell the evidence of magick makes him uncomfortable.

"This is your cousin's house?" asks Lambert, looking around the kitchen.

"Yes," I answer. "She's the physician who treated Marguerite until the sisters took her back to the convent."

"But . . . your *cousin?*"

"I didn't know until recently, but I'm half Selenae," I explain. "They reached out to me when Magister Thomas was imprisoned."

His eyes widen. "I know who you are," Lambert whispers. "Your father was that physician who kidnapped the Gallian girl and . . . seduced her."

"He didn't kidnap her," I say, trying not to be irritated. "And he didn't seduce her, either. They were married."

Lambert frowns doubtfully. "My father's records say the Selenae killed the woman and her child when her family tried to rescue her rather than pay the demanded ransom."

I raise my eyebrows. "There was no ransom. She refused to return home, and my mother's people led a mob into the Quarter that killed more than a dozen Selenae, including my father. Then she died in childbirth. And as you can see, I'm also alive."

He swallows. "I guess I only ever heard one side of the story."

"You and the rest of Collis." It's not full acceptance, but it's a start. "What's more important is finding Remi and Oudin."

"Oudin?" Simon asks in confusion. "Why are we looking for him, too?"

"They left together," I answer. "They're part of the group patrolling with the city guard, looking for you."

"And you've led them straight to us."

Athene stands in the door to the washroom. Her expression is neutral and her tone flat, so I don't know if she's truly angry, but her words paint visions of burning houses and bodies in the street. "The city guard is here?" I gasp. "In the Quarter?"

"Not yet." Athene turns her kohl-lined eyes on Lambert. "But you've brought the provost's son. They're sure to follow."

"No one knows I'm here," says Lambert.

"Your assurances mean nothing, Hadrian." Athene focuses on me. "Catrin, your birth brought destruction on us, but you were innocent then, and we did not blame you. You are not innocent now. All of you must leave, immediately."

I take a step toward her. "But where else can I hide Simon?"

"That is not our concern."

"But—"

"It's all right, Cat," says Simon. "Your family has done more than enough."

"We don't need to worry about finding Remi," adds Lambert. "He'll eventually come home. We can hide Simon and deal with Remi in the morning after I talk to my father."

I suppose he's right. "Where can Simon stay until then?"

"The Sanctum?" suggests Lambert. "That building is huge. Surely there are areas that no one goes in regularly."

There are many such places, especially in the older sections. I kick myself for not thinking of the Sanctum sooner, but Simon couldn't have climbed to any of them with his ankle last night.

"Yes, that's a good idea," I say. "But getting there will be tricky with all the patrols." I feel guilty asking, but Athene might be willing if it gets rid of us. "Can we borrow your moonweave cloak again?"

She sighs and turns back into the washroom to fetch it. "At this point I may as well give it to you."

I follow her, wanting a private word. "Athene, I'm sorry for causing so much trouble."

"You should be." She takes the cloak down from the peg by the back door. "I understand that the Hadrian world is in turmoil right now, as are you, but you've piled risk upon risk on us without considering the consequences."

"I won't ask for anything more," I promise. "You have my word."

"That is not the solution, either, Catrin," she says. "We need you as much as you need us."

"Is this about your hopes that I will save Selenae magick from extinction?"

"Partly," she admits. "But it's also about you and what you possess." She holds the cloak out to me. "A gift misused is a curse. Never forget that."

I fold the moonweave over my arm. "How do I know if I'm misusing my gifts?"

Athene considers for a moment. "That's complicated to answer, but a good way to judge is whether you are feared by those you love. It's one thing to fear what someone is capable of, it's another entirely to fear what someone will do with that capability. A weapon is only dangerous in the wrong hands."

I think of Magister Thomas, who knew some of what I was—or might be—capable of, and yet his faith in me never wavered. Marguerite accepted that magick might be good only after she knew I had it. Simon isn't afraid of me, even knowing more than anyone else.

"I'll remember that," I tell her.

Athene nods. "I have to get back to the song before Gregor becomes suspicious." She pulls the moonstone dangling on the silver chain from around her neck and places it over my head. "This isn't as strong as it could be, but I had it in the pond for a good hour tonight. It's in better shape than the one you have."

As soon as it touches my skin, the magick in my blood responds, bringing the world into sharp clarity. Simon is tying his boots in the next room, having removed the wrap and bloodstones. Lambert's heart beats rapidly; he's eager to leave. "Thank you," I say. "I promise to use it well."

"I'd rather you promise to bring it back."

"That, too."

Athene opens the door and pauses with her hand on the latch. "Always remember what you are, Catrin."

"What is that? A bridge between Hadrian and Selenae?"

"Exactly." She nods as she steps into the moonlight. "A bridge."

Athene pulls the door shut behind her, leaving me slightly puzzled. She's said that before. Why bring it up again?

Then I understand.

I hurry back into the kitchen, where Simon and Lambert are waiting patiently. "I think I know how to find Remi tonight."

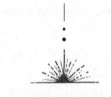

CHAPTER 60

We take the most direct route to the Sanctum to save time. I want to get inside ahead of the call to prayers shortly before midnight, otherwise we'll have to wait another hour for the building to be deserted. Even under a moonweave cloak, every minute Simon is outside is a risk.

When we reach the square, I start for the far end and the window, wondering if Lambert will be able to squeeze through, when he pulls a ring of keys from his pocket. I gape as he leads us to one of the doors in the south transept tower. "Where did those come from?"

"The provost has access to all public buildings," Lambert explains. "I took them from my father's desk. Doesn't the architect have a set of his own?"

"Well, yes. Remi has them now." Being they weren't anything I ever needed, using them never occurred to me.

Lambert fumbles with the first key in the moonlight. "I'm not sure which is the right one for this door."

I itch to take them from him, knowing my sight will make this much faster, but Lambert knows more than enough Selenae secrets. He doesn't find the correct key until the fourth try, and just as he opens the door, pounding footsteps echo across the square.

"Quickly!" Lambert whispers, shoving Simon and me inside. "I'll distract whoever it is."

The door slams shut, leaving us alone. Since he can't see nearly as well as me, I guide Simon to the spiral staircase. I have a hiding place in mind, but first I want to go to the tower while the moon is still visible to most of the city.

"Please don't tell me we're going all the way up," he whispers as we pass where I took him out to walk along the gutter.

"No, just here," I say. We step out onto the next level, even with the peaked ridge of the roof which runs to the squat tower over the center of the Sanctum, the crossing point for the transept arms and the length of the building. I move into the moonlight coming through the tall windows. "There's something I need to try, but I'll need your help."

Warrior kings and queens could cross a bridge of moonlight to the mind of another person.

The connection with Nichole happened when she and I saw the moon at the same time. If Remi looks up at it, I might be able to enter his mind and see where he is.

Last time I was lucky to have fallen over backward rather than tumble out the window. I lead Simon to the edge where I'll be able to see best. "Stand behind me, please, and hold on."

Simon pushes the cloak back over his shoulders, then puts his hands at my waist. "What is the rope for?"

My safety line is still there. I briefly consider taking it off, but I don't want to lose time. "Closer," I tell him. "And tighter."

He inches forward and puts his arms all the way around my middle. "Like this?"

His heartbeat against my back and his breath on my ear are very distracting. I'm tempted use the voidstone to rid myself of everything but sight, but I'm not sure how that would affect what I want to do. "That's perfect."

"Now what?"

"Just keep me from falling over."

"Is this moon magick?" he asks.

"Yes. Are you afraid?"

"I'm afraid if you think you need my help," he says. "What are you going to do?"

I take a deep breath and focus on the moon. "I'm going to try to find Remi."

Suddenly it occurs to me that my connection to Nichole had started with the moon in her vision, but then I'd been trapped in her mind until she died—while looking at the moon again. If I manage to get into Remi's mind, I may not be able to get back out.

And what happens if I stumble into someone else's mind? If this ability is something out of legend, there's no one alive who could ever guide me through this. It's too dangerous to try while so much is at stake. Lambert was right—we don't need to find Remi tonight.

I close my eyes. It's not worth the risk.

But when I open them again, I'm not in the south tower anymore.

— • ✳ • —

The moon stares at me through the long window like an eye, casting a shaft of light on the web of wooden beams around me. Until it had appeared, I had no concept of time, waiting for death to surprise me, but now I can judge the minutes as the moon sinks lower and lower. I preferred not knowing. I can also see my feet dangling over the edge of the wide beam and how far it is to the floor.

They'll think this is a suicide, given what happened with the ceiling the other day.

Mum, I don't know what they're going to tell you when they find me, but I'm sorry.

A pair of tears slides down my cheeks to soak into the tight, thick gag. My jaw aches and the rope around my neck itches like hell—minor irritations compared to everything else. With my legs half asleep and my hands tied behind my back, any movement could make me lose my balance. Once more I consider just leaning forward and getting it over with, letting myself fall and have the noose catch me, but I'm scared. I don't want to die. There was so much I was going to do.

The graceful curves of the bronze in front of me are green with age. Magister Thomas says a young, polished bell sounds bright and hard, like a town crier, whereas "Eirish moss" gives it the deeper intonation of a learned statesman, but I always thought of it like the difference between harsh sunlight and soft moonlight.

I snort. Death makes a man wax poetic, apparently.

How many swings will it take before the bell is high enough to knock me over the edge I'm sitting on? That's a morbid calculation. It probably depends on which religious brother's turn it is to yank the rope. Old Martin might take a dozen pulls to get it going, but Brother Vincent could probably have it ringing in two or three.

I've avoided looking at the moon, not wanting to see how far it's moved, but my eyes are drawn to the window like a moth to a flame.

Will you cry, Cat? Will you miss me? Will Lambert be the one to—

——— · ✳ · ———

I leap for the moon as soon as he focuses on it. Remi's surge of anger and the thought of Lambert drags on my mind like an anchor, disorienting me. Rather than return to myself, I view my body from the outside first, with Simon holding me in a close embrace, the moon shining like a halo around his head.

"Cat," Simon pleads. "Please—oh Light."

—*Simon. That penniless, half-sane bastard. Why? Why him?*—

My head snaps backward like I've been struck, and my knees give out. I feel myself being lowered to lie across Simon's legs as he kneels. His face comes into focus over mine, white as bleached linen in the moonlight. Relief floods into his eyes, and a second later his lips are on mine. "Hell beyond," he gasps. "I thought you were dead."

I blink. "Dead? Not yet, but it's only a matter of—" I stop. Those are Remi's thoughts.

Simon helps me sit up. "You were stiff as a corpse," he says. "I thought you were having a seizure. What happened?"

Oudin and Lambert are watching us with wide eyes from the top of the stairs. Lambert has his hands on his brother's arm as though to hold him back. "Did it look that bad?" I ask.

"It actually looked like you were enjoying it," says Oudin sourly.

I scramble to stand. "Why are you here?"

"I'm looking for Remi," Oudin replies. "We got separated a couple of hours ago."

Lambert blinks like he's coming out of a trance. "I told him we were looking for him, too."

"He also said Simon has convinced you Remi is the killer," Oudin growls, and Lambert tightens his grip on him.

Simon rises to his feet beside me. "Cat thinks it's Remi, but I'm certain her reasons are solid." He touches my elbow and lowers his voice. "Did you . . . see him?"

"Yes." I push Remi's lingering emotions aside and try to recall what he saw. A long tall window. Shadows. Wooden beams like a spiderweb. A bell.

He's in the tower at the far end of the Sanctum. When the bells are rung for prayers, he'll die.

His fear and despair. His thoughts of his mother. Of me.

"*Remi!*" I throw Simon's hand off my arm and dash for the far window. "Remi, I'm coming!"

At the edge I take a flying leap onto the Sanctum roof, landing lightly on the rounded peak. Behind me, Oudin swears and Simon frantically calls my name as I sprint along the crest of the transept arm to the squat, boxy tower in the middle. When I reach it, I skirt around its narrow ledge until I get to the longer ridge leading to the western facade.

The moon shines on me from the gap between the two towers as I run toward them—the one to the left is where I'd spent that glorious hour with Simon, to the right is the bell tower, where Remi waits for his death. I'm not sure I'd dare doing this in daytime, but in moonlight like this, with so much magick flowing through me, it's easy. Natural. I have no fear of misstep.

As I near the end, I stretch out my hearing. Lambert, Oudin, and Simon didn't try to follow me, instead going down and making their way to the front of the Sanctum from inside, but I'm way ahead of them. Shuffling footsteps on the tower stairs are a bigger concern. The bell ringer is coming.

Between the towers is a walkway with a low stone wall which I hurdle over and turn right. The tower door is closed and locked, and I pound on it, screaming, "Remi! Don't move! I'm coming!"

A muffled sob echoes back.

Lambert won't get here with his keys in time. I move to the front of the walkway and throw a leg over the railing to climb into the decorative alcove with a wingless chimera inside. Clambering over its back, I find the distance to the arching windows risky, even for me, until I see the storm cable tucked in the corner. Like a buttress redirects the force of thousands of pounds of stone, the metal wire draws the explosive energy of a lightning strike from the rod on top down to the ground. I grab ahold of it and swing around, stretching my leg and arm until they reach the edge of the window.

It's still too great for me to manage, but there's no going back. I push off with my back foot and lunge for the opening. My chest hits the bottom edge, and my hands and arms splay out on the floor, seeking any hold. Fortunately, while the Sanctum's outer walls are smooth and fitted so tightly a thread couldn't be worked between them, the floors no one sees are much less so. My fingers find an uneven place between stones and grab on. The toes of my boots have enough traction to lever me up until my whole upper body is inside and I can pull myself the rest of the way in, heart pounding.

That's when I realize I still have my safety rope around my waist. Had I remembered, I could have used that somehow. Too late now.

I stand and look around. Several smaller bells are arranged at my height, and I weave around and through them, peering up into the framework placed by the first builders decades ago. The largest bell in the center blocks most of my vision, but beyond it, near the top, I spot the bottom of a pair of boots. Remi sits across from a bell of medium size and weight—medium being four feet in diameter and weighing over two thousand pounds. It will have no trouble knocking him over.

How in the Light did the killer get up there?

Narrow walkways run between the beams, but the spiral staircase to the top of the tower is enclosed by long metal bars, so it's useless for getting to them. In the opposite corner lies a wooden platform attached to a series of pulleys for lifting a person up to inspect the bells.

Its ropes have been severed.

More ropes run up the wall and out to the wheels on the sides of the bell yokes. Their ends go down through the floor to the bell ringer's room. Even with my enhanced eyesight, the tangle is impossible to sort, otherwise I would just cut the one leading to the bell in front of Remi. The trapdoor must be bolted from the underside because it won't budge.

Climbing up the framework doesn't frighten me, but it will take time. When I pull myself up to a lower bell's yoke, my weight tilts it enough that the clapper strikes the side, ringing out.

From a distance, a small bell like this has a soft, pleasant sound. This close, surrounded by stone walls and magick, the reverberation is deafening, not to mention the actual vibration of the metal itself, which conducts painfully through my body. A number of pigeons roosting on the surrounding beams burst into flight.

"Hang on, Remi!" I shout through my rattling teeth. "I'm climbing up to you!"

I'm halfway to the top when Simon, Lambert, and Oudin finally reach the tower, entering from the trapdoor below.

"Cat!" Simon shouts. "Where are you?"

"Up here!" I call back. "Remi's trapped! Stop the bell ringer before he's hurt!"

Lambert and Simon both run back down the way they came, but Oudin stays, looking up for me. The moon has passed out of the window, leaving the inside of the tower almost completely dark. Athene's moonstone is the only reason I can still see.

A bell strikes below as Oudin begins climbing up as I did. The birds which had resettled explode into the air again, and I fling one arm across my face to protect against feathers and claws, losing precious seconds. By now I'm even with the top of the largest bell. Remi's feet are only another arm's length away when I see the round mouth in front of him begin to tilt.

The bell is being pulled.

"No!" I scream. "Stop!"

It swings back, going farther. Even if I can get to Remi in the next few seconds, there's not enough time to get him down or out of the way, nor can I stop that much weight.

But now I can see which rope leads to the wheel.

It's a short leap to a close-set pair of beams, which I run across to the other side. I grab the rope to stop its movement, but the weight of the swinging bell drags it through my clenched hands, leaving searing marks across my palms and fingers.

I'll have to cut it. I reach for the knife at my waist, realizing at the last second it isn't there—I loaned it to Remi.

The bell swings again, tilting even higher, and the clapper brushes against the side, singing a note of warning.

No time. Anything sharp will do.

I dig into my pocket for the voidstone, but my fingers are burned so raw I nearly drop it as I settle it in my palm. Grasping the rope with my other hand, this time I make no attempt to stop it, moving up and down with it as I saw on it from below. The first twist of rope parts as the bell strikes again, louder. My ears ring as I press harder and drag the glass-like edge across the fibers, hearing and feeling more break with each stroke.

A second cord splinters apart. Only one remains.

Out of the corner of my eye, Oudin comes level with me on the walkway. I give the rope one more vigorous slash, severing the last strands with a single stroke. There's not even a split second of relief before the voidstone continues, slicing into my forearm.

The world goes dark.

CHAPTER 61

For several seconds I think I'm dead. I can't see or hear or even smell. Nothing I was touching is there anymore. Then warm wetness drips down my arm, and I realize I've cut myself with the voidstone, and it took all the magick from my blood, leaving nothing. After having so much power, normal senses are so inadequate I can barely tell which way is up.

The next strike of the clapper is soft as a whisper, though perhaps because I've lost my hearing, but it won't swing any higher. I've saved Remi.

But now the real killer is only feet away.

As I ran along the roof to the tower, I'd tried to understand who could have done all this. The only possibility was Oudin. He despised Juliane like he despised his own mother. He knew all the women who had died. He hated Simon. His friendship with Remi drove him to frame Magister Thomas for the crimes so Remi could advance to master architect faster. And if he knew how Remi felt about me, going after Mother Agnes almost made sense, as her death would leave me with no one else to turn to but him.

But why this now? Perhaps Oudin told him what he'd done,

and Remi wasn't as grateful as he thought he'd be. Then damaging the Sanctum and attacking me was a message that Oudin could destroy us, too, but Remi still intended to go to the provost with what he knew, and so he had to die.

I shove the voidstone in my pocket and pull Athene's necklace out of my shirt. If exposing my blood to moonlight is the only way to get the magick back, maybe I can do it with the stone. I press it against the wound in my arm, and to my relief the world appears again, though with much weaker light. Oudin is right where I last saw him on the walkway, reaching for Remi's feet to pull him down.

"*No!*" I scream and tackle him from the side. Oudin is too solid for my weight to have much effect, but he's standing on his toes, and I surprise him so much he loses his balance and stumbles over the edge, just managing to catch himself with one hand. He looks up at me, terrified, as I smash his fingers with my fists until he loses his grip, vanishing like he did from the scaffolding at the Sanctum the night he tried to kill me.

His fall is broken by the large bell, and he rolls down and then off of it. There's nothing for him to grab at until the last row of bells which he hits with a *crack* that echoes through the tower. He bounces off the crossbeam to land on the floor like a sack of flour and doesn't move.

Crawling out from under the still-swinging bell, I push to my feet and grab Remi's boot. "I'm here, Remi! Let me figure out how to get you down."

I haul myself up to his level and sit beside him, straddling the beam with my legs. He sobs with relief as I pull the noose off, and I feel down his back to his bound wrists. My fingers are raw from trying to stop the bell rope, but I manage to loosen the knot enough to slide one loop over his hands, and then it's easier to get the rest off. Once he's free, Remi immediately reaches up to hug me, but his arms and hands are clumsy from being tied up for so long. I rise to my knees to pull his head to my chest as he cries. "Shhh, Remi. It's over. You're safe."

My big, stupid Remi who loves me more than he ever had the courage to say. How could I have thought he was the killer?

He tries to speak around the gag, and I turn his face up and tug the wet, twisted cloth around his jaw and down.

"Cah," he says, but his tongue and lips are as useless as his arms. "Am hur."

Blood from my forearm is smeared across his face, but the wound isn't deep. "I'm fine," I say. "It's just a scratch."

"No, Cat." Remi stretches his face in several directions. "Lambert."

"What about him?"

"He did this to me." Remi shifts his legs and groans. "He grabbed me on the street and put something on my face and the next thing I knew I was being hauled up here."

"Lambert." I stare at him, confused. "*Lambert Montcuir?*"

Remi nods as he works his jaw.

"Not Oudin?"

"Of course not Oudin." Remi pauses to swallow, peering down at the dark shape barely visible below. "Is that him who fell?"

I sit back on my heels, still trying to understand. Not Remi. Not Oudin. Not even the Comte de Montcuir.

Lambert.

Who is now with Simon.

CHAPTER 62

"Where are you going?" Remi tries to follow, but he's stiff and slow, and I can't afford to wait or answer as I scramble down the framework. My sight is as good as it would be in here during the day, but the moon is gone from the window and full power is literally just beyond my grasp.

I jump the last several feet to the floor, landing next to Oudin, who groans and rolls over. There's no time for apologies or explanations as I dash to the opposite corner of the tower and the trapdoor. At the bottom of the steps, a Brother of Light holds a lantern to the frayed end of a cut rope. "Who are you?" he demands as I come flying down the stairs. "Did you do this?"

Simon and Lambert are nowhere to be seen. "Where are the two men who were just here?" I gasp.

Neither of us care about the same thing. He drops the rope and comes at me, shaking his fist. "The high altum will hear about this."

Before he can grab me, I seize his robes and shake him, shouting, "*Where did they go?*"

Startled, the brother smacks at my hands and points at the

door leading to the interior of the Sanctum. "That way! Now get out!"

I release him without a word and bolt in the direction he indicated, cursing my partial blindness.

Down another set of stairs and I'm on the triforium, the balcony level over the gallery walkway. Though mostly decorative, it's the highest passage that goes the length of the building. Lambert could have taken it on either side all the way to the other end of the Sanctum or gone down. I move to the center of the facade, my back to the circular window, bright with the glow of the moon behind it. The colored glass blocks any chance of regaining my more powerful senses, but I can hear movement echoing off the stone walls. I close my eyes and listen.

Footsteps. One set. Treading heavy, especially on one leg. After years of working at a construction site, I know the sound of a person carrying something bulky. Lambert is heading toward the unlocked door in the transept tower, probably with Simon slung over one shoulder. I can't hear any indications of struggle, so Simon must be unconscious—and alive, otherwise there's no reason for Lambert to have taken him. I hope.

Trotting swiftly to the other side of the nave, I peer down the triforium walkway, striped with the shadows of the arched columns in groups of three. A hulking shape vanishes at the far end. I sprint at it, my mind trying to put the pieces together in a way that makes sense.

Simon was right that Lambert fit the description of the killer he'd built—even I can admit that now—but what I can't understand was *why* he did all this. He had everything most people strive for: money, power, and soon would have a marriage that increased both. What was it he wanted? Like before, I feel I'm missing something vital, though it may be because I'm running so hard I can barely think at all.

My lungs are ready to burst by the time I reach the transept arm. I swing around the corner to the stairs, gasping for breath, and stop to listen again. Pigeons rustling above. Disturbed by something.

Lambert went up, toward the place where I crossed into Remi's mind. I hold one hand to the stitch in my side as I follow. Now I realize when I'd tried to go back to my own body, I'd passed not through Oudin's thoughts but Lambert's as he stared at Simon holding me in his arms. He'd been stunned and angry at what he saw. He hated Simon, and it hadn't started tonight, either.

Lambert's attempt to kill Remi may have failed, but he won't leave anything to chance with Simon.

The stairs open to the first landing, where the windows are level with the bottom of the main roof. I pause to extend the voidstone wound on my arm into the moonlight, letting the magick flood into my bloodstream again.

To my surprise, rather than going higher into the tower, Lambert walks along the wide gutter at the bottom edge of the roof toward the east end of the Sanctum. Simon's limp body hangs over his right shoulder, and, thanks to the moonlight, I can hear he's still breathing. He's alive, but one heave of effort is all it will take to cast him from a fatal height.

Yet somehow I know that simple end won't be enough for Lambert, not after seeing what his rage made him do to his other victims. Ironically, that works in my favor.

Simon's weight slows Lambert down, but he still reaches the end ahead of me. Sliding behind Pierre, he continues along the covered portico over the stained glass wheel which matches the one at the western facade. Unlike the walkway in the front of the Sanctum, however, this has no railing. One could step off the edge as easily as stepping from the street into the gutter, only the fall here is eighty feet. Below are the forges of two blacksmiths with vertical racks holding dozens of iron and steel rods for making nails and hooks. No one would survive the landing.

I grab onto Pierre at the corner to stop my momentum. "Lambert!"

He turns around from halfway across and smiles. "Yes, my dear Catrin?"

Like the voidstone in my pocket, his tone has a sharp and cruel edge as it did the night he pressed the cold blade against Ysabel's throat. *I want you to die.*

I slow my breathing with effort, keeping the statue between us. "Where are you going?"

The wind whistles through the arched columns like Perrete's last cry for help as Lambert glances around idly. "I suppose this will do." Almost casually, he slings Simon down off his shoulder. There's a thud as Simon's head connects with the stone walkway.

I grip Pierre's stone wing to keep myself from running to him. "And now what will you do?"

He stares at Simon's pale face. "I will end this."

Fury twists in my gut like a knife. "Rather unsporting to kill the winner of your sick game, don't you think?"

"He didn't win." Lambert raises his gaze to meet mine. "I simply realized the prize wasn't worth having."

Prize? There can't be a prize unless both sides want the same thing. I'd assumed the contest was between hunter and killer, with the loser either caught or wrongly blamed. Lambert had been playing a different game entirely, but for what?

It's not until I see the loathing in his eyes that I understand. "You wanted *me*?"

Lambert raises his eyebrows. "Why else would I have done all that work?"

All that work. Killing Mother Agnes, imprisoning Magister

Thomas, driving a rift between me and Simon, taking away what gave me purpose . . . "You sought to win me by destroying everything and everyone that was important to me?" I ask incredulously.

He snorts. "They kept you from understanding how low you were. You never would've left your precious architect or the Sanctum, and if you lost those things, you could still go back to the abbey." With the toe of his boot, Lambert nudges Simon's chin, turning his face upward. "This one practically threw you from his presence, and after Remone blamed you for the collapse, you were supposed to go to the only person who never judged you. The one who always listened, who helped you when no one else would."

"The one who tried to kill me that night?" I challenge.

He rolls his eyes skyward. "I wasn't going to kill you, Catrin. You would have been allowed to escape, though until that platform broke, it looked as though I'd have to leave you unconscious but miraculously alive. I thought I might even return to rescue you, if I had time."

Rescue. As soon as he uses the word, I realize the connection between all the victims. Juliane had described Lambert's romantic vision of raising a woman from poverty as his father saved his mother. *That* was what he went seeking with Perrete, Ysabel, and Nichole, yet somehow it had gone wrong.

Lambert looks down at Simon again. "But it wasn't me you came to for help that night," he snarls. "It was *him*." He makes a noise of disgust as he shoves Simon's face away with his foot. "You betrayed him and he sent you away, and you still went crawling back to the man who could offer you nothing." Lambert shakes his head. "Then Remone forgave you. Oudin told me he even proposed, and you didn't say no."

Remi wasn't a threat until there was suddenly a chance I

would choose him over Lambert. Then he had to die. That was why Simon would.

If Lambert now hates me as much as he hated them, revenge is what he wants most. The question is whether, given a choice, he would kill me or kill Simon. And if it's me, how do I survive that? I have one idea, but to make it work I need distractions and time.

I reach for my waist where the statue blocks his view. "What about the other women?" I ask, counting seven loops of the safety rope with my fingers while I try to keep him talking. "How did they offend you?"

"You act like you would have deigned to speak to any of those . . . *women*." The last word drips with contempt. "But they disgusted me, too. Willing to do anything if money was involved. Not one of them could have told me from my brother in the dark. Do you know Perrete even offered to let us share her?"

To them he was only a source of quick and easy money. "They didn't appreciate what you offered," I say.

"Exactly." Lambert shakes his head. "I wasn't going to lose this time. I just had to be more deliberate with how I offered myself."

What the killer needs *will not change.* Simon had said. *How he goes about getting it may.*

I wouldn't see myself as needing to be rescued until I was stripped of everything I had and left with nowhere else to go. Same madness, different method.

Lambert nods to the motionless form at his feet. "Even when you came to Simon, I still believed I had a chance. Until I saw you with him tonight. Then I realized everything you did was an act to get what you wanted. I was a fool. You were no different from the others."

He was right to some extent. I'd used his liking of me to get into the gaol, and I'd not discouraged his small advances—but that didn't mean he owned me.

Lambert takes a sudden step in my direction, murderous rage in his dark eyes. Reflexively, I move back, blurting out the question I still need answered. "What about Juliane?"

His expression changes from wrath to agony in an instant, and he curls inward like he's been struck. "Juliane?" he whispers.

I step up to Pierre again, the unhooked clasp of my safety rope in my hand. "Didn't you love her?" I call from across the statue's back. "She loved you."

He flinches. "It was mercy. More than once she'd begged me to end her suffering."

No, it wasn't, and he knows it. Perrete, Ysabel, and Nichole had been victims of rage. The others had been methodical removals of people who were in his way.

He may have made Juliane's death as painless as possible, but it's how he left her—lovingly covered and posed like she was sleeping—that tells me she was his ultimate sacrifice in chasing his prize. Juliane he regrets.

She's the key to pulling him apart. But I'm not ready to do that yet.

"I never got the impression she was hopeless," I tell him. "In fact, thanks to Simon, she was more optimistic than she'd been in years."

My gamble pays off as Lambert's eyes are drawn to Simon, and I unwrap one loop from around my waist. Each will give me approximately three feet, which means I'll need two more.

"Simon was madder than her," he mutters. "He was just better at hiding it."

I wince at his referring to Simon in past tense but push a hard edge into my tone. "If Simon was so mad, what does it say that he understood you?"

Lambert throws back his head and laughs, the mirthless sound echoing around us. A second loop comes off my waist, and I press it against Pierre's flank to keep it out of sight. Lambert flings one arm in Simon's direction. "If he did, he wouldn't be lying there right now. Simon never even considered me."

But he had. It was my denial and his own fear of bias that made him discard his theory. And if Simon was right about that, he was probably right about other things, even if he didn't understand why. "He knew about Beatrez," I say.

That makes Lambert pause. "He did," he admits. "That was clever. Or maybe just lucky." Bitterness twists his face. "I learned the most from her. Namely that no woman is worth begging for."

"They should come begging to you, is that it?" I lean against the statue, every nerve in my body quivering. "Except no one does. Even your own sister preferred Simon."

It might be a coincidence, but at the mention of his name, Simon's head turns slightly. To my horror, his face tenses around the bruise forming on his temple. I could use a diversion, but Simon waking would be the worst possible one.

"Cat!" Remi's voice floats on the wind over a distance. "Cat! Where are you?"

Remi will be a better distraction than Simon. In the meantime, I need to keep Lambert's focus on me.

"Which is the real reason you killed Juliane," I throw at him. "Once Simon came along she didn't need you anymore."

The accusation hits the mark or very close to it. I have every ounce of his attention.

"And then," I continue, "when you feared her madness would stop me from accepting you, she became just another obstacle keeping you from claiming your *prize*."

This angle is dangerous, though, as my own anger rises to an uncontrollable level.

"Because that's what Mother Agnes was, wasn't she?" I shriek into the wind. "A woman who did more good in a day than you've done in your whole life was an *obstacle*?" My voice cracks, and I can't say Marguerite's name. "A sister who was beautiful and sweet and loving was an *obstacle*?"

"Cat!" Remi's coming this way, running along the gutter on the opposite side of the roof. Someone else approaches much slower from the direction I came, probably Oudin. Lambert turns his head to look, and a third loop comes off my waist.

Almost ready.

Simon groans, one hand drifting to his face. Lambert shifts to look at him again, and I hastily wrap the end of the rope over Pierre's outstretched paw and clasp it to itself.

I'm out of time.

"Lambert!"

He faces me as I step around the statue, leaning to pass under its wings as close as I can.

"Do you know what I think?" I stand straight and hold the rope against my back to prevent it from slacking around my waist. "You never loved Juliane. She just made you feel better about yourself."

I move to the edge of the walkway, angling to block his view of the rope leading back to Pierre. "And she saw right through you. That's why she preferred Simon. That's why she preferred me."

Lambert's eyes dilate until they're almost solid black, and his body tenses. He doesn't notice Simon twisting to look at me, blinking rapidly as he struggles to focus.

I set my heels only inches away from the drop behind me. "And that's why no one could ever love you."

Remi appears on the far end of the walkway, and Simon's eyes widen in horror as he realizes what's happening.

"*No!*" they both shout as Lambert lunges at me.

Rather than move out of the way, I embrace him.

It's what he wanted anyway.

CHAPTER 63

We fall.

My feet are off the walkway and I'm spinning, the last three and a half loops around my waist unwinding like a spool of thread.

A thread that can rip me in half.

I push Lambert away, using both hands and feet. By the third twist, we're separated enough that when the rope runs out, his effort to hold on to me fails and we come apart.

A narrow force stops me instantly while momentum flings my limbs downward and my head lashes forward and back like a whip. Lambert continues plummeting seven more stories to the ground, landing across a rack of vertical iron rods. Several tear through his flesh with sounds I wish I couldn't hear and will never forget. He lies facing up, two thin poles extending through his torso and another coming out of his neck.

One hand reaches for the metal piercing his throat, but Lambert's upper arm is also pinned and his fingers only manage to brush against it. He gurgles and strains as blood bubbles on his lips and spreads out from the wounds on his chest. Frantic, unfocused eyes search the sky, unable to find whatever it is they seek, until he suddenly gasps and ceases to struggle, his wrist slackening to rest on his shoulder. Finally, his whole body relaxes with the release of one long, shuddering breath.

His heart beats once more.

And stops.

I dangle high above, bent over the rope at my waist with the reopened wound bleeding down my left arm to my fingertips. Several drops land on Lambert's face to trail back like tears.

"Cat!" Remi shouts from above. "Cat! Are you all right?"

I groan. "I may have actually broken something. A rib. Or two." I twist around to shift the pressure of the rope from my stomach to my back, and it slides up to my armpits. For a moment, the relief it gives me washes out the residual pain.

Remi's face looks over the edge of the portico, his green eyes so wide they're white all the way around. Simon appears next to him. "Hang on. We're pulling you up."

I release myself to gravity, arms and legs hanging limply, and barely notice as I slowly drift higher. Then hands are grabbing my arms and hooking under my shoulders to lift me onto the walkway. Simon pulls my legs away from the edge as Remi cradles me in his lap, crying. "Why the hell did you do that?" he sobs.

"Wouldn't you have done it for me?" I ask. Breathing hurts less now that all my weight isn't supported on a thin line.

Oudin leans over Remi's shoulder. Half his face is swelling with bruises, but he looks better than I expected. "What happened? Where's Lambert?"

Remi explains what he saw as Simon carefully pulls me into his own arms. To my surprise, Remi lets me go without a fuss.

"You're bleeding," I tell Simon, noticing the wound on his left temple. Lambert must have struck him there.

"Never mind that." Simon bends down to hug me. "I'm

sorry," he whispers in my ear. "I should have known it was him. I failed you."

I bury my face in the collar of his shirt. "Neither of us wanted it to be true. And you did know. The only part you got wrong was what he wanted."

Simon eases away enough to look me in the eye. The flaw is lost in the shadow of his brow. "And what was that?"

I sigh. "Me. He was trying to leave me with only him to turn to." I offer Simon a weak smile. "But his plan didn't include you forgiving me."

"How could I not?" Simon strokes my cheek. "I've never known anyone to fight so hard to protect those they love."

My skin warms under his gentle fingers. "Do you remember the question you thought in the kitchen? About whether I would protect you?"

Simon's hand freezes. "You heard that?"

"Yes." I reach up to touch the scab at the corner of his mouth. "You were bleeding."

He frowns. "It's not very nice to listen to someone's thoughts without their permission."

"It was an accident. I didn't know what I was doing." Sort of.

"Hm." Simon glances at Remi and Oudin, who are peering over the edge of the walkway at Lambert's body, speaking in low tones.

"Do you remember my response?"

Simon looks back at me. "Is that why you said 'yes'?"

I nod. "I meant it. If you want me to."

When Simon doesn't respond, I skim my hand from his jaw to the trickle of blood sliding down his cheek. "May I listen to what you're thinking right now?"

His mouth twitches. "If you're sure you want to know."

"I do."

He doesn't resist as I push my fingers over the bruise on his head and into his hair. For a long moment I close my eyes and listen. When I open them, he's watching me with something like hope. I smile. "I want the same thing."

Simon pulls my hand away, breaking the connection, but barely a second later his mouth is on mine, and I don't need blood to know what his answer is.

CHAPTER 64

"Ahem."

Simon stops kissing me to look up. Both Oudin and Remi are averting their eyes. Thankfully, Remi appears more resigned than angry as he watches Simon help me sit upright.

"It won't be long before the city guard finds my brother." Oudin tilts his head to indicate the bloody scene below. "We need to decide what we're going to say."

"The truth," I tell him. The muscles in my stomach ache so fiercely I have to lean against Simon for support. "Lambert murdered all those women, caused the collapse, and tried to kill Remi and Simon and me. Now he's dead. Justice is done."

He raises his eyebrows. "Where is your proof of any of that?"

Simon—and pain across my middle—keeps me from sitting forward more than a few inches. "You don't believe it?"

Oudin rolls his eyes. "It doesn't matter what's true, little Cat, unless we can prove it."

"He's right," Simon whispers in my ear, pulling me back to his chest. "We're rather short on evidence."

I lean on him again but refuse to relax. "Isn't what he did to Remi proof enough?"

"It's our word against what my father will want to believe," Oudin says, more rational than I've ever heard him sound. "And that's not a battle we'll win. Not when he can blame everything on Simon here."

"Maybe that's better," says Simon. "No other innocents will get tangled in this mess."

I turn to face him. "You are not giving yourself up."

He shakes his head with a soft smile. "I wasn't planning on it."

Something tells me he might if he felt it was necessary. Remi clears his throat. "Blame is irrelevant if the comte can't find you. We know plenty of places you can hide."

Remi's not just offering to protect Simon, he's acting like he intends to.

Oudin agrees. "Just lie low for a few days, and we'll get you out of the city. I think I can keep Father from pursuing you too vigorously."

"How?" I ask.

He smiles ironically. "Lambert and Juliane aren't the only secrets our family would rather keep. And now I'm the only son left. He can't afford to lose me."

"So you *will* tell him the truth."

"Of course."

Maybe my mind is addled by exhaustion, but I don't understand. "A few seconds ago you said he won't believe Lambert's guilt."

Oudin chuckles darkly. "Oh, he'll believe it. He'll just do anything to keep everyone else from finding out."

"We need to be smart about it," says Remi. "The price of our silence will be clearing Magister Thomas and setting him free."

Movement and voices tell me the commotion we made is being investigated. "The guard is here," I tell them. "Or will be in a matter of minutes. We can't let any of them see Simon, even from the ground."

"I'll take care of that." Remi pushes to his feet and offers Simon a hand. "I think the best place to put you is in the walkway around the center tower."

After gently setting me against the wall, Simon accepts his help. "Any particular reason?" he asks.

Remi grins as he pats the ring of keys on his belt next to the two-colored braid of hair. "Because it's behind two locked doors, and we'll have to walk across the central rib of the vaulted ceiling. It's unnerving if you don't know it's actually the most stable place to put weight."

Simon shudders a little but gestures for Remi to lead. "You're the expert on ceilings."

The compliment isn't lost on Remi, who gives me a brief nod of assurance. He knows I'd never forgive him if Simon is captured, but that's not his primary motivation for helping, and that makes me happier. While Remi may struggle with some of the finer points of life, he always does what he believes is right. I knew that about him, yet I was more willing to believe he was the killer than Lambert. I'm not sure what that says about my judgment.

As if having similar thoughts, Oudin scoots to rest against the wall beside me, though he keeps his distance. "Some of this is my fault," he says, gazing out at the stars. "I knew how Lambert felt about Beatrez. I should have said something when Simon put her name on the list."

I turn my head to look at Oudin, wincing as pain shoots through my neck. "Lambert was in love with Beatrez?"

Oudin snorts. "Half the men I know were at some point. That was her . . . specialty." He shifts uncomfortably. "She gave first timers a confidence-building experience."

It's odd to see him so awkward considering how uncouth he normally is. "And Lambert went to her?"

"I arranged it. He needed something normal after . . ." Oudin shakes his head rather than finish that thought. "I even paid in advance, so she could make a show of returning Lambert's money." He gently probes his swollen lip. "He proposed to her, but most of her besotted customers did."

"And soon after that she chose to marry," I say.

Oudin nods. "He was devastated. I never imagined he would kill her, though."

Simon had described most first murders as panicked and often unplanned. "I'm not sure Lambert thought he would, either," I say.

That was how it started. Lambert had seen Beatrez as a woman he could rescue, but she rejected him in favor of someone undoubtedly lower, and he couldn't stand that. After killing her, he retreated to his previous quiet, awkward demeanor, still obsessed with the idea but too wounded to try again. His engagement forced him to make another attempt, but things must have gone terribly wrong with Perrete, and he killed her in a rage. With Ysabel and Nichole, the disgust and lust for blood had come quicker. Emeline was silenced before she could tell Simon anything she knew that connected them all. Sun only knows how many more women he would have gone through if I hadn't caught his attention.

I was a far more appropriate candidate and had a few things in common with his mother; I was even raised at the same abbey. That his competition for my affection was Simon made it more exciting—Lambert could defeat both his rival and his hunter. Yet, in the end, it wasn't him I went to, it was Simon.

I was Beatrez all over again.

"You said Lambert needed something normal," I say. "Did you mean after your mother's illness?"

Oudin nods, his eyes blank. "Juliane's delusions were strange but easily dismissed as nonsense. Mother's were more insidious.

Or maybe we were just more impressionable. Lambert was the only one she loved, but I gave up trying to please her when I saw what that meant." He shivers and pulls his knees closer, almost to his chest. "Unnatural things sons should never do with mothers."

I don't want to know. Fortunately, Oudin isn't inclined to elaborate.

"Her despising me was actually my protection," he continues. "It's sad to think I was the lucky one."

"Oudin," I whisper, and he turns to meet my eyes for the first time. "Did Lambert kill your mother?"

"No, that was Father." Oudin grimaces. "He couldn't lie to himself anymore about what was happening. I think he believed it was the only way to free Lambert from her influence. Except his way of getting Lambert to please him was to criticize. My brother couldn't handle that either."

Shouts below tell us Lambert's body has been spotted.

Oudin pushes himself up the wall to a stand. "I think we should tell everyone my brother fell while searching for Simon, but we shouldn't say Simon was actually here. Then we can push the idea that he's long gone from the city." He offers me his hand, but when he sees how raw and scraped mine are, he grasps my forearms.

"We'll have to tell Remi before we go down." I wince as Oudin gently raises me to my feet. It would be much easier to list the few places I'm *not* scraped or bruised. Oudin waits until I'm steady before releasing me, his civility disconcerting. "I imagine you could really use a drink right now," I joke feebly.

Oudin blinks, but his surprise isn't directed at me. "For once in my life, I actually don't."

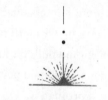

CHAPTER 65

Though we should keep the appearance of mourning, I can't bear to sing along with the crowd as the Sun dips below the horizon at Lambert's funeral. Neither can Remi, who stands next to me with his collar pulled up to hide the raw marks on his neck from the noose. My hands and other wounds are already healed thanks to Athene's bloodstones.

"Enjoy your place in hell," Remi mutters as the last of the orange light vanishes. I glance around nervously, but no one seems to have noticed as they draw out the last note of the hymn.

"Someone could have heard that," I hiss once everyone nearby has moved out of earshot.

Remi snorts. "I hate this pretending. All those speeches about what a loss he is to his family and the city, how the Beyond has gained a soul of Light."

Officially, Lambert's death was a tragic accident while searching the Sanctum for a criminal, but coming so close on the heels of Juliane's death, there are already whispers that it was a suicide. Oudin denies it but not too vigorously. Either explanation is preferable to the truth.

"If we want Magister Thomas released, we need to show we're

willing to play along," I remind Remi. "The provost will be watching us."

"I don't think he's watching anything."

I'm inclined to agree. The Comte de Montcuir stares blankly at the fading horizon. He looks like he aged twenty years in as many hours, but I have little sympathy for the man after what Oudin told me.

The mourners depart quickly, as they did two nights ago with Juliane. It seems grief is as uncomfortable for people to witness as mental affliction. The last to leave is Lady Genevieve d'Ecre's family, and I'm surprised to see Oudin giving his brother's fiancée extra attention and holding her hand longer than I would expect. "What do you think that's about?" I ask Remi quietly.

He shrugs.

At last everyone else is gone, and the comte returns to the house without a word. Oudin rubs his face tiredly as he walks to meet us. "Would you mind giving me a hand?" he asks Remi. "We can talk about the deal I had to make." His dark eyes shift to me. "Cat should stay, too, as it concerns her."

I glance at the blue-violet sky to the east. Gregor and his companions will retrieve Simon from the Sanctum soon, before the full moon is high enough to shine on the reflecting pool. My promise to join the song tonight was his condition for the rescue, and I'm eager to fulfill it for more than one reason. "If it won't take too long," I say.

We follow Oudin inside. Lambert's coffin was closed just before sunset, but within it he's dressed to hide his wounds, including a scarf around his neck. Oudin leaves briefly and returns with a hammer. Remi offers to hold the nails while his friend sets the first in place.

"I'll start with the good news," Oudin says. "The magister will be released tonight."

I almost weep with relief. "Thank you."

He drives the nail home with one blow of his hammer. "Don't thank me yet."

Remi offers him the second. "I imagine your father set certain conditions beyond our silence."

"Not just for you." Oudin takes two tries to hit this nail, missing completely the first time. "It's not settled yet, but I'll probably be marrying Lady Genevieve in Lambert's place."

I don't know which of the two to feel more sorry for. "How do you feel about that?" I ask. "How does she?"

Oudin shrugs. "She didn't cry, so that's a start." He holds a hand out, and Remi drops a nail into it. "I guess we'll both make the best of it."

"That's a big sacrifice," Remi says cautiously. I think he's asking if his friend intends to give up his night life.

"It's funny," says Oudin, focusing on the casket. "But it doesn't feel that way. For the first time in my life, I don't have a sense of being trapped. The only things worse than what happened in our family—that *were* happening—was having to pretend they didn't. Maybe that's what drove my brother to his madness. I preferred drink and *skonia*." He strikes the nail with a loud *bang* as though to emphasize.

We all live in cages. Only those of us who are lucky get to choose which ones.

Oudin looks up. "Our secrets aren't gone, of course, but they're in the past. Now that I don't have to live every day in a lie, I don't mind being sober. I actually feel hopeful."

Remi offers him another nail. "Then I guess I should say congratulations."

"Thank you. I just hope it lasts." Oudin avoids looking at me as he moves to the lower end of the coffin. "That wasn't the only thing I had to agree to."

We wait and he clears his throat. "I have to lead a hunt for Simon tomorrow." My heart punches my ribs like a clenched fist. "I have a week to return with his body, or one that looks like it."

I gasp. "You're not going to—"

"Kill anyone?" Oudin chuckles humorlessly. "Of course not. There are plenty of dead out there to choose from."

"The prisons in the capital would be a good place to start," says Remi. "Lutecia is huge."

Oudin nods. "That's what I was thinking. If not the gaols, then the beggars' hospitals should have someone suitable."

The next three nails are placed without comment. "Was there something else?" I finally ask.

Oudin sighs and stands upright. "You know none of this was your fault, right?"

Part of me will always feel responsible, but I nod.

He tosses the hammer on the lid of the coffin, speaking through gritted teeth. "Father blames you for Lambert's insanity. He also says people associate you with Simon now, and you'll always remind them of him. It's really his own association. Collis will move on."

I shrug. "I have more important things to worry about than what people think."

Like magick and my Selenae family and repairing the damage to the Sanctum.

Oudin shakes his head. "He can't stand the sight of you, Cat. And he'll always consider you the biggest risk in keeping the truth about Lambert hidden."

"So I'll stay away from him. Remi can show him around the Sanctum when necessary."

"No, Cat." Oudin finally looks at me. "That was Father's third condition for releasing the architect. You have to leave Collis."

——— · * · ———

I stand in the shadows on the edge of the open area of the Quarter, watching Selenae dance in the light of the full moon. Weavers and dyers sing on the sides as they work looms and stir pots of moonflower essence. Dozens of moonstones glow from the pool in the center, absorbing the light from above. Gregor spins past, his arm linked with a middle-aged woman's. His cheerfulness probably has a great deal to do with expecting my arrival, but he hasn't noticed me yet.

Three days. That's all I have.

Then I've lost the magister, Remi, and the Sanctum. Mistress la Fontaine and Marguerite. The family I'd only just begun to know.

Both Oudin and Remi assured me I could come back someday, when the comte was dead. He's past fifty, so theoretically that might not be very long. Or it could be twenty years. He could outlive Magister Thomas.

"Cat?" calls a soft voice behind me.

I turn to see Simon walking toward me, arms outstretched to feel along the wall in the dark. He trips on the uneven street, and I step back to guide him to a place beside me. The dark Selenae outfit he wears hangs on his lanky frame and exposes his wrists with too-short sleeves. Water drips from his hair onto his shoulders. "I guess you've had a bath?" I ask.

He ducks his head. "Your cousin said the dust and bird droppings would choke anyone who came within ten yards."

"She's right," I agree.

Simon looks over the bustling plaza. "Do you want to join them?"

"Not yet. We should probably talk." I step farther away from the moonlight. "Have you decided where you'll go?"

He shakes his head. "Mesanus is the only other town I know, but it's probably the first place they'll look for me."

I nod. "We have to decide soon, though."

"We?" Simon wrinkles his forehead.

I explain the terms of Oudin and the comte's agreement and my banishment.

Simon exhales slowly. "Oh, Cat, I'm so sorry. I know what it's like to lose your home and family." He takes my hand. "Does anyone else know yet?"

"Remi does. He's probably telling Magister Thomas right now." As much as I wanted to see him tonight, I know he'll understand why I'm honoring my promise to Gregor. The first thing the architect will want to do is take a bath and sleep in his own bed anyway. I clear my throat. "I realize we don't know each other that well, but I was thinking we would be better off together than alone."

"That's difficult to argue with," he says, rubbing his thumb over the back of my hand. "And I'll be glad for your company. Even if it's not the way I wanted any of this to happen."

"Nor I."

"Catrin." My uncle stops in the moonlight several feet away. "Are you coming?"

I hurriedly brush the tears from my eyes. "I'm not in the mood to dance."

Gregor grimaces in sympathy but doesn't press for an explanation. "The moon is only here for a few hours. Whatever troubles you can wait." He gives Simon a brief nod and rejoins the crowd.

Simon watches him go. "He's right. You should enjoy your magick while it's at its strongest. We can talk about leaving tomorrow."

I look down at the edge of the shadow. "Are you afraid?"

"Less than I was when my father died." He shrugs.

"No, I mean of me. Of my magick and what I can do."

Simon tilts my chin up until I meet his eyes. The brown flaw doesn't draw my attention like it used to. It's just part of him. "Are you afraid of *me*?" he asks. "Of my 'gifts'?"

"Of course not. I know you."

He smiles. "And I know you." Then he steps out, drawing me with him into the moonlight.

CHAPTER 66

My three days are up. Every night until this one has been full of songs and stories and lessons in moonlight, but this time the darkness is needed to hide our departure. A moonstone of my very own hangs from a silver chain around my neck, though the new voidstone bracelet remains in a pocket. I'm still a little afraid of it. My cousin says I don't need to trim my magick as most Selenae do, but I should practice in case someday I need one sense above all others.

Athene hands me a small bag. "Some extra moonstones," she tells me. "And some bloodstones. Try not to need them."

I tuck them in my vest. "Thank you. For everything."

"I wish we had more time. There was so much I wanted to teach you." She settles a satchel on my shoulder, her usual brisk manner noticeably gentled. "But the Selenae community outside Londunium trains the best physicians. You'll do fine there."

That's where we've decided to go. The Brinsulli capital isn't that far away, but it's across the narrow channel, and the chances of Simon being recognized are much smaller. Between the Selenae and some of Magister Thomas's old colleagues, we hope to find a place to live and work. I also have a special letter tucked deep in my bag for the architect's wife, if she's still living. He doesn't expect her to come back after all these years, but he hopes she can at least forgive him.

Gregor stands awkwardly next to Athene. We'd quarreled again when he insisted I could stay in the Quarter and the provost wouldn't be the wiser, but I refused. I think my uncle believes I'm choosing Simon over my Selenae family. Maybe I am, but it's not out of spite. As I pivot to face him, Gregor pulls an embellished moonweave pouch out of his shirt and tugs the drawstring open. A pearlescent glow from within tells me what's inside.

"How many moonstones do you think I need?" I ask, trying to lighten his solemn expression.

He tips the bag out into his hand. "This one is different."

The stone looks the same until the moonlight hits it and casts the light back with a rainbow sheen rather than a soft white radiance. A closer look with enhanced sight shows me the colors splitting inside the stone and bouncing around as through an endless maze of corridors. It's beautiful.

Gregor wraps his fingers around the stone and closes his eyes for a few seconds. Then he reopens both and offers it to me. "It is the most rare kind of moonstone. What it absorbs it holds forever."

I swallow. "And what is that?"

"Thoughts," he says. "Memories."

Gooseflesh rises on my arms as he places the colorful stone in my hand. "Whose does this hold?"

"Mine." Gregor nods. "Go ahead."

I close my eyes and clench the moonstone against the white scar on my palm, wondering if there is something else I should do, when the image of two people appears in my mind. The woman has waves of chestnut hair and a laughing mouth set over a straight and narrow nose I've seen in mirrors. Her eyes are hazel like mine are—or were—while the man holding her close has the silver ring around his irises that I know is coming to dominate mine. He looks like I would expect a young Gregor to appear, were he not so scarred or his nose crooked. The smile he wears is more shy than the woman's as he gazes at her. He leans down, and she runs a pale hand through his dark curls. They kiss, and their skin is silver and gold where it meets.

"Stella," Gregor whispers. "And Iason."

Tears come so fast my eyes are forced back open. Though Athene had told me my parents' names, I never heard my uncle utter them until now. The pain in his voice tells me it was grief, not anger, that chained him for so long, and it was that anguish— not resentment—that had made him give me up seventeen years ago. I nearly drop the memory stone in my haste to wipe my cheeks. "Thank you."

"It's been so many years it's almost impossible for me to remember their faces without help." Gregor takes the stone back and drops it into the moonweave pouch. Then he ties it shut and holds it out to me. "I want you to have it."

I shake my head. "I can't. That's your memory."

"Which makes it mine to give."

I glance at Athene nervously, but she nods. Finally, I accept my uncle's gift. Saying thank you again seems trite, so I hold it to my lips before putting it in the pocket closest to my heart. "I'll take good care of it."

He smiles, and I see my father's in it. Then he offers an arm to Athene, and they leave for the Moon Pool together without further words.

Remi has been waiting impatiently for his turn, and he sweeps me off my feet and into a hug as soon as their backs are turned. "I'll miss you more than you know, Kitten."

I squeeze back just as tightly. "You promised never to call me that." Truthfully, I don't mind anymore.

"Yes, well, that was a conditional promise." Remi sets me back down, then blinks several times and kisses my forehead hastily, before turning to Simon. "Farewell, Venatre."

Using that title was definitely meant to needle Simon, but he only nods. "My thanks for everything you've done."

Now Magister Thomas embraces me, his tears soaking his beard and my hood, and suddenly what I'm leaving behind is more than I can bear. "I don't think I can do this, Magister," I gasp.

"But I know you can, my dear." The architect leans back and frames my face with his hands, and I notice a third streak of white extends back from the hair by his left ear. "And I'll see you again someday. That's why I can let you go."

"I love you," I whisper.

He kisses my forehead as Remi did. "And I love you."

I back away so Simon can shake the architect's hand, some silent exchange happening between them as their eyes meet, and they both nod. Then we walk down the vine-lined alley to the street. As soon as I see the abbey wall, I realize what I almost forgot.

"Wait!" I leave Simon and dash across the road to the repaired gate and ring the bell. Midnight prayers have just ended, and one of the sisters heading back to bed comes when I call, though she has trouble seeing me in my moonweave cloak. "I need to say goodbye to Marguerite," I tell her.

She fetches the keys and lets me inside, and I run around to Marguerite's cell just past Mother Agnes's old sitting room. They haven't elected a new prioress yet, so her chambers are still empty.

"Marga?" I call softly from the door. She wouldn't have gone to the liturgy, but that doesn't mean she didn't say prayers from her bed. "Are you awake?"

She turns her head on her pillow, eyes alight. "Cat!"

I rush to her side before she harms herself trying to sit up. "I came to say goodbye."

Marguerite sighs. "Sister Alix told me you were leaving Collis, but I didn't realize it would be so soon."

"I'm sorry I didn't come until now." I stroke her hand. "But I promise to write." If the abbeys have one thing I admire, it's an efficient system of sending messages to each other.

"Please do." She settles back into her pillow, her eyes slightly out of focus from the earlier movement. Without bloodstones, her recovery is slow. Marguerite points to the small table next to her bed. "There's something for you in the drawer."

I open it, expecting prayer beads or similar, but find a dirt-crusted bag full of coins—the one I'd buried behind the garden shed over five years ago. "How did you know about this?"

"Because I know you." She smiles fondly. "Take it. You'll need money."

Magister Thomas gave me more than enough. I shake my head and put it back. "You keep it. It's not as much as your hair would have brought, but you can put it toward a new loom."

She sighs. "There's no way I can talk you out of that, is there?"

Her forehead is still bandaged, so I lean down to kiss her nose. "Not a chance."

I wish I had more time, but Oudin is waiting outside the city with a pair of horses, probably very impatient by now. Promising again to write, I squeeze Marguerite's fingers and whisper my last goodbye, then hurry back to the gate, thanking the sister who let me in.

The moonflower vines across the street are dotted with flowers open to the waning moon, their fragrance tickling my nose.

From beyond the walls comes the sound of singing, and I can distinguish Gregor's baritone, heavier than usual. Simon stands straight from where he leans against the abbey wall and hoists his travel bag back onto his shoulder.

"I couldn't help thinking," he says softly as he steps into the moonlight. "You could stay here, at the abbey, if you wanted. The comte would never know, and you could visit your family as much as you want."

I shake my head. "You know I don't belong there."

"No," he admits. "But I'm not sure you belong with me, either."

"We'll figure that out together." I take his hand, lacing our fingers. "Are you ready to do this?"

Simon's pulse echoes up my arm from our joined wrists. "No," he says. "But I'm ready to do this with you."

AUTHOR'S NOTE

Depicting mental illness is never an easy task, even when—or perhaps *especially* when—one has personal knowledge of those affected by it. The characters of Juliane, her mother, and Simon's father are in no way meant to definitively represent schizophrenia. Each case is as individual as the person and depends greatly on their environment, but such conditions have been recorded going back thousands of years. Their treatment varied widely based on religion, individual societies, how important the person was, and whether they had family to take care of them. Too often, those stories are tragic and heartbreaking for everyone involved.

Schizophrenia can be difficult to diagnose even today, but it is often treatable with medication and therapy, though a support network is critical. Like Juliane, many sufferers are highly intelligent and even aware that much of what they experience isn't real. While some are able to build successful careers, most hide their condition from all but those closest to them. It's quite likely you know or work alongside a schizophrenic person, and I sincerely hope if they share their secret with you, you will honor that trust. I owe a mountain of appreciation to my sensitivity reader, Nadhira Sitaria, for her kind words and personal expertise in depicting this complicated topic. If you would like more information on the subject, I recommend *The Man Who Mistook His Wife for a Hat* by Oliver Sacks and *The Center Cannot Hold: My Journey Through Madness* by Elyn R. Saks. The latter is a memoir of schizophrenia, and I am grateful for Professor Saks's candor in revealing the inner workings of such a personal journey. Though I have borrowed the tone of some of her delusions for Juliane, they were very similar to ones I've seen—up close and personal—from the outside. But in the words of Forrest Gump: That's all I have to say about that.

—— • ✳ • ——

Simon's home of Mesanus is based on a real place in Belgium. While I have fictionalized and imagined some details, they have all been in keeping with the spirit of the city's history.

According to legend, Geel is the resting place of St. Dymphna, whose martyrdom in the seventh century at the hands of her insane father was as described by Mother Agnes in Chapter 12. For over a thousand years, her tomb has been a pilgrimage site for those seeking cures from mental afflictions. Before and after her canonization in 1247, the Catholic Church built several hospitals to care for those brought for miracles, many of whom were left behind by their families.

Over the centuries, Geel became known worldwide for its compassionate, deinstitutionalized approach to treating mental illness, so much that Vincent van Gogh's father considered sending his troubled son there in the late 1800s. To this day, the city's residents actively participate in the care of patients (called boarders), taking them into their own homes and giving them the stable interaction of family life.

Ironically, Geel's thousand-year-old practice is considered too revolutionary to establish in other places. In a society where people's "knowledge" of mental illness comes primarily from Hollywood dramatization, the stigma is still too difficult to overcome. We have made progress, but not enough. Yet.

ACKNOWLEDGMENTS

Dear reader, you've finished it. Thank you for finding this book and entering its world for a few hours. If you picked it up because you loved my previous stories, then I owe you double and triple thanks. I was able to continue writing because of you.

What a strange world this has become. I know every book is different, but one written while living in a foreign country during a global pandemic and throughout upheaval in the publishing world . . . well, it's been surreal. My mental health owes a great deal to the intercession of St. Dymphna, whose own story made it into this book. The idea of psychologically profiling criminal behavior is very recent, dating back only to the late 1800s. Including it in a historical setting (even a fantastical one) is anachronistic, and I had to find a believable reason for it to be used. Without my previous knowledge of the saint, her shrine, and the city of Geel, I'm not sure how this plot would have developed. Funny how it worked out. Or maybe not funny but meant to be. But anyway, thanks to Dymphna and also St. Francis de Sales (the patron of writers) and the four Thomases, this story was possible. *Deo Gratias*.

I also leaned heavily on my superagent, Valerie Noble, who is always in my corner, ready to fix anything. Farewell and following seas to my beloved Imprint team, especially Erin Stein, Nicole Otto, and John Morgan—the publishing world is less without you. But thanks to FSG for picking up the orphaned manuscript on their doorstep, and extra thanks to my new editor, Wes Adams, especially for video chats outside East Coast business hours and during a long drive through the Korean mountains. More gratitude for the team beyond—designer Veronica Mang, production editor Helen Seachrist, copyeditor Amber Williams, publicist Brittany Pearlman, marketing manager Gabriella Salpeter, proofreaders Susan Bishansky and Rosanne Lauer, and production manager John Nora—most of whom I haven't met (yet), but who created and fixed the guts, plus jaw-dropping awe at Sasha Vinogradova's cover. I hope to earn my keep.

A debt of gratitude to John Douglas and his pioneering work in criminal profiling for the FBI and the books he wrote on the subject. If he ever actually reads this novel, I hope it doesn't make him cringe. Thanks also to the welcoming community here in Busan, South Korea, though it is already fragmenting from people getting orders to new places and being sewn back together with fresh arrivals. Somehow I became the "old salt," but by the time this book is in print, I, too, will have moved on. Such is the military life.

Thanks to my parents and my in-laws for taking care of our college spawn. I know you didn't count on the university closing and forcing them to move in with you when you volunteered to be their home base, and I'm eternally grateful. They, in turn, faced a pandemic while eight thousand miles from Mom and Dad.

The other three kids have navigated a new world with a very different language and a school so small each grade fills a single classroom, all through COVID-19. I'm so proud of you all for weathering it with good humor and leaning on one another, even from the other side of the globe.

And Michael, you've sacrificed for us all more than you should have had to. Without you, none of this would be possible.